MEANWHILE GARDENS

MEANWHILE GARDENS

AN URBAN ADVENTURE

CHARLES CASELTON

Matador
5 Weir Road
Kibworth Beauchamp
Leicester LE8 0LQ, UK
Tel: (+44) 116 279 2277
Email: books@troubador.co.uk
Web: www.troubador.co.uk/matador

ISBN 978 1848764 354

British Library Cataloguing in Publication Data.
A catalogue record for this book is available from the British Library.

Typeset in 11pt Sabon by Troubador Publishing Ltd, Leicester, UK
Printed in the UK by TJ International, Padstow, Cornwall

Matador is an imprint of Troubador Publishing Ltd

To the Macdonald family! Lots of love to you! Charlie xx

For My Family

1

HUMDINGER THE III

For the third morning in a row Ollie Michaelson woke up with *Bringing in the Sheaves* playing in his mind with all the insistence of a church organ.

As the phone rang he looked at the alarm clock beside his bed and saw 9.45 flashing red on the display. Ollie knew who it was before he picked up the receiver. The first of his concerned morning calls.

"It's a beautiful day," the woman's voice was firm but friendly with a hint of Jamaican that betrayed her childhood. "Join me for coffee."

Ollie yawned and stretched.

"Hi Auntie Em."

"I know you weren't out last night. And you certainly didn't have company."

"Auntie Em – "

"If you're not going to join me I'll bring something back for you."

"I – "

"And we'll go for a walk. Your young friend will need to. You can't stay in and mope for ever."

Without waiting for a reply she gently put down the phone. Auntie Em knew that if you gave people the option they would invariably take it.

Sometimes it was best not to give it to them.

Ollie stayed in bed for another half-hour, enjoying the gentle breathing and warmth of Hum, the 'young friend' Auntie Em had alluded to, the young friend who twisted and turned in his sleep next to him.

Ollie appreciated the regular checks by his neighbours and friends. Afterall it had now been nearly a month since his best and oldest friend had been killed. Perhaps it was about time, Ollie thought, to focus on his own life.

Or if not on his life, on the life of Hum who slumbered beside him.

Hum, the last living link to his dead friend. James' death had thrust parenthood on Ollie and, he realised, he must be responsible and think for two now.

Hum's full name was Humdinger the III. He was nearly three years old, adorable and mischievous in equal measure – part German Shepherd, part Briard and all wonderful.

Ollie remembered the day James had got Hum and proudly brought him round, a two month old pup with attitude. It seemed natural to call him Humdinger – what other name would fit? And as for 'The lll' – well, the pup had such a confident air, such an unshaken belief in himself, such unhesitating charm that they both agreed he needed an appropriately American name. All the most confident Americans had 'The lll' after their names and so, it was agreed, should Humdinger.

Ollie drew the sitting room curtains and looked down the little cobbled mews. From his vantage point at the entrance he could see all five houses, each with a brightly painted door. Cornering the bottom of the mews was a C-shaped house where Auntie Em lived with Gemma. They were known to all as Auntie Em and Auntie Gem. Or Gem 'n Em for short. Greenery spilled over the railings of the narrow first floor balcony that ran the length of their pretty house, the largest in the mews.

Noticing movement in Ollie's windows Nicky waved at him from her studio across the way. She put her forefinger to her thumb and bent her wrist as if drinking from a cup.

Christ, Ollie thought, all my friends want to do is turn me into a caffeinated wreck. He waved back and gestured for the photographer to come over.

"She said I couldn't stay in and mope all day. Why the hell not? Why can't I?"

"She's right."

"Well of course she's right Nicks, but...." Ollie's voice trailed off.

"Sweetheart, we all miss the hell out of James and no-one's begrudging you the right to grieve but you're -? – you're moping not grieving. You're using this as an excuse to – to "

"To what Nicks?"

"Just to put off whatever you're putting off, to put off living."

"I *do* live."

"No sweetheart what you do is eat," Nicky prodded him in the waist. "I can hardly feel your ribs."

"It's been a crap summer," Ollie blustered, "everyone's a bit heavier. It helps to keep out the cold."

"It hasn't been that cold, besides there are other things to keep out the chill like the thinnest cashmere, like silken thermal underwear, like – "

"Like porridge?" Ollie asked hopefully.

"Sure – as long as you don't overload it with cream and sugar."

Nicky went to the garbage, lifted the lid and peered in. Inside the heavy stainless steel can were the packaging, wrappers and empty boxes that told of Ollie's burgeoning girth.

"Bramley apple pie with cinnamon," Nicky read out loud. "Rhubarb and blackberry crumble – family size – "

"I was going to ask you over – " Ollie said defensively.

"- cherry, strawberry and raspberry thick crust – cherry, strawberry AND raspberry?" Nicky looked at Ollie and raised her eyebrows.

"It's good, you should try it Nicks."

"An extra large tub of clotted cream – "

"It's half-fat!"

Nicky smiled and put back the lid with a clang.

"Elvis, Oprah and the Notorious B.I.G. are worthy role models for their talent but perhaps not for their dietary habits. C'mon Ollie, you're growing tits for Chrissake," Nicky poked him again, once in each breast. "Male boobs are not a hot look."

To his shame Ollie could feel the flesh jiggle.

"Yeah, well, it's comfort food," he grumbled.

"I can see that sweetheart," Nicky put her arm around Ollie's shoulder, "but you can get comfort from other things, like – "

"I'm not dating anyone, I'm not answering any ads, and it's too cold for Hampstead," Ollie said hurriedly.

" – like, exercise."

Ollie looked at his friend with suspicion.

"You've been talking to Auntie Em haven't you?"

Before Nicky could answer Hum barked a surprisingly loud bark and raced down the stairs to the front door. Ollie sighed and made to follow, but Nicky beat him to it.

"I'll get it."

She bounded down the stairs, returning seconds later with a small sellotaped carton which she put on the kitchen table.

Inside were four custard tarts from the neighbouring Portuguese café.

"These were on the doorstep – "

"They must be from Auntie Em."

"- along with a note."

Ollie grabbed for the slip of paper but Nicky pulled it out of reach.

"Be ready in an hour," she began to read. "No is not an option." Nicky flashed the note at him to show there was nothing else.

"Fresh air and custard tarts."

"Auntie Em's answer to everything."

Ollie looked out of the kitchen window at the modernist 60's tower block that loomed over the mews.

On one side of the enormous structure, separated from the main building by parallel walkways two storeys apart, was the lift shaft and stairwell looking for all the world like the handle to a transistor radio.

The main building with its white-framed windows, its balconies and criss-crossing concrete lines appeared as an extraordinary grid against the sky.

These two features combined to make the block of flats look like some mammoth ghettoblaster on its side.

"I often think that someday a giant in seven league boots will come along, pick up Trellick Tower, sling it on his shoulder and rock on his way."

Nicky paused to let this thought filter through her mind.

"Like the guy in the KEEP ON TRUCKIN' poster?" she asked.

Ollie clinked his mug to Nicky's.

"You got it."

Everything was so different in London.

For a start there were so many people. So many people! Where had they come from? And where were they going with their briefcases, their brollies and frowns?

Rion had snuck a look at an A to Z in WH Smiths at King's Cross to confirm where she was.

As if she needed to.

Everyday for the past month, ever since she had finally decided to leave home, Rion had gone to Bridlington library and asked for the London A to Z. She knew exactly where she was. And exactly where she was going.

What she was going to do when she got there was another matter.

It looked easy on the map. Just turn right out of King's Cross station and keep going.

Straight. Straight. Straight.

It was 10:40 when Rion passed Madame Tussauds. People, five abreast, queued in a thick line that stretched the full length of the building.

Tanya Bishop had said there was a lifesize waxwork of Tom Cruise inside! Rion hoped it was a larger than lifesize model for the original was a notoriously abridged version, at least to Tanya Bishop who preferred her movie stars on the large size. Whilst Rion admired his compact quality she feared she would tower over Tom Cruise should she ever meet him.

Standing five foot eleven in bare feet made this an inevitability.

Judging from their accents, as much as from the coaches setting them down, Rion noticed that the majority of the people in line for the waxworks were French. She took this as a sign, a good sign, for the man she was going to see today, the man she hoped would have the answers, was French.

"Rion," she said her new name to herself – it was Rion now. She had dropped the preceding 'Ma' on the train from Bridlington.

Marion had always felt like the wrong name for her. It was somehow displaced, she thought, a name from a bygone age, an age that just didn't exist anymore – and to Marion's mind bygones should be bygones.

From now on there would be no 'Ma' for Rion.

And thankfully no Pa.

Outside the waxworks the smell of frying onions reminded her of how little she had eaten since leaving Bridlington 5 hours ago. She had had a kit-kat for breakfast. Not the usual four finger kind, but a promotional two finger kind. In dark chocolate. Now she was hungry.

Counting her money Rion found she had £3.27.

Exactly.

Three £1 coins, a twenty pence piece and seven pennies.

Before she approached the burger van Rion caught sight of her reflection in the display windows of the wax museum. She pulled down her sleeves to cover the bruises and adjusted the collar of her thin fleece.

The reasons for her flight would remain concealed.

"Yes, darlin'."

The words addressed to her were more a statement than a question.

"How much for a cheeseburger?" Rion's Yorkshire accent seemed somehow out of place on the busy Marylebone Road.

The youth, his hair greased into a kisscurl over his forehead, insolently tapped the board on the side of the fold-down counter.

"£5.50. Fries are £2.20."

He called chips – fries, and £5.50 for a cheeseburger! Although inwardly staggered at the price Rion realised, with some pleasure, that this was another reminder she was no longer in Bridlington.

Rion plucked up courage and smiled. "Could I have half a portion of ch – " she corrected herself, "fries – and some onions for £1.25?"

"This isn't a market darlin'," he sneered. "If you want a bargain go to Portabella."

Rion walked away, the youth's laughter following her.

"Eee oop Yorkshire, you're champion lass! Aye," he mimicked to her back. The youth shook his head violently and tutted in disbelief.

The kisscurl remained firmly in place.

Rion was down to £1 by the time she got to the roundabout at the start of Bishop's Bridge Road. She knew London would be expensive but even so £2.26 seemed steep for an apple, an orange and a small Mars bar. She should have had a pound and a penny but one of the small dirty coins had turned out to be a Canadian cent.

Another sign. Another positive sign. For Canada was the scene of her hero's greatest triumph.

Looking up Rion saw an enormous billboard for a removals company covering the top half of the building above her. The huge poster showed a tightrope walker tiptoeing across the Earth with the slogan: TAKE A STEP IN THE RIGHT DIRECTION AND MOVE WITH US.

'Take a step in the right direction – ' Rion mimicked the tightrope walker above and for an instant forgot her troubles. It would all be worth it.

"Please God," Rion whispered, "give me one more sign just...."

And then she saw it. The fourth and final sign.

In the window of the greasy café below the billboard were the words, '*Omelettes our speciality*.' Now there could be no doubt! Her hero's favourite meal spelt out in bold letters right before her eyes. Right before her eyes!

"Thank you Lord," she murmured.

First the *French* tourists, then the *Canadian* cent, followed by *Take a step in the right direction...* and finally *Omelettes.*

Ignoring her blisters Rion hurried on. The man she was going to see would have the answers. Now she was sure.

The young girl raced through the passages of the underpass, expecting to be mugged at any second. She had seen CrimeWatch and knew what to expect from grimy London subways but to her relief there was no one around.

Or would she be safer if there were people around?

Was it safer in a crowd?

But then again didn't people vanish in crowds? There was that story the other week of a girl, not much older than herself, who was kidnapped in broad daylight and later found – well, she flinched, it just didn't bear thinking about.

Finding herself in the open basin of Little Venice Rion was relieved to see a man on a bench overlooking an island. Posh three storey houses lined the far side of the inland waterway, a series of lowlying non-descript council blocks edged the near. Remembering her last encounter with a Londoner, the greased youth from the hamburger van, Rion took a deep breath and approached.

"Excuse me," her voice-sounded nasal, her attempt at flattening her accent not entirely successful.

"Excuse me," she tried again, this time with more success,

sounding, she thought, like someone on the telly. "Could you tell me where – "

As the man turned round Rion knew she had made a mistake – his eyes were red and weepy, snot encrusted his nostrils, his breath just a mass of fumes. The man picked up a bottle and waved it at her.

"Do I look as if I know where I'm going?" he slurred. "Go on gerrrout of it. Piss off girlie."

Rion's asthma and blisters slowed her down on the other side of the canal where she stopped to catch her breath beside a line of longboats. The names of the brightly coloured barges initially soothed her and her inflamed alveoli.

'Morrisco'; She smiled, no doubt a Latin step danced by sweet old couples.

'Longfelloe'; Probably refers to the size of the boat, although the spelling struck her as slightly odd.

'Home Sweet Home'; Home Sweet Home? Was there such a place?

Rion shuddered and carried on her way.

Another twenty minutes of limping found her at the back of an enormous bunker of flats, thirty storeys at least she thought, higher than anything she had seen in her life. The towering concrete block was set in its own park complete with meandering two-tiered pond.

As she approached a man bounded up the steps that joined the park to the canal ten yards in front of her. He was in his mid-twenties she guessed, and quite handsome in his way, although he could lose a few pounds, maybe even a stone. A woman, perhaps his mother, followed.

They looked trustworthy Rion thought. She would ask them how far she had to go. Again she pulled down her sleeves to hide her bruises and pulled up the collar of her fleece. Rion took a deep breath.

"Excuse me," Rion smiled nervously. "Could you tell me how far it is to – " she couldn't finish the end of her sentence before the man shouted at her, "Hum!"

Rion looked nervously at him, "I beg your – "

"Hum goddammit!" the man's eyes bulged alarmingly as he seemed to look through her. Rion's breath caught in her throat. Who was this madman and why did he want her to hum?

Rion looked to his companion for support but the woman simply yelled, "Hum!" in the same authoritative tone.

Her eyes brimming with tears Rion began on the only tune that came into her head. She falteringly hummed the first few bars of God Save The Queen before she seized her chance and dashed away.

"Hum!"

She heard the man order again but Rion was hobbling away as fast as she could, hoping to God they wouldn't run after, catch her and – oh my gosh, ghastly images again filled her mind. Rion half ran, half-limped round the bend in the canal and away from the deranged couple.

By now Rion was convinced that everyone in London, absolutely everyone, was either mad or horrible.

Or both.

"Hum!" Ollie shouted again before looking after the young girl. "Hey!" he called to her back but Rion had vanished around the corner with no intention of returning. Ollie shrugged his shoulders and gave one final yell, "Hum!"

This time he was rewarded by a glimpse of Humdinger the III under Carlton Bridge faraway in the distance.

"Auntie Em, he's over there."

Within ten minutes Rion had crossed over the canal. She

skirted the funeral merchants on the busy Harrow Road before finding herself in front of some open iron gates painted white. With trembling heart she entered the small building to the right, handed over the last of her money for a map, then walked through the triumphal arch into the calm of her destination.

She had made it.

Kensal Green Cemetery.

2

STRANGE BUT UNDENIABLY HANDSOME

It was peaceful here. The cemetery had none of the emptiness, none of the gloom, of the stony patch attached to St Kilda's church in Bridlington. There, the graveyard was filled with stolid headstones of people awash with decency and thrift. Here Rion could see that thrift was neither desired, nor indeed a consideration. For as far as the eye could see there were temples and obelisks, marbled family shrines and miniature chapels for the dead, all laid out along elegant, tree-lined avenues.

Rion saw on her map that her hero's grave was at the far end of South Avenue, on the other side of the cemetery. Excited now, she set off.

After a few steps the plucky runaway had the peculiar feeling she was being watched. Rion looked up but the only people she could see were a rather incongruously jolly little group beside a grave on what, after a hurried look at the map, she deemed to be North Avenue.

She carried on, her attention taken by a romantic stone canopy nearby. Rion turned off Centre Avenue onto the soft, slightly springy wood chips of a smaller path. Again she felt she was being watched, but again a furtive glance revealed no one.

Within moments she was standing in front of a sculpted comforting angel that guarded the grave beneath the canopy.

"George Augustus Frederick Percy Sydney Smythe. Seventh Viscount Strangford and Second Baron Penshurst," she read out loud the lettering carved in stone.

"He died before he was forty, you know – "

Rion jumped, startled by the young man who had appeared suddenly beside her. The young man ignored her look of surprise and continued, " – of brandy, dissipation and consumption. He was a journalist as well as a Tory politician – who would have thought eh?" he said wrily. "Plus ça change – " he paused for a moment in reflection. "What do you think dissipation is?"

From her previous encounters with Londoners Rion thought it best to remain silent.

"Whatever it is," he continued, "it doesn't sound very now does it?"

Rion turned to look at the young man who appeared oblivious to her silence. He was roughly the same height as her although much, much older – at least twentysix she reckoned. He wore a raggedy sweater over paint spattered jeans. His black hair bounced in thick curls over his forehead.

"I used to know a gardener years ago called Percy," the young man paused in thought. "You don't get too many Augustus's – or should that be Augustii? – now do you? You did then though. Another Augustus, George 111's sixth son – the Duke of Sussex – is buried here. It's said his house was full of singing birds and chiming clocks and that during his final illness he survived on a diet of turtle soup and orange sorbet! Imagine that!"

Rion began to imagine if he would ever stop talking.

"Some of these graves go down sixty feet or more and have spaces for generations of the same family."

Rion overcame her nervousness. "How do they get down there?" she asked curiously

"Ropes and pulleys. There are also catacombs under the main chapel but I don't know much about them." Jake gazed over the acres of tombs and monuments. "I could show you around if you'd like."

"Thanks, it's ok," Rion said hurriedly. "I'm just trying to find the grave of – "

"He was known as a dazzling, handsome rake."

"Sorry?"

The young man gestured to the elaborate grave, "George Augustus Frederick Percy Sydney Smythe, Seventh Viscount Strangford and – "

" – Second Baron Penshurst," Rion finished for him.

The young man smiled. "It is also said he fought the last duel in England. Nifty huh?"

Nifty? Rion felt herself warming, somewhat against her will, to this talkative young man. Anyone who could use the word 'nifty' – and get away with it – might just be ok.

"I'm Jake by the way."

Rion avoided his eyes and didn't offer her name.

After a pause he asked, "Would you mind if I accompanied you?"

"Really, it's ok, I – "

"Well, as long as we're both going in the same direction. Shall we?"

He took Rion gently by the elbow and turned her round to face the burial places lining the other side of the small path. After a couple of steps he stopped before a white marble grave locked inside some railings.

"William Makepeace Thackeray," Jake announced.

Rion looked up, interested. She peered closer. "We were reading Vanity Fair at school."

"Ah, Vanitas vanitatum – " Jake said sombrely.

"- all is vanity," Rion finished the closing sentence of the novel for him intrigued. Who was this gentle-mannered, undeniably attractive, but undeniably strange, man and what was he doing in a cemetery? "I was going to take my GSCE next summer."

"Was – ?" he enquired.

"Well, it's, I don't think – I'll….nothing – " she flustered.

Jake put his hand up to stop her. "It's none of my business is it?"

"No it's just, yes, I mean – "

To stop her embarrassment Jake gently took her by the arm again, "This you must see."

He led her back to where the main avenue branched to the left. In front of them was a compact, ornate shrine.

"Now this man knew about life."

Rion looked at the carved stone tomb, decorated with shields, that lay on blocks of green marble. The whole was enclosed by red columns that supported a canopy of arches, gargoyles and other flourishes.

"Who was he?" she asked, awed by the overdecorated Gothic shrine.

"Commander Charles Spencer Ricketts 1788 -1867. He ran away to sea when he was seven years old, served under Nelson at Trafalgar, quickly rose to the rank of commander, married an heiress and retired at twentyseven."

Jake paused to let the information sink in before continuing in a tone half-admiring, half-envious. "Now tell me that wasn't a great life plan? I mean, who could want for more? Marrying an heiress and retiring at twentyseven – it's every man's dream."

"They must have been the celebs of their day."

"Yeah, but they got it by doing great things, extraordinary

things, not by being kicked out of a reality show in week three."

Suitably impressed Rion followed Jake as he ambled down the avenue, pointing out the graves of notable people as well as their foibles.

Finally they arrived under a large evergreen oak where the cemetery bordered the canal. This could be the moment, Rion thought, where she could thank him for his company before setting off to find her hero's grave.

"Are you a guide here?"

Jake smiled. "Not exactly."

Rion noticed Jake's attention had been taken by something behind her. The girl followed his gaze to see a taxi coming down the main avenue in the distance.

"What do you do then?"

"I thought we agreed to no questions," Jake replied goodnaturedly.

"Well, do you live round here?"

Jake rolled his eyes.

"I know it's none of my business, and I wouldn't normally ask," Rion said hurriedly, not wishing to appear forward. "It's just I'm trying to find somewhere to stay and – "

Jake again raised his eyes skywards.

"Sorry, I know, no questions."

"No, it's not that but – " Jake paused for a moment, unsure. He then looked her level in the eye. "Can I trust you?"

Rion felt her cheeks redden as she returned his gaze. Embarrassed she looked at the ground before forcing her eyes to meet his again, "Yes."

Jake again looked into the ivy-clad tree. "This is where I live," he pointed out the evenly spaced notches at the back of the trunk that led to the lower branches and the dense foliage.

Squinting upward Rion could just make out some planks camouflaged green some way above her head.

"You live – " she jerked her eyes up, amazed, "– up there?"

The taxi was at the top of Terrace Avenue now, slowly making its way down the muddy track towards them.

"Damn," Jake said, "she's early." He paused for a moment before leading Rion away from the approaching taxi.

"I know a place you can stay. It's unusual but quite comfortable."

"I – " Rion began.

"Don't worry, there'll be no funny business."

They had reached a cluster of gravestones away from the tree. Jake motioned for Rion to sit beside one, "She doesn't like to see anyone around when she arrives. Come back in an hour."

Jake began to walk away. After a second he turned back, "What's your name?"

"Rion."

"Rion?"

"Like Marion but without the Ma," Rion added helpfully.

Jake again began to walk away before turning once more as if he had forgotten something.

"Oh," Jake paused, looked at the ground then looked back at Rion and smiled. "Don't come knocking if the tree's-a-rocking," he winked at her. "Know what I'm saying?"

Rion felt her face flush a deep red.

From her hidden place beside the grave of Emmeline Pilkington, whose tombstone was inscribed with a beguiling '*In fragrant memory*', Rion watched Jake shin up the notches of the imposing tree and vanish from sight.

Through curious eyes she saw the taxi stop beneath Jake's

tree. A slender woman, thirties, stepped out, paid and quickly looked about her. She was dressed in a well-cut jacket, tailored trousers and turquoise pumps. Shading her eyes were an owllike pair of dark glasses. A large bouquet of flowers peered out of the elegant pink shopping bag she held in one hand. On the side of the bag were the words GHOST written in big white letters.

"Come back at four o' clock sharp," Rion heard the woman say authoritatively.

As the taxi slowly bumped and rattled up Terrace Avenue the woman, looking for all the world like a bereaved widow, placed the bouquet of flowers beneath the tree. When the taxi made its way out of the distant main gate Rion saw the woman look around before taking off her dazzling turquoise pumps. She put them in the pink bag where the flowers had been, put the bag over one shoulder and had a final look about her. Satisfied she wasn't being watched Angie Peters went to the back of the tree where, to Rion's amazement, she nimbly stepped up the notches and away from view.

Rion stayed beside the tombstone of the fragrant Emmeline for a minute wondering if what she had seen had really happened. Deciding it had done, and deciding that Londoners really took the biscuit, Rion walked back to the mysterious tree. Without looking up into the prolific vegetation that concealed she couldn't imagine what, Rion picked up the bouquet of flowers and hurried away.

Gorby watched with interest as Rion wound between the colonnades of the Anglican Chapel. From his groundfloor window the guard saw her reach the gateway and vanish from sight. If he was lucky she would return. Gorby patted his large stomach in an attempt to massage away the mid-afternoon rumblings. It wouldn't be long now until –

"Tea!" a shrill voice called from down the corridor.

The guard removed his peaked cap to give his magnificent strawberry birthmark a good scratch. With the rumblings increasing Gorby loped along the stoneflagged passage towards the promise of cake and digestives.

Rion counted her way along the burial plots of West Centre Avenue. Within moments she had reached grave 31398, square 140, row 1.

Upon seeing the simple red granite monument Rion was immediately disappointed. And then immediately guiltridden for feeling so disappointed.

She had some funny notion, she thought to herself, that her hero's tomb would somehow be worthy of the huge amount of inspiration she had received from him.

But it wasn't.

It was elegant, yes, and simple, yes, but it was neither the grand nor grandiose shrine she had imagined.

Rion peered closer to make sure this was indeed her hero's final resting-place.

The inlaid gold lettering confirmed it was.

Jean Francois Gravelet (1824-97)
Of Niagara House, Ealing

On either side of the monument were silhouette marble medallions, portraits of the man she had come to see and of his wife who had died ten years before him.

Why was it, she wondered, that a century ago women died ten years before their men, whilst now women died ten years after them?

Rion placed the elegant bouquet between the marble portraits and offered up a prayer for guidance. She sat on the low walls of the grave, waiting for some message, some thunderbolt that would tell her what she was to do. She waited. And waited.

And waited.

The mid-afternoon sun warmed her as she slipped further and further down until she lay sheltered by the low walls of the tomb.

Rion stretched out, enjoying the feeling of the cool stone beneath her. It had been a long day but now she had made it to where she wanted to be.

Secure in the arms of her hero Rion could keep the tiredness away no longer. The last thing she saw as she drifted off was the large angel smiling at her from atop the memorial.

Within seconds she was sound asleep.

Within seconds she was dreaming of rocking trees, of ugly sisters, of angels and brutes and tightrope walkers, all spinning round, all grinning, all telling her to hum! Hum goddamnit! Hum!

Gasping, Rion shook herself awake.

"You'll catch a chill if you lie there much longer."

Rion looked up to find Jake sitting behind her on the low walls of the tomb.

"Granite, marble, any stone really," he continued, "but especially smooth polished ones, the cold just goes right through you."

Rion rubbed her eyes, unsure for a second of where she was.

Then it all came back to her.

She had made it to London, she had made it to her hero's grave, and this curly-haired, friendly-faced person in front of her was called Jake and he somehow lived in a tree house in the cemetery.....?

This last bit seemed unclear.

Rion shook her head as if to jolt her thoughts into place, but the information remained: Jake lived in a treehouse where the cemetery bordered the canal. There was also something about a woman with dazzling blue pumps – ?

Rion shuddered and sat up.

"It looked like you were having a bad dream."

"How did you know where I was?" Rion asked, her hands shielding her eyes from the late afternoon sun.

"When you didn't show up at four as arranged...."

Rion hurriedly looked at her watch and saw it was twenty past – she had slept for an hour!

"I spied you here from home. You can see most of the cemetery from there."

"Of – of course."

"You said you wanted a place to stay?"

The young girl looked up at the silhouette medallion of her hero. Could she trust this man? she silently asked.

"What are you doing here anyway? I mean, why this grave out of all the others? What's so special about Jean Francois Gravelet?"

Rion smiled at hearing her hero's true name.

"No one calls him that!" she said.

"OK, apart from being the most famous tightrope walker in the world, what's so special about Blondin?"

As Rion unzipped her fleece and reached into an inner pocket Jake saw the mottled yellow bruising around her neck. He was curious but knew not to ask questions.

From her fleece Rion brought out a thin, plastic wallet which she unfolded, carefully removing a much-creased piece of paper. Ever so delicately she lay the paper on her knee and smoothed out the creases before passing it with much gravity to Jake.

The paper consisted of a faded engraving of a mustachioed man balancing on a tightrope above a raging waterfall. What was peculiar about it was the man appeared to be cooking something in a frying pan in the middle of his traverse.

Below the picture was the caption: *Blondin cooks an omelette. Niagara 1860.*

"That," Rion declared, "has got me through some of the roughest times of my life."

Jake took another look at the picture which, to him, seemed more comical than inspirational. He nodded at Rion to continue.

"It's just that he makes it look so easy doesn't he? There he is risking his life hundreds of feet above treacherous, swirling waters when one wrong move, one inch, half-an-inch, even a millimetre of miscalculation would mean a fall to a certain death, battered and bludgeoned by the torrent on the rocks far below." A shudder went through Rion as she thought of it.

"Whenever I've been at the end of my tether – and believe me being the youngest of four girls and with parents like mine – " she shook her head vehemently. "There've been many times when I – " her voice drifted off. "It's just that if he could manage to cook and eat an omelette – to cook *and* eat – whilst doing something so difficult, then I can survive anything."

"There's more to it though, isn't there?"

"More?" Rion asked astounded, sounding for the entire world like the orphanage beadle in a production of *Oliver*.

Jake nodded. "After Blondin cooked the omelette in the middle of the falls he took a bite then lowered it, by rope, to the Mayor of Niagara who waited with other dignitaries in the rescue boat far below."

Rion hadn't heard this part of the story.

"What did they think?"

"They pronounced it among the finest of omelettes they had ever tasted!"

Rion laughed with delight. "No-one in Bridlington understood about Blondin, no-one except my friend Tanya Bishop – she owned the hair salon I ran to whenever I could – *she* understood."

As Rion reached for the crumpled picture her sleeve pulled back to expose two painful scabby red circles on the side of her wrist. Jake held Rion's arm for a closer look, "Those are nasty cuts."

But they didn't look like cuts to him.

"Yeah, well – " Rion hurriedly pulled down her sleeve to cover the unsightly marks. "Are you sure about this place to stay?"

Jake nodded.

"And you're sure there'll be no funny business?"

Jake pulled Rion to her feet, "I promise."

They walked back through the colonnades of the Anglican Chapel and were soon on Terrace Avenue heading for Jake's home in the trees.

"The cemetery closes at five this time of year – pretty soon. There are a couple of guards so it's best not to be too visible."

"Why do they have guards?" Rion asked.

"To stop the ritual slayings and grave robbings," Jake rolled his eyes and fluttered his hands like some spectral figure until he saw Rion blanche. "Just kidding," he winked at her and smiled.

Rion held her rucksack tightly to her back and nervously pulled her fleece around her.

"It's because some of the monuments have been vandalised over the years, their stone wreaths, bronze busts, grieving angels – anything really – stolen. There's a large market for them as garden ornaments it seems."

Rion, shaken by the mere mention of ritual slaying – wasn't that what her Mum said happened to girls that ran away from home? – was having second thoughts.

"Perhaps I should find somewhere else."

Jake stopped. They were almost under his tree.

"I didn't mean to frighten you, it was a silly joke – I'm sorry," his voice was earnest now. "I don't know what you're running from, that's your business right?" Jake stared at Rion who avoided his eyes. "You look like you need a place to stay. I can help."

Rion peered into the tree.

"Not with – ?"

"No, not with me. On your own. You'll be safe don't worry." Jake saw Rion was still unsure. "You can trust me, don't you think you can?"

Rion looked Jake level in the eye for the first time. She didn't answer but in a funny way she felt she could trust him – well, at least more than anyone else she had met in London.

"Wait here. You'll need some things." Jake disappeared into his tree where Rion could hear him rummaging around. Within moments he was beside her again. A rolled up sleeping-bag inside an elegant, pink *GHOST* carrier in one hand, a plastic Sainsburys bag in the other.

Rion followed Jake who headed past the grave of the fragrant Emmeline and down towards the canal. He slipped onto a smaller path, wound his way between a few headstones in this untended part of the necropolis and was soon at the imposing fence that marked the cemetery's border. Beyond were the tree-covered banks of the Grand Union Canal.

Jake eased himself between a broken railing, squeezed through a row of tightly planted saplings and vanished from sight.

Rion took a deep breath and followed.

She found herself in a narrow space between two rows of willowy saplings. To her back the tall young trees screened the cemetery from sight. All she could see were the tops of the iron railings.

In front of her she could see water through the young trees and beyond them, above and on her left, were two huge gasometers.

Several yards in front Jake beckoned for Rion to join him. The saplings to his back had been replaced by a brick wall some ten feet tall. In front of him was a gap in the trees lining the canal.

"This is the only place where people can see you from the other side."

Jake gestured across the strip of water to a towpath that followed the line of the canal. Further down the path Rion could see a couple, oblivious to their presence, walking hand in hand towards them. A small figure – an old lady? Rion thought, or an old man? – approached away in the distance.

"So be careful."

The path between the trees became narrower, forcing Jake to turn and inch through sideways. Rion put down the pink *GHOST* bag, took off her rucksack and carried it above her head as she pushed sideways after Jake.

Within feet Jake had reached an opening that led through to a tiny clearing. A rustic fence, at least six foot high, of branches and twigs woven through the saplings, created an additional barrier from people on the towpath opposite.

"Here it is," he announced with a fanfare, "'Heron Point'." Jake looked back at Rion to try and gauge her reaction but the girl's face was blank. "This might not be your style but how long is it for?"

"I – " How long would it be for? Rion had no idea. "I'm not sure."

"Well, it's shelter and it's sort of clean and dry."

Rion watched as he descended a few roughly hewn steps into what looked like a cave. She crouched down by the entrance and looked inside.

Jake stood in the dimness of an underground chamber. He took two small white candles from the carrier bag and placed them in an alcove. When he lit the candles their flames flickered shadows over the low ceiling, revealing a room of surprising depth.

In the corner was a simple metal-framed bed with mattress. A small chest of drawers stood next to a rickety table to one side. A shelf of what looked like driftwood lined the wall above the bed.

"It hasn't been lived in since September when Old George – er – " How could he put it in a way that wouldn't frighten the young girl? "when Old George – er, moved on."

Rion came down the four steps into the chamber. "You mean he died? In here??"

"Yes, I mean no, I mean yes he died, but not in here."

Rion saw above the bed a picture of Jesus, his arms outstretched, an enormous red heart in the middle of his chest open as if awaiting surgery.

"I'll help you clean up in the morning," Jake patted the mattress, which threw up a cloud lightly dusting the religious picture above. He delved into the carrier bag and began removing objects which he placed on the table: a box of candles, a large box of matches and a lighter, a pencil torch, a bottle of water, a tin mug, two apples, a spoon and fork and a chipped plate.

Jake then took out something wrapped in metal foil. "Do you like Cuban?"

Rion looked at him, confused, "Cuban what?"

"Food – fish and rice and dumplings normally," Jake sniffed at the foil. "It should be ok, it's fresh on Wednesdays and Sundays."

Jake then pulled out a roll of loo paper from the bag.

"Old George used the canal – downstream of course – but there are alternatives."

Rion looked up hopefully.

"Sainsburys has a loo and a couple of pubs round here have decent toilets." Jake went up the earthen steps to the banks of the Grand Union Canal. "If you need anything – " he whistled four notes that sounded like a cross between some tv theme tune and a door chime. " – whistle. Can you do that?"

Rion whistled the four notes. And again.

"I'll always announce myself like that. If you hear noises and don't hear the whistle, lie low ok?"

Rion nodded. There was no way she was going to investigate any strange sounds – especially on land bordering a cemetery.

"I'll be going out later for a drink – care to join me?" Jake asked.

Rion again averted her gaze.

"No, thanks, I," she stumbled through her words. "I'm really tired and I have a lot of thinking to do.

"And you'll be ok?"

"Yeah." Rion would be ok – she knew it.

"I'll bring breakfast in the morning. It'll be Cuban again but it'll be fresh this time – and we can talk if you want. There are some things – tricks really – you should know."

Jake paused, feeling suddenly like an old boy on the first

day of school showing a new student round, or like a bellhop taking a guest to her room.

"If you need anything or – whatever, something frightens you, not that it will," he added hurriedly, "just whistle. Got it?"

Rion nodded. She didn't want to ask what she should do if something frightened her while he was out – that would be like tempting fate wouldn't it?

"You're sure you'll be ok?" he asked again.

From deep within her Rion pulled up what she hoped was a confident smile. "Thanks for – " Rion gestured around her, "just thanks."

Jake grinned and left.

Rion heard him push through the saplings and then he was gone. She was grateful for his help but grateful too that he had left her alone. In peace. In silence.

Silence.

Rion listened but all she could hear was some birdsong and the distant flash of a train. She closed her eyes, it was hard to believe she was in the middle of a city

"I'll be alright, I'll be alright, I'll be alright," Rion chanted softly to herself before opening her eyes wide. "No I won't!"

Suddenly scared she raced after Jake. Quickly retracing her steps Rion squeezed through the narrow stretch of saplings to the place where the path widened, to the place where a gap opened over the canal. Rion tried to quell her rising panic. She looked around anxiously, unsure of where she was.

And then she saw it. Her welcoming present, her first London prize – the pink bag from the shop whose clothes were coveted by 'women in the know' – or that's what it said in Vogue, Glamourista and the other magazines she devoured in Tanya's salon.

Rion clutched the bag to her, immediately comforted by its presence. She stared into the sun setting across the canal, not seeing the small figure on the shadowy towpath opposite.

Auntie Gem was transfixed by the ethereal vision before her – a virginal girl with long flaxen hair. Across the young girl's chest were the words *GHOST*.

The old lady felt her heart pound. She closed her eyes, feeling distinctly unsteady. When she opened them she gasped in horror. The spirit had vanished into thin air!

Auntie Gem crossed herself three times and made for home, made for the calm of Meanwhile Gardens Mews.

3

CAUGHT BETWEEN HEAVEN AND HELL

Ollie thought the phone calls should come later on Sundays.

But they didn't.

The alarm clock again flashed 9.45 as the phone jangled into his sleep.

"Auntie Em – " Ollie began, "didn't – "

But an entirely different voice cut him short.

"Oliver it's Candida."

The cold clipped tones of James' sister felt like ice down his back. Ollie blinked and sat up, suddenly wide awake.

"Oliver?" the voice asked again.

"What can I do for you Candida?" Ollie tried being cordial but relations between him and Candida had never been good.

The fact that James had made him co-executor of his will, a role he shared with Candida, hadn't helped matters.

"Could I come to see you this morning?"

"Well, I – " Ollie thought furiously.

"It's important Oliver."

"I'll be out until twelve then – "

Candida didn't wait for him to finish his sentence, "I'll be there at twelve fifteen."

The phone clicked off.

Seconds later it rang again.

"Who were you on the phone to at such an early hour?"

"Auntie Em, didn't your mother tell you never before ten or after ten?"

"Plans for the day angel?"

Ollie stretched, "Well, I'm – "

"Are you going to your TQ lunch?"

Ollie thought for a moment. He hadn't been to the weekly TQ sessions since before James' death. The lunches, held amongst the brunching families at the Hungry Hearts Diner on Kensington Park Road, were attended by about a dozen local gay men.

Over copious Bloody Marys each vied, with stories of their tragic lovelives and previous week's disasters to win the title, 'Tragedy Queen of the Week'.

The winner went on to enter, 'Tragedy Queen of the Month'.

The twelve winners went on for the annual top prize: 'Tragedy Queen of the Year'.

But today Ollie wasn't up to their relentless bonhomie.

"I don't think so Auntie Em, I'm – "

"But you haven't been in ages."

"Maybe next week. I'm – I'm going jogging."

There was a silence at the end of the line before, "Darling, that's wonderful! Remember start off very easy."

"Of course."

"And do some warm-ups. Are you going down the canal?"

"I'd be too self-conscious to go anywhere else Auntie Em. I'm not up to jogging along the Portobello that's for sure."

"You do know that Auntie Gem saw a ghost last night don't you?"

Ollie snorted. "No, I – " he tried to keep his voice serious. "Where? Is she ok?"

"She's a bit shaken up and has been praying more than usual. She's already been to two masses today."

"Two down, four to go," Ollie smiled, knowing Auntie Gem's fondness for the circuit of Sunday masses – six in total – whenever anything even remotely disturbed her. "The ghost wasn't of a tall, dark, handsome man was it?"

"In your dreams dear boy – "

That's about all where he would be, Ollie sighed.

" – it was a virginal girl with long flowing hair 'caught between Heaven and Hell' is how Auntie Gem described her."

Rion would have agreed what an apt description this was for her current state.

"It was along the canal further on from the gasworks," Auntie Em continued, "in front of the knoll with the bench overlooking Little Wormwood Scrubs."

"I'll be careful," Ollie said.

Will you be joining us for lunch?"

"Of course."

After his new style breakfast – a banana and natural yoghurt at home in place of a fry-up at the Golborne Café – Ollie felt well on the way to fitness.

He changed into raggedy tracksuit bottoms and a Keith Haring sweatshirt, suitably low-key dress for what, he hoped, would be a suitably low-key jog. Maybe in the future he could invest in some garish trainers and skintight allweather jogging bottoms, but for now it was comfort over performance.

Slowly, slowly, much to Hum's amusement, Ollie lunged and pulled and stretched. As he threw his arms from side to side the dog barked and jumped up, becoming increasingly excited, so excited in fact that he ignored the repeated knocking on the door.

"Hum!"

But the hound, his eyes glittering with excitement, simply barked at Ollie, nipping his legs as he ran down the stairs to see who it was.

Nicky stood on the doorstep. She cast an admiring eye over Ollie's running kit, "So you are going jogging. Auntie Em said you were but I didn't believe her. I guess you must have taken our little heart to heart yesterday more seriously than I thought," the photographer smirked. "I was going to ask you to Café Feliz but – "

"It's mainly because of Café Feliz that I'm going jogging." The neighbouring Portuguese café, with its custard tarts and full frontal calories, was a favourite refuelling stop. "Give me a second and I'll walk you round."

Closely followed by Hum Ollie went back upstairs. He grabbed his ipod, scrolled down to 'Sixteen Stone' by Bush and joined Nicky at the door.

They were soon on the bridge. "If I'm not back by – " Ollie glanced at his watch: it was ten thirty, "by twelve – "

"By twelve?" Nicky exclaimed. "How far are you planning on going?"

" – send a search party ok?"

"Of strapping men?"

Ollie nodded.

"In uniform?"

Ollie nodded again, "Yes please. With shiny brass buttons if possible."

"You got it sweetheart," Nicky blew him a kiss and headed towards the Portuguese café.

Ollie and Hum went in the opposite direction, under

Trellick Tower, into Meanwhile Gardens and onto the towpath of the Grand Union Canal.

⁂

Rion had been awake since eight o'clock, woken by the chorus of Canada geese on the canal. She had slept surprisingly well. The long day, the fresh, slightly damp air, the darkness of her new lodgings and the warmth of the down sleeping bag had brought about a deep, seemingly dreamless sleep.

"I am in London, I am in London, I am in London," Rion had repeated to herself since she woke up, smiling more and more every time she said it. The longer she was away from her family the stronger, the more confident, the more 'herself' she felt, even though she wasn't at all sure who 'herself' was.

At least not yet.

Jake's four-note whistle alerted her to his arrival. Rion heard him push his way through the saplings into the little clearing outside Old George's old home, which might, she thought, be Rion's new one.

In his hand he carried a package wrapped in metal foil. If it was again Cuban food, if it was again as good as the fish and dumplings he had brought last night, then Rion would be happy.

"Good morning, nice morning!" Jake exclaimed with the exuberance of a barrow boy. He found Rion, motionless, looking intently through the rustic fence at something on the canal.

Rion put a finger to her lips, "Shhhh!"

Hidden from the canal by Old George's screen of branches and sticks Rion gazed at one of the birds that gave the place its name.

The heron had not been disturbed by Jake's arrival. It

continued wading on its long thin legs, occasionally spearing the water with its beak, searching for eels, for carp and small pike.

Rion was transfixed. The bird had a tufted crown, a badger stripe running down the back of its head and what looked like a rough necklace of different sized feathers hanging at the top of its chest.

She gestured to the heron's feather necklace. "It's like something Hitherto Williams would use isn't it?"

The awkward silence that followed was broken by a high-pitched woman's shriek coming from the other side of the cemetery wall. The heron looked up, flapped its enormous wings and flew lazily to the other bank.

Upon hearing the shriek – a cry more of wonder than of fear – Jake cocked his head to one side and smiled, "Senora Padilla."

Rion didn't understand. "Excuse me?"

"That's Senora Padilla," Jake gave a short, mischievous laugh, "confirming her belief in spirits."

"Sorry?"

"Near my tree there's a large, double-fronted family grave in grey marble," Jake explained, "perhaps you saw it yesterday?"

Rion shook her head.

"It's the resting place of the Padilla family, although the grandfather, Jose Gabriel, is as yet the only occupant. His grieving widow comes to talk to him and to pray every Wednesday and Sunday."

The picture was becoming clearer to Rion. "And she always brings food right?"

"Lovingly prepared by her hands – didn't you think it was good?"

"Well, yes," Rion had to agree it was.

"If I didn't take it, the foxes and crows would get it."

"But – "

"It's not like I'm stealing or anything."

"Yes, but – "

"And she doesn't see me, I mean, she's praying, eyes firmly closed, when I take it."

"But it's wrong!"

"Why?"

"Because – "

"How do you know that she's not praying for something like that to happen? How do you know she's not hoping that when she opens her eyes the food will be gone, that the very act of the food vanishing doesn't somehow reaffirm her faith and comfort her?"

"It's still wrong."

Jake opened the envelope of metal foil. The fragrant smell of tomatoes and herbs wafted over to Rion.

"So you won't be having any then?" Jake asked.

The memory of last night's Cuban offering, the crumbly fish, the delicate sauce and the soft, almost creamy dumplings, made up Rion's mind for her.

"I didn't say that."

She nipped down the steps, brought out the chipped plate and cutlery and neatly divided Senora Padilla's graveside offering into two.

"Spoon or fork?" she asked Jake.

"Fork."

They ate from opposite sides of the plate.

For a few uncomfortable seconds their faces came within whiskers of each other as they lent down to scoop up the delicious food.

Instinctively they both pulled back.

"Sleep ok?"

Rion nodded between mouthfuls.

"The sleep of the just."

"Or the dead," Rion replied hesitantly. "I was exhausted."

Using one finger Jake eased the last dumpling onto his fork. "You know – "

Rion put up her hand to stop him, "Wait." She put her head to one side and listened. In the distance was the sound of barking.

And then she heard it.

The muffled sound of someone angrily shouting, "Hum!"

Ollie staggered down the towpath. Beside him were the enormous rusting gasometers, on the other side of the canal the broad expanse of the cemetery. Glancing at his watch for the umpteenth time he saw it had taken him fifteen minutes to get this far.

Fifteen minutes!

Almost the same time as it would have taken to walk.

Ollie's thighs and lungs burned, his breath came in painful rasps, his eyes blurred, his mouth was parched and his calves ached; Bush pounded on his ipod which, spitefully, seemed to be stuck on full volume and the hound was driving him mad.

Completely mad.

For every step of the way Hum, barking in feverish excitement, had leapt up and down right in front of his feet. With every stagger, every lurch that Ollie took, the dog threatened to trip him up.

Repeated admonitions had achieved nothing.

Ollie resigned himself to shouting the dog's name in the hope of getting him to behave, shouting the dog's name louder and louder, louder and louder above the blasting, blasted ipod.

Any second now he would turn back, he promised himself, any second now.

With relief he saw the knoll overlooking Little Wormwood Scrubs. That's where I'll turn round, he told himself, and not before. If I can just make it to -

But Hum had other ideas.

The mischievous hound, foaming at the mouth from exhilaration and exertion, came in just too close.

Ollie's right foot became wrapped in Hum's front feet. He tripped and stumbled. Flailing at the air, arms windmilling like mad, Ollie tumbled to the ground in what seemed to him like slow motion.

The headphones were ripped from his head. His ears buzzed in the newfound silence.

Above the sound of his curses and groaning Ollie was sure he could hear a girl's laughter. The strange thing was it seemed to be coming from the cemetery.

But that was impossible.

On the other side of the canal rows of tightly planted saplings lined the high brick cemetery wall. There was hardly enough room for a goose let alone a person.

Then something struck him.

Ollie quickly looked around. He was in front of the knoll, further on from the gasworks – there was no one else in sight.

Could it be Auntie Gem's spirit? The ghost of the young girl caught between Heaven and Hell?

Could it?

Ollie slowly got to his feet.

"Don't be stupid Ollie," he said out loud, "of course it's not." He reattached headphones to ipod, gave a last look at the saplings and limped back the way he came.

Hum ran ahead, ignorant of the damage he had caused.

Rion and Jake peered through the rough fence of branches Old George had woven between the saplings closest to the canal. They watched as Ollie shuffled around the corner.

"He won't have seen us but he might have heard you."

"Do you know him?"

"No, I've seen him around though. I recognise the dog."

Rion was dying to wash her face. She had been tempted to splash canal water on it then, mindful of what Jake had said Old George did in the canal – even though it was downstream – decided against it.

Who knows how many people upstream were doing what Old George did downstream?

Also she had managed to pee in the bushes but now something more urgent called and she wasn't doing *that* in the bushes.

"You know what you mentioned about Sainsburys and where I could, you know," Rion looked at the ground, "have a wash……"

"You don't get sea-sick do you?"

Sometimes, Rion thought, Jake said the oddest things.

"Er – no, at least I don't think so."

"Good. Get your things then and meet me near the broken rail."

Jake pushed his way through the saplings and was lost to sight.

Rion grabbed her toothbrush and toothpaste, some cotton wool, a bar of Boots' gentle cleanser and pushed through after him.

Further on from the broken railing leading to the cemetery she found Jake struggling with something stuck in the reeds.

With a final huff Jake pulled the object free.

Rion's heart sunk.

It was a two-man canoe in battered, yellow fibreglass, patched with glue and thick silver masking tape in several places.

"It's quite safe," said Jake cheerfully. He pulled a paddle out of the canoe before holding it above his head.

Water trickled from the front position.

"I got it from the scouts. They threw it out."

Now there's a surprise Rion thought.

He dropped the canoe, which landed with a smack on the water. "I often use it at night, it keeps me out of the guards' way – I just paddle across and leave it in the bushes under the towpath wall." Jake turned to Rion, his hand outstretched, "You get in first."

Rion looked at the canoe wobbling in the shallows, "No, I'll walk, I'll – "

"If you walk you'll need to go out through the cemetery, onto the Harrow Road and across the bridge. It'll take you fifteen minutes. In the canoe it'll take less than two."

That did it. She couldn't last fifteen minutes. Sometimes Nature doesn't call so much as shout, she thought unhappily.

Dispelling her fears Rion took Jake's hand and stepped into the leaky craft.

4

UNWANTED AND GOING FOR A SONG

It was 11.25 by the time Ollie got to Café Feliz.

He saw Nicky before she saw him. With the Sunday papers open on her knees the photographer sat in animated conversation with her usual lot outside the small café.

There was Liv who made stripy T-shirts and flip-flops with plastic flowers wound into the toe that 'le tout' Notting Hill clamoured for; her friend Isa, a brittle brunette who was something in PR; an American whose name Ollie always forgot who was involved in hair and make-up; the perma-tanned Ger who seemed to spend all his time in Goa or Thailand and Clive Fairland, a partying heterosexual fashion student with a penchant for drag.

Ollie's heart raced faster for a few beats upon seeing who sat with Clive. Even though he had cropped his formerly tousled long hair there was no mistake.

It was Will.

Ollie didn't know his last name but he did remember he was called Will. They had spent the night snogging drunkenly at a dreadful New Year's party, two – or was it three? – years ago.

There could be no doubt. It was the way the way he held his chin, it was his languid amused smile, and it was his dimples. His dimples!

"Sweetheart!" Nicky got up. She was about to put her arm around him when she saw his grazed knee.

"It's nothing," Ollie said before she could ask. "Hum tripped me up and – "

"Crash?" Nicky finished for him.

Ollie shook his head sorrowfully, "Yup."

"Want a pastry?"

Ollie looked at the custard tarts flaunting themselves in the window. He salivated, imagining his teeth sinking through the thin layers of pastry into the rich custard.

"No," Ollie said, "No." And then again to convince himself, "No thanks."

Nicky gestured to the people at the table, "You know everyone – "

Ollie nodded to one and all. He smiled at Will who lowered his eyes, "It's Will isn't it?"

Clive laughed, "Ollie you're terrible with names. This is Andy. Andy, Ollie."

Shaking hands seemed such a naff thing to do so Ollie just grinned stupidly. Andy? His name can't be Andy.

"Whatcha been listening to?" Clive asked.

Ollie realised with a shudder that they were all members of the style police. Something as potentially unhip as Bush would not go down well at all. He held the ipod tightly to him.

"Er – "

"Give us a clue at least," Liv pressed. "A lyric perhaps –"

"Hum a bar," Nicky suggested.

"Name that tune!" cackled Isa.

All attention was now on Ollie.

"Well," he squirmed. "I'm never quite sure if the line is: 'The cupboard is bare we *really need* food....' or: 'The cupboard is bare *my willy* needs food....'"

The group pondered in silence.

"That depends on whether it's heavy metal or some singer-songwriter. I mean, if it was Green Day – " Ger offered.

"Well, it's obviously not Green Day," Liv argued, "they're American and they wouldn't use a word like 'willy' would they?"

"Unless it was Vance Pashun, she's got balls – "

"And probably a willy too!" said Nicky.

" – she'd use it wouldn't she?" Clive looked to the others for confirmation.

All nodded and turned to Ollie.

"Is it Vance then? Is it 'Pashun'?" Clive asked.

Ollie shook his head, "No."

"Vance – the original Number 1 Fan," Andy muttered.

"Could it be Lily Allen?" inquired the American whose name Ollie never could remember.

"For 'we really'? or 'my willy'?" Isa giggled.

"Neither. You've had two chances and now I have to go I'm afraid," Ollie looked at Nicky. "Candida's coming round in half an hour – "

"Ouch!" Nicky got up to join him. "You'll need some support then."

" – and I want to have a shower before she arrives."

As Nicky folded her paper and picked up all the supplements from the floor Liv asked, "Who was it then? On your ipod? You can't leave us not knowing."

Ollie breathed a quiet sigh of relief. "Next time!" he grinned as he took Nicky's arm and left to a chorus of disappointed groans.

After a few yards Nicky stopped in her tracks, struck by a sudden realisation.

"Oh I know who it is," she said turning to face the group.

"Shhhh! Nicks, let's go."

"Ollie and I play air guitar to it."

"C'mon Nicks we really must be – "

"It's Bush."

Ollie could feel himself blushing like a schoolgirl.

"Bush?? That sub-Nirvana tosh?" Ger raised an eyebrow in exaggerated surprise. "Kinda retro I guess."

"Post-retro more like," Liv took Ollie's side. "The amount of times they're listed as influences these days."

"Yeah, well, I needed something to throw me down the canal."

"It's a wonder you didn't throw yourself in it!" Clive howled.

Nicky looked at her friend, "It *is* Bush isn't it Ol?"

Ollie didn't reply. He looked back at the table, taking in Will's – Andy's – chuckle and gave a resigned wave of farewell.

He could still hear their amusement as they crossed the bridge.

"You could have been a bit more supportive," Ollie grumbled, "and said it was Florence and the Machine or Bat for Lashes or someone."

"But it wasn't Ol."

"Next time I'll give them a bar from a Miles Davis song, that'll get them."

"And you can really hum freeform jazz can't you?"

"Well," Ollie blustered, "well – ". He quickly changed the subject, "What do you know about Andy?"

"Not much. I've seen him around though. He's a drummer or something. Funny how you thought his name was Will."

"It was Will," Ollie insisted. "I know it's him Nicks. He snogged me rotten at Spider's New Year's party a couple of years ago – we had a joke about his name, '*Will* he, won't he? *Will* I? *Will* you?' you know, silly drunken humour."

"How many people have you drunkenly snogged?"

"That's an unfair, loaded question."

" – at New Year's parties?"

Ollie glared at her, "Ok, I give in."

"Think about it Ollie. Maybe it was someone else."

But Ollie wasn't listening any longer. His attention had been taken by a brown Mercedes jeep parked outside the blink-and-you'd-miss-it entrance to the mews.

The front door to Ollie's house was open. Hum, growling, bounded past the workroom and up the stairs. Ollie and Nicky followed.

"Soi fort mon ami," Nicky squeezed his hand.

As always when he was nervous Ollie began whistling the theme tune from *Bewitched*, the sixties hit tv show turned into noughties flop film.

Coming up the stairs into the sitting room Ollie found Candida on a stepladder by the shelves next to the fireplace.

The lower shelves were crammed with books, but the upper one had a selection of prints and sketches that he had picked up over the years from his travels, from markets and auctions.

It was the upper one that Candida appeared interested in.

Hum, a dangerous glint in his eye, had made it to the third rung of the ladder that now wobbled precariously.

"Call him off Oliver."

"Hum. No."

But Hum was intent on going further.

"Oliver!"

Ollie went over to the stepladder, picked up Hum and firmly put him on the floor.

"On your bed," Ollie commanded but Hum stayed where he was. "On your bed!" he said more loudly. The dog smiled at Ollie, gave a last snarl at Candida and moved reluctantly to his leopard-print snug under the table.

Ollie helped Candida down from the stepladder.

"You have quite a good little collection, of no value of course," she sniffed disdainfully, "but interesting."

"Still working at Sotheby's Candida – or is the Hermès scarf just for effect?" Nicky was unable to keep the sarcasm out of her voice.

"Still taking little snaps?" Candida cooed in return before turning back to Ollie. "I found a key in James' things Oliver, I was early so thought I'd better let myself in. I hope you don't mind," she smiled sweetly, immediately putting Ollie on edge. "I'll get right to it. James was given a miniature by great Aunt Wilhemina before she died. It's a portrait of a young woman in a silvery fur wrap – you haven't seen it by chance?"

"No Candida," Ollie lied.

"James didn't leave it here or – "

"No."

"It's just the portrait is of one of my ancestors. It's worthless and is only of value to us, the family. We're anxious to keep it as a historical reminder and – "

Ollie cut her short, "If I see it I'll let you know."

"The funny thing is I'm sure James said he gave – lent it to you?" Candida looked Ollie straight in the eye.

Ollie tried not to blink but couldn't. To ease his nerves he again whistled a few bars of *Bewitched*.

"Oliver," Candida's voice returned to its normal coldness, "I know you have it."

"Listen Miss La-di-da Nose-In-The-Air," Nicky moved between them. "Ollie said he doesn't have it, and besides, if your brother gave this painting to him, he obviously wanted Ollie to have it didn't he?"

Excited by Nicky's raised voice Hum emerged, tail wagging, from under the table.

Ollie gestured for Nicky to calm down, "It's ok Nicks."

"No it's not ok! She lets herself in, snoops around, practically accuses you of theft. It's not ok."

"There's an easy way of doing this, Oliver, and a hard way."

"Candida, if I see this miniature – "

"If?" Candida repeated scornfully. "I can see you're going to choose the hard way." She grabbed her Bill Amberg bag of soft tan leather and made to leave. "I never did understand your relationship with my brother. You loved him and he didn't love you – wasn't that it? That's not a relationship Oliver, that's pathetic."

Ollie felt his eyes welling up.

Candida turned at the top of the stairs and gestured to Hum who began to bark and snarl. "You know if it wasn't for me you wouldn't have the damn dog. I could have had him put in a home, I could have had him put down."

Hum took this opportunity to deliver a light nip to Candida's ankles.

"And if that's drawn blood, he will be."

Nicky had to restrain the snarling, snapping Hum.

"Candida?" Nicky pronounced it 'Candeeder' knowing it would annoy the hell out of her. "Haven't you forgotten something?" Nicky held out her hand palm up and gestured to James' sister.

Candida grimaced. She unballed her fist, threw the front door key at Nicky's feet and stomped down the stairs.

As the door slammed Nicky put an arm around her friend, "It's no wonder they named an ailment after her."

Ollie pulled Nicky to him and began to cry.

"You got the key back I hope?"

Ollie nodded to Auntie Em's question. He sipped the Bloody Mary that he was so fond of and she was so good at making.

"Well, Nicky did actually. She was great. You would have been proud Auntie Em," Ollie raised his glass in salute to the photographer. "Candida had obviously planned this. I told her I'd be out until twelve."

"Maybe she *was* just early – "

"Half an hour early?"

"Well, it is Sunday afterall, perhaps the traffic might have been easier than she thought?"

"She lives in Holland Park Auntie Em."

"So it wouldn't take her more than – "

"Even with the road works on Ladbroke Grove it wouldn't take more than five minutes."

"And you got back at?"

"About 11:40 wasn't it Nicks?"

The photographer nodded, "She must have been there for a while already. She'd even been through the bedroom."

"And the studio," Ollie added.

"The little sneak. If I catch her snooping around again she'll regret it." Auntie Em went to her bedroom. When she returned she had in her hands the miniature of the girl in the silvery fur wrap.

Auntie Em turned the painting over.

"'Merlijnche de Poortje'," she read from the underside. "Unless the family are Flemish – ?" she looked to Ollie for confirmation.

"German through and through. They were Hapsburgs."

Nicky was impressed. "You mean like the kings, queens and emperors kind of Hapsburgs?"

Ollie nodded. "You can almost tell from her jaw can't

you? There's something positively Teutonic about the way it juts out."

"God you can be a bit of an anorak Ol," Nicky tutted sadly, "like I know the facial characteristics of European royalty."

"James always said they were a very minor strain. It's an enormous family apparently. Anyway they were Hapsburgs until the First World War when they changed their name to–"

"Hapshill," Auntie Em finished for him.

"Don't believe a word of what Candida said. It's not a family heirloom. I was with James when he bought it at a rather cheap and nasty auction in Brighton," Ollie looked at the painting, "It was unwanted and going for a song. James fell in love with it."

"Is it by any one famous?"

"Some Dutch school apparently – but that could mean anything."

Nicky looked at the miniature, "She looks so calm and poised doesn't she?"

They all admired the painting with its striking use of shadows and light.

"What do you think Candida's up to Ol?" Nicky asked

Ollie shrugged, "Until we find out Merlijnche de Poortje might be safer here. Auntie Em – would you?"

Auntie Em topped up their glasses, "It would be a pleasure."

Auntie Gem's favourite Sunday mass was the one with the Sisters at their chapel in St Charles Square. She hadn't missed their mid-morning prayers for – for? Auntie Gem wracked her brain but she couldn't remember, all she knew was that it had been many, many years.

This morning Sister Margaret had asked for special prayers for those lost and alone. Auntie Gem immediately thought of the ghost of the poor young girl she had seen in the cemetery and offered up a prayer for her deliverance. What with seeing the ghost, and with her concern about Ollie, this could turn into a six-mass-day she thought.

After the service and a cup of tea with the Sisters, Auntie Gem crossed Ladbroke Grove into the two storey Victorian shopping terrace of Golborne Road. Even on a Sunday the little street was busy, its Portuguese cafés, delis and North African street vendors doing a steady trade from regulars and incomers alike.

Gem bought some black olives marinated in lemon juice, Emma's favourite kind, from the friendly Moroccan. She could never call Emma 'Em' like others did. She quite liked 'Auntie Em' – but she couldn't call her charge 'Auntie' could she?

Auntie Gem chuckled at the thought.

Emma would always be her charge, would always be the mischievous creature she had cared for since a baby, had cared for, in fact, for all of Emma's fifty three years – the first nineteen of which had been spent in Jamaica. After 'the accident' as Auntie Gem referred to it – she had never believed Emma's father had committed suicide – they had been forced to come to England where they had been for the last thirtyfour years.

Thirtyfour years.

Even though England was certainly her home and she was settled here now, Auntie Gem harboured thoughts of returning to Redlight, the tiny village of her birth, in the Blue Mountains above Kingston.

Perhaps next year after she retired, she thought.

Perhaps.

Auntie Gem picked her way through the crowds outside the cafés amazed at how, with the first hint of sunshine, the people outside Café Feliz wore shorts and t-shirts. She shivered, adjusted the brim of her brown felt hat, tightened her chunky knit scarf and pulled her quilted coat around her. It would take a lot more than autumn sunshine to get Gemma Nelson into something lighter.

Entering the small cobbled mews she could hear voices coming from the large corner house she shared with Emma.

"And how was your run angel?" Auntie Em refilled Ollie's glass.

"Well, it wasn't so much a run Auntie Em as a jog," Ollie's brow furrowed slightly. "Actually even jogging is overstating things. It was more like a cross between walking and falling. I staggered and stumbled along the canal, literally bouncing off the walls. "

"Something you'll be doing regularly then?"

"Perhaps. If you see a sign on my door saying 'gone lurching' you'll know where I am," Ollie paused to take a sip from his Bloody Mary. "This might sound ridiculous – "

Nicky and Auntie Em looked over. They both liked things that sounded ridiculous.

" – but I think Auntie Gem's ghost might exist."

Auntie Em stopped refilling Nicky's glass to give him an amused look, "Really?"

"I didn't have a chance to tell you before but when I was jogging – "

No one had heard Auntie Gem come in. She had hung up her coat by the front door and was about to make her presence known when she overheard Ollie's remark about the ghost.

Feeling guilty for listening Auntie Gem remained motionless in the stairwell. She heard Ollie recount how he heard a young girl's laughter coming from the cemetery opposite the knoll overlooking Little Wormwood Scrubs.

"But the funny thing was the laughter seemed to have an otherworldly quality," he continued. "It just seemed to hang in the air."

"Couldn't someone have been on the other side?"

"No, you would see them. It's where the iron cemetery fence turns into a brick wall. The canal bank just there is hardly big enough for a goose let alone a person."

Auntie Gem could bear it no longer.

"Hello?" she called up.

"Not a word about the ghost," Auntie Em hissed to Ollie who nodded. Hum awoke from his slumber and trotted over to greet the elderly, but ageless, black lady as she came up the stairs into the sitting room.

"Doesn't he bark?"

"Only at people he doesn't like Auntie Gem," Ollie took an envelope from his jacket and gave it her. "A little present for you. Open it later."

It was closer to seven when Ollie and Nicky finally left. Trellick Tower loomed large above them, its crown of aerials half-shrouded in mist.

"Are you sure you won't come? The new Almodovar is showing at The Gate."

"There's something I have to do Nicks."

"We'll be at The Cow later."

"Maybe I'll join you."

Nicky kissed him on the cheek, "Liar."

Ollie watched Nicky walk out of the mews. Without looking back she put one arm in the air and waved – just like Sally Bowles in *Cabaret* Ollie thought, smiling as he let himself into his house.

Closing the door he realised he could put it off no longer.

"Hum," Ollie called.

The dog sat down obediently at the bottom of the stairs and looked at his master.

"It's time isn't it?"

Ollie took a deep breath and opened the door to his workroom.

It's surprising how neglected something can look in just a few weeks, he thought. Dust covered the surfaces, his tools huddled in disarray, sketches lay scattered over the desk and floor.

Spiders' webs stretched over and between the work in progress – an Empire table for Mrs Harrison, a cabinet for the Delameres, some elaborate arrow curtain rods and door handles for Lady Fairland, a coffee table – heavily inspired by Allen Jones – for Johnson Ogle and eight dining room chairs to match the table he delivered in July for Donal O' Keane.

The answerphone flashed urgently with weeks of messages. Faxes, curling over and over, buried the dusty machine. Ollie booted up his neglected laptop, watching in dismay as three hundred and forty three emails flooded his inbox.

He looked around, took another deep breath and set to work.

In the corner house Auntie Gem took Ollie's envelope and sat before her shrine. She knew what was in it before she opened it.

Ollie never disappointed.

Inside was a picture cut from a magazine, a picture she hadn't seen before. It showed a tall, fair-haired woman with extraordinary eyes. She wore an evening gown, simple diamond drop earrings and a radiant, radiant smile.

Auntie Gem found a place for it with the many others that made up her shrine. All the pictures were of the same elegant woman taken at various points in her life.

Auntie Gem wouldn't be going to any more masses today, she decided. She would stay in front of her shrine, the warmth of the woman would calm and ease her soul.

Auntie Gem lit a candle and asked forgiveness for eavesdropping on the others this afternoon, she asked for the young girl's wandering soul to find its home and she asked that Ollie be comforted in his sorrow.

Auntie Gem looked into the eyes of the woman smiling down at her.

Diana 'the Queen of Hearts, the People's Princess' would help – Auntie Gem knew she would.

5

VILLAINS, ROGUES AND ROYALTY

Rion couldn't have imagined she would ever feel this good.

She could hear Jake clattering plates, cutlery and pans as he washed up by the canal. The taste of the fish and vegetables he had cooked remained with her. The blackened billy atop the small fire promised tea within minutes and the stars pinpricked the darkness above. Rion pinched herself hard to make sure she wasn't dreaming.

Was it really less than fortyeight hours since she had left home?

Home was such an ugly word, it sounded as though it was always a place meant to be left. Rion shivered, lightly feeling the cigarette burns on her wrist – a souvenir of 'home'.

But here she was. And no one from 'home' knew she was here.

Jake had helped her clean out the chamber. The mattress had been scrubbed and aired, the table, chest and shelf wiped down, the floor swept and when the candles were lit – well, you could be anywhere.

Rion smiled with a sense of pride as she looked down the steps into the candle-lit space. It was really rather cosy she thought. The picture of Blondin was pinned under the one of Jesus with the open red heart. Her thin trousers of black and white checks, her socks and assorted tops were neatly laid out on top of the chest of drawers. Her washpack and prized mini-ipod were on the shelf by the bed. The collection of magazines from Tanya's salon (dog-eared copies of year-old Vogue, Glamourista and Hello) and her favourite self-help book were on the rickety table. The only thing Rion had put away was her underwear, which she had placed in the top drawer of the small chest.

Jake had given her a faded pink blanket which was now tied back over the open doorway. As long as it didn't rain, or at least didn't rain too hard, she would be ok.

The clattering stopped. Within seconds Jake pushed into the small, fenced clearing.

"If Blondin inspired you there are several others here you should know about."

Rion held out her hands over the flames, enjoying the warmth of the fire, "Like who?"

"Like Dr James Barry for a start."

Rion shrugged her shoulders, "Who's he?"

"Who's he?" Jake laughed. "Don't you mean who's she?"

"She?" Rion shook her head in disbelief. "James isn't a woman's name!"

"Marion isn't a man's name but it was John Wayne's."

"John Wayne – the actor?"

"The icon," Jake carefully put two measures of tea in the bubbling billycan and left it to stew. "Dr James Barry – " Jake let out a loud sigh of appreciation, " – was way cool. She disguised herself as a man and had a hugely successful army career, eventually becoming Inspector General of the Army Medical department."

"Didn't anyone know?"

"Not even her landlady or her servant. The truth only popped out, so to speak, when she died."

Rion giggled. "But someone must have guessed, must have suspected, I mean they *must* have."

"She even fought and won a duel with a fellow officer at the Cape of Good Hope."

Rion paused for a while to take in the extraordinary information. "I guess if there were doubts," she conceded, "fighting a duel is a pretty good way to remove them."

"It's a typically dumb male thing, fighting a duel I mean, not a very feminine response is it?"

"And her name was Dr James Barry?"

Jake nodded.

"There are other characters here like – Wilkie Collins?" Jake looked over at Rion.

Rion shook her head. She hadn't heard of him either.

"He wrote *The Woman in White* – acclaimed as the first detective story. He was a friend of Dickens and Thackeray and is buried here *with his mistress.*" Jake glanced at Rion who wasn't shocked. "He was extremely tall and due to a difficult birth had a huge head and tiny feet – feet so small that he could wear women's shoes."

"Did he? Wear women's shoes I mean?"

Jake didn't think so but to make the story more interesting said, "Embroidered with red roses I hear!"

Rion clapped her hands in delight.

"Throughout his life he suffered from rheumatoid arthritis and so was prescribed laudanum – an alcohol/opium mix and very popular in Victorian times – which he took to like a natural. His fondness for laudanum increased his tolerance and he was forced to take it in ever larger measures, so much so that when, at the end of his life, his housekeeper mistakenly swallowed half of his draught she keeled over and died!"

"I bet she didn't mistakenly swallow it."

Jake smiled, "Probably not but I bet she regretted it!" He poured the tea into two mugs, "Milk and sugar?"

Rion nodded, "One please."

Rion felt herself relax. Sipping the hot, strong tea she listened as Jake told of villains, rogues and royalty. There was something rather calming about someone else doing all the talking. Rion's heart went out to the sadder stories, amongst them Princess Sophia, unhappy daughter of George 111, who was seduced and made pregnant by a scheming courtier more than twice her age. Almost exiled to Europe she led a lonely life and was, towards the end, totally blind.

There was also an infant prodigy pianist by the name of Elizabeth Soyer who took fright, poor thing, during a tremendous thunderstorm and died; but perhaps saddest of all was the story of Mary Hogarth, Dickens' sister-in-law to whom he was devoted. She died of a heart attack at the age of seventeen in her carriage on the way back from seeing one of his plays. Her death at such a young age affected the great writer for the rest of his life.

"And he never, ever got over it." As Jake finished he looked over at Rion who was clearly entranced.

Rion took a last sip of her now cold tea. She swirled the tea leaves around the bottom of the mug before tipping them out on the ground. Straining her eyes to see them in the darkness she realised their pattern would hold no clue to her future. Rion slowly raised her eyes to the tousled young man in front of her, "And how did you come to be here Jake?"

Jake laughed at her question. "You realise if I tell you my story I'll expect to hear one in return..."

Rion weighed this up. His story must be more interesting than hers, she guessed, and besides when the time came to tell her story she could plead tiredness or – ? Or? Something would spring to mind.

"Are you sure that's fair? I mean, the story of how you came to be living in a treehouse in a cemetery in London will take some b – " Rion was going to say 'beating' but the word was abit too familiar for comfort, "will take some topping."

"It's not a competition Rion."

He said Rion! That was the first time she had heard someone say her new name.

"Would you say that again?"

Jake's face glowed in the firelight. "Wha – ?"

"I'll tell you about it – perhaps in my story."

"Perhaps?" Jake asked.

Rion gave in, "Perhaps certainly."

"It's not a competition."

Rion gestured for him to continue, "It's not a competition– ?"

"It's not a competition, Rion."

Perfect. It sounded perfect she thought. And natural. Perfectly natural.

"Ok. Where to start?" Jake was silent for a moment and then began his tale. "I dropped out of university in my second year and I've been here ever since. It was easier then, there were no guards and there were more of us – well, just Old George and me were here but under the gasometers was a whole secret community. You'll see on the other side of the canal there's an old cherry tree – its main branch twists over the towpath wall – well, you could just hop over there and you would be in this hidden world. There were also many more people living on canal boats then too."

"But why here?"

Jake didn't have to think to answer. "Because it's so easy. There's everything I could want here. Fish, eels, duck and goose eggs, Cuban meals twice a week, even spliffs and rum."

Rion wrinkled her nose. She knew what a spliff was even though she hadn't tried one. Or wanted to.

"Where do you get those from?"

"From the grave of a Caribbean bandleader, Mr Marks, amongst other places. His funeral was packed. Packed! I've never seen who leaves them but they're regular – not as regular as Senora Padilla, but not infrequent either. And I love it here. It's so quiet and where I sleep moves and creaks with the tree. Where else in London could I get that?"

Rion didn't know. Feeling that it might be her turn soon she stretched and gave an exaggerated yawn.

"And I do P & D – painting and decorating – there's always work." He pulled a mobile phone from his worn jean jacket, "I get a call – I'm there. I've got work for the next month."

"And your family?"

"Haven't seen them in years. We're not compatible – you know?"

Did she ever.

Rion stifled another heavy yawn. "What about your friends?"

"A couple know. Most don't. If they want me," Jake tapped his mobile phone, "they know where to find me."

"What about...." How could she put this? "What about, 'when the tree's rocking, don't come knocking'?"

Jake chuckled, "That's personal." With relief Rion saw him get up to leave. "I'm going to turn in, I can see you're tired too."

Saved, Rion thought.

"I'm working early tomorrow. There's a couple of apples in the bag, longlife milk, sugar and – are you up to making tea?" -

Jake could see the thought of bubbling billycans, fires and

pan holders, even in daylight, was not an attractive one to Rion.

"If not you'll have to wait until about five. I'll bring some supper but you'll have to sing for it."

Oh God, Rion cringed, he can't possibly mean karaoke can he?

"And you're ok?"

Rion nodded.

Jake smiled and was gone.

Rion stayed beside the dying fire until it lost its warmth. With a real yawn she went down the steps, got into the sleeping bag, blew out the candles and was soon fast asleep.

6

REVELATIONS

Auntie Gem didn't mind Mondays. Unlike others who dreaded the start to the week Auntie Gem looked forward to it. She liked the fresh feelings Mondays brought, no matter what the weather, like slipping into clean sheets in an old bed.

She had worked at Peters & Peters ever since she had come to England with Emma. Every day she walked to and from the factory that bordered the canal on the other side of the cemetery. Auntie Gem was sure the daily walk, rain or shine, blow or snow, was the reason she was so rarely ill.

For the first time in three generations there was only one member of the Peters family in the business. The company, makers of 'Peters Garden Helper – the Spray the Garden Loves!' and 'Peters Kitchen Helper – the Spray the Kitchen Loves!' amongst numerous other snappily named and advertised household cleaners, was run by the last of the line, her boss Sir Edwin Peters.

Auntie Gem was in charge of the executive trolley for teas, coffees and biscuits. She would also bring Edwin his meals when he was too busy to come to the dining room. Despite his recent knighthood she still addressed her boss as 'Mr' Edwin, a fact that both endeared her to him as well as annoyed him. It was easy work and Gem enjoyed it.

Walking down the canal on her way to work this Monday morning she was struck at how her daily life so often turned her thoughts to the Queen of Hearts.

Ollie's dog Hum made her think of Diana. His eyes, large, trusting and sometimes sorrowful were so like the princess' – especially when he looked up at her through his heavy eyelids. Could human souls move into animal souls?

Could they?

Auntie Gem wondered. Afterall Ollie had said Hum had been born on the tenth anniversary of Diana's death.

Had the soul of the Diana, Princess of Wales, somehow moved into Ollie's dog?

Such a bizarre notion was too weird, especially for Mondays. Auntie Gem immediately felt guilty for thinking such a thing. She quickly crossed herself and carried on.

Another reminder of Diana was the heron she almost always saw on the way to and from Peters & Peters. If she didn't see the heron she felt disappointed and strangely abandoned. Seeing the slightly sinister looking bird always took her back to the eve of Diana's funeral, a clear, cool Friday evening in early September at least ten years before, when she had gone with Emma to Kensington Gardens.

Auntie Gem remembered that painful time so well. She had taken a week's leave, spending most of it in the tribute-filled gardens in front of the palace, and had especially wanted to be there for the princess' last night in her home.

As the sun set over Kensington Palace Emma had pointed out the heron, wings closed over its body like a monk's cowl, beneath one of the three enormous stone urns on the roof above Diana's apartment.

At first they had taken it for a decorative sculpture until it changed position and shook its pointed beak at them – right at them! Silhouetted against the dying sun the bird remained guarding the princess until night fell and they watched it slowly fly northwards – northwards to this section of the Grand Union Canal.

Since that time Auntie Gem had wondered if what she now called 'her heron' was indeed the one atop Kensington Palace that night.

Was it? she asked herself. Could it really be the same bird?

As if to confirm this the ring of a bicycle bell interrupted her musings. As the cyclist sped past Auntie Gem looked up and there, watching motionless from the opposite bank, was the heron.

But that wasn't all that got her attention.

Auntie Gem saw that she was now just further on from the gasometers. With a shiver she looked over at the opposite side of the canal, at the tightly planted saplings lining the cemetery wall.

And then she heard it. A young girl's tuneless singing. All Auntie Gem could think of were the lost and lonely warblings of Ophelia before she threw herself in the river and drowned. The words were indistinct, the voice unclear as it dipped then grew in intensity, seemingly lacking in rhythm or rhyme.

More proof of the wandering soul of the poor young girl.

Ollie had heard the otherworldly laughter, she herself had seen the spectral, virginal figure and now here was further proof.

Auntie Gem kept her eyes straight ahead. She blocked her ears and quickened her step, relieved to see the chimney of Peters & Peters beyond Mitre Bridge in the distance.

Unaware of the ghostly status she had attained Rion sang along to her favourite songs, playing and replaying the same tunes but now, she realised sadly, the battery in her ipod was fading.

Remembering batteries can be recharged if left in the sun Rion took the headphones off, removed the powerpack from the music player and placed it in the brightest bit of sunlight.

She had had another good night, finished Jake's last apple and now wondered what she was going to do. Even though she had no money she knew something would turn up, besides Tanya would send the savings she had been entrusted with, but – where would she send them?

Old George's Cavern, Kensal Green Cemetery, London?

Rion smiled and picked up her wellworn copy of *Face the Fear and Eat It* – the book that had propelled her to London in the first place.

Sitting in the sun Rion was unworried. It would all be ok. The realisation that her family could no longer touch her made her smile and smile.

Today she was enjoying her freedom, the sun on her face and doing nothing. Absolutely nothing.

And as for the storytelling later?

Rion stretched and wiggled her toes, she would think about that when the time came.

Ollie was in his workroom when the phone rang.

"I'm not disturbing you am I sweetness?"

Ollie looked around him. He had been up since early that morning, returning calls, replying to the most urgent of faxes and emails, placating angry clients. "No, Auntie Em."

"I've just put the phone down on poor Gem. It seems she had another haunting experience on her way to work this morning."

"Another one?"

"At exactly the same place apparently."

"Further on from the gasworks?"

"So I believe, she was a bit upset and it was hard to understand exactly, anyway, she's refused to walk back."

"I could go and get her Auntie Em."

"Thanks for offering angel," he was such a kind boy she thought, "but I'm going to collect her from work later, the thing is – I need a favour."

"Ask away."

"Well, Auntie Gem has refused to walk down the canal until – well – until that part is exorcised."

The penny began to drop, albeit slowly.

"And you want me to – ? Auntie Em you know how terrible I look in priestly garb, remember Nicky's Halloween party? I mean I just can't carry it off and besides – "

"Sweetness, I was only going to ask you to investigate – just so we can tell Gem there is no ghost and nothing to be afraid of…"

Ollie wasn't exactly thrilled but he felt he had to satisfy his own curiosity anyway. "It'll have to be later on."

"You're an angel, angel."

It was close to four thirty when Ollie knocked on Nicky's door. He could hear music coming from her studio which normally meant she was working.

Nicky opened the door and looked him up and down.

"You've got quite good legs you know – "

Having decided his tracksuit bottoms were too cumbersome Ollie had changed into shorts.

"– but shouldn't you have a day's break between exercise?"

Ollie closed the door behind him and followed her into the large open room on the ground floor. "Well, if I stop now I'll never start again. I'm not disturbing anything am I?"

The studio was set up for a shoot. Hum raced to the other side of the large piece of black material that split the room in two.

"I was just taking some pictures of – you two know each other don't you?"

Ollie stuck his head around the screen to see an instantly familiar face. Dressed all in black, with vibrantly patterned pink socks, the man sat on a stool in the middle of the space. Hum sniffed him curiously.

It was Will.

Or was it Andy?

"Oh. Hi," Ollie nodded, his heart beating furiously.

"Andy needed some shots done. He's off to Japan later this month."

Trying not to show too much interest Ollie looked at the floor and grunted.

"Hey," Nicky was unable to contain her excitement. "Angie just called – the shoot with Vance has been confirmed!"

"Do you think it'll happen this time?" Ollie asked, still not daring to lift his eyes from the floor.

"We've been told she'll be in town for the Awards at the end of the month – so a step closer."

"That's great – I really hope it happens," Ollie said, before remembering why he was there. "Could I borrow your ipod Nicks? Mine's bust."

"Don't worry, I've got some Bush tunes," Nicky nudged him in the ribs and grinned. "It's on the counter."

Acutely aware of Andy's presence Ollie looked through Nicky's downloads – a mixture of old, new, borrowed and blue. He scrolled to a selection that would satisfy even the strictest of style police, flashing the screen as proof. "It's Al Green," he kissed Nicky on the cheek. "Don't talk about me," he whispered.

Ollie whistled for Hum and made his way out. He was dying to say something to Andy – but what? Turning at the edge of the screen Ollie said, as coolly as possible, "I love your socks."

I love your socks? Did he really say that?

With Hum barking excitedly in front of him Ollie jogged through Meanwhile Gardens and onto the canal. After the shortest of times his legs began to ache. Nicky was right, perhaps he should have rested for a day or two.

He had just lumbered under Ha'Penny Bridge when Al Green began to croon about how tired he was of being alone. Deciding Al was a touch close to the bone Ollie muted his ipod and continued in silence.

After half-a-mile he turned off the canal and walked breathlessly over the bridge at the top of Ladbroke Grove. Ollie entered the cemetery through the small gate by the Dissenters' Chapel and quickly made his way along the woodchip paths until he saw he was opposite, but further on from, the huge gasometers.

The graves were neglected here. No authors' societies, no ennobled families, no loving relatives tended these forgotten tombs.

Snuffling happily Hum skirted several overgrown headstones before arriving at the iron-railing fence that marked the cemetery border. Without looking back Hum squeezed through a loose railing and vanished into the rows of tightly planted saplings on the other side.

"Hum!" Ollie barked angrily but the hound had gone.

Ollie could see a small trail stopped at the fence and then carried on the other side. Wishing he had brought a bottle of holy water with him, Ollie pushed the weak railing to one side and went through.

Despite having been in the sun for most of the day the battery hadn't re-charged. It figures, Rion thought, the only thing I can remember from science class and it doesn't work anyway. Disappointed she took off the headphones, realising she couldn't get any more batteries until Tanya sent down her savings.

Again she wondered – where would Tanya send them?

A rustling and a panting broke into her thoughts. A black, shaggy dog, obviously young, bounded into the tiny clearing and over to her. Tail wagging, it sat at her feet and gave her a paw. She could see large brown eyes grinning up at her from behind its unkempt fringe.

Rion immediately recognised the dog. Panicking slightly she realised that its owner couldn't be far behind.

A more ungainly huffing, puffing and crashing announced Ollie's arrival. "Hum!" he called in annoyance as he pushed through the increasingly narrow path between the saplings. To his relief he saw an opening ahead. With a final thrust Ollie propelled himself through.

He staggered into the clearing to find a young girl with long, long hair looking at him with apprehension. Ollie knew who it was. Immediately. The girl who had stopped him on the canal a couple of days ago.

With some annoyance he saw Hum sitting contentedly at her feet.

"So you're not a ghost?" Ollie smiled, relieved, not that he had ever seriously entertained the notion, all the same the proximity to the graveyard had caused him to think more than twice.

Rion stayed silent.

"You've been scaring my elderly neighbour half to death. She's convinced you're a lost soul wandering between Heaven and Hell." Ollie grinned again to show her he meant no harm but the young girl again stayed silent.

By the ashes of the dead fire in front of him Ollie saw a well-thumbed book. He reached down for a closer look, picked it up and saw it was *Face the Fear and Eat It* – the bible of the self-help set. "Any good?" he asked.

Rion nodded nervously.

"A friend of mine saw his wife reading this – a week later she served him with divorce papers."

Rion didn't know what to say so simply looked at the ground.

Sensing his presence was unnerving her Ollie made to leave. "Anyway I didn't mean to disturb you. Hum!"

He noticed the young girl freeze slightly. The beginnings of a small smile spread over her lips before fading as abruptly as they appeared.

"I don't mean you," he joked. "Hum!" Ollie ordered again but the hound simply lay on his back and stretched.

"It's your dog's name isn't it? Hum?" Rion asked.

"Short for Humdinger – Humdinger the Third that is." Ollie felt slightly embarrassed. "I know – pets' names, where do they come from? – but at least he's not called Truffles – "

" – or Nero." For the first time he heard the girl laugh. "Hum," she smiled as she bent down to stroke the dog's stomach. "You know when I bumped into you a couple of days ago I thought you, and the woman you were with, were telling me to hum."

Ollie let out a yelp of laughter before chuckling apologetically, "Sorry."

"I was getting upset because the only tune I could think of was the National Anthem!"

"You must have thought – " Ollie laughed. "Well, what did you think?"

"I thought you were all mad," Rion smiled remembering the incident. "It's my first time in London you see."

"And your mother told you we'd be like this?"

Rion tensed. How did he know that's what her mother had said?

Ollie looked around the small clearing. Behind the girl he could see an opening, half-screened by a pink blanket, through which he could make out some sort of chamber. "What brought you to the city?"

The girl pointed to the book Ollie held in his hand. "Well, that book played a large part."

Ollie looked again at the worn copy of the self-help bible, "So it *is* that good." He gestured to the pink blanket tied across the opening, "And you live – here?"

"It's meant to be a secret really. Jake said – "

"Your boyfriend?"

"No!" Rion said quickly, feeling her face turn a bright red. Why couldn't she control her blushing, she asked herself for the thousandth time. "Just a friend. He helped me find this place actually."

As if on cue the four notes whistled into the clearing.

Rion gently whistled back. She looked at her watch. It was just after five. "Here he is now."

Ollie watched as a young man, a Sainsburys bag held tightly to his chest, squeezed through the narrow opening. Ollie judged him to be about the same height as himself but more ruffled, more sloppily handsome.

"I hope you're ready for – " Jake began before doing a doubletake upon seeing Ollie. He looked quickly at Rion.

"I was just talking about you," she smiled at Jake to let him know everything was all right. "This is Jake, I'm Rion and you are – ?"

"Ollie. Ollie Michaelson."

Rion peered into the supermarket carrier. "Is there enough for three?"

As the sun went down Jake built and lit a fire with the speed and ease of someone who had done it many times before.

"Lucky I bought a couple extra eh?" Jake took several potatoes from the carrier. He wrapped them in foil before placing them away from the main flame but still in the heat of the fire.

"You live near here don't you?" Ollie asked.

Jake wondered how much Rion had told him. "Yes," he replied truthfully. Ollie didn't have to know how near.

"I thought I'd seen you before." Through the woven mesh of branches Ollie could see the sun's dying rays reflected in the canal. "You'd never know this place existed from the other side, there just doesn't look to be enough room."

Jake pulled out a small bottle of Appleton's rum and two matchstick-sized joints from his army trousers.

"Are they from Marks?" Rion asked knowingly.

Ollie looked over at the tiny cigarettes, their ends rolled into twists. "And Spencers?" he asked amazed. "Which branch do you go to?"

Jake grinned, "Mr Marks the bandleader. He's buried –"

"He's dead?"

Jake nodded, "One of his supporters leaves an offering every now and then." He took a swig from the rum before offering it to Ollie.

Feeling curiously like an egyptologist in the Valley of the Kings Ollie looked at the bottle, "This isn't graverobbing is it?" Deciding it wasn't he raised the bottle in a toast to the departed steelband leader, "To Marks!" He took a gulp, nearly choking as the 150 proof Jamaican rum burned his lungs and throat. A shudder started in his shoulders worked its way down his spine through his groin and all the way to his toes that curled involuntarily.

With eyes watering he offered the bottle to Rion. "How old are you?" he gasped.

Rion took the bottle. "Old enough," without taking a sip she passed the rum to Jake, "and wise enough."

Another rum judder sent heat coursing through Ollie's body. He waited for the aftershock to subside before asking Jake, "Are there any other – er – things people leave?"

"Lots of flowers of course, some Cuban food – "

"Cuban – ?"

"Yup, food, it's delicious," added Rion.

"Letters and mawkish poems – "

"You read them?" Rion asked Jake

"If they're not sealed sure, why not? Don't you ever read other people's postcards?"

Ollie and Rion spoke at the same time.

"Yes!" Ollie said.

"No!" Rion answered.

Not that she had the chance, Rion thought. No one in her family ever got sent any cards. The only card she had ever received was from Tanya when she went to Greece two summers ago and everybody had read that before it got to her.

Ollie was still curious to find out about the young girl. "Rion was just going to tell me her story when you arrived." He looked over at the young girl, "Could we continue?"

"How much time do you have?"

Ollie opened his hands palm up as he looked at Jake, "I'm not going anywhere, are you?"

"Nope."

Although slightly hurt that Rion felt she could open up to Ollie when she had only just met him when he, Jake, had done so much to earn her trust, Jake hid his feelings. He picked up one of the small joints, lit it and gestured for Rion to go ahead.

As Rion vanished behind the pink blanket Jake passed the joint to Ollie who took three quick puffs before handing it back.

"To Marks," Ollie toasted again, struggling not to cough. Within seconds the small spliff had sizzled to an end, the sinsemilla mingling with the rum to produce a most enjoyable buzz. Ollie and Jake stretched out in the fireglow and waited for Rion to return.

They didn't have to wait long. When Rion returned she had with her the cutting of Blondin crossing Niagara. She knelt on the ground beside the fire and took a deep breath.

Rion told her story quickly and simply. She looked at the fire, occasionally glanced at the picture of Blondin in her hand, but steadfastly avoided Jake and Ollie's eyes.

"I'm the youngest, by several years, of four girls. My mum says my dad always took a lot of stick from his mates about his three girls and no boys. They somehow questioned his masculinity at not producing any sons so I was sort of his last ditch attempt at proving himself."

Ollie nodded. He understood the fragile male psyche.

"Anyway when I came along my dad took even more stick."

"Producing three girls might be regarded as foolishness but four looks like carelessness?" Ollie enquired.

Rion smiled but still refused to meet their eyes. "Something like that," she paused for a moment to gather her thoughts. "So growing up I was a constant reminder to him of his failure. He always went on about wanting a 'pride and joy' – that's what he called his longed for son – and I most certainly wasn't that – "

Jake interrupted, "In his eyes."

"Sorry?"

"You might not have been *his* pride and joy – "

"I'm no-one's pride and joy," Rion shook her head vehemently. "No-one's. Ever since I can remember my dad picked on me and when my sisters saw it was alright to pick on me, in fact that my dad seemed to encourage it, well there was no stopping them. They were like a pack together and I was outside it."

Ollie and Jake listened in silence, the Jamaican spliff heightening their empathy with Rion. Then Ollie asked something Jake had wanted to ask but hadn't dared.

"Is that why you have cigarette burns on your arms?"

Rion instinctively hugged herself as if to hide the telltale marks. Then she relaxed, she wasn't going to hide them any longer.

Rolling back the sleeves and collar of her fleece Rion displayed the marks of her abuse. Even in the firelight the twin scorched circles of skin, scabby and painful, were clearly visible on the soft white underbelly of each wrist. Further up her arm and around her neck were mottled splotches of bruising.

Ollie and Jake winced audibly.

"They don't hurt. At least not any more."

"How can people do that?" Ollie asked in horror.

"Without them I wouldn't be here, so in some strange way– " Rion lightly circled the burns with her finger, "I'm quite proud of them. They're what got me out of there." Rion pulled her sleeves down and her collar up. "As with anything else you get used to it." The girl seemed unfazed by the burns and the bruising. "I knew I'd get out sometime and look – " she smiled at them both, " – here I am."

Jake whistled between his teeth. "How did you survive?"

"By dreaming, by spending every second I could in Tanya's salon – and if I wasn't there I was in the library, anywhere apart from home," Rion explained. "Tanya's my friend, my only friend. I used to clean up, help with the shampooing, coffees and the like. Tanya used to give me all the magazines, 'Vogue, Tatler, Glamourista, ' – you know, all of those – in which I used to escape."

"So that's how you know about Hitherto Williams?" asked Jake.

"And 'Ghost', 'Browns' , 'Giles Deacon', 'Killer', 'John Galliano' 'Henry Holland' 'Preen....' Rion continued to reel off the names of designers and exclusive boutiques until Ollie held up his hand to stop her.

"But what are you going to do here in London?"

Rion knew she hadn't come to London to camp out in a cemetery, no matter how many worthy, inspirational people were buried there and no matter how kind and attractive Jake was, but if she told them – would they laugh?

"Well," Rion began before looking closely at the two young men sitting opposite her around the fire. "This is going to sound stupid but," she looked at the picture of Blondin before saying quickly, "I want to do something in fashion, hopefully work in a great shop, learn about cut and fabrics and people – how it all works." The words came out in a jumble. Rion quickly put some kindling on the fire. She watched intensely as the flames took hold, waiting to hear Ollie and Jake's derisive laughter which never came.

"And you'll be ok till then? You have money?" The September evening had turned cold. Ollie shivered and moved closer to the fire, silently cursing himself for not wearing his tracksuit bottoms.

"Yes, I mean no, I mean yes I'll be ok, living here is nothing if not cheap and Jake's a huge help." She smiled shyly at Jake who grinned back. "Tanya's been looking after my savings, she's going to send them down."

Ollie interrupted, "To where? She can't exactly send them here can she?"

"No, but – "

"Have you family in London?"

Rion shook her head.

"Friends?"

Rion looked at the ground, "Apart from you two, no," she said softly.

"Well if you trust me you can tell Tanya to send them to: 3 Meanwhile Gardens Mews, W10." In case Rion hadn't understood Ollie added helpfully, "That's where I live."

Rion looked over to Jake who nodded his agreement.

"One second," Rion again drew back the pink blanket. She descended into the candlelit space, returning with a pad of notepaper, a pencil and the down sleeping bag which she put around Ollie's legs.

Rion quickly wrote down his address while she still remembered, "Ollie Michaelson, 3 Meanwhile Gardens Mews W10?"

Ollie nodded and wrapped the sleeping bag around him, "Thanks. You know," he began to smile, "my friend Nicky takes pictures for Glamourista."

"Does she?" Rion flinched. This was all too much. "Would you..? could I?.... will..." she stammered, feeling her chest freeze up. Luckily Ollie knew what she wanted to say.

"I can't promise anything but she meets alot of people, maybe one of them is looking for someone."

Rion began to tremble slightly. She offered up a quick prayer of thanks. "So the streets of London are paved with gold?"

Ollie again held up his hand, "No promises but give me your number –" Ollie fumbled in the pocket of his shorts, pulled out a super-thin phone and nodded at Rion, "You've got a phone don't you?"

The young girl slumped slightly, thinking of the old Nokia Tanya had given her – and her sisters' delight at its destruction. "Not any more," she said sadly.

"I might have an old one at home, it won't have a camera or – "

"That's ok," Rion said quickly.

" – but we'll find one for you anyway."

With the pick from his Swiss Army knife Jake pierced the potatoes and smiled in satisfaction. He removed two packets of the supermarket's *beef bourguignon* from the carrier, turned the contents into a battered saucepan which he expertly placed over the fire. With Ollie's hunger already heightened by the marijuana the sizzling smell of stew set his tastebuds racing.

"Hungry?" Jake asked.

Ollie nodded perhaps a touch too eagerly. "Starving," he confirmed.

"Well, house rules are that you sing for your supper. I told my story last night. You've just heard Rion's, when we finish we expect to hear yours."

After the trio had wolfed down the stew, the mini pots of fromage frais were practically swallowed whole. Within seconds Jake and Rion looked at Ollie who knew his time had come.

Ollie reached for the bottle of rum, took another quick swig and waited for his juddering insides to calm down. "Well," he coughed lightly to clear his throat. "I – " Where to begin he wondered, his memory annoyingly clear even after the spliff and industrial strength rum.

With the firelight glowing on the faces in front of him Ollie began his story. The only reason he mentioned his public schooling on a vast Palladian estate near Buckingham was because it was there he met James. Ollie lightly touched on his family life, how his parents weren't suited and how he had been mainly brought up by his grandmother in London.

"Is she still alive?" asked Rion.

Ollie nodded, "Oh yes."

"And living in London?"

"Some of the time. She's taken to cruising like a," Ollie cleared his throat, "duck to water but if she's in town Gran can be found anywhere there's a Dior make-up counter."

"And your parents?"

"My father remarried when I was four and lives in the States. There's little contact or love there," Ollie said matter-of-factly. "My mother works for UNICEF. I see her occasionally for a couple of minutes on tv whenever there's a crisis." He raised his hands palms up, "That's that side of things."

Rion and Jake listened enthralled as Ollie told them of his travels with James after leaving school – trekking around India before wandering though Burma, down into Thailand, to Sumatra, Java, Bali and finally to Australia.

"After coming back to England we lived together at James' place in Holland Park, but soon realised we fancied other people: James – women, me – men."

"And you were ok with that?" Jake poked the dying fire, which obligingly flared into life.

Ollie took a deep breath – had he been ok with it? "Sure. There's often more love in friendship than friendship in love."

Jake stoked the flames with some well-placed branches. "And then what?"

Ollie looked at the fire for a while, mesmerised by the embers glowing a blistering red. "I went to Cornwall to study carpentry. When I returned I shared a house – not lived with – James but it was too complicated. I moved out and into

Meanwhile Gardens Mews where I've been for the past five years."

"And James?"

Ollie didn't answer the question immediately.

"You know even though we weren't living together or anything like that we were still very protective of each other. There were many times when we used to sleep in the same bed – nothing else mind – just because to wake up to a loved one's face is one of the joys of the world, no?"

Rion listened agog. Is this what people did? It all sounded so civilised, so grown-up.

"Anyway – "

Ollie looked them level in the eye. He quickly decided it would be too much of a downer to tell them James had been killed in a car crash not five weeks before, the front seat passenger in a car driven by StJohn StJohn, a complete wanker who was way over the limit and who, in the manner of things, escaped without a scratch.

" – James isn't here anymore."

"Where's he gone?" Rion asked interested.

Ollie avoided their gaze. "Just away," he smiled weakly.

"But where?" Rion persisted.

Jake tapped her on the forearm, "Away will do."

Before Rion could inquire further Jake launched into a lively anecdote that soon had the young girl's attention. Ollie listened, soothed by Jake's easy way and Rion's laughter. He was glad the focus was off him, off James. There might come a time when he could bring himself to tell them but tonight wasn't it.

The chocolate-brown Mercedes jeep stopped outside the entrance to the mews. Trellick Tower, lights glittering from balconies, rose into the darkness above them.

"He lives at number three," Candida pointed into the little cobbled street.

"The one with the yellow door?" Her companion was a man in his late twenties. His dark blue jeans and clean white T-shirt, stretched over his chest, couldn't hide the powerful body underneath. From his collection of baseball caps (ironically featuring the logos of American football teams) he had chosen the 49'ers – his favourite.

The woman nodded. "Let's just see if he's back yet shall we?" She took out the mobile from her soft leather bag and dialled Ollie's number.

"Hi, you've reached – " She didn't need to hear the rest of the message and she certainly didn't want to leave one.

Candida parked the jeep on the road outside. "Stay here," she said firmly. Candida got out of the jeep and crept to the entrance of the small mews. James' sister smiled in satisfaction upon noticing no lights were on in any of the houses. All was silent.

Seeing her enter the darkened threshold her companion switched on the radio. He quickly found the Sports Station. This was going to be an easy job, he thought, and she's paying well. He smiled, scratched his crotch and listened to Arsenal beating Chelsea.

Not quite sure why, when there was no sign of life in the mews, Candida tiptoed over to Ollie's door. She felt slightly ridiculous but was aware of Hum's possible presence. And she certainly didn't want to disturb him.

Reminding herself that it is better to let sleeping dogs lie Candida gently pushed open the letterbox and peered through.

"Can I help you?"

The voice came from the house opposite.

Candida remained on her knees. She ran her hands over the doorstep as if she had lost something, then gave up. Her father had taught her to be honest if caught – or lie, lie, lie like hell.

Candida decided on a mixture of the two.

"No, I was trying to see if Oliver was – "

Nicky immediately recognised the cold, clipped tones of James' sister.

"We had an appointment and – "

" – you turned up half an hour early to snoop through his stuff again? Is that it Candida?"

She straightened up and turned to face Nicky. The photographer stood at the window of her first floor sitting room opposite.

"You don't understand anything," Candida grimaced and began walking out of the mews. She hadn't got halfway to the jeep when she heard a door slam behind her.

"What I do understand is that it is an offence to enter someone's house without their permission."

Candida quickened her step. She didn't look round but could hear Nicky come out of the mews behind her.

"If I, or anyone else, see you snooping round here again Candida, we'll call the police."

Trying to keep as much dignity as possible Candida opened the driver's door and hopped up into the Jeep.

She switched off the radio and fired the engine.

"But they were just – " Wayne complained.

"In your own time bud," she snarled, her fondness for American cop shows suddenly revealing itself. With a satisfyingly dramatic squeal of tyres she did a u-turn and headed for Holland Park.

Wayne, adjusting his baseball cap, sulked next to her.

7

SPOOKS

The shower cleared his head, the hot water pummelling away the marijuana hangover that fogged Ollie's brain. Although the rum had quickly run out, Jake had kept a steady supply of remarkably sweet-tasting grass going Ollie's way.

It was only later, after Jake had told him the batch was called 'headstone home-grown', that Ollie found out where the 'home' in home-grown was.

No wonder he had had strange dreams.

He didn't want to think about all the exceptional nutrients the plants had fed off to grow that sweet. Whatever the site specific minerals were he was fairly sure you couldn't get them in a florist.

Ollie thought back to the night before. He had a hazy memory of being ferried across the canal in a leaky canoe with Hum barking excitedly and a message from Nicky – something about Candida?

That part remained unclear.

What was clear, however, was the image of two newfound friends.

Towelling himself dry Ollie wandered through to the sitting room. He must tell Auntie Gem about her 'ghost'! He must tell them all, but it was only fair Auntie Gem knew first.

The phone rang before he could find the number for Peters & Peters.

"Nice to see you were out last night." Few things slipped past Auntie Em.

"I had a great time too."

"Good angel, you need to enjoy yourself more. Anyone I know?"

"No," Ollie smiled, "but you've heard of one of them."

"Ah, any more clues than that sweetness?"

Ollie couldn't stop himself, "Oh Auntie Em – I have monumental news!"

"I'm listening."

"I can't tell you until – can you and Auntie Gem come round tonight at about – " Ollie remembered he had arranged to deliver the Allen Jones table to Johnson Ogle in Hampstead at 7:30, add in the required stopover time for chat and fitting – he would be lucky to be out of there by 9.

"– 9:30?"

"I'm sure we can sweetness."

"I'm out most of the day, I'll try and phone Nicky but would you tell her if you see her? It's important."

"My, but you are being mysterious."

"I might be late so let yourself in and Auntie Em?"

"Yes angel?"

Ollie was in two minds to whether to tell her the news now or not. He paused and decided against it, "Nothing."

"Are you sure you don't want to get it off your chest now, I won't breathe a word – "

"Tonight Auntie Em."

As Ollie clicked off the phone Auntie Em realised she hadn't told him about Candida. Still, she was sure Nicky would have told him and besides, Merlijnche de Poortje was safe with her wasn't she?

Ollie kept a close eye on Hum. Meanwhile Gardens was full of jagged chicken bones, a reminder of Notting Hill Carnival weeks before when millions of people crammed into West London to drink, dance and eat jerk chicken the remnants of which, it appeared, they threw as one into the small park. A faint smell of cooking oil still hung in the air, grease still stained the walkways, waiting for the autumn rains to cleanse the space.

Although he had a duty to do his attention was soon taken by a figure near the pond. Ollie hadn't seen the man before. He was sure of that. Such a figure, hulking and masculine, wouldn't have slipped easily from the storeroom of his mind.

But even without the powerful body and chiselled looks the man would have been memorable: full Aussie cowboy drag – hat, drizabone, moleskins and shiny brown boots, the whole lot topped by a natty pair of sunglasses – was just not normal attire for morning constitutionals in Meanwhile Gardens.

He also seemed to be scratching his crotch.

Alot.

The funny thing was Ollie thought he recognised the dog – a little Jack Russell, white with brown blotches – called Maisie.

The dog sort of ruined it for Ollie. Any guy that big with a dog that little had to be limpwristed. He probably did needlework, Ollie thought, his fantasy rapidly deflating. Not that he had anything against limpwristed needlework champions, he told himself quickly, it's just they did nothing for him.

Hum bounded over to say hello to the Jack Russell, making conversation between the two men an inevitability. Ollie steeled himself for the destruction of his fantasy.

"Is this Maisie?" Ollie asked.

Wayne seemed thrown for a second, before immediately recovering, "No, it's – er – Dorothy," he said in the accent he'd been working on for days.

The man's voice betrayed no sign of mincing nor effeminacy. It bore the lazy, strangled tones of a Kiwi/South African hybrid, tempered by a satisfying East End gruffness that immediately rekindled Ollie's fading fantasy.

Ollie smiled, "Does that make you a friend of Dorothy?"

The joke was lost on Wayne.

"She's not mine," Wayne said quickly, realising what he was there to do. "She belongs to my aunt who had a bad fall. I'm just walking her."

The bedridden aunt was Wayne's own invention and he was proud of it. Trying to think of something more to say he smiled his warmest of smiles at Ollie, put his hands in his pockets once more and jiggled away.

Ollie looked at the man playing pocket pool in front of him and raised an eyebrow.

"I haven't got crabs," Wayne said hurriedly. "It's just I shaved my – " he looked around him to make sure no one was in listening distance but the two men were alone in the park. Suddenly self-conscious Wayne stared at the ground before whispering, " – my balls yesterday and they itch like crazy."

Ollie smiled quizzically and carried on.

Wayne left Meanwhile Gardens near the Cobden Club. Waiting near the park gates was a young boy with cropped hair and an Umbro shirt. He looked about twelve but smoked a cigarette with the attitude of a sixteen year old.

"It's a tenner now. You were longer than you said," the young boy took Maisie.

Wayne began to argue then quickly handed over two five-pound notes. What did he care? He would claim it as expenses and let Candida reimburse him.

"He said what?" Nicky asked.

Ollie stood on his neighbour's doorstep and repeated what the man in the park had said.

"Is that like code?"

"Does it sound like code Nicks? Come on, if there was a message there it certainly wasn't hidden."

"How should I know? You guys with your nods, your winks, hankies, active this, passive that...."

Ollie knew what she meant. He sometimes felt you needed a dictionary more than a personality to negotiate a relationship these days.

"Could it have been a line?"

"Nicks – if you wanted to come on to someone the word 'crabs' wouldn't come anywhere near your chat up line would it?"

"Not unless it was linked to 'soft-shell' 'ginger' and 'Chinese restaurant on Queensway'. Give me a break Ol, I've been in the darkroom all morning." Nicky breathed in the fresh air, relieved to be out of the little room under the stairs and in the daylight once more.

"Those chemicals getting to you?"

"And that shabby red light," Nicky shivered at the thought. "Anyway maybe the guy was just tongue-tied for chrissake."

Ollie chuckled reproachfully, "I'm not the sort of guy that makes other guys tongue-tied..."

"You will be if you carry on with the jogging."

"He could have been out of practice I guess," Ollie conceded. "With a body like that he probably hasn't needed chat-up lines in years."

"Did you get my message? About Candida?"

Ollie had a vague recollection of struggling with his voicemail the previous night. "Sort of."

"She was snooping around again."

"Was she alone?"

"There was some guy in the jeep – either that or an incredibly butch woman."

"Candida always gets what she wants you know."

"Maybe not this time." A smile crossed Nicky's face.

Ollie followed the photographer into her studio which took up the whole of the ground floor. He gasped upon entering the large room.

"They're beautiful Nicks."

Hanging on a line across the back window were large black and white photos of Andy, the results of the previous day's session.

"I still say his name is Will though. Did he – er – "

"Mention you?" Nicky asked, momentarily raising Ollie's hopes. "No sweetie, he didn't I'm afraid."

Ollie moved closer to the pictures.

"Which is your favourite?" Nicky asked.

Ollie studied each one: Andy smiling, looking up, looking down, winking sexily, staring moodily into the distance, slapping his thigh laughing, his face half in shadow.....

There was no doubt in Ollie's mind. He immediately pointed to the one in the middle.

Nicky unpegged the photo of Andy winking sexily. "Auntie Em says there's a pow-wow at yours tonight," she waved the photo in front of Ollie's face, "I'll give you this if you tell me what's going on."

Ollie took the picture from her. "9:30 Nicks. Don't be late."

Rion spent the early morning exploring the cemetery. She was particularly fascinated by the grand graves in front of the Anglican chapel. Families of people who hadn't been loved during their lifetimes hoped to hide their neglect with elaborate funerary arrangements. Enormous stone caskets sat on solid bases, raised biers proclaimed superiority whilst the occupants' social standing had long since crumbled to dust.

It was only when she played around the tomb of Princess Sophia that Gorby saw her for the second time. The guard pulled his phone from his pocket, quickly set it to video and filmed Rion as she chased her shadow around the enormous raised sarcophagus.

The English weather put an end to these games. What started off as mid-morning drizzle had by lunchtime turned into steady rain. Rion returned to Old George's chamber. She felt secure in Heron Point but, more importantly, she felt dry. Although the wet weather made the chamber feel damp, Rion noticed with satisfaction that there wasn't a drop of water inside at all.

Outside was another matter.

From time to time Rion pulled the blanket back and peered out. The clearing had taken on an increasingly soggy appearance. By six o'clock it lay under nearly two inches of water.

By seven o'clock Rion was starting to feel fed up. And very bored.

She had read the self-help book again. That made five times she had read *Face the Fear and Eat It* since Tanya had given it to her some months before.

Rion had faced the fear and eaten as much as she could. She knew she had. She was here in London but doing what exactly?

She had finished the crosswords in all the magazines, read

and re-read articles, even attempted Sudoku, but now her eyes were tired – and so were the batteries in the torch.

She couldn't write by candlelight and it was best not to use the torch unless she had to.

The food Jake had brought the night before was nearly finished and, she realised unhappily, he wouldn't be back until much later.

Hoping to God she was wrong Rion felt the familiar ache in her shoulders that normally foreshadowed a bout of illness.

She curled up in the sleeping bag and dreamt of her new life in London, of working for Glamourista, of expensive make-up and beauty treatments, of friends, of feathered gowns by Hitherto Williams....

Rion felt the rumbling grow and grow from deep inside her. Her breath constricted in ever shorter wheezes, her lungs expanded to their full capacity until, unable to contain the pressure any longer, she let out a magnificent, yelping sneeze.

Outside it continued to rain.

It was still raining when Ollie turned into the drive of Johnson Ogle's large house on Heath Road. For an interior decorator, or 'lifestyle enhancer' as Johnson insisted on calling himself, he had done incredibly well. Although his many critics complained that the only lifestyle he had enhanced was his own, Johnson nevertheless had a following of loyal, and very rich, clients from Moscow to Mustique who required their various houses 'doing'.

Often once or twice a year.

He had now reached the enviable stage of being in the same financial bracket as a lot of his clients, a fact represented by the beautiful corner house, with half-a-dozen winding red brick chimneys, that backed onto Hampstead Heath.

A houseboy Ollie didn't recognise showed him into the hall where Johnson awaited.

"Coffee in the conservatory please," the lifestyle enhancer ordered before kissing Ollie on both cheeks. "I was so sorry to hear about James." He took Ollie by the arm, leading him through to the rear of the elegant house, "You got the chocs?"

Ollie nodded. He had never seen such an enormous box of chocolates as the ones that had arrived from Godiva the week of the funeral.

"I thought you would find them more comforting than flowers which are just too *deadly* at such a time."

The conservatory, a Victorian affair Johnson had snapped up at a Scottish country house sale and had transported down, "at vast expense," he always said proudly, lined the entire back of the building.

Johnson gestured to the orchids that filled the room. "Cate gave me one when she was here and I've since gone *completely* mad for them. Of course you know Meryl has nothing else in her Manhattan bedroom, apparently they do wonderful things with ionisation – no more plugging in ugly little boxes 'cos these babies," Johnson surveyed the plants, "do it naturally."

Upon hearing a gentle rattling Johnson turned to Ollie, "Tell me what you think of the new 'boy' although, as you can see," Johnson smiled, "I use the term loosely."

The houseboy entered wheeling a trolley upon which was an elegant silver coffee service. Ollie studied the young man in the crisp black uniform of the Ogle household. With his fresh face and tightly cropped hair he was no different from a thousand other personable young men.

Johnson waved the boy away. "We'll do it ourselves thank you – " he winked at Ollie, " – Leila." Johnson, in that drawl so favoured by the English who travel constantly, made the name sound like 'Lyle-a.'

Ollie assumed it must be some pet name, either that or he had misheard. He looked after the departing houseboy. "Apart from the fact that he's not called Gerardo and is not Latin American – ?"

"Lesbians," Johnson hissed, "they're the way forward."

Ollie tried to digest the sentence.

"They don't want to mother you like straight women do and you don't want to sleep with them like – " Johnson fluttered his hand in the air, "Gerardo."

"Or Eduardo, Rodolfo, Diego ...." Ollie added.

"Exactly. It always ends in tears. Just too much trouble. And so – " Johnson fluttered his hand again as he tried to find the right word, " – temperamental," he said finally.

Yes, Ollie thought, all of your lovers had tempers and all tended to be mental.

"But lesbians – they're perfect, they love to wear uniform and they're reassuringly dependable which, of course, fits in perfectly with my own modus operandum."

Ollie had heard Johnson's philosophy spiel before. He made the decorator stew for a few seconds before asking, "Which is?"

"Well," the decorator began, happy to tell his story again, "you know the secret of my success is to be reassuring and dependable. I can always be relied on to find something 'just so' for a library or guest suite, and I'm always there to walk them to the opera or some ghastly ball and they *know* I'll make them enjoy it."

Listening to Johnson Ollie could see what his clients saw in him. Everything about him was reassuring, his voice was calm and rich, his looks were ruggedly Harrison Ford – albeit Harrison Ford on a bad day as Johnson always said.

"Or Harrison Ford on a fag day," Ollie joked.

"Harrison doesn't have fag days," Johnson smiled at his guest, revelling in the ease with which he dropped the star's first name. "But Harrison on a bad day is better than 98% of men on their best days."

Ah, that ever-elusive 2% of men – wherever were they? Lulled by Johnson's warm manner Ollie looked at the rain outside and wondered how Rion was coping. With Jake's experience he was sure she was doing just fine.

"And of course I'm gay, which the wives find reassuring – they know that with me they're not going to get some minimalist crap pressed on them by some devoutly hetero family man with an obnoxious puritanical streak, no, with me they can swag and tassell with handmade Venetian fabrics until they drop."

Ollie looked around him. Apart from a riot of gilt, some dubious trompe l'oeil columns and the odd tiger print cushion, Johnson's house betrayed more of the minimalism his clients hated than the swagging they loved.

"And the husbands find it reassuring 'cos they know that I'm not going to jump their wives and that, whilst with me, their wives are not going to jump the lithe surfer poolboy or the studly stable manager with the sexy Gloucestershire burr – Lady Chatterley is still an inspiration to *many* of these women."

Ollie's thoughts wandered once more to the wellbuilt guy in Meanwhile Gardens. Did what he said really classify as small talk? Ollie was brought back to the conservatory in Hampstead by the clapping of hands. He looked up to find Johnson beaming at him.

"But let's see this table shall we?"

Ignoring Hum's reproachful look from the passenger seat

Ollie opened the back of the van. He observed the new house'boy' as she helped carry the two carved wooden pedestals, and the blanket-wrapped plate of glass that fitted securely on top, into the morning room.

The only thing Ollie noticed was the complete lack of spots or the beginnings of stubble that the seventeen-year-old boy she looked like would have. But then being twenty-two and female her hormones would be entirely different.

Johnson looked at the pedestals, "Do I know the model?"

The two wooden bases, both exactly the same, showed a male form on his knees, his muscled back flat over his body. His head and neck were straight as if looking at something on the floor in front of him. The figure's arms were curled behind him, his hands demurely covering his backside.

"Not unless you're 2000 years old."

Johnson looked in one of a pair of gilt Louis XV mirrors. "That reminds me," he put his hands beneath his temples and lifted them up to make the already smooth skin on his face even smoother, "it's about time I saw Dr Richardson."

"Dr – ?" Ollie gave Johnson an enquiring look.

Johnson lightly slapped his temples. "Fillers," he explained.

Ollie lifted the sheet of glass, easily slotting it into the two prepared grooves at the base of the man's neck. The table was now in place.

"Bit modest isn't he?" Johnson sniffed. "I was expecting something more fully frontal."

"But it's not for you is it Johnson?"

Johnson hummed and hawed, certain if Ollie knew they were for someone else he would raise the price, "Weeeell..."

Ollie took out his ever-present notepad and pen.

"Is this more what you had in mind?" He quickly sketched an upside down man in the crab position. "I could make a pair of mainly decorative tables which, by making the stomach really flat, you could put a mug on – "

"It's a cup and saucer in this house."

" – but perhaps little else, or," Ollie gestured to the table he had just assembled, "I could make them bigger, more of the coffee table size – "

"Hmmmmm," Johnson examined Ollie's sketch. "Let's go for the decorative tables for the time being but," Johnson took Ollie's pen and drew in a more bulging crotch, "make them more like this ok?"

Johnson looked at the rain pouring down outside and gave an oversized sigh. "Such a shame the weather's so foul. I was hoping to go for my exercise."

Ollie knew this was a cue for a compliment. Johnson looked at him with big eyes, waiting.

"I thought you looked well Johnson."

Johnson smiled. "Well I've been going for regular aerobic exercise, what we in Hampstead call, – " he paused then whispered conspiratorially, " – blow-jogs."

Ollie hadn't heard the term before but the words were self-explanatory. Just in case he had missed the meaning Johnson explained, "Everybody's at it this time of day. All the City boys and dealers come back from work, jog up to the Heath and – "

"I get it. I get it."

"There must be a lot of spouses mystified as to why their partners are still as unfit as they were before. It's taken over from walking the dog as the favourite excuse and not a moment too soon. There's nothing more offputting than having someone go down on you only to have Fido come sniffing round...."

Unwilling to hear any more of the sex lives of Hampstead denizens Ollie got up, "I have to go Johnson. I'll let you know about the tables."

❧

By nine o'clock Rion was ready to move out. Water had started trickling over the high first step about half an hour before. In the flickering candlelight she could see several large pools on the chamber floor – several large pools getting larger, she realised unhappily.

It was time for action.

Wriggling out of the snug sleeping bag Rion was surprised at how cold it was. With her throat beginning to burn and her limbs feeling suddenly heavy, Rion struggled into her black and white checked trousers, pulled on her fleece and swung her legs over the edge of the bed.

The first disappointment was finding her trainers, an island of shoe in one of the large pools beneath the bed. She shivered. There could be nothing worse than squeezing cold feet into already wet sneakers.

Rion felt she was starring in her own Gothic horror film as the guttering candle threw uncomfortable shapes over the ceiling and walls. She grabbed the pencil-torch from the shelf, pulled on her white pac-a-mac and drew back the now sodden, heavy pink blanket from the doorway. The accompanying breeze blew out the already sputtering candles.

Switching on the torch Rion was dismayed to find its weak beam barely pierced the darkness. "Here we go Rion," she said to herself, strengthened by the sound of her own voice. "Think of Blondin, think of crossing – " the next word came surprisingly naturally as Rion took her first step into the pool that had once been the little clearing, "the Niagara," she said miserably, feeling the cold water slosh into her shoes and around her feet.

To keep the demons away Rion began to whistle and then

sing one of her favourite songs. It was a chirpy number by Candi Staton that always lifted her spirits, but this time her voice struggled hoarsely with the tune.

Before she got to the end of the second line her foot met with one of the stones around what was once the fire. With her toes well and truly stubbed Rion did a hop of pain. She momentarily lost her balance, slipped and landed bum first in the unfortunately refreshing water.

A second later she heard a small splash which, with a sinking feeling, she realised was the torch.

Deciding it would be useless to look for the torch which, in any case, would now be completely unworkable, Rion made for the dimness of the opening. Thinking she couldn't get any wetter she pushed through the dripping saplings, realising once more, how wrong she could be.

Now completely soaked Rion found her way to the fence, squeezed past the broken railing and entered the cemetery. Shivering she knocked into several headstones as she headed for the mass of Jake's tree. He would want her to go there, she told herself, to get warm and dry, perhaps a change of clothes...Rion quickened her step – a change of clothes! The notion at first sounded so remote it appeared inaccessible.

Lost in the dream of warm dry clothes Rion didn't notice the headlights coming down the avenue.

Until it was too late.

From the interior of the guards' jeep Rion appeared lit up as an eery ghoul. Toy figures, masked and dancing, dangled from the jeep's rearview mirror.

"What the hell is that Gorby?" Beck, the young guard, turned to the driver.

"Beats me," Gorby replied winding down his window. "Hey!" he shouted into the night.

Rion turned round to be blinded by the powerful lights.

Panicking she ran onto the woodchips of a smaller path, the lights of the jeep showing her the way between the tombs on either side.

Hearing a door slam behind her she ran on, ignoring the voices calling into the night. Her wet clothes hung cold and heavy against her, restricting her progress, her waterlogged trainers chafed her feet, but Rion ran as fast as she could.

When she was out of the jeep's glare she turned round to see two powerful torches searching the night in her wake. Rion squelched on, soon ducking behind an ornate mausoleum to catch her breath and get her bearings.

She figured she was on a small path off South Avenue, not far from the main entrance gateway, that would, at this hour, be securely locked.

What had Jake told her again? She wracked her memory. Something about another escape route through the fence near the Reformer's Memorial? Or was it the Dissenter's Chapel? They were both in the direction she was going – she would find out when she got there.

Rion could hear the guards coming closer and closer. She held her breath, certain they could hear her beating heart.

Or her chattering teeth.

She saw the torches light up grieving angels and marble steles, the powerful beam flashing over burial plots and into corners in their search for the trespasser.

Feeling another huge sneeze come on Rion watched, eyes watering, as the two guards gave up the search. Halfway to the jeep Gorby turned round and flashed his torch at the ornate tomb. The momentary adrenaline rush scared the sneeze away although Rion wasn't sure if she had jumped back fast enough.

"She's vanished," said the younger guard.

“Spooks always do,” Gorby replied, although he wasn’t so sure. He was intrigued though – this ‘spook’ could be just what they were looking for.

8

AN UNEXPECTED ARRIVAL

Ollie had only been back for five minutes before Hum barked ahead of an urgent knock on the door. He opened it to find Nicky on the doorstep.

"Come on! Come on!" Clutching a bottle of wine she pushed past him, "Don't you know it's raining out there?"

Ollie looked at his watch. It was quarter past nine. "You're fifteen minutes early," Ollie grumbled as he followed Nicky up the stairs and into the sitting room.

"Yeah, well, I thought I might get a headstart on the news if I arrived early." Nicky rummaged through the cutlery drawer, found the corkscrew and quickly opened the Cabernet Sauvignon.

"Not until Gem 'n Em get here."

Nicky poured a glass for Ollie and then one for herself, "How was Johnson?"

Ollie began telling her about the lifestyle enhancer and his blow-jogs when again Hum's bark preceded another series of knocks.

"So when you say you're going jogging we're not going to find you, trousers around your ankles, in the bushes along the canal?" Nicky called to Ollie as he went down to open the door.

With a smile Ollie swung open the door to let in Auntie Gem and Auntie Em.

"We're not too early are we dear?" Auntie Gem asked.

"Nicky's already here. She thought I might spill the beans before you arrived."

"And did you?" Auntie Em kissed him on the cheek and went up the stairs.

"He wouldn't, would you child?" Auntie Gem tickled his ribs as she followed Em up to the sitting room.

"Of course not."

The two very different ladies – Auntie Em, white, tall, in her early fifties and Auntie Gem, five foot one, black, closing on seventy – settled themselves on the sofa.

Nicky handed them a glass of wine each, "Don't worry he hasn't told me anything."

"Now precious," Auntie Em began, "what is this 'monumental news'?"

"Firstly, it's just – " Ollie began pacing up and down in front of the fireplace. "What would you think about if – and that's all it is at the moment an 'if' – someone moved into lA?"

His question met with silence. Even Nicky was quiet. 1A, the house next to Ollie's, was known as the 'unlucky house' due to the mishaps that befell its residents. It hadn't been lived in since the McGuires left four years ago.

Auntie Em was the first to speak. "You know how we feel about that angel."

Ollie did know. Auntie Em, in some way, felt responsible for the unhappiness that had affected the inhabitants of lA. In her eyes everyone who had moved in there had met with misfortune.

Two had ended up in addiction clinics, one had been sectioned, the Robinsons had divorced, prior to that Lily McGuire's son had met with that *terrible* accident – Auntie Em linked a whole catalogue of wretchedness to the 'unlucky' house.

"But if you think about it Auntie Em some of those disasters were actually blessings. Harriet and Sasha have been clean now for several years, Martin got the help he needed, the Robinsons – well, they weren't really suited anyway and Lily's boy – when they removed the spike they found he had a much more serious condition which, if left untreated, would have been potentially fatal."

Nicky came to his aid, "Sasha and Harriet say getting clean was the best thing that happened to them."

"Who is it that wants to move in?"

"Well, that's just it Auntie Gem. I haven't told her – this person – about 1A but I have a feeling she needs our help, or will do soon."

"Ollie, this isn't one of your lost causes is it?" Nicky asked, her tone had changed from one of support to one of suspicion.

"You're very sweet, angel, but you can be too trusting sometimes," Auntie Em chimed in.

"And too nice. Remember Stan?"

Ollie really didn't want to. "But he – "

"Remember Stan?" Nicky persisted.

"Yes," Ollie said crossly, remembering the builder who came to replaster the sitting room ceiling, moved in with Ollie before promptly moving out with his stereo, record/cd and dvd collection, alongwith one of Nicky's cameras. It was only after some diligent sleuthing that they found everything at the Record & Tape Exchange in Notting Hill Gate.

"We got it all back though."

"That's not the point Ol."

"Why don't you tell us a bit more about this person?" Auntie Gem asked. She refilled Auntie Em's glass, before standing to top up Nicky's.

"Well," Ollie said, "you sort of know her Auntie Gem."

It was at that moment Rion chose to make her entrance.

Having made it to Meanwhile Gardens Mews she found the door to number three was open ajar. From his bed at the top of the stairs Hum opened one eye and half-heartedly wagged his tail.

As Auntie Gem moved round to pour some wine into Ollie's glass she felt a blast of cold air come up the stairwell. She looked over the banister.

What she saw froze her blood.

Seeming to hover halfway up the stairs was the ghostly figure of the young girl from the cemetery, but this time, Auntie Gem noted, she looked like she had crawled through the gates of Hell. Large, haunted eyes looked up at her, her mouth opened beseeching, beseeching, croaking some satanic message from the otherside.

Rion's long bedraggled hair was matted to her mud spattered face, her white-pac-a-mac floated around her in the current of air. With her sore throat killing her she tried to call Ollie's name but nothing came out apart from a dreadful hoarse growling. Looking up Rion saw a horrified black woman holding a bottle of wine.

With a scream Auntie Gem collapsed back into the sitting room and fainted dead away.

The rain had finally slowed to drizzle when Jake made it home to Kensal Green Cemetery. The house painting in the wilds of Stoke Newington would take another three days at least. If they finished before the weekend the actor whose house it was had promised a handsome bonus. It would be another early start in the morning.

Jake looked at his watch to see it was nearly twelve thirty. He had to be away by six which meant, he realised, five hours sleep maximum.

He had tried to convince himself all day that Rion would be all right. After all Old George had seen off much worse weather with never a drop on the chamber floor.

He had tried to convince himself but failed.

Underneath he had this nagging feeling that Rion wasn't ok, that something unfortunate had happened to the young girl.

Squeezing through the railings and the dripping saplings Jake whistled his arrival. He wasn't too put out when there was no welcoming whistle in return – Rion would surely be wrapped up in the sleeping bag, fast asleep.

When he found the clearing under water he realised things might be worse than expected.

"Rion," Jake whispered, then louder, "Rion!"

There was no reply.

He pulled back the heavy blanket from the doorway. When he flashed his torch inside Jake saw something he had never seen in all of the years he had known Old George.

The floor of the chamber was completely under water, not a dry patch of ground to be seen.

The beam from his torch bounced around the space but there was no sign of Rion. His hopes rose for a moment upon seeing the sleeping bag on the bed but it was clear, even from the doorway, that no one was inside.

Jake splashed into the chamber. He could see Rion's now sodden clothes were still there – she couldn't be too far away. He looked in vain for a note but there was none.

If nothing sinister had happened to her there was only one place he surmised she could go. To Ollie's. He hoped with all his heart that was where she had gone.

Rion was curled up in the spare room of Gem 'n Em's house at the end of the mews.

"How is she?" Ollie asked as Auntie Em emerged leaving the door open ajar.

Auntie Em sunk into the sofa beside Nicky. "She's sound asleep but has quite a temperature."

Ollie poured Auntie Em a cup of tea from the freshly made pot.

"Mmmmmm," she took a sip of the soothing hot drink, "thanks sweetness." Auntie Em leaned back and closed her eyes. "What a night it's been," she murmured. Ollie and Nicky could only agree. What a night indeed.

The young girl had run from the house upon hearing Auntie Gem scream. She had hardly got out of the front door before Ollie realised who it was and what was going on. He managed to bring her back upstairs to the sitting room where Auntie Em and Nicky tried to bring Gem round by splashing water on her face.

After much fluttering of eyelids Auntie Gem opened her eyes to see Rion directly in her line of vision. The thought that she had woken up in Hell occasioned another bout of screaming.

This in turn brought on an uncontrollable bout of sneezing from Rion. What with Auntie Gem screaming and Rion caught in a spluttering sneezing frenzy, the only thing left was for Hum to join in.

Which he did with delight.

Excited by all that was going on around him the dog threw himself into the centre of things and barked like mad.

Auntie Em thought the world was coming to an end.

After much persuading Auntie Gem understood that the bedraggled girl in front of her was not a spirit sent from Hell. Rion's wheezes subsided as did Auntie Gem's screams until the old lady's whimpers were matched by the young girl's sobs.

Still shaken but much calmed down, Auntie Gem was taken to her room, given a sleeping pill, some hot tea and tucked up in bed where Ollie read her stories about Princess Diana until the old lady fell asleep.

While this was going on Nicky and Auntie Em gave Rion a hot, very bubbly, bath and one of Ollie's long t-shirts to sleep in. Ginger tea with a dash of rum, a double dose of Uniflu, clean sheets and a large duvet soon had Rion in the land of Nod.

With relief Ollie, Nicky and Auntie Em drank their tea. The only sound in the house the gentle wheeze of Auntie Gem snoring.

After a while Nicky asked, "Does she have family?"

"Bridlington or somewhere I think," Ollie replied. "Up north anyway."

"Shouldn't we contact them?"

Ollie breathed out heavily. "I think that would be the worst thing we could do. Didn't you see her body?"

Both Auntie Em and Nicky shook their heads.

"She was adamant we turn around when she got in and out of the bath," Auntie Em said.

"And made sure there were lots and lots of bubbles," Nicky added.

"Well – " Ollie shook his head, he couldn't understand how people could do that to anyone let alone their own children. " – there's bruising around her arms and neck *and* two very nasty cigarette burns – "

Nicky stopped him. "Cigarette burns?" she asked in horror.

Ollie nodded, " – on the underside of each wrist."

Auntie Em winced.

Ollie told them all he knew about Rion, about her family, about Jake. When he had finished Nicky and Auntie Em sat staring straight ahead.

"It's not surprising she ran away," Nicky said.

Auntie Em welled up, "The poor, poor child."

"Anyway she's the one I told you who needed our help, the one I thought might move into number 1A."

"She's staying here for the time being and that's that." There was no arguing with Auntie Em when she used that tone of voice. "We'll think about 1A if and when – ok? At the moment let's just get her better."

After Ollie and Nicky had left Auntie Em went in to the spare room. Rion was muttering in her sleep. The words didn't make sense to Auntie Em. Something about omelettes and what sounded like 'Blondie'.

Auntie Em wiped the sweat from the girl's brow. Before settling herself in the armchair in the corner of the room Auntie Em lifted up Rion's wrist. There, like Ollie said there would be, were two sullen red scabs.

Auntie Em grimaced. This one wasn't going to be taken away from her, she vowed, not this time.

9

JUST WHAT WE'RE LOOKING FOR

Gorby arrived for work early the next morning. In the daylight the birthmark that gave him his nickname was visible. It spread magnificently over the left side of his bald head like a Rorschach test in red ink.

"I thought you weren't on until later?" one of the night guards enquired as Gorby changed into the off-green uniform of the cemetery keepers.

Gorby smiled and tapped his nose, "Overtime."

Senior grunted and returned to his paper.

Gorby made his way past the tombs of Oxford Avenue, carrying on all the way down until he had almost reached the canal. The only burial place of note in this otherwise unvisited section was the simple grave of Marigold Churchill, the infant daughter of Sir Winston and Lady Clementine.

This was about the place, he reckoned, where he had seen the young girl the previous night. Over the years several homeless men had bedded down in the cemetery only to be thrown out by the guards. But this was different.

This was a young girl.

If she were homeless she would be perfect. No one would miss her. No one would know she had gone.

It didn't take him long to notice the track snaking through

the overgrown headstones. He followed it until he came up against the iron railings of the boundary fence. Seeing the path continued on the other side Gorby pushed the broken rail, squeezed through and carried on along an increasingly narrow trail between the trees.

Thinking he could go no further Gorby turned sideways, inching towards an opening on the other side of which he could see an open space.

Gorby pushed through to find himself in an overwhelmingly muddy clearing. On one side he could see a dirty pink blanket hanging across what looked like a doorway.

"Hello?" he moved closer to the opening. "Kensal Green Keepers, is there anyone there?"

Gorby pulled the covering to one side, his nose wrinkled automatically at the rank, dank smell of the chamber.

He tied the heavy blanket back and entered, immediately realising that this was where the young girl had been hiding.

Gorby opened the chest of drawers, reached in and took a souvenir.

He smiled in satisfaction. She would be perfect.

Entering the cemetery Ollie knew he had to find Jake. The only clue Jake had given him was that he lived, 'round here', and that the marijuana he grew was called, 'headstone homegrown'. Where on earth would he start? Looking at the sea of graves and mausolea before him he wondered if he should rephrase the question.

Perhaps, 'Where in Heaven?' might be more suitable.

Or, he shivered, 'Where in Hell?'

Deciding Jake might be in the chamber by the canal or that, at least, he might have left a note there for Rion, Ollie thought it best to head there first.

Seeing there was no-one around he let Hum off the lead. As soon as he had done so he realised it was a mistake. The dog immediately raced after a squirrel, scattering graveside vases of flowers in the process.

"It's dog-training for you," Ollie cursed under his breath. He felt like crossing himself as he saw Hum cock his leg over several simple tombs in the distance. He watched as the hound made instinctively for the broken railing in the border fence and jumped through.

Arriving in the same spot Ollie saw a man emerge from the direction of the chamber. The man was dressed in the dull green uniform of the cemetery guard. He was wiping his nose with what looked like a handkerchief which, upon seeing Ollie, he hurriedly stuck in his pocket.

"You haven't seen a dog in there have you?" Ollie tried desperately not to look at what was an exceptional birthmark on the man's head. "Black, shaggy, mischievous?"

"All dogs must be kept on leads," Gorby said gruffly, annoyed at the owner of the dog that just moments before had nipped at his heels. "Didn't you see the signs at the main gate?"

"No , I – "

The man squeezed past the broken railing and pushed past him. "Well read next time. They're put there for a reason."

Just as Ollie thought of something snappy to say in return Hum appeared, barking in delight at seeing him. The dog jumped through the railings, sat at his master's feet and looked up at him with twinkling eyes.

"*Now* you're good aren't you?" Ollie clipped the lead securely to Hum's collar.

As he headed towards the Anglican chapel in the middle

of the cemetery Gorby looked round to see the owner petting his dog by the fence.

The guard reached in his pocket, took out Rion's flimsy white underwear, caressed it between his fingers and carried on his way.

With the guard no longer in sight Ollie thought it safe to venture forward. Just as he was about to push the railing aside a four-note whistle-stopped him. Ollie turned to see Jake coming out from behind a large tree about fifteen yards away.

"Is Rion with you?" Jake asked concerned.

"I was coming to tell you she's ok."

Ollie could see the relief on Jake's face.

"I knew she'd be with you if she had any sense. It's best if she stays there for the time being too. That guard'll be back."

"Well, she's sort of ok."

Jake's face dropped.

"I mean, she will be ok," Ollie continued, "she has a terrible fever and – "

Ollie thought it unnecessary to fill Jake in on how Rion looked when had she staggered into his house the previous night, nor about the chaos and confusion that ensued with Auntie Gem.

" – she's tucked up in bed at my neighbours'. The worst thing that can happen is she'll be mothered to death." Ollie suddenly thought of Rion's family history and wondered if he couldn't have phrased Rion's condition a little more delicately. Luckily Jake hadn't noticed.

"I wasn't sure of your address but I was sure I could track you down," Jake smiled for the first time that morning. "There can't be too many Ollie's, nor too many mews beneath Trellick Tower."

"People know the dog," Ollie bent to scratch Hum between the ears. "They might not remember me but they always remember Hum."

Jake headed for the chamber, "We'd better get her stuff. They'll be back and soon."

It didn't take long to get Rion's worldly possessions. The few clothes packed easily into the plastic knapsack, the old magazines, now damp, and the dog-eared copy of *Face The Fear & Eat It* went into the elegant GHOST carrier.

"I should have been in Stoke Newington hours ago but I had to make sure Rion was ok." Jake took something out of his overalls and gave it to Ollie. The simple business card advertised his services as a painter/decorator with the well-worn slogan *No job too big or too small.* A number for a mobile lined the bottom. "Let me know how Rion's doing, get her to call if she can. The next few days are the worst for me," Jake grimaced, "and I'm working late all week." He quickly glanced at his watch, "I have to run."

"Wait," Ollie tore off a small piece of Jake's card and wrote his number on it. "Just remember Meanwhile Gardens Mews, mine's the only house with a yellow door."

Jake put the paper in his pocket and disappeared.

Ollie took a last look around the muddy chamber. Without Rion's presence and belongings it looked sadly uninhabitable. He was about to leave when something caught his eye. Moving to the bed he carefully took down the treasured cutting of Blondin crossing the Niagara. He decided to leave the picture of Jesus with arms outstretched and open heart. Whoever stayed here next might benefit from His presence.

Ollie was just about to knock on Gem 'n Em's door when

it opened in his face. Dr Gidwani came out followed by Auntie Em.

"The infection will go but she needs rest. Call me if the condition gets worse. I'll check back after surgery hours Miss Nelson," the doctor nodded at Ollie before leaving.

"What's the diagnosis Auntie Em?" Ollie asked but Auntie Em just looked at the handsome Indian as he walked out of the mews. "Such a nice man," she sighed, lost in thoughts of multi-coloured saris, incense and writhing acrobatics.

"Auntie Em?" Ollie prompted but it was a few seconds before the elegant woman returned to reality. When she did she seemed surprised to see Ollie in front of her.

"Auntie Em," Ollie began once more, "what did the doctor say?"

"Nasty chest infection coupled with 'flu of Asian origin, sweetness, and everything aggravated by asthma."

"So – ?"

"Lots of rest, antibiotics and few visitors," Auntie Em again smiled and looked into the middle distance. "Be an angel, angel, and get this from the chemist," she fished in her pocket and gave Ollie a recently written prescription.

Rion was barely awake when Ollie came in, his arms full of magazines.

"They're all this month's," he put the glossies on the bedside table before sitting beside the pale young girl. "Did Auntie Em tell you I got your stuff?"

Before Rion could speak Ollie put up his hand to stop her. "She says you're not to get tired – doctor's orders. Just nod for 'yes', shake the head for 'no' – ok?"

Rion nodded then shook her head. With her finger she spelt out J in the air.

"Jake?"

Rion nodded.

"He knows you're ok. He'll be in when he can but he's working late all week." Ollie stroked Rion's hand, "I have a surprise for you."

He stood up, smiled, and retrieved something from the confines of his wallet. Ollie carefully smoothed out the creased piece of paper before asking, "Where shall I put it?"

When there was no answer he turned round to find Rion, her head lolled to one side, her eyes closed, deeply asleep.

Ollie put the cutting of Blondin on top of the magazines and tiptoed from the room.

Gorby quickly showered in the tiny cubicle before changing into a fawn pair of slacks and a dark green turtleneck. He pulled on his favourite cardigan that, luckily, was also the cleanest, opened his back door and stood on the stern of *Longfelloe*, the longboat that was his home. Gorby inhaled deeply. He loved this time of the evening when the day slipped into twilight and the dull waters of the canal changed to a slick black.

Waving to his neighbours several boats down, Gorby crossed the gangplank linking him with the adjacent larger boat. He gave his familiar knock and pushed open the door to *Morrisco*. Entering the cozy interior he found his friends busying themselves around a table set for supper.

"Bang on time!" Ted turned with a grin, his neck forever stooped by the barge's low ceiling.

"What can I get you? Wine, orange squash or – " his wife called shrilly, " – tea?"

"I think he drinks enough of that at work eh?" Ted smiled at Gorby and handed him a glass of red wine.

Gorby raised his glass to his immediate bosses, "Cheers Ted, Mary."

He looked at the couple he had known for many years. Gorby often wondered how old they were. He figured they must be between sixty and seventy five years old – although how close or far from those ages he could never tell. One thing, though, that he knew would never change would be their love of tweed. Ted was kitted out in worn tweed trousers with a cotton tweed shirt, whilst Mary looked fetching in her tweed blouse and skirt, her outfit garnished by a tweed apron in shiny plastic.

"Oh," Ted winked at Gorby, "listen to this!" He nodded at Mary who smiled.

"A woman called the cemetery twice this week claiming she had seen a ghost!" Mary hooted with delight at the thought. She put one arm through Ted's, "How long have we been there darling?"

"Nearly twenty years."

"And how many ghosts have we seen?"

"None!" Ted said triumphantly.

"The spirit sounded interesting though – a frail young thing with long blonde hair," Mary smiled at Gorby. "You haven't seen anyone answering that description have you?" she said jokingly.

"Well, I have noticed a young girl hanging around."

Ted looked up while the smile froze on Mary's face.

"You should have told us," she scolded.

"I was going to," Gorby replied, "but I didn't want to get your hopes up until I was sure."

"And?" Mary's voice had a harshness to it.

"Now I'm sure."

The smile returned to Mary's face.

"Really," she said slowly.

"Yes. I've found out where she's been hiding."

"How old is she?" Ted asked.

Gorby shrugged, "Sixteen?"

"Did she look untouched?"

"Unplucked?" Mary added.

"Positively vestal I'd say."

Ted and Mary exchanged an interested look.

"Really," Mary said again, although this time even more slowly than before.

"Was she – " Ted tried not to get his hopes up. "Was she alone?"

"As far as I could tell," Gorby pulled his phone from his pocket. "See for yourself."

Mary and Ted couldn't take their eyes from the screen where Rion chased her shadow around the raised tomb.

"Could she be homeless?" Mary asked breathlessly, watching the short film again.

"If she is – " Ted began only for Mary to finish the sentence for him, " – she could be just what we're looking for."

All three smiled at each other as the same thought filtered through their minds.

Mary raised her glass, "To the ghost!"

"The ghost!" Gorby and Ted echoed. They clinked their glasses and sat down to supper, excited at the thought of a homeless young girl and all that could entail.

10

LADY PETERS!

Having spent the last nine days soaking up the glorious Indian summer in Brighton, Wayne was feeling good about things. He could even handle the phone call which, the screen on his mobile told him, was from the person who had been chasing him all week.

"Where on earth have you been?"

Wayne moved the phone away from his ear but still the clipped tones of his employer were clearly audible.

"I've left numerous messages and – "

"I engineered the first meeting." Wayne loved using this sort of language, it made him feel so clever.

Slightly mollified Candida asked, "What did you wear?"

"I wore everything."

"Even the hat?"

"Everything."

It had been expensive kitting Wayne out at the Australian clothiers in Covent Garden, but Candida hoped it would be worth it. How could Ollie resist a body like Wayne's in hulking cowboy boots? She figured correctly that Ollie must have a rancher fantasy somewhere in his psyche.

"How did it go?"

Wayne thought back to the previous week in the park and

Ollie's quizzical expression. "He was in a bit of a hurry but it went ok."

Immediately after he said 'ok' he knew he'd made a mistake.

"Ok?" Candida's voice went even colder than usual. "Ok?" she repeated. "I'm not paying you to be 'ok'."

"What I mean is it went quite well."

"Quite well?" Candida's icy tones sent a shiver down his spine.

"Yes, I – " Wayne thought for several seconds to get the phrasing just right. "I scoured the terrain, preparing traps to open doors."

Candida correctly surmised that her exceptional looking lure had spent the unusually hot weather out of London. Still, if he had a tan to go with that body she would soon have the painting she was after.

"Make sure you do – open the doors I mean. I want results, Wayne. Results."

Wayne coughed. "There've been expenses."

"Keep the receipts and an explanation."

"You don't get receipts for information." Wayne knew how women such as his employer liked being deferred to. Deciding it was time to tug a forelock or two he added, "Miss."

That was something Candida liked about Wayne. Being called 'Miss' in her mid-thirties made her feel almost coy.

"When are you seeing him again?"

"Tomorrow Miss."

Ah, that 'Miss' again. Candida softened for a second. Then she snapped out of it. "The next time you see him hum *Bewitched*."

He had dressed up in cowboy clothes which, admittedly, he had quite enjoyed; he had booked an appointment with the hairdresser's and tanning salon for a radical change of image and now he had to – what?

"Sorry Miss?"

"You know *Bewitched*, that sixties tv show – " Candida began to whistle the theme tune and was relieved when Wayne joined in. He had seen the re-make on the flight back from Tenerife the previous year.

"Just whistle that when you see him ok?"

The newly appointed editor of Glamourista put her turquoise pumps on the desk and gazed out the window. In the square below secretaries ate sandwiches and drank Diet Coke in the sunshine. Some – were these the popular ones or merely the desperate, she wondered – snogged pimply young men called Gary or Kev who lived in Leytonstone and hadn't the faintest idea about skincare.

There were no sandwiches on the editor's desk. In front of her was an exquisite lacquered Bento box, its small compartments filled with no-fat Japanese delicacies.

Eschewing chopsticks for fingers Angie Peters marvelled at what a title can do for a girl. Ever since her husband had been knighted for Services to Industry earlier in the year, her rise through the ranks of contributing editors had been swift.

Astonishingly swift.

Chins wagged, heads nodded, phones rung, positions offered. As such Angie had jumped over numerous 'Mrs', several 'Ms' and a couple of 'Hons' until here she sat in the hallowed leather chair, her position personally appointed by Luca Mortimer, the owner of the publishing empire in which Glamourista played a small, but glittering, part.

She thought of phoning Jake on his mobile and talking

dirty. It was unfortunate, even downright unfair, that he was working all this week but in some strange way the fact that she couldn't dictate the terms made the relationship even more enjoyable.

Being in charge at the magazine, she mused with a smile, meant she could probably hire him as a personal trainer – or 'bonkmaster-to-the-editor' as he would be known behind his back – and let Luca pick up his salary, but she knew Jake would never consent to that.

Besides she didn't want him around *all* the time.

Also she loved the wonder of the treehouse amidst the Gothic splendour of the decaying Victorian cemetery. Its exquisite proximity to Edwin's office at Peters & Peters made it all the more delicious. That and the fact that no one knew it was there.

And no-one knew she was there. Yes, all in all it was pretty damn perfect.

The chime of the office intercom calmly interrupted her reverie. Again she thanked God that her first task had been to change the cardiac inducing buzzer to a more zenlike gong.

"Yes Miranda?"

"I have Johnson Ogle on line one Lady Peters."

Lady Peters! She still hadn't got used to the title and certainly never tired of hearing it.

Angie swivelled in her chair before clicking through. She had met Johnson at Wanda Mozzoni's the previous week. Over several glasses of Krug she had said the magazine would be interested in the celebrated lifestyle enhancer doing a regular column on design.

Which they would be. Johnson was always good value.

He was also one never to let an opportunity for self-promotion slip by.

"Johnson sweetie."

“Angie,” the decorator’s rich voice oozed charm. “You don’t still have that chaise- longue in last year’s leopard print do you?”

Whilst Angie was considering the best way in which to answer, Johnson continued, “Because I have an offcut of *the* most beautiful thick golden raw silk that a certain someone – the most I can say is that her daughter is named after a certain place of pilgrimage.... are you with me?”

Angie hoped he meant Madonna and not Ada Collaren, the WAG queen who followed suit and named her daughter Medugorge after the faux Yugoslavian site. The style-bereft Ada, whose husband’s millions and the attention of the world’s top stylists had still not hidden the fact that she was the dernier cri in naffness, was a renowned bandwagonjumper. Whilst Angie was quite happy for the hapless Ada to appear in her magazine looking frightful in assorted frocks, she did not want to appear linked to her in anyway. Even sharing fabric from the same decorator would be too close.

As if reading her mind Johnson hinted, “Her initial is M not A.”

That did it.

“Johnson, you’re so clever. I was just going to have it re-covered,” Angie lied.

“Let me do it for you darling. Send it to the showroom *a toute vitesse*. It’ll be my welcoming present.” With the trivia out of the way Johnson got to the real point of the call. “Now about this column you mentioned at Wanda’s.”

“Interested?”

“Hmmmm – ” Johnson hummed and hawed. He knew what the editor really wanted – but it was not something he was prepared to give. “You’re not after design tips are you Angie?”

Johnson knew the game too well.

"Mainly, but not entirely." What Angie really wanted was high quality gossip for herself and her readers. She figured that being editor of Glamourista should entitle her to be privy to the secrets of the rich and famous.

And Johnson was famously well connected.

He was also famously discreet.

"Johnson you know I wouldn't dream of asking you for any tattle, at least not in print."

The lifestyle enhancer was tempted. It was risky though. His top clients didn't want anything on their houses in any magazine.

"Anything about footballers, their wives and boob jobs – fine. But anyone else?"

"We won't go there," Angie finished in her most soothing of voices. She could tell he was nearly snared.

"Do a profile on me and we'll talk further. Get Nicky Dixon for the photos – did you see her shots of Jim James?" The weight of the hearthrob popstar (real name Dimitri Constanzos) was a national talking point on a par with the weather. "She took at least fifteen pounds off him – and – "

Angie waited for some ludicrous demand.

"Think about where you're going to put the chaise-longue. The silk shimmers beautifully at sunset."

11

RETURN OF THE COWBOY

Rion stood at the sitting room window. Halfway down the cobbled mews she could see Auntie Em talking to Ollie who lay in his y-fronts on a lilo in the sunshine. Hum lay in the shadows beside him.

It had been ten days since she had been outside, ten days of unusually hot weather which she hadn't been able to enjoy. Although she was still feeling weak she was much, much better. Rion knew she was well on the road to recovery and it was all due to her new friends. Still, Doctor Gidwani had said to stay inside and Auntie Em was making sure she did.

She had quickly learnt there was no arguing with Auntie Em. It was easier to get round Auntie Gem but Auntie Em? No way. Rion didn't mind their strictness, which she knew was borne of love and was really, 'for her own good'.

Her parents had often used that expression, 'for her own good', but Rion didn't understand how a beating could be for anyone's good, especially when she had done nothing to deserve it. She had often wondered what her parents were trying to beat out of her.

She didn't have to wonder anymore. Rion had decided that it was all in the past and in the past it would stay.

What Rion did wonder about though, was the nature of the conversation in the mews below.

Ollie squinted up at Auntie Em who was filling him in on Rion's progress. In her hand she held a circular chain jammed with keys. "It's too early of course, sweetness, and for the time being she's certainly staying here but – " Auntie Em pulled off a large rusty key from the chain, " – would you see what needs doing in lA? I'm sure it's just a question of clearing out the pigeons but it would be best to see."

Ollie smiled and took the key, "Consider it done Auntie Em."

As Auntie Em went back up the mews to her house, Ollie, in an effort to tan the white strip running from his armpit to his waist, moved onto his side and stretched his arms over his head like a highboard diver.

With eyes closed he stayed in this most uncomfortable of positions until a vaguely familiar voice roused him.

"The sides are always the worst aren't they?"

Ollie opened his eyes, blinking into the sunshine to see a shockingly blond, strikingly tanned, man smiling down at him. Ollie shielded the sun with one hand to make sure that what he was seeing was real. He tried not to stare but it was impossible not to. The man had the most amazing body, toned and strong, squeezed into t-shirt and jeans that were bulgingly tight without looking sprayed on.

"Excuse me?" Ollie closed his eyes for a second, making sure to brand the image on his brain. If all else failed he would at least have this picture on file to provide happy moments on otherwise dull days.

"The sides," the man gestured dangerously close to Ollie's body, "need extra attention don't they?"

Ollie decided to play along. "They sure do."

"Can I park my van here for a couple of hours?" the man flashed a dazzling smile at Ollie. "I'm doing some work on Golborne Road and they've started clamping. It'll just be for an hour or two until," he looked at his watch, "four at the latest."

Ollie knew Auntie Em's policy about strangers parking in the mews but desperate times called for desperate measures.

"Well," he didn't want to appear too eager but it was difficult not to, "if you park outside my house," Ollie gestured to the yellow door behind him – was that too keen? "it'll be ok. Just this once though," he said, smiling to make sure that wasn't necessarily the case.

The man quickly returned with a pick-up that rattled into the mews and parked outside Ollie's.

"I'll be back at four," the man said dazzling Ollie with another smile. "I owe you one mate."

Wayne nearly jumped when he saw himself reflected in the pick-up's side mirror. He still hadn't got used to the blond hair nor the extreme tan. Putting phase two of the plan into action Wayne sauntered out of the mews whistling the theme tune to *Bewitched*.

"I can't believe you let him do that."

Ollie turned to see Nicky coming out of her door opposite. In one hand she carried a metallic case filled with photographic accessories, in the other her crash helmet.

"Did you see – " stuck for words Ollie gesticulated with his hands, " – that?"

"You wouldn't have let him park there if he was ugly." Before Ollie could protest Nicky held up her hand, "You wouldn't have done," she said firmly.

"I have an ulterior motive."

Nicky rolled her eyes.

"It's that builder fantasy isn't it Ol? The one where they wear nothing but a hard hat and a belt full of spanners and you talk about equipment and erections and – "

"No!" he said mustering as much indignance as he dared, "that's the scaffolder's one anyway. If you must know Auntie Em asked me to check out lA, see if any work needs doing."

"And you think he might do the business so to speak?"

"That would be up to Auntie Em, but it would be tempting fate not to find out. 'See a builder pick him up and all day long you'll have good luck,'" Ollie recited.

Nicky slotted the case into one of the panniers of her black Honda 550, pulled her helmet on and straddled the bike, "I can't believe you have a rhyme for that." She started the powerful machine, clicked down the visor and eased her way out of the mews.

The hunk was as good as his word. On almost the dot of four he ambled down the mews. Ollie immediately phoned Auntie Em.

"He's here."

"I can see that sweetness."

Ollie looked out to see Auntie Em, phone in hand, at her sitting room window.

"And this has nothing to do with the way he looks?"

Ollie knew he'd be fooling no one, least of all Auntie Em, if he protested.

"We do need someone."

"I'll be there in a sec angel."

Ollie clicked off the phone. Going outside he found the man hovering about as if waiting to see him. Waiting to see him! This was getting better and better.

"You couldn't have a look at something for us could you?" Ollie blushed slightly at how the question could be construed. Behind the man Ollie could see Auntie Em approaching from her end of the mews.

"I'd be happy to," the man winked at Ollie leaving him

slightly breathless. What does a wink mean again? He must ask Nicky.

"There's a property at the end that's been empty for ages and could do with some attention," Ollie again struggled against the unintended double entendre which had, he half-hoped, gone unnoticed. He had taken a quick look at 1A earlier on. Apart from having pigeons, both alive and dead, and some plastering that needed redoing, the house had weathered its neglect pretty well.

With relief he saw that Auntie Em was now beside them. "This is the owner, Ms Nelson."

The man turned to Auntie Em and shook her hand with just enough strength to show he meant business but without crushing her.

"Wayne Watson."

He then turned smiling to Ollie, "We haven't met."

As Ollie took the outstretched hand he felt a shiver followed by a spasm to the groin. The builder's hand had a rough firmness to it and Ollie was sure he felt Wayne's middle finger graze the soft underside of his wrist. He couldn't believe people still did that, it seemed so seventies, so closeted.

But it felt surprisingly sexy.

"I'm Ollie."

Lost for words he looked at Auntie Em who took charge.

"Follow me Mr Watson."

Entering the house at the top of the mews, they moved through the narrow hallway where a child's toy gathered dust in the corner.

"How long since it's been inhabited?" Wayne asked as they filed up the stairs.

"Well, the old stabling part downstairs was used for

storage by some market traders but not for at least three years," Auntie Em explained. "They used to wake people up at five in the morning and so had to go."

"I can never understand how people can be so cheerful at such an hour," Ollie said.

"Unless you haven't been to bed," Wayne remarked.

Ollie wondered if he was the only one who noticed how Wayne stressed the final word.

Coming to the top of the small flight of stairs they stepped into the large sitting room that made up most of the living area. 1A had the same layout as the other houses in the mews, except for Gem 'n Em's larger C-shaped house at the end.

As in the others a kitchen opened off the large central space. On each side of the kitchen, large enough for a stove, fridge and small table, was a door leading to a small bedroom. At the top of the stairs an opening led to a bathroom that contained a sink and an old, rather battered, claw-footed bath.

Wayne looked around. He immediately spotted the hole in the corner of the high ceiling where the pigeons came in and sometimes, judging by at least two feathered skeletons, failed to leave.

As he peered into the two small bedrooms on either side of the kitchen Auntie Em whispered to Ollie, "I bet he knocks on the wall." As if on cue they heard a series of taps. Auntie Em rolled her eyes, "Cowboy!" she hissed, unaware of Candida's recent expense in Covent Garden.

"Give him a chance Auntie Em."

Wayne moved quickly through the sitting room to the tiny bathroom.

"Where are you working now Mr Watson?"

Wayne had already prepared the answer to this inevitable

question. "Just round the corner on Portobello. D'ye know the old greasy spoon opposite the florist?" he returned to the large central space.

Auntie Em and Ollie nodded.

"Well it's being refurbished, all bleached beech and bare brick – there's alot of that round here isn't there?"

"It's a bit far to park your van isn't it?" Auntie Em asked.

"When the clampers are out it's any port in a storm I'm afraid Ms Nelson." Wayne gave the room another once-over, "The only major thing is the damp in the bathroom ceiling which'll need to be proofed and replastered. Apart from that, and the loose tiles which shouldn't be a problem, everything is pretty much surface stuff – nothing a good clean and a couple of coats of paint wouldn't put right."

Ollie looked pleadingly at Auntie Em.

"Should take ten days/two weeks maximum."

Auntie Em moved down the stairs followed by the two young men. She strolled in thought to Wayne's blue pick-up, "Give us some references and a written quotation Mr Watson, in the meantime why don't you two – " unseen by Wayne she winked at Ollie, " – exchange numbers."

Wayne slung himself into the driver's seat of the pick-up and rooted around in the glove compartment. "I'm fairly sure I gave out my last card yesterday," Wayne scribbled his number on a scrap of paper.

"I haven't even got one," Ollie said apologetically.

Wayne smiled as he handed over the scrap of paper, "You'll have to phone me then won't you?"

Ollie was sure his gulp must have been audible.

"Where do you live Mr Watson?" Auntie Em continued her questioning.

"Dagenham."

"And you'd travel in every day?"

"If I got the job I'd try and find somewhere local to overnight in."

Ollie could feel Wayne's eyes burning into him.

Wayne slammed the driver's door shut. A quick wave and he reversed slowly out of the mews.

"Well at least he didn't whistle through his teeth." Auntie Em turned to Ollie, "Let me know what his quote is but I'm not going above seven fifty. That's final."

Auntie Em was nearly at her front door when Ollie called down the mews. "Thanks for getting his number for me."

"I'd watch him, angel. Those Dagenham boys – they're at least three stops past Barking."

Ollie waited three days before calling. When he did he made sure to have Auntie Em next to him.

The phone was answered on the third ring.

"Wayne? It's Ollie here from – "

Wayne cut him off, "Hi mate! I thought you'd found someone else for the job."

Ollie was pleasantly taken aback at the warmth of the greeting.

"I was going to stop in but I've been on the other side of town," the builder continued.

So that explains why he hadn't seen the pick-up, Ollie thought. He had wandered past the restaurant site several times a day for the past few days hoping to bump into Wayne, but hadn't seen hide nor hair of the builder.

"I could do the job for seven hundred and fortyfive all in."

"One second," Ollie put his hand over the mouthpiece and looked at Auntie Em. "Seven forty five?"

Auntie Em returned his look with more than a hint of suspicion, "You didn't tell him he couldn't go above seven fifty did you sweetness?"

"No!" Ollie grinned. "I thought about it though."

"Well, if he's useless we'll know soon enough. When can he start?"

Ollie uncovered the mouthpiece. "When can you start Wayne?" he tried to keep from sounding overenthusiastic.

"Monday alright for you?"

"Monday?" Ollie mouthed to Auntie Em who grimaced her consent.

"Monday it is then," Ollie, smiling, clicked off the phone.

Auntie Em sighed, "There's something about him...."

"Isn't there just?"

"I know lust is blind, angel, but I can't quite put my finger on it," Auntie Em shook her head. "It's probably nothing," she muttered, but something was definitely troubling her about the builder.

Wayne yawned, stretched and got out of bed. He could get used to these jobs and this one was turning out a treat. Candida Hapshill was paying him for information on, and the possible retrieval of, some stupid painting AND he was going to be paid for doing a glorified cleaning job.

He looked at himself admiringly in the full-length mirror and smiled, "You're a genius Wayne Watson, there's no doubt about it."

12

LIES DAMN LIES

Today was the first day that Rion was officially allowed out of the house. And she was going to take full advantage of it. In what she hoped would become a regular habit Rion collected Hum from Ollie and walked Auntie Gem along the canal to work. She breathed in lungfuls of air, happy that the painful wheeze had finally gone.

They had just passed Ha'penny Bridge when Rion saw the first one.

"What's that Auntie Gem?" Rion pointed to something floating amongst the rushes.

Auntie Gem moved closer to the canal bank. Squinting past the cans and burger cartons in the reeds she saw a greyish/black object bobbing in the water. "It's a pipe, child, rubber tubing or whatnot."

Rion moved closer but pulled back suddenly when Auntie Gem's rubber tubing turned belly up to reveal a white-scaled underside.

"Ugh!" Rion could see that, apart from having scales, the object had the ugliest of faces.

Auntie Gem could now see the thing for what it was. "It's an eel," she chuckled. "One of the fisherman probably caught it and threw it back."

"What a waste!" Rion said disgusted both by the loss of

life and by the eel's countenance which was one of the most hideous things she had ever seen.

"A heron'll get it, or a gull. Someone will have it for supper don't you worry!"

Rion noticed several other dead fish on their way up to the bridge at the top of Ladbroke Grove but didn't mention it to Auntie Gem who was rattling on about her childhood in Jamaica.

Arm in arm they walked past Canalside House where Hum, in one of his favourite tricks, ran down the gentle slope to scatter the pigeons being fed outside Sainsburys. The dog carried on to harass the swans and geese who hissed and spat at his impudence.

"He'd better go on the lead, child," Auntie Gem advised. "All the young are out once we're over Cardiac Arrest."

"Cardiac Arrest?"

Auntie Gem gestured to the end of the walkway where a sharply rising humpback bridge spanned the entrance to a lock. "That's what I call it anyway."

With the chunky old Nokia Ollie had given Rion feeling secure, but heavy, in her pocket, they huffed and puffed over Cardiac Arrest and were soon on the green of the towpath once more. Auntie Gem was right. On this section proud pairs of ducks and moorhens swam with their tiny, fluffy offspring. Further on two geese shared duties over a creche of at least a dozen goslings.

Auntie Gem and Rion watched as the baby geese, heads down, tugged and pulled at the grass on the towpath. In a sudden burst Hum tugged out of Rion's grasp and raced for the birds.

"Hum!" Rion turned to Auntie Gem in anguish, "The poor birds what'll – "

"It's not the birds I'd be worried about, child."

They watched as the young dog, grinning from ear to ear, raced for the birds.

Upon seeing Hum the two creche-keeping geese reared up in the water. At their honk of alarm their charges scurried for the canal. All except one who continued to tug at the grass. With the lead flying Isadora Duncan style behind him, the dog charged at the unfortunate gosling that kept feeding unawares.

Rion clutched Auntie Gem's arm. "Just our luck," she wailed, "the poor thing's deaf!"

"Hum!" they both called as loud as they could but the dog had no intention of stopping.

The honking of the two guardians had now spread up and the canal bank, all the geese united in an abrasive chorus of alarm.

Hum was nearly upon the gosling when the more fiercesome of the two guardians reared up onto the bank. With beating wings and neck stretched like Concorde the avenging goose reached its doomed charge just ahead of the dog. Spitting and jabbing like a cobra the protector sheltered the gosling and herded it back to the canal.

Having the time of his life Hum continued to dance on the riverbank, barking at the geese who hissed their rage from a safe distance.

"He'll learn sometime won't he Auntie Gem?"

The old lady patted her tight curls as if worried some had gone astray. "Or he'll be taught a lesson. If they're lucky the young always are."

Rion ran to the excited hound, caught the lead and dragged him away.

Sporadic honking followed Auntie Gem and Rion as the geese gabbled amongst themselves, looking forward to the day when they would get their revenge.

On an instinct Gorby had come down to the chamber beside the canal. He had come here nearly every day since the girl's disappearance but today somehow felt different.

Gorby stared through the rustic fencing at the willowy girl and the small black woman on the towpath opposite.

He knew she would return. He was glad he hadn't had to wait too long.

Work still hadn't finished on Mitre Bridge. It seemed the labourers had been strengthening the structure and nearby railway wall for months.

Auntie Gem watched as the young girl and Hum made their way through the gauntlet of admiring comments and wolf-whistles. Next time she would make sure Rion didn't accompany her this far. Gem knew Ollie would probably welcome such attention, and Nicky could certainly handle it, but Rion – it wasn't right for a young girl, no matter how well intentioned.

Upon entering the Peters & Peters compound she waved as always to Mr Henry, the company guard – or Chief of Security as he was now called. He normally smiled and waved back but this time he came rushing out from his cabin.

"Miss Gemma," the guard seemed unusually anxious, "the boss, he's in a terrible mood today. He's already fired Miss Doreen."

Auntie Gem was not unduly worried. Doreen always took the brunt of Edwin's anger. She was fired at least once a month from the secretarial pool. It didn't seem to change anything. Doreen simply moved her things behind the large plastic ficus at the end of the office and did her work from there. Edwin normally calmed down within a couple of hours and had forgotten everything by the following day.

"*And* Miss Kitty," the guard wrung his hands as if drying them above an air vent.

"And Kitty?"

This was different. Kitty was Auntie Gem's assistant and the reason why Gem could come in mid-morning instead of half past eight with the rest of them.

"But she's still here?"

"No!" Henry opened his eyes wide. "He walked her out himself!"

This was even more unusual. Edwin never threw people off the grounds. Quickening her pace ever so slightly Auntie Gem crossed the yard towards the main building.

The change in feeling was apparent when she came out of the lift on the first floor. There was none of the chatty buzz that normally greeted her. Apart from a few muted phonecalls all worked in silence. From here she could just make out Doreen in her place of banishment behind the giant plastic plant.

Eyes pleaded with her as the trolley slowly squeaked towards Mr Edwin's office. Even before she was halfway there Gem could hear her boss' muffled angry voice.

Sitting rigidly at her desk outside was Miss Collins, Edwin's personal assistant. The normally irrepressible PA waved Gemma over.

"Is it as bad as I've been told?"

"Worse!" Miss Collins replied her voice just above a whisper. "Have you any arsenic?"

Auntie Gem chuckled, "He'd taste it Liz."

"It's for me silly!"

Auntie Gem gave a hoot, which she quickly suppressed. "What started it off?"

"At first we thought it was about Lady Peters but then

something arrived in the post. Something he wouldn't even let me see."

"And Kitty?"

The PA waved her hands to minimise the firing, "I've spoken to her already. She'll be back on Monday."

Again the rumbling of Edwin's voice carried through the office walls.

"Who's in there now?"

"Mr Paul but he shouldn't be – "

At that the office door swung open and the young assistant manager strode out, his face like thunder.

Miss Collins raised her eyebrows, " – too long." As Auntie Gem wheeled the trolley in Miss Collins stage-whispered after her, "Don't forget to call him Sir!"

Sir Edwin looked up from his desk when he heard the squeaking trolley. "Ah Gemma, it's you." He returned to the papers on his desk, "I had to let Kitty go."

Knowing her assistant would be back on Monday Auntie Gem pacified her boss, "I'm sure she deserved it." After a pause she added, "Sir Edwin."

Sir Edwin's naturally suspicious features narrowed further at this unexpected acquiescence. After a worrying few seconds he smiled, "That's the first time you've used my title Gemma."

Auntie Gem bobbed her head in a slight bow of deference, "Sir Ed-win," she repeated but this time separated his name in two in the Jamaican lilt he liked. She poured a milky tea, put three digestive biscuits on a plate and placed them in front of him.

"Everybody says you're in a filthy mood," again she paused before his name, "Sir Edwin."

Looking at the honest face of the lady who had worked first for his father and now for him, Sir Edwin Peters sighed.

Holding a large brown envelope he stood up and paced along the huge window that looked over the canal.

"It's just some damn scientist," the chairman of Peters & Peters shook the envelope in his hand, "has made allegations – without any evidence to back them up I might add – about us. They're lies, damn lies, and he's threatening to print them."

Auntie Gem shook her head, "Well if they're lies," she began.

"It doesn't matter if they're lies or not. If he prints them it would harm us."

Sir Edwin used the 'us' when he meant 'me'. When there was trouble to be shared he used the collective pronoun, the singular when there was glory. "Some of it would stick, it always does," he said glumly.

"Can't you sue?"

Sir Edwin didn't care if his sigh was deemed demeaning. He spoke slowly as if explaining something very difficult to a very simple person, "That would take ages by which time the damage would have been done. We would only get a retraction anyway – by then it would be too late."

"Bribery?"

Her boss smiled icily but said nothing.

Auntie Gem thought it best to change the subject. She knew the thought of food often improved his temperament. "What will you be having for lunch?"

Sir Edwin felt some of his bad mood coming back. "It's Friday isn't it?" he snapped.

Auntie Gem nodded.

"What do I always have on Fridays?"

"Fish."

"You know how I value tradition. I'm not changing now." Sir Edwin felt a familiar burning pain in his bladder. Flinging the envelope on his desk in dismissal he walked quickly across the office to his adjoining bathroom and closed the door.

Never one to let something private of Edwin's escape her attention, Auntie Gem went over to his desk. She opened the brown envelope to find it contained a bound dossier. As she was about to open it she heard the toilet flush. Sliding the dossier back in the envelope she hurried back to her trolley.

Just in time.

Sir Edwin came back to find Auntie Gem poring over the cups and saucers. Much as he liked her, well as much as he could like any of his staff, she did tend to hang around.

"I thought you'd gone," he said in a tone that implied he wished she had.

Auntie Gem straightened up. Smiling she placed a small white bowl on her boss' desk, "Cheer up."

She was almost out the door when Sir Edwin called her back, "Gemma."

Auntie Gem turned back into the office.

"The fish," her boss asked nervously, "it's not caught locally is it?"

"I don't think so Sir Edwin, but I'll ask cook."

Auntie Gem chuckled as she left the office.

"He's having a bad day alright," she said to Miss Collins.

The PA rolled her eyes, "We knew that Gem!"

"He was worried the fish for lunch was caught in the canal!"

Sir Edwin didn't notice the envelope was in a different place on top of his desk. Instead his eyes were drawn to the bowl the tea-lady had left. It contained his very favourite things: fruit pastilles.

13

IT'S NOT UNUSUAL

The weekend had dragged by for Ollie but finally it was Monday morning. He could hear Wayne whistling the theme from *Bewitched* as he cleared out number lA, right next door.

Right next door!

It was funny how Wayne seemed to be as fond of the tune as he was. Ollie took this as another sign of how compatible they were.

Or could be.

Ollie was determined to find out which this week. And he was determined to have fun trying.

Ollie noticed that the whistling had stopped. Hearing a series of knocks he imagined Wayne on his doorstep, shirtless, dust stuck to his sweat-clad muscles, gagging for a cuppa or ...whatever.

He gave himself a quick glance in the hall mirror, ruffled his hair – no, too tousled – then ruffled it back, but then it looked as though he had just got out of bed – too suggestive, at least at this stage. Looking round frantically he spied a comb next to his keys and quickly pulled it through his fringe.

Again the door was rapped three times.

Fixing a natural grin on his face, Ollie took a deep breath and opened the door.

Rion and Hum stood before him. The dog jumped up at seeing his master. "Come for a walk with us," the girl said with a bewitching smile.

Ollie glanced up and down the mews but there was no sign of Wayne.

"I can't Rion, I'm working."

"But you were working all weekend," the girl complained.

"So I could have this week free to help Wayne."

"He'll be there when we get back and besides," she cupped her hand to her mouth and lowered her voice to a dramatic whisper, "you don't want to appear too keen. Let him come after you."

"Is that what it says in your magazines?"

"C'mon. Pleeeeease," Rion stretched the word out as long as she dared. "I want to see Jake but I can't control Hum off the lead."

"I can't always control him either."

Seeing the young girl's downcast look Ollie changed his mind. She was right. Wayne would still be there when he got back. Besides he had never followed any advice given in magazines and look where it had got him.

"As long as we're back for lunch."

Rion laughed happily, "Easily!"

Ollie grabbed his keys and closed the door.

As they passed lA they could hear Wayne clattering about on the first floor.

"One second," Ollie said to Rion before knocking on the door of what was the unlucky house.

When Wayne appeared at the open sitting room window Ollie had been right. The builder looked like he should be in a Diet-Coke ad.

"I'm going out for a while," Ollie tossed his keys to

Wayne who snatched them out of the air. "Let yourself in if you want anything."

"Thanks mate," Wayne smiled. Ollie, Rion and Hum were escorted out of the mews by the whistled strains of *Bewitched*.

Wayne waited for at least five minutes before letting himself into Ollie's next door. Although he knew no-one was there he still crept up the stairs until, feeling foolish, he straightened up and entered the first floor sitting room as if it was his own.

Again he looked at the glossy reproduction Candida had ripped from a book. Somewhere, in one of the many libraries in Kensington and Chelsea, a study on seventeenth century Dutch painting was missing a page. The image of the pale young girl in the white stole gazed back at him from the shadows. Merlijnche de Poortje didn't look like anything special to Wayne.

He made a cursory glance through all the rooms to make sure the miniature wasn't in plain sight. Having determined it wasn't Wayne set to work, starting on the sitting room cupboards.

They were almost at the bridge running across the top of Ladbroke Grove when Ollie couldn't contain his curiosity any longer.

"What on earth are you looking for?" he asked Rion who had been gazing intently at the canal ever since they had left Meanwhile Gardens.

The young girl didn't answer for a second. Her attention had been taken by a moorhen and her two young bobbing amongst the rushes below them.

"Are they called moorchicks d'you think?" she asked.

Ollie looked at the tiny birds beside their mother. "If they're not I think they should be."

The calm of the scene was broken by Hum who charged up barking happily. The moorhen and her chicks paddled out to the middle of the canal and safety.

"There's one!" Rion exclaimed pointing at what, to Ollie, looked like just another bit of floating rubbish.

"Haven't you seen an empty can of coke before?"

"Not that! I mean next to it."

Ollie looked again but all he could see was an unfortunate perch turned belly up.

"It's a dead fish isn't it?" Rion asked.

"Yes," he said slowly, "you sometimes get them along here."

Rion's face dropped slightly. "So it's not unusual?"

To be loved by anyone? Ever since Ollie had seen Tom Jones squeezed into leather at some awards ceremony the Welsh singer popped into his thoughts at the slightest provocation.

Ollie smiled, "Fish aren't immortal you know."

"It's just that when I walked Auntie Gem to work yesterday I saw a couple more and a dead eel."

"It happens Rion."

Quickly putting Hum on the lead they crossed the bridge, entering the cemetery through the side door next to the Dissenter's Chapel. Hum practically choked himself as he strained against the leash.

"Aren't you going to let him off?" Rion asked.

Ollie pointed to a sign stating that dogs must be kept on the lead AT ALL TIMES.

"I got told off by some creepy guard on my last visit."

"What's the worst he can do –" Rion giggled, " – ask you to leave?"

In some perverse way the thought kind of appealed to Ollie. "I've never been thrown out of a cemetery before," he mused, imagining himself being bounced out of the graveyard ('And don't come back') by two burly minders, "but it's best we don't attract too much attention."

Following the path below South Avenue they skirted Thackeray's gleaming white grave and were soon within sight of Jake's tree.

As they came closer Rion signalled her arrival with the four-note whistle. The chirpy reply was almost instantaneous. Arriving beneath the overgrown leafy tree they looked up to find their host half-hidden in the branches above them.

"Will Hum be quiet if you leave him down there?" Jake asked.

Ollie and Rion looked at each other and shook their heads. "No," they said in unison.

"Especially not if he's tied up," Ollie added. The thought of the headstrong dog roaming the cemetery off the lead and by himself was surely an ejectable offence.

"Wait a sec then."

They watched as Jake vanished further into the tree. Not for the first time Ollie cursed Hum. Fired by what Rion had told him he was dying to have tea in the treehouse, with its driftwood, rugs and spyhole to check out visitors.

Jake was beside them in a jiffy. In one hand he held a battered tobacco tin. "Shall we?" he gestured for them to follow him the short distance to where a bench overlooked a simple tomb.

Ollie read aloud the inscription on the plain grave that was almost exaggerated in its austerity; "'George Cruickshank – For thirty years a total abstainer and ardent pioneer and champion by pencil, word and pen of universal abstinence from intoxicating drinks.'"

"Do you think he would have approved of this?" Jake opened the tin, which Ollie could see was filled with marijuana. "I've called this one Mausoleum Madness. It's grown at the back of a circus owner's tomb and always has a bit of zip to it," he smiled wickedly at Ollie. "You haven't got major plans for the day do you?"

I don't *now*, Ollie thought, looking at the tin of grass. "Just helping someone do some cleaning."

"You said you had to finish some work!" Rion exclaimed indignantly.

"Plans change," Ollie gave a helpless smile and shrugged his shoulders.

Jake took out a packet of small blue Rizla from the tin, removed a single rolling paper and began filling it with the pungent weed.

"Don't worry, this isn't skunk, it won't knock you out for twentyfour hours."

Ollie dismissed his concern with a wave of the hand, "I really get into cleaning when I'm stoned."

Rion sighed in disgust.

"What's going on at that house anyway?" she asked. "I mean, why is Wayne cleaning it out?"

Obviously Auntie Em hadn't told the young girl what was happening. And if Auntie Em hadn't told, Ollie realised it wasn't his place to tell either.

"I think Auntie Em has some plans for it. I'm not sure what," he lied.

"I'm going to have to find somewhere soon aren't I?"

"Think about that later. Wait until you get better first."

Jake rolled the joint between the fingers of one hand,

lightly sealed it and twisted one end. "Is she better?" he asked as he passed the joint for Ollie to light.

"Yes," Rion said firmly.

Ollie wasn't convinced, "But fevers can boomerang back – you don't want that do you?"

Rion shook her head.

"And Gem 'n Em aren't throwing you out are they?"

"No but I can't stay there forever."

"At the moment Heron Point is out of the question I'm afraid," Jake passed a box of matches to Ollie. "One guard in particular is always down there."

Rion's sigh expressed her dismay.

"You can always stay with me if you do need somewhere," Ollie reassured her, "or with Nicky, she wouldn't mind."

"Thanks," she squeezed his arm in appreciation. "Did you ever ask her about – " Rion looked away as if somehow embarrassed, " – you know?"

Ollie racked his brain but nothing came back to him.

"Remember that first night when we sat around the fire and – " Rion prompted him again, " – you know!"

"I remember smoking lots of homegrown," Ollie admitted but realised that probably wasn't very helpful.

"Which muddles your memory doesn't it?" said Rion unhappily.

Jake turned to Ollie, "Were we smoking Headstone?"

"Sounds might familiar," he replied with a smile.

"Yeah, it's not great for the recall."

Rion cleared her throat in an effort to get back into the conversation. "Anyway, you said Nicky sometimes works for Glamourista and she might know someone..."

Ollie remembered now to his shame.

"I haven't asked her but I will. Remind me though ok?"

Jake had waited long enough. He nodded towards the

joint that Ollie still held, unlit, "Are you going to light that or what?"

After a pleasant morning spent with Jake, Ollie and Rion made their way back along Centre Avenue. Ollie lagged behind Rion and Hum, unable and unwilling to wipe the smile from his face. Although they had only smoked two small grass joints Ollie felt as if they had finished the whole tin. All the better to do the cleaning with, he reasoned, besides the grass should also take the edge off his over-enthusiasm for Wayne and make him approach the situation with a touch more mellowness.

Fat chance of that.

He followed Rion and Hum out of the main gate, stepping aside at the last moment for a taxi entering the cemetery.

Ollie exchanged a look with the elegant lady in the back of the black cab. He was sure he had seen her before, but where?

With his brain buzzing on the marijuana Ollie knew it would be useless to ask it anything as basic as memory retrieval.

In the back of the cab the editor of Glamourista flicked a speck of dirt off her turquoise pumps. She shivered at the prospect of the next hour spent with Jake in the house in the trees that moaned and groaned in time as they made love.

14

SUCH GUILE

On the previous Saturday's trawl through the market Nicky had picked up a battered copy of *The Guide to Feng-Shui* for a pound, but now she felt feng-shui'd out of existence. She had moved the mirror, put flowers in front of the TV, hung crystals in the window and moved the bed to face the northeast but still she felt restless. Yes, vitality was flowing into the financial side of her house, and yes, her career had a certain amount of vigour at the moment but the upshot of all this energy was that it made her irritable.

In this frame of mind Nicky pushed past the plants that crowded the room and went down to answer the door upon which someone was knocking with uncommon enthusiasm.

Her mood vanished immediately upon seeing who was on the doorstep. Ollie, a broad smile on his face, a bouquet of lilies in his arms, beamed at her.

"These are for you," her neighbour handed her the flowers with an exaggerated flourish.

"For what?" Nicky asked, her irritation vanishing by the second. Flower power worked for her every time.

"For all the lovely Tuesday mornings in the world," said Ollie as he kissed her on both cheeks. "May I come in?" Without waiting for a reply he slid past her and took the stairs, two by two, up to the sitting room.

Lacking his sparkle Nicky followed at a more sedate pace.

She came up the stairs to find him already on the sofa. He had his hands behind his head, his feet up and that broad grin on his face that normally only meant one thing.

"I take it Wayne succumbed?"

Ollie beamed, "No."

"No? Then why the cheesy grin?"

Ollie swung his feet onto the floor and sat up. "He likes art, Nicks."

Nicky got the large vase down from the top shelf and began filling it with the mainly closed stems of lilies.

"When I came back yesterday I found the glossy book on the Dutch Masters – "

"The one James gave you?"

Ollie nodded.

" – open on the table. He couldn't work the kettle – "

"Ah. Bless," said Nicky with more than a touch of sarcasm.

Ollie ignored her and carried on, " – and so had to boil up a saucepan for his cuppa. While waiting for the water to boil he saw my books and – "

Again Nicky interrupted sarcastically, "Just couldn't stop himself?"

"Yes!" Ollie said triumphantly. "You should have seen his face when I asked him about it. Oh Nicks, he looked so sheepish. This tough builder with calloused hands – "

"How do you know what his hands are like?" she asked.

Ollie ignored the question.

"This tough builder with calloused hands likes art. A real man Nicks, not some airy-fairy wittering on about space and lines and what it means to him claptrap. He's a – "

Nicky put up a hand to stop him. "Don't say it Ol, not a rough diamond."

Ollie looked hurt for a second before breaking into a smile. "A diamond in the raw."

"A diamond geezer?"

"Do you know what this means?" Ollie could hardly contain his excitement. "Sunday mornings at Tate Britain, lazy afternoons holding hands in the Hayward. We've already made plans to see the Masters of Light exhibition–"

"The Dutch stuff?"

Ollie nodded, " – at the National on Friday."

"Let's backtrack a bit here O1. You didn't sleep with him?"

"No!" Ollie sounded indignant. "Wayne went back east last night anyway, but he phoned to tell me he was getting in the shower. What's that mean?"

Nicky put the artfully arranged lilies on the table. "That he's had a hard day and needs a wash?" she asked tentatively.

"He said that so I would think about him *in* the shower don't you think?"

Nicky wasn't sure.

"Perhaps," she said, not wanting to burst his bubble.

"And then he winks at me every now and then. What's that all about?"

"It could mean everything or nothing or all points in between."

"And – "

Just as Nicky thought she couldn't bear any more on wonderbuilder, Ollie put his head to one side. Flashing a grin at Nicky he ran to the window.

"He's here!"

Ollie gave Nicky a big kiss on the cheek and ran out of the room.

"Phone me later," she called after him, but her friend was already down the stairs and out the door.

In her newly aligned existence there was one household item that still bothered Nicky – the phone. Where could she put the damn thing where it would reflect and empower her?

Flicking through the 'Guide's index of household appliances she found there were three listings for the telephone. Before Nicky could decide whether the phone on the answering machine was cordless, handheld or other – when it was patently all three – it rang.

"Sweetness I'm not disturbing you am I?"

Nicky smiled. She knew only one person who asked her that. Everyone else, it seemed, assumed you were dying to talk to them.

"Of course not Auntie Em. I was just – "

Nicky stopped herself. It sounded too ridiculous to even mention. What would she say? 'Oh, I was just trying to figure out the optimum position for the phone and I was using a directory to do it?'

" – It's not important. What's Rion up to?"

"I sent her off to Ledbury Road."

Over the past few years this once shabby Notting Hill Street had seen an influx of smart shops move in, including the one that Rion seemed very fond of.

"She's probably got her nose pressed up against the window of GHOST as we speak."

"Hopefully she's inside asking if they want anyone. We need to find her something to do." Auntie Em paused rather pointedly before continuing, "You don't know of any jobs going do you angel?"

"Well," Nicky had been promising herself an assistant for ages. "I've got a couple of things that she can help me with this week."

"I knew you'd be the right person to ask. Rion's still a bit shy and you can't be backwards...."

" – in coming forwards can you Auntie Em? If you want something done...."

" – you've got to do it yourself," Auntie Em ran her fingers through her hair and smiled. She and Nicky had had this conversation many times before. "I hear you're doing some work for Glamourista."

Nothing got past Auntie Em Nicky thought. "Yes, do you know Ollie's friend Johnson?"

"The decorator?"

Nicky gave a short laugh. "That's not what he calls himself but yes – they want me to do some pictures of him."

"Glamourista don't need anyone do they angel?"

"I don't know, I'll ask if you want."

"It's just Rion has this thing about working for them and – "

"No problem Auntie Em. I have to phone Angie anyway. It's a pretty nasty office though."

"In what way treasure?"

Nicky thought for a second. How could she put this? "Class-driven backstabbing ambition?"

"They're all like that aren't they?"

"Hmmm. Some are worse than others though."

"She'll have to learn about that sometime – this is England after all – perhaps it's best she does it whilst she has our support."

"I'll ask Auntie Em, but no promises."

"Of course not sweetness. And Ollie didn't mention this?"

Nicky shrugged her shoulders, "Not that I remember."

"Rion says he promised he would."

"Ollie's had other things on his mind though, hasn't he?"

Auntie Em knew she meant Wayne. Precious little else had entered Ollie's consciousness recently.

"Yes," Emma said in a voice that couldn't hide her disapproval, "that he has." She allowed herself a quick frown before continuing, "What do you think of that 'thing' our boy has on his mind?"

"Lust?" Nicky hung onto the word as if by doing so some of its qualities might rub off on her. "It has its place doesn't it? Ollie could do with a good going over I reckon."

"No sweetness, I meant what do you think of Wayne?"

"Oh," Nicky thought for a second. "He is quite stunning in that East End bit of rough sort of way, but he doesn't float my boat. Any guy who has a chest bigger than mine doesn't do it for me – but he's like a walking wet dream to Ollie."

"Do you trust him though?"

"To do some simple building work? Probably. He doesn't seem too much of a cowboy. His work's ok isn't it?"

"Yes, but – "

"But with secrets, something important?" Nicky shook her head, "Probably not."

"I don't trust him Nicky. I just don't trust him. He was in Ollie's for ages on Monday."

"Apparently he couldn't work the kettle so had to boil up some water."

"Kettles aren't that difficult to operate are they angel?"

"Well Ollie's kettle is a bit odd Auntie Em, you know there's that button underneath – "

Auntie Em gave a snort of disbelief.

"I have to admit I thought the same thing," Nicky agreed. "And then Ollie said Wayne got sidetracked by his art books. Apparently Wayne's a bit of a gallery gazer."

"So he felt it was ok to rifle through Ollie's belongings?"

"I don't know if it was quite like that."

It was all starting to make sense to Auntie Em.

"Last night when Kanwar dropped me off – "

Nicky couldn't let that pass unnoticed. "Kanwar?" she repeated.

"Doctor Gidwani."

"How long have you been seeing him?"

"That's not the issue here sweetness, suffice to say that a rather touching friendship started up when he was treating Rion, but I'm sure we saw that man – "

"Wayne?"

Auntie Em nodded, "Up at the Gate. It was about midnight. He was talking to someone in a brown Mercedes jeep."

Nicky was incredulous, "Candida?"

"I couldn't see to be sure but yes, it was a woman."

Nicky was about to wisecrack, 'Then it couldn't be Candida.' when she thought better of it. This was all too strange. "But why? Do you think – "

"Sweetheart I'm not sure what to think, but – what was Candida trying to get from Ollie?"

"The miniature?"

"Yes angel, and when she found he wasn't going to hand it over?"

"Ollie's dreamboy shows up? Auntie Em you don't really – "

"I'm not saying anything sweetness. Just think about it."

Nicky didn't have to think for long.

She knew Candida was capable of such guile, she knew she was after Merlijnche de Poortje, and what had Ollie said? 'What Candida wants Candida gets.'

"What are we going to do?"

"I have a plan angel, but I'll need your help."

By the time Auntie Em had finished telling Nicky of the ruse the photographer was won over. More importantly she believed Wayne would go for it. Her only concern was for her friend.

"But what are you going to tell Ollie?"

Auntie Em sighed, "It's a difficult one but for the moment nothing. He's in no danger. Let him have his fun."

Nicky wasn't entirely happy but she knew it was the best way.

"Besides he's practically incapable of lying isn't he?"

Nicky nodded. Auntie Em was always right.

15

LIES DAMN LIES

Café Feliz was normally quiet at elevenses. The workers had long ago grabbed their espressos and headed for the office while the slackers were still nursing hangovers in bed, leaving the little café with a token presence of mothers with prams, a party of Somalis and some grufflooking Portuguese.

Clutching their milky coffees in tall glasses, and a custard pastry each, Nicky and Ollie sat at one of the wrought-iron tables outside. The only other people were an elderly couple seated one empty table away but one.

Ollie inhaled deeply and smiled, "I love this time of year. I love the smell of burning leaves that you get everywhere in the city."

"It's exhaust fumes Ol."

"It doesn't matter where you are – in Camden, Chelsea or darkest Soho," he took another deep breath, "the smell is so autumnal."

"Stop being such a romantic Ol, it's traffic pollution," Nicky glared at him. "And I wish you'd wipe that smile off your face, you'll force me to put my shades on and then I'll look like part of the fashion pack."

Ollie was unable to stop beaming. "But you are part of the fashion pack Nicks."

Nicky rummaged around in her bag, "That does it."

After a few seconds she pulled out a pair of this year's very dark owlshaped glasses in tortoiseshell frames. Giving them a quick wipe she plumped them on her nose. Nicky sighed in relief, "Aaaaah....I sometimes wish I could have these surgically attached."

"When did you get back last night?"

"Late enough for there to be no lights on in your house," Nicky took a sip from her coffee. "I noticed Wayne's pick-up was still parked outside though. Funny, I would have thought 1A was still too fumey to sleep in – some of those paints should carry a health warning."

"They do Nicks which is why," Ollie took a deep breath and puffed out his chest, feeling immensely proud all of a sudden, "he's been staying at mine for the past couple of nights."

"But," the photographer said in mock innocence, "there's no bed in your spare room is there?"

Ollie rolled his eyes, "Enough already!"

"So dish, sweetheart."

"Well," Ollie thought back to the past two wonderful nights. "It started on Tuesday. He asked me if he could have a bath at mine so – "

"Good Samaritan that you are you said yes?"

Ollie shrugged his shoulders, "I could hardly say no could I? Anyway I saw him putting candles round the bath which I thought was kinda sweet."

"He put candles round the bath?"

Ollie nodded. "I'm telling you Nicks, he's not the philistine you think he is."

"Carry on."

"So I busied myself in the kitchen."

"Right," Nicky said in a disbelieving voice.

"Just as I was about to go downstairs and check on something in the studio – "

"Yes?" she egged him on.

"He asked me if I would scrub his back."

Nicky almost choked on her coffee. "Scrub his back?! That's a good one," she exclaimed loudly.

The elderly couple two tables away had remained motionless, cups to their lips, since Ollie had started the story.

"So I did and – well, you know how it is..."

Nicky wasn't going to let any details go. "Tell me."

Ollie sighed, "Well, I got wet, had to take my shirt off – "

"And?"

Ollie wasn't dishing. "Use your imagination Nicks."

The elderly couple put their cups down in disappointment.

"You know what the nicest thing was though?"

"Are you going to tell me or will I have to use my imagination?"

"After we had splashed around he wrapped me in that big towel and rubbed me dry. It was so – " Ollie searched for the right word, " – so – "

The elderly couple again had their cups to their lips, poised for any salacious titbit they might later tell their friends.

" – so fraternal."

Nicky snorted. "With brothers like that who needs incest right?"

"And then – "

"There's more?"

"We were feeling hungry."

"I bet."

"So I phoned up Rotisserie Georges for some chicken and dauphinois."

"Mmmmm."

"And he went to collect it!"

"Don't they deliver though?"

"Yup but he *really* wanted to."

Nicky remembered what Auntie Em had told her.

"And this was on Tuesday night?" she queried.

"Yes."

"About midnight?"

"More or less."

Ollie saw Nicky's face drop.

"Are you ok Nicks?"

The photographer smiled weakly. "Sure."

A honking of horns alerted them to Wayne's arrival. The blue pick-up swerved over from the other side of the road and double-parked outside the Portuguese café.

Wayne, looking striking in worn jeans and ripped t-shirt, jumped out smiling, "I got the paint. Nu-Line had run out but I got it in Queens Park." He nodded to Nicky, "Hi Nicks."

Nicks? The photographer thought to herself – who the hell said he could call her Nicks?

"So are you going to help me again today?" Wayne winked at Ollie.

"Ah, how sweet," Nicky gave Ollie a cheesy grin, "Wayne's little helper." As Ollie blushed Nicky asked him, "You haven't seen Candida have you?" Although Nicky directed the question at Ollie she made sure to look at Wayne to see if there was any reaction to the name.

There wasn't.

"You don't know any Candidas do you Wayne?" Nicky asked, ignoring Ollie's confused look. Although her manner was joking she was watching Wayne like a hawk.

"Don't get too many of those where I come from Nicks."

The photographer again flinched at this unauthorised shortening of her name.

"I haven't met a Tara before either," Wayne continued, "or even a Sophie come to that, my sister called her daughter Caroline though – "

As Wayne winked at Nicky she felt a frisson that must be a hundred times stronger in Ollie's body.

" – but I think she was on a bus going down Sloane Street at the time!"

Either he was very good, Nicky decided, or totally ignorant. For selfish reasons she wanted to think he was totally ignorant – afterall someone couldn't look like that and be clever could they? Someone couldn't look like that and fool all of them could they?

She had the horrible feeling that they could.

Ollie still looked confused at the way the conversation had gone.

"Are you coming mate?"

Crossing the bridge behind Wayne, Ollie could see Aunties Gem 'n Em with Rion.

"I'll be there in a sec," he replied.

With that Wayne hopped into the pick-up and screeched over the bridge. What was Nicky asking him about Candida for? He wondered if it was coincidence or did she know something?

What had started off as a cushy little job was becoming more complicated by the day. In spite of the pay he'd be glad when it was over.

Before Ollie could find out what Nicky had meant by asking Wayne about Candida, Hum had spotted the approaching trio. The dog knew it was time for his walk along the canal.

Auntie Em had hardly stopped at the café before she moved on. "Can't dally," she kissed Ollie on the cheek and gave a conspiratorial smile to Nicky, "I have to go to the framers."

It was time to put the second part of the plan into practise.

Deciding he could do with the walk Ollie accompanied Auntie Gem, Rion and Hum past the orderly council blocks and down the canal.

"I read somewhere that a brisk walk is just as good as a jog for burning the calories."

Auntie Gem cackled, "You'd better go ahead then." She put her arm through Rion's, "We amble don't we child?"

"Yes we do!" Rion said happily. "Normally anyway. But today – "

Much to Hum's enjoyment Rion began skipping up and down the towpath. The dog, excited by any sort of activity, jumped at her heels.

" – calls for something more!"

"What are you so happy about?" Ollie asked but Rion just kept skipping up and down, only now she was whistling some tune of unsurpassed chirpiness.

Auntie Gem linked her arm through Ollie's, "Hasn't she told you?"

"Told me what?"

As Rion skipped by Ollie tried to grab her but, laughing, the girl jumped out of reach.

"I've got a job!" she called back. "Well," she corrected herself, "it's a sort of job."

Ollie realised that he hadn't spoken to Nicky as he had promised. He smacked his hand against his forehead, "Rion I'm sorry. I still haven't asked – "

"But I have!" Slightly out of breath Rion slowed to a walk beside them, "Nicky wants me to be her assistant tomorrow. She said a friend of yours – Johnson Someone-or-other – "

"Ogle."

"'scuse me?"

"His name is Johnson Ogle."

"Yeah, anyway this Johnson is coming to the studio tomorrow to have his picture taken for – " Rion stopped, opened both arms wide and gave a fanfare, "Ta-da-da!" She looked questioningly at Ollie and Auntie Gem.

The old black lady cupped her hand and whispered to Ollie, "I know the answer to this."

"For?" Rion asked again.

Ollie shrugged his shoulders. Neither Johnson nor Nicky had told him anything.

"Glamourista!" Rion said triumphantly. "And Nicky said she would ask if there was an opening there, and if that didn't work," Rion spun round in excitement, " – she said your friend Johnson is like this – " the girl crossed her middle finger over her index, " – with the editor and would put in a good word for me."

Ollie felt slightly left out. After all Johnson was his friend and if anyone was going to put in a good word for Rion it should be him.

"Why didn't anyone tell me?"

Rion sighed in great exaggeration as if the answer was painfully obvious.

Auntie Gem playfully squeezed Ollie's arm. "The way I've heard it if the subject isn't a certain builder," she nudged Ollie in the ribs, "you're not interested."

"Now wait a minute," Ollie began, "that's unfair."

"Is it?" Auntie Gem asked smiling.

"Yes," Ollie said crossly. He then remembered Auntie

Em's comment at Café Feliz and Nicky's pointed remark earlier. "Well," he conceded, "perhaps I have been preoccupied with the work at lA."

"Is it just the work that's been occupying your time?" Rion asked.

Auntie Gem couldn't suppress her mirth, "Or the worker?"

Rion and Auntie Gem looked at each other and burst out laughing.

Ollie put up his hand to stop them, "Ok. Ok," he felt ganged up on all of a sudden. "So I don't see people for a couple of days and all of a sudden no-one tells me anything?"

Auntie Gem put her arm through Ollie's, "We just miss you that's all."

They carried on walking in silence. Ollie, his feathers ruffled, occupied himself with counting the number of dead fish. It was only when they had passed Sainsburys that he realised he had counted thirty within as many feet.

Moving closer to the water for a better look he shrunk back by what he saw.

"Jeez," he gasped in horror.

Lining the canal bank below him, out of sight from the towpath, was an unbroken band of dead fish. They were mainly on the small side but Ollie could see there were some larger ones and eels amongst them.

"There are more and more every day," Auntie Gem shook her head sadly.

"You said it's not unusual," Rion's voice had taken on an accusing tone.

Ollie again allowed Tom Jones a momentary streak through his mind before returning his attention to the horrible sight in front of him.

"Well," he hesitated, "the odd one or two isn't

uncommon, but I've never seen anything like this."

"What could cause it?" Rion asked.

"It sometimes happens after a long hot spell," Ollie shrugged his shoulders feebly, "something about oxygen levels in the water."

"But it hasn't been *that* hot."

Rion was right. In a bid to make up for the season-that-never-started the weather had given England a balmy Indian summer. Whilst pleasant it was hardly fish suffocating weather.

Ollie gestured to a lone fisherman further up the path, "Let's ask him."

"What's he doing fishing when you can pick them out with your hand?" Rion asked.

"Something to do with sport," Ollie said dryly.

The man sat on a fold-out chair surrounded by the paraphernalia of his hobby. In the grass by his side were a large net, a rest for his long pole, various tupperwares full of wriggling maggots, open tins of feathered flies and a small hamper containing what they could see was a packed lunch. A metal bucket nearby was almost full of freshly caught fish.

As usual Hum broke the ice. Despite calls to the contrary the dog made straight for the writhing maggots and gave them a good sniff.

"Sorry," Ollie pulled Hum back by his collar.

"He's alright," the angler replied, "I've not had need of them today. The fish are practically leaping onto the hook."

Ollie guessed the man was in his late forties. He had a pinkish complexion and the round body of someone who spent days sitting on riverbanks.

"It's almost like a mass suicide attempt. They can't wait to get out of the water," the man made a rather unpleasant gurgling sound which Ollie only realised, after a few seconds, was a form of laughter, "but then that's not surprising is it now?"

Rion peered into the metal bucket containing the angler's catch, "Ugh!" she wrinkled her nose in disgust. "Why do they have those – " Rion pointed to the puffy growths some of the fish had on their bodies, " – things?"

"Why isn't it surprising?" Auntie Gem asked the fisherman.

"Well, would you like to stay in there?" the man pointed to the canal.

Ollie looked at the dirty water, "It would be preferable to your bucket I imagine."

"But what's caused them all to die?"

The fisherman turned to Auntie Gem, "You know the work they're doing on the bridge further on?"

Auntie Gem nodded.

"As I heard it the workmen didn't tie up a bag of chemicals securely enough, some kids found it, chucked it in the water and – hey presto! – dead fish by the dozen. Those that haven't the sense to kill themselves haven't the wits not to!"

Ollie, Rion and Auntie Gem left the man gurgling at his luck and continued on their way.

The thin line of dead fish edging the canal had turned into a thicker stripe by the time they had got to Mitre Bridge.

To their disappointment there were no workmen to be seen.

"They've probably been sent home," Ollie said.

"If they're here when I finish I'll give them a piece of my mind," Auntie Gem said, but all knew the possibility of workmen still being on the job at four o'clock was so small as to be infinitesimal.

"Perhaps they'll be back tomorrow."

Auntie Gem's face brightened at the thought.

Ollie and Rion watched from the canal as Auntie Gem crossed Mitre Bridge above them and headed the short way to the entrance of Peters & Peters.

Rion and Ollie made their way back along the towpath. Ollie gave a half-hearted wave and Rion shuddered as they passed the gurgling angler.

"I still don't understand what he's doing," the young girl shook her head, perplexed. "I mean, if catching fish is his thing, why doesn't he simply scoop armfuls out of the water?"

"Ours not to reason why – you know?"

Rion didn't but grunted as if to indicate that she did.

It was when they got to Sainsburys that something happened that would change Hum's life forever. Admittedly, the situation had been building for weeks.

As usual the hound charged excitedly along the canal walk, barking at the swans and geese that hovered in the water waiting to be fed. He ran like mad into the pigeons and that is where he, literally, came unstuck.

Pelting up the gentle slope Hum slipped on the morass of bird droppings. Ollie and Rion watched amazed, and then horrified, as Hum careened out from the cloud of pigeons. The dog's momentum propelled him up the slope where, unable to stop, he slammed into the railings and fell into the water several feet below.

The birds couldn't believe their luck.

They were on him in a flash. The swans were the first. They raced over, their powerful wings beating the water, their necks outstretched, their eyes narrowed in fury.

The geese weren't far behind. Remembering the abuse

they had suffered ever since Hum had showed up they fell on him eager to exact revenge.

Even the moorhens got in on the action. Diving beneath the water they pecked at the hound from underneath.

Hum had soon disappeared beneath a flurry of wings and jabbing beaks.

He never really stood a chance.

"Do something!" Rion implored Ollie. The young girl was in tears.

Hum had vanished from view. A tail, an ear, a paw would surface occasionally before disappearing once more beneath the angry birds.

Ollie ripped off his shirt and began waving it ferociously at the swans.

"I don't think a shirt's going to do much mate," a voice sniffed behind him. Ollie turned to find an old man at his shoulder. He recognised him as being the one who regularly fed the pigeons when Hum charged into them.

"You want to be careful," the old man continued with more than a hint of a smile, "swans can break a man's arm with their wings you know." He peered over the edge at the frantic splashing, "Imagine what they could do with a dog and a young 'un at that. It's best to let him go."

"Let him go where?" Rion wailed.

Ollie continued beating at the birds with his shirt but his onslaught wasn't making much of an impression.

Looking round frantically he spied a freshly bought baguette sticking out of a shopping bag. To the woman's surprise Ollie grabbed the stick of French bread leant down and began battering the swans with it.

"'Ere, you can't do that mate," the old bird-feeder muttered, annoyed at thinking Hum might get away with it, "they're a protected species."

Ollie continued beating at the ferocious birds with the baguette while flailing his shirt in his other hand. His aggression had the desired effect. Giving a last vicious peck the leader of the geese backed off, his minions at his tail.

Before the swans could put in their parting shot Ollie struck the larger of the two on the head with the baguette. Seeing they had lost the support of their friends the swans hissed violently but moved on.

The cowardly moorhens were nowhere to be seen.

"Is he still alive?" Rion asked tearfully as the hound's bedraggled body rolled to the surface.

"Hold my legs," Ollie instructed Rion.

He leant over the edge, stretched for Hum but couldn't quite reach him. As he wriggled further he felt another pair of hands on his ankles to stop him falling in.

With the added support Ollie was now able to touch Hum. He pulled him closer, got a grip with his hands and twisted back to put the dog on dry land once more.

It was then he saw the extra pair of hands belonged to Andy. His body was already od-ing on adrenaline, he hoped it could handle more.

"He's not moving!"

Rion was right. There was no movement from the dog at all. She had to bite her fist to stop herself from screaming at the sight of Hum's body. The poor dog was beaten and bruised. Numerous cuts bled into the water dripping from him so that soon Hum lay in a red pool growing larger.

But the thing that really got Rion was how skeletal Hum looked. With his fur flattened by the water the hound seemed a fraction of his normal size. It didn't seem like he could fight off an under-the-weather Chihuahua let alone a gang of marauding geese.

"I have my car," Andy gestured to the car park at the front of the hypermarket.

"He's not breathing Ollie!"

The only thing Ollie could think to do was put his head to the dog's chest and listen for a heartbeat. He began to massage Hum's bony chest but it was apparent there was just one thing that could save him now.

Mouth-to-mouth.

Digging deep for the memory of the Red Cross course he did long ago Ollie clamped his fingers over the hound's nostrils, tried not to think of where Hum's mouth had been recently, opened the small jaw and blew in. And again. And again.

Nothing.

It was only after the seventh time that Rion shrieked, "He blinked!"

Ollie gave one more breath and pulled back. Just in time. Hum spluttered, coughed then retched up pools of murky canal water over Ollie's trainers.

The crowd cheered.

Hum weakly wagged his tail, tried to stand but couldn't.

Ollie wrapped the dog in his shirt and held him in his arms. He looked at Andy, "Could you take me to the vet?" Ollie stammered, feeling slightly self-conscious of his shirtless self and of Andy being so close by. "It's not far and – "

The drummer took control of the situation.

"Just tell me where," he said firmly.

Rion followed as they hurried through the crowd to Andy's car and away.

16

UPCHUCK

Angie's body tingled. It had been another energetic session at Jake's. As the taxi rattled out of the city of the dead she felt alive, she felt sexy and she felt her phone vibrate.

"Hello?" she purred into the receiver.

"What are you doing in the cemetery?" her husband's voice contained a hint of mirth.

Angie quickly looked around her. How the hell did he know where she was? "Edwin!" she exclaimed, drawing on the quickthinking skills for which she was renowned. "Er – I'm just leaving actually. We're doing a piece on funerary chic, black being the new black 'n all."

"Is that going to be your big project?"

"How did you know I was here?"

"You're Lady Peters my dear and I have a lot of staff. I can probably see you from my office."

Angie desperately hoped he couldn't.

"I still think you should find a top model, do a nationwide search, find a new face to rival Lily and Natalia."

Angie thought back to the previous night when they had dozed off in front of yet another tv reality show aimed at finding the next model/designer/catwalk star. That was something about Edwin that she rather liked. He was solid, yes, and dependable, definitely – but imaginative? It just wasn't in his brief. She quickly pooh-poohed the idea.

"How many shows are there at the moment with the exact same aim? Let's list them: 'Make Me a Supermodel', 'The UK's Next Supermodel', 'From Supermarket to Supermodel'……"

Edwin cleared his throat, "Just trying to help darling."

"….'Project Runway', 'Top Model 8' 'Model Behaviour', 'Britain's Next Top Model', 'Find Me the Next Doll'……."

"Join me for lunch then."

"It's Friday – I've never liked the way your chef does fish."

"We could go to E & O."

The thought of chilli salt squid and people watching was an appealing one but having spent a couple of hours out of the office Angie knew she had to get back.

"I just can't today Edwin – I'm running behind already. I'll see you at home. I should be back before nine."

Angie clicked off her ultra-slim phone, settled into the back of the cab and wondered how long her fling with Jake could last. She also wondered whether she would keep her title should divorce ever be mentioned – the title wasn't hereditary afterall – but, well, Heather had kept hers, hadn't she?

In some ways it had been the perfect affair. They had known nothing of each other at the beginning and now, six months later, apart from first names and numbers of mobile phones, they knew little more.

Of course they had discovered all the fleshy, deliciously sensitive nooks and crannies of each other's bodies, and had exchanged secrets normally kept hidden from the world, but apart from that, they knew next to nothing of each other's lives.

Perfect!

It really had been perfect.

However the time had come to end it. The affair had lost some of its flavour, some of its sparkle. The treehouse in autumn was not as alluring as it had been in spring and whilst the notches up had done wonders for her agility, not to mention her calf muscles, Angie knew it was time to quit.

Things had also started to get a bit too close to the real world recently. Favours had been asked which was always a sign that everyday life couldn't be far behind.

And whenever everyday life intruded on an affair the magic died.

But the last and most compelling reason for ending it was career instinct: what if the Press were to find out? What if they were to dig deeper, printing her true age and details of her Edgware childhood? All the lies she'd told, the facts she'd hidden to get where she was would become common news. Angie shuddered, realising unhappily that 'common' was the word they would pick up on.

The thought was too horrible to contemplate.

The tabloids would have a blast. She could imagine the headlines – 'Magazine Editor in Torrid Tombside Trysts'? or 'Toy-Boy Sex Secrets of Ghoulish Aristo'? or, her stomach quaked, 'Suburban Council Estate Past of new Lady Peters'?

What would her boss do then? Luca Mortimer wasn't known for his soft side. A speedy return to contributing editor status would be on the cards but it would be on one of his lesser titles. This time she'd be lucky if she made FOLK – the magazine of country dancing, 'Seamstress Monthly', or that editorial graveyard; 'Home Recipes and More!' Angie never knew what the 'More!' was – or why it needed such a prominent exclamation mark – but she had a feeling, if the story ever leaked, she would be sure to find out.

Jake had started to feel ill before Angie's message came

through. He always kept the mobile on silent/vibrate when he was at home. Something as insistent as a ringing telephone would distract even the most devout mourners from their duties.

As he pressed the speed-dial for Angie's number he felt his stomach seize up.

"It's me," Jake managed to croak, the bile burning his throat.

In her swish office overlooking Berkeley Square the editor of London's best-selling woman's magazine checked the screen on her mobile. It was Jake's number all right but it certainly didn't sound like him.

"Jake?"

"You phoned?" he managed to splutter.

"Yes – are you alright?" Angie used her conciliatory tone, her carefully prepared words all planned, but this croaky voice threw her slightly.

"Just a touch of – " Jake covered the mouthpiece to mask the sound of his dry retch, "'flu."

It didn't seem fair to break off the relationship if he was ill but fairness, Angie justified, was a luxury at her level.

"Whilst it's been fun – " with her voice as soothing as a funeral director's Lady Peters went into her speech.

Unfortunately as soon as she began Jake, gripped by another stomach spasm, covered the mouthpiece and held the phone away from him.

He managed to put it back to hear, "I really think it's best that we – " but his gut contracted robbing him of his breath.

Jake didn't have to listen to the words though, he could tell from her voice what Angie was saying.

At the other end of the phone all the editor could hear were what sounded like muffled chokings. Lady Peters was surprised. She didn't think he would take it this badly.

With his eyes streaming Jake put the phone back to his ear. "So we're breaking up?"

Angie had prepared for this moment. With her voice at honey pitch she breathed into the phone, "Yes but don't – "

She wasn't allowed to finish before Jake, feeling the approach of another spasm, choked out, "Fine," and clicked off his phone.

Angie was surprised, and not a little disappointed, to have the conversation end halfway through her farewell. It wasn't like Jake to suffer from pique.

The break-up hadn't been as fun as she had expected. There was no sense of victory, no hint of the pleasure she had been looking forward to, the pleasure of knowing you are going to hurt somebody but also of knowing there's not a damn thing you can do about it.

Putting down the phone Jake rushed to the plastic bucket that served as his bin and threw up. In the milky clear upchuck were pieces of his lunch: fish caught the previous night from the canal.

They buried the heron that evening.

It was a simple ceremony. Ollie dug a grave in the soft earth bordering the two-tiered pond in Meanwhile Gardens. Gem 'n Em, Nicky, Ollie and Rion placed lilies on the bird's body before Ollie gently lowered the heron to its final resting place.

He had found the dying bird at the start of his daily jog. Poisoned, the heron lay in the rushes below the towpath at the back of the job centre on Kensal Road. The bird's feathered necklace was bedraggled, its eyes were lifeless, its elegant wings, now crumpled around its slender frame, would no longer swoop down the canal.

Gem was inconsolable. This was her heron. This was her

direct link to Princess Di, or so she'd always thought. What would she do? What could she do?

Although vengeance wasn't in her nature, revenge was firmly on her mind.

17

A SMALL PARCEL

"Auntie Em he's on next!" Rion sat glued to the tv. The local news, following on from the national and international items, was about to begin.

Behind her, next to the fireplace, Hum lay sedated in his fluffy leopard-print bed. Given antibiotics and solace by Doctor Alexander in his surgery off Westbourne Park Road, Humdinger had now retired, his wounds well and truly licked, to sleep off the nightmare.

It had been decided the hound would recuperate at Auntie Em's. Ollie was still giving Wayne a hand at lA which, even with the windows open, was too full of dust and fumes for a recovering hound and Hum certainly couldn't stay alone at Ollie's.

It was best the dog stayed where Rion could watch over him. Having recently been nursed back to health herself Rion was anxious to pass on some tlc to someone else – whether that was animal or human was immaterial to her.

"Auntie Em!" Rion again called through to the hall where Emma stood at the window waiting for an important package.

Uncharacteristically nervy Auntie Em looked at her watch, sighed and came through to the sitting room.

"Have you set the machine?"

Rion nodded hesitantly, "I think so. I followed the instructions anyway."

The dvd player had been set for Auntie Gem to watch later. She had phoned mid-morning to confirm her boss' appearance on *Around You at Two*, the popular local news slot.

Auntie Em checked the machine and was satisfied to see it had started recording.

"Do you think Gem'll be on as well?" Rion asked.

Auntie Em smiled as the fanfare announced the start of the programme.

"I think she'll give it a damn good try don't you?"

They watched as the perky reporter introduced the featured stories. The lead item concerned the London restaurant awards being presented that night. The second was about the Halloween fireworks party on Primrose Hill over the weekend. Item three was the one they had been waiting for.

From the studio 'perky reporter' flashed a brilliant smile at the camera.

"Our third story comes live from West London with our reporter at large Alvin Baker – Alvin?"

A clean-cut young man in fashionably oversized glasses appeared on screen.

"He's in front of the factory!" Rion squealed.

The reporter stood beside the Peters & Peters factory logo. Next to him stood Gemma's boss.

"That's Edwin," said Auntie Em.

Around You at Two's science correspondent began his piece to camera.

"I'm here in West London with Sir Edwin Peters – "

"Sir!" Auntie Em laughed disdainfully.

" – Managing Director of the family firm at the heart of

the pollution controversy devastating this stretch of the Grand Union Canal."

Edwin nervously adjusted his tie at the mention of 'pollution', 'controversy', and 'devastating'.

"What do you say, Sir Edwin, to the allegations that it is your factory causing the death of all the wildlife on this stretch of canal? Herons are a protected species as I'm sure you're well aware."

Sir Edwin visibly bristled as Alvin Baker shoved a microphone in his face. "Firstly there is no truth to these allegations and anyone furthering them will be receiving attention from my legal advisers."

Sir Edwin thought it best to throw that one in straight away: broadcasters, especially the smaller, local ones, were averse to the threat of legal action and damages.

"I have it on very good authority from independent pollution monitors that the the destruction of the wildlife has nothing to – "

As Sir Edwin went into his spiel Auntie Em said, "He's already pulled his ear three times." In reply to Rion's questioning stare she explained, "It means he's lying."

From then on Rion was more interested in what Gemma's boss was doing with his hands than in what he was saying.

" – is due to the addition of chemicals into the canal environment by a certain railway company – "

"And stroked his hair," Auntie Em pointed out.

" – chemicals which of course we as an organic – "

"And again!" they both protested.

" – manufacturer couldn't use. A report from the independent monitors is available – "

Rion gestured at the tv, "Scratched his nose!"

" – and thank you for giving me the chance – "

At this the factory gates behind him opened.

" – to clear up any misunderstandings."

The camera followed Sir Edwin as he entered the compound. Helping the security guard close the gate was a figure they both recognised.

"It's Gem!" Auntie Em laughed.

Just before the gate closed on the cameraman Auntie Gem stuck her head out and smiled.

Auntie Em hugged Rion, "I knew she would!"

As the screen cut back to 'perky' in the studio Auntie Em switched off the dvd player. Behind them Hum whimpered in his sleep.

"Poor love," Auntie Em went over to stroke the hound. "He's probably re-living the whole ghastly experience."

"The vet said he'd sleep all afternoon. Will he be ok with you?"

Auntie Em nodded, "I'm going out later for tea though."

"I should be back by then," Rion bent to kiss Hum between the ears. "I said I'd go and see Jake that's all."

From the hall window Auntie Em saw her visitor with the all-important package coming down the mews. She followed Rion down the stairs.

"Send him my love, angel." Auntie Em had met Jake several times when Rion had been ill and thoroughly approved of the young man.

Opening the front door Rion found Nicky almost on the doorstep. In one hand the photographer carried a small parcel wrapped in plain brown paper.

Nicky smiled upon seeing Rion, "Have you seen Ollie today?"

"Just a wave every now and then."

"Is he there at the moment?"

Rion put her head to one side and listened. She could hear the radio coming from 1A but it wasn't too loud.

"And working by the sounds of it. They switch the radio up when they're – you know – " Rion felt herself blushing, " – at it."

"Ah," Nicky said slowly as if pennies were dropping left, right and centre. "I was going to ask them to turn it down this morning. It was blasting for ages."

"That was when Ollie came back from his jog."

"Well, our boy looks rather fetching in his shorts doesn't he?" Auntie Em said.

"Especially with sweat dripping down his body," Rion giggled.

"Let him have his fun while he can," Auntie Em took the package from Nicky. "I have a feeling it won't last too long."

Auntie Em waved Rion off down the little cobbled mews. Before the young girl had turned the corner Auntie Em had closed the front door.

"It's damn good I think," Nicky whispered then wondered why she was talking so softly.

Closely followed by Nicky, Auntie Em hurried up the stairs into her bedroom where she ripped open the package. The contents made her gasp admiringly.

"I'm not sure which I prefer," she turned the object around, looking at it from all angles.

In her hands she held an exact copy of the miniature Candida and Wayne were looking for. Auntie Em took the original from her bed and placed it next to the fake. "We even got the frame almost exactly right."

Nicky had cleverly constructed the fake by photographing the original on matt paper, dulling the colours and then carefully sticking it to a piece of canvas stretched across board. With the glass, frame and a touch of ageing here and there it looked remarkably similar.

"It won't fool Candida for a second."

"But the hired hand will go for it don't you think?"

"Without a doubt," Nicky said with certainty. "When do we do it?"

Auntie Em thought for a second.

"Let our boy have another night of fun."

"Tomorrow then?"

Auntie Em nodded slightly wearily. "He won't thank us for it."

"He won't tomorrow but maybe next week he will," Nicky put her arm around Auntie Em. "I hate to sound so parental here but – " the photographer cringed at the approaching cliché, " – it's for his own good."

Auntie Em smiled weakly, "Yes. Yes," she murmured as she closed the bedroom door leaving both Merlijnche de Poortjes side by side like disjointed twins.

Before going out Auntie Em looked at herself in the bedroom mirror. She was pleased with what she saw but something was missing – what else could she use that would increase her allure? After a few seconds thinking it came to her.

A scarf.

Rifling through the second shelf in her dressing room she tried on several before settling on a red, gossamer, silky scarf with a light yellow and blue pattern – a nice little Nina Ricci number acquired from Killer, the vintage clothes shop at the base of Trellick Tower.

Placing the scarf over her head, she knotted it under her chin and again checked the mirror. This time the image reflected was of an attractive but demure woman. Attractive but demure – just what she wanted to put over.

Leaving the mews she was stopped by a voice calling her.

"Auntie Em!"

She looked up to see Ollie standing at the sitting room window of lA.

"Where are you going looking so Grace Kelly?"

Ollie always knew the words to charm her.

"Never you mind, sweetness."

"Stay right there!" he ordered. Ollie's place at the window was taken by Wayne.

Before Candida's henchman could speak Emma addressed him. "Mr Watson," she said curtly, hoping to God he wasn't going to call her Auntie Em, "would you go and see Nicky this evening at six?"

The builder smiled down at her, "Sure Auntie Em."

Emma gritted her teeth. Before she could remind Wayne of the employer/ employee relationship Ollie had flung open the front door.

In some strange way it hurt her to see how well he looked, knowing his happiness was based on deception.

"Well?" Ollie enquired, arching his eyebrows in a playful fashion. "I've been hearing rumours….."

"So have we dear," Auntie Em hid her sadness well. "Something about the radio increasing in volume from time to time?"

Ollie burst out laughing, "That obvious huh?"

"Not to me it wasn't," Auntie Em said tactfully before mentioning, "Nicky's feeling abit left out sweetness."

Ollie avoided Auntie Em's gaze, "I know, I've been stupidly pre-occupied lately."

If you only knew Auntie Em thought.

"Anyway she says to remind you that Johnson's going to the studio tomorrow."

"I know."

"Did she tell you Vance cancelled?"

"No. Ouch – but she should be used to that."

"Go and see her tonight, she needs company."

Ollie's face lit up before falling. "I can't. Johnson gave me his tickets to *Love Never Dies* – I'm taking Wayne."

"Do you think that's his sort of thing angel?"

"Auntie Em. It's not like you to judge a book by its cover," Ollie said crossly. "Just because Wayne's from Dagenham and obviously works out doesn't mean he's thick or uncultured. He loves Dutch painting you know."

Auntie Em sighed, "So we've heard sweetness."

"Besides it's Lloyd Webber, not Pinter or anything difficult – he's hardly going to drift off during the pauses – and it's a musical. I think Wayne can handle a couple of songs for heaven's sake."

"Of course he can angel," Auntie Em gave him a peck on the cheek. "You go and enjoy yourself. Don't worry about Hum, he'll be fine with us."

Rion screamed when she saw Jake. She couldn't stop herself. Her friend was barely coherent, his lips had a scary bluish tinge and she was sure she could see specks of white at the corner of his mouth.

He was also incredibly pale.

"Jake!" she shook him by the shoulders but Jake had lost control of his muscles and flopped around like a rag doll.

It didn't take Florence Nightingale to realise he needed medical help.

Rion grabbed Jake's mobile phone and dialled 999. The emergency services answered promptly.

"Police, Fire or Ambulance?" the efficient voice at the other end enquired.

"Ambulance!" Rion choked.

"Where to Madam?"

Rion wailed, "The cemetery!"

The voice at the other end turned cold, "I suppose you'll be telling me next that it's for a dead friend?"

"I'm not sure, I think he might be – how did you know?" Rion gasped with relief.

There was an icy silence from the operator.

"We don't appreciate these hoax calls Madam. You're blocking the lines for people that might really need us."

"But I do!"

"I could report you for wasting our time and I will do if you call again," the emergency operator clicked off the phone. It was the fourth joke call since his shift had started.

"This is not a hoax!" Rion protested before realising she had been cut off.

Remembering what they did in films Rion lightly slapped Jake on the face but it seemed to do no good. She looked in his eyes and saw they were almost fully glazed over.

What else did they do?

Quelling her rising panic she remembered they always made people walk – but how would she do that?

"You've got to help me Jake," Rion put her arms around his waist and tried to help him up. "We're going to go and get help you and I," she spoke slowly and clearly.

Jake lolled his head in what Rion took for a nod. He tried to speak but all it did was increase the foam building at the corners of his mouth.

Jake appeared to switch on autopilot as they half-clung, slid and fell down the vast tree trunk. Rion was grateful it wasn't Senora Padilla's day for visiting her dead husband. Seeing a young girl and a ghostly white dribbling figure fall out of the tree above her would no doubt have speeded the Cuban widow's entrance into the spirit world.

With Jake lurching semi-conscious against her Rion struggled along the small path adjoining the canal. She looked around frantically for a cemetery guard but, in the manner of law enforcement officers everywhere, there wasn't one around when needed. After what seemed an age they were through the gates of the Dissenters Chapel and on the bridge at the top of Ladbroke Grove.

"Help me!" she pleaded with the first people she saw.

The couple glared at Jake and Rion before hurrying past.

The few other people coming their way crossed to the other side to avoid them. Rion tried to flag down a lone taxi that slowed down, then sped up, upon seeing the state they were in.

With Jake getting heavier and heavier against her, Rion decided the only thing to do was to head down the towpath for Meanwhile Gardens Mews.

But didn't Auntie Em say she had to be somewhere for tea? And what if – oh God, please no – what if the volume on the radio had been turned up?

Praying for someone to be there – and not having sex – Rion staggered down the canal. She was acutely aware that Jake's breath was getting slower and slower.

Auntie Em looked forward to these chaste romantic assignments. They made her feel so girlish, a quality she had never sought for herself, and normally abhorred in others, but at the moment it felt, well, it felt just delicious.

Slipping her hand into Doctor Gidwani's she felt a pleasant tingle as his thumb caressed hers.

"You know Kanwar," she said to the handsome Indian, "if we continued walking, and walking, and walking," Emma dreamily gestured up the canal, "perhaps for several days, we would end up somewhere in the middle of England."

Auntie Em felt her knees buckle slightly as the doctor turned to look at her with those deep brown eyes.

"It would be Heaven to spend several days alone with you, my love," Kanwar Gidwani smiled, "but if we finished up in Birmingham my cousins and aunts wouldn't give us a moment's peace."

Auntie Em was silent at the thought of a break spent alone with the strikingly handsome, gentle-mannered doctor.

"Perhaps we could?"

"Spend a few days in Birmingham?" the doctor flashed a smile of unrivalled brilliance at her.

Emma laughed gently, "Spend a few days alone."

Kanwar pulled her to him and nuzzled her face, "There would be nothing I would like more," he murmured, placing an elegant finger under her chin. Auntie Em was sure he was about to kiss her for the very first time when he froze.

"Kanwar?"

"Isn't that – "

Doctor Gidwani looked up the canal where it appeared a man had his arms around a young girl and was refusing to let go.

"Isn't that Rion?"

Even though the body of the man obscured the girl's face Emma knew immediately who it was.

"Yes. Yes. It is, and it looks like she needs help."

Auntie Em began hurrying up the canal towards the couple. "Get off her!" she shouted in her most authoritative of voices.

But the man didn't pay any attention.

"Auntie Em!" Rion shrieked. "It's Jake. I think he's dying!"

Doctor Gidwani was first on the scene, "Has he taken any drugs?"

"No!"

"Rion you can tell me."

"You won't get into trouble," Auntie Em said slightly out of breath.

Doctor Gidwani began muttering as he looked into Jake's drooping eyes, going through all the conditions that could bring the young man to such a state.

"Jake's not a druggie," Rion said almost crying. "He may smoke an awful lot of grass but – "

Auntie Em turned to Kanwar. "That couldn't do – " she gestured to Jake's crumpled body, " – this, could it?"

"No," Doctor Gidwani rummaged in his jacket pocket for his mobile phone, "not unless it was laced with paraquat." He pulled Jake roughly to his feet, "Keep him standing."

Jake had now lost all control of his muscles and was slipping in and out of consciousness. Whilst Auntie Em and Rion struggled to keep him upright the doctor barked instructions into his phone. As soon as he had finished he rushed to take Jake's weight from the woman and young girl. "Help me walk him to Ha'penny Steps, that's where they're meeting us." Although Kanwar's voice was calm Em could tell he was growing very concerned.

With Jake propped between Doctor Gidwani and Auntie Em, they made their way the short distance back to the old tollbridge.

"Will he be alright?" Rion asked, skittishly following the ungainly trio.

Doctor Gidwani looked at his watch. He was beginning to get more flustered. "I've informed St Mary's and if we can get him there in time he'll probably be ok."

"Probably?" Rion said, unable to envisage the 'probably not'. "Probably?" she choked again, horrified.

Kanwar looked at his watch again and strained to hear the ambulance but there were no sirens to be heard.

"There's no way it can be called the unlucky house now," Ollie surveyed the work they had done in lA.

Wayne called through from the bathroom, "Unlucky what?"

"It's Auntie Em's name for the house," Ollie explained walking over to the small room which, apart from having no door, was almost finished. "The reason why – " Ollie stopped himself as he entered and just looked. He never got tired of the sight of Wayne.

The builder, shirtless, flecked with paint, was busy adjusting the thermostat on the shower. "The reason why?" he looked up questioningly.

"It's – er – a long story and not important."

With a final twist of the screwdriver Wayne wiped his forehead and stepped out of the cubicle, "It should work now." He turned on the tap and leapt out of the way as a stream of water burst from the showerhead.

Ollie gingerly tested the water with his hand, "And it's warm!" He grinned at the builder, "Should we christen it?"

Wayne answered by simply slipping the belt from his work trousers and letting them fall to the floor.

They didn't bother turning up the radio.

Nicky hurried down the stairs hoping it would be Auntie Em. There was an element of the plan that concerned her.

"About time," she said as she opened the door but instead of Emma Nelson she found Wayne.

"Am I late?" the builder looked at his watch. "Auntie Em said to come over at six."

Auntie Em? It grated almost as much as him calling her Nicks.

"Sorry. Come in," she said, taking in how presentable he looked in one of Ollie's shirts over black jeans.

"Best leave it on the latch," Wayne said before she could shut the door. "Ollie'll be over in a minute."

Following him up the stairs Nicky caught a whiff of a familiar lemony smell. She was sure it was from the bottle of Issey Miyake she had given Ollie for his birthday.

"What needs doing then?"

In an effort to make sure Wayne stayed until everything was in place Auntie Em and Nicky had decided to tempt him with more work.

Nicky moved to the mantelpiece where Merlijnche de Poortje cast her sad gaze over the room.

"A complete overhaul really. Repainting for starters."

"Where?"

As Nicky gestured to the whole of the space she made sure to run her fingers along the gilt-framed miniature, but Wayne still hadn't noticed. "Everywhere."

"Woodwork too?"

Nicky nodded. "And varnishing the floors in the kitchen and bathroom."

"The works then?"

Unable to wait for him to spot Merlijnche de Poortje Nicky knocked the small painting from the mantelpiece.

"Whoops!" she said catching the miniature with great relief before it hit the floor, "Ollie would have killed me." With great exaggeration Nicky placed Merlijnche de Poortje back on the mantelpiece. "Apparently it's quite valuable."

Wayne turned to see Nicky pointing to the picture of the girl in the white fur stole.

"Didn't Ollie show this to you?" Nicky asked.

The builder's attention had most certainly been captured. He moved closer to the miniature and looked at it curiously.

"Funny. He said you were into Dutch painting."

"Some," the builder grunted.

"Do you like Vermeer?"

Wayne was still fixated by Merlijnche de Poortje. "Sorry Nicks, I've just had a shower," he shook his head as if to clear excess water from his ears. "Do what for you?"

That settles it Nicky thought.

"Nothing," she murmured.

At the rattle of the letterbox Nicky shouted down, "It's open."

The sound of the stairs being taken two by two preceded Ollie's arrival in their midst. He burst into the sitting room looking freshly washed and scrubbed.

"Are you ready?" he asked Wayne before going to greet Nicky with a kiss on the cheek.

She tilted her head to one side and looked at him admiringly. "Where are you off to looking so dapper?"

"To see *Love Never Dies*."

Nicky couldn't hide her disappointment.

"I thought we were going to go and see that Ol," she said crossly. "I could do with an up night in the West End, especially after the last few days."

Wayne snuck another quick look at the miniature. There was no doubt this was the one in the picture Candida had given him.

"I could make a start on those quotes if you really want to go Nicks."

I bet you could Nicky thought.

Wayne put his arm around Ollie's shoulders. "Nicks might want me to do some work for her."

"Tonight?" Ollie asked incredulously.

"No. No. You go to the theatre," she said quickly. Things weren't set up yet anyway. "Maybe tomorrow night – we'll all be at the fireworks on Primrose Hill."

"So will Wayne!" Ollie protested.

It would be better tomorrow night, Wayne thought, when no one was around. "Let's see how things turn out." He picked up the miniature and turned to Ollie, "You never told me about this."

"Ah Merlijnche," Ollie's face lit up upon seeing the miniature. "She looks good here doesn't she? I've borrowed her for a few days from Auntie Em."

Wayne turned to Ollie. "Has she been looking after it for you?"

"Yes, Auntie Em thinks someone is – "

"You'd better be going O1," Nicky hurriedly shooed them from the room, "you don't want to be late."

As Wayne went down the stairs Ollie hugged the photographer, "Sorry about tonight Nicks, I'll make it up to you I promise. And thanks," he gave her a resounding kiss on the cheek, "for keeping Wayne here."

"It's not sure yet," Nicky said cautiously.

"I know you're doing it for me."

Nicky guiltily returned his hug. "I hope you'll thank me for it later," she managed to mutter.

Ollie blew her a kiss and left.

Wayne was able to make the call during the interval of the hit show. An answerphone clicked on immediately but it was unmistakably Candida's voice on the message.

The builder kept it short. "I've eyeballed what you're looking for. It'll be in your hands before too long." Through the crush he could see Ollie approaching with the drinks, "Call me tomorrow."

Wayne clicked off the phone. He would miss Ollie but the bonus would make it worthwhile.

18

A HOMECOMING

Ollie and Rion sat on Auntie Em's sofa anxiously listening in to her phone conversation. They could hear a steady stream of soothing tones that obviously belonged to Doctor Gidwani, followed by a voiced breath signifying Auntie Em's digesting of the information. This carried on for several minutes before Auntie Em thanked Kanwar and put down the phone.

"Well?" Ollie and Rion asked in unison.

"Jake had a good night. He's stabilised although very weak. Apparently he has severe septicaemia."

"Which is?" Rion asked.

"Blood poisoning," Auntie Em replied. "The blood literally turns black."

Rion wrinkled her nose, "Ugh!"

"Poor Jake!" Ollie exclaimed. "What do they think caused it?"

"Well," Auntie Em sat down in the overstuffed armchair. "They've found incredibly high levels of delanquine in his body – apparently it's some chemical normally used in crop spraying and the like. They can't understand how he came to have such toxic levels in his blood."

"Did you say crop spraying?" Ollie asked.

Auntie Em nodded.

"Maybe," Ollie suggested, "maybe the cemetery guards found one of Jake's grass patches and sprayed it."

"Then he smoked it," Rion said.

Auntie Em was puzzled. "Wouldn't the plant show signs of chemicals? Withered leaves? Yellowing?"

"Not if it was harvested soon after it was sprayed," Ollie sat back. "That's the only explanation."

"But that must mean Jake would have had to have been practically following the guard round."

Ollie threw up his hands, "Stranger things have happened."

Auntie Em remained unconvinced, "Not that strange. Jake didn't strike me as being a simpleton."

"Anyway visiting hours are mornings eleven until one and evenings five 'til seven."

Rion turned to Ollie, "We could go before the fireworks!"

"Sure," Ollie said. While they were at St Mary's Wayne could do Nicky's quotes and meet them at Primrose Hill he thought.

"Don't forget we've got something to do before then," Auntie Em arched her eyebrows knowingly at Ollie.

"I won't," Ollie stood up and smiled back.

"Won't what?" Rion asked.

"Shhh! Your first job has arrived," Ollie pointed out the window to Johnson Ogle. The lifestyle enhancer was just getting out of his silver Mercedes 500 he'd parked outside Nicky's.

More worryingly he had just spotted Wayne.

"We'd better go," Ollie said knowing how similar Johnson's tastes were to his own.

Johnson slowly looked Wayne up and down. "Is this the reason you haven't been phoning?" he asked Ollie.

"Johnson, Wayne has things to do."

"And I bet he does them very well," Johnson said in that mid-Atlantic drawl that was part of his charm.

"This is Rion – Nicky's assistant – she'll take you in."

But Johnson couldn't take his eyes off Wayne.

Ollie put his arms around the decorator's shoulders and forcibly turned him in the other direction, "*Now* Johnson."

The tall man sighed, "And I was thinking he could do something for me."

"That was obvious my friend. Now go, Nicky's waiting."

This would be an easy session. She had snapped Johnson on two previous occasions and he had been a darling – charming, affable, full of stories and, most importantly, fast.

Nicky had borrowed some furniture from Ollie's workroom with the aim of getting him a credit which, since Ollie had taken Wayne for a night in the West End instead of her, she thought was being overly generous.

"No blusher! I don't need it."

She could hear Johnson behind the screen where Naoko, the Japanese make-up girl Nicky used for such occasions, was dusting him.

"Nao – give Johnson what he wants," she called through, "he has excellent skin."

"Thank you Nicky," Johnson came out with the make-up cover still round his shoulders. Rion hurriedly removed it as he walked round the studio.

"I thought we'd use some of Ollie's furniture in the pictures."

"Just as long as you remember who the star is Nicks."

"As if I could forget," Nicky smiled. "Why don't we try the bench first, Rion?"

With Rion's help Nicky moved the simple bench with the

lion's paw feet to the centre. "Are you coming to Primrose Hill with us tonight?"

As Johnson sat, lay, put one foot on the bench, Nicky began snapping away.

"I wasn't asked," he sniffed, "which is just as well as I'll be at Elton and David's for dinner. Their chef excels in – well in practically everything actually. She does the most gorgeous Thai thingies..."

Rion listened agog as the names she had only read about dropped thick and fast.

The young girl remained unaware of the frantic activity taking place outside where Auntie Em, assisted by Ollie and Wayne, readied lA for her occupation. A bed was moved in, cupboards wiped down, curtains put up, a fridge installed and filled, flowers put on the table – it seemed there was an endless list of things to be done in such a short time.

"How did you get Jim James to look so slim? You know what the real scandal was about that film?"

To the dismay of his many female fans, and to the delight of their boyfriends, the teen hearthrob had been caught on amateur video in a compromising, and frankly rather uncomfortable, position with another man in a Hyde Park shrubbery.

"Apart from the fact that he was cruising some serious monsters, which in itself was ridiculous," Johnson continued. "I mean he could have a platoon of marines washed, oiled and sent to his suite and no-one need know about it, no, the real scandal was how out of shape he was. Am I right? A millionaire pop star letting himself go like that? That was the disgusting part, that was the real scandal, no?"

Nicky called to the Japanese girl who stood beside Rion

in the corner, "Dust him ever so lightly Nao. You're starting to glisten around the forehead Johnson," she explained.

"Nicks, sweetheart, weren't you ever told that women glisten, men perspire and horses sweat? Of course when I'm around men sweat, women gossip and horses – well, they just stay in the stable don't they?"

Nicky adjusted the lights, "I want to do some profiles Johnson and then we're done."

"You know it's my left side I prefer?"

Nicky nodded.

"And then I'm finished?"

"Yup."

"It's just I'd like to ask Ollie's – " Johnson cleared his throat, " – builder – "

Nicky laughed, "Really Johnson, you make him sound like someone's 'financial adviser'."

Johnson tutted.

"Financial advisor is so a couple of years ago Nicks, now its 'personal trainer' to indicate you're shagging which, of course, has taken over from 'therapist', 'stylist'- "

"'Counsellor' – "

"And soon it's going to be 'casting agent'."

"Really?"

"Count on it Nicks, haven't you noticed how many of them there are around?"

Nicky chuckled. "Seriously though, would you take Ollie out on Sunday?"

"Could do I suppose – any particular reason?"

"I just think he'll need some support."

"Looks like he's got some firm support if you ask me," Johnson drawled as he posed for the last shot. "Who's your silent assistant by the way?"

"Rion. Isn't she excellent? I'd be lost without her."

In the corner Rion tried not to look too thrown. Be cool she told herself. Perhaps no-one else had noticed but she hadn't done a damn thing – how could she be excellent?

"She looks so like Jerry's eldest daughter – you know the one modelling for Vivienne?" Johnson smiled at Nicky. "You'll lose her if you're not careful."

"I've lost her already Johnson – she wants to get a job at Glamourista."

"What ever for? It's a terrible office, a real piranha-fest."

"That's what I told her. I asked Angie if there was anything going but she said there wasn't."

"She just didn't want to owe you a favour Nicky, but she owes me one already." Johnson turned his gaze to Rion, "Would you like me to ask her for you?"

Rion had lost her powers of speech. Great, she thought, all I have to do is say yes and I can't even do that. Feeling her chest freeze she just nodded furiously.

"That's settled then. I'll let Nicky know."

"Th – th – thanks!" Rion managed.

As Nicky walked Johnson out of the studio she said, "Don't forget to ask Ollie about Sunday – he's setting himself up for a fall."

Or we are, she thought unhappily.

Nicky opened the front door to find Auntie Em, a variegated ficus in her arms, hurrying across the mews. She anxiously peered over Nicky's shoulder.

"Don't let Rion out yet," she said in a loud whisper. "We're not quite ready and Auntie Gem's not back. I'll let you know!"

Auntie Em continued on her way. She squeezed past Ollie who was sweeping the hall of 1A and vanished up the stairs.

Johnson turned to Nicky, "I love this place – it's always so full of intrigue."

She ignored the impulse to tell him just how much. Johnson and secrets just didn't go together.

"Yes," Nicky sighed, "isn't it?" She kissed him on the cheek, "I'll call when the pictures are done." Nicky returned to her studio before Rion could see what was going outside.

As Johnson went to greet Ollie a mobile phone rang close by. Johnson checked his but the ringing came from inside lA. Ollie traced it to Wayne's jacket hanging from a nail in the hall. "Wayne?" he called up but there was no reply.

"Better get that O1," Johnson advised.

"Wayne Watson's mobile," Ollie answered cheerfully. "Hello?" he said again but the other person clicked off without speaking. Ollie looked at the number fading from the mobile's screen – he was sure he recognised it, but couldn't quite pin from where.

"I'm taking you to lunch on Sunday Ollie. No arguments. Perhaps your handsome friend might care to join us?"

"Wayne's being a bit weird about Sunday – you'll have to settle for me."

Johnson got into the silver coupe. He wagged his finger at Ollie, "Sunday lunch!" Reversing out of the mews Johnson waved once and was gone.

"Was he really going to have supper with Elton John?" Rion asked.

"If he said so."

"And when he said David Bowie – is he the one married to Naomi Campbell's mum?"

"I think you mean Iman?"

Rion nodded.

"She's like the original Naomi Campbell."

"He said you looked like Jerry Hall's daughter!" Nao was impressed.

This was all too much for Rion to take in.

"When Johnson said Vivienne," she asked hesitantly, slightly worried about all these first names, "did he mean Vivienne Westwood?"

"That would be the only Vivienne he knows."

Rion couldn't stop herself blushing.

"Now why don't we make use of Nao while she's here and finish off this film?" Nicky switched the lights back on and led Rion to the centre of the studio. Putting the light meter against her she fiddled with the lens.

"On me?" Rion couldn't believe what was happening.

"Nao," Nicky called to the make-up artist. "Let's do some little girl looks like you did for Linda at the Cerruti shows, and then maybe something wilder, something glossy pink, something more Chloé, more Berardi. Ok?"

Nao knew exactly what the photographer wanted. This was more fun than doing Johnson Ogle. She got out her brushes and went to work.

The telltale knock summoned Nicky to the door.

"We're ready!" came the whispered message.

Returning to the studio Nicky was struck by how beautiful Rion was. What Johnson had pointed out now seemed glaringly obvious. With her long hair pulled away from her face the young girl had the pale pinched cheeks so loved by the camera, not to mention the tall, youthful frame favoured by designers and editors everywhere.

Nicky simply stood and stared.

"What are you looking at?" Rion asked shyly.

Nicky snapped out of it, "You're stunning Rion. You really are."

"No I'm not," the young girl looked at the floor but

couldn't hide her happiness for long. "That was such fun!" Rion span around, her long blonde hair shimmering under the lights.

The telltale knock again was heard but this time it sounded more urgent.

Nicky smiled and took Rion by the hand, "The best is yet to come." She took a scarf from the coatrack and blindfolded the young girl with it.

Rion giggled, "What are you doing?"

"You haven't seen 9 1/2 Weeks have you?"

"How long?"

Earlier in the year Ollie and Nicky had rented the celebrated eighties movie, becoming slightly obsessed with scarves in the process.

"No worries," Nicky replied.

Rion knew she was on the mews by the cool air on her face. She also knew Auntie Em was nearby from the sound of her whisper.

"Mind the step," a familiar voice advised.

So Ollie was there too! But she thought they had gone further on from his house.

Hands guided Rion up the stairs, which smelt very strongly of fresh paint. Now she knew where she was.

But what was she doing here?

"Ok," Auntie Em said. "You can open your eyes."

Blinking slightly Rion opened her eyes to find herself in the sitting room of lA. A banner had been hung over the fireplace. Its message was short and succinct, spelt out in brightly coloured letters,

WELCOME HOME RION!

Before she could take it all in, Nicky and Auntie Gem

threw streamers at her while Ollie opened a bottle of champagne with a loud POP.

"It's yours for the time being," Auntie Em offered Rion a key on a small red velvet cushion. "Or until you find something better."

When the enormity of what they had done hit her, Rion collapsed onto the sofa. Her eyes welled up. What started as a trickle quickly turned into a torrent until soon she was bawling her eyes out. Perhaps she had a real family at last.

Wayne looked on from the corner, embarrassed at witnessing the genuine emotion before him. His phone came to his rescue. Hearing it ring Wayne went down the stairs for some quiet.

It wouldn't really matter how loud the surrounding noise was, this voice would always come through loud and clear.

"Wayne, it's Candida."

With the real Merlijnche de Poortje hidden under her coat Nicky hurried past Ollie, Wayne and Rion towards the house at the end.

"It's on top of the dresser in my bedroom," Auntie Em whispered as the photographer went past her and ran up the stairs.

"Come on Nicks!"

Nicky could hear Ollie and Rion calling impatiently from the mews. She ran into Auntie Em's room. By the light of the lava lamp she could see Merlijnche de Poortje's white stole gleaming atop the dresser. She made her way towards it in the eery glow and put the miniature down ready to swap it with the fake one.

"Nicky?"

The photographer jumped as the hall light went on behind her.

"There's a light by the bed."

"Auntie Gem!" Nicky grabbed the miniature in the darkness and put it under her coat, replacing it with the one she bought. "Gotta rush!" she kissed Gemma on the cheek and hurried out.

Again she ran past Wayne, Ollie and Rion who stood talking to Auntie Em.

"I think I left the stove on!" she gasped as she rushed into her house.

"Get it together Nicks," she heard Ollie call from outside. "We're late as it is."

Now completely out of breath Nicky placed the miniature on the mantelpiece. The fake felt almost exactly the same as the original she thought. Almost exactly the same! Smiling at a job well done she went to join her friends in the mews.

"Phew!" Nicky put her arm around Ollie, "Let's get out of here."

"When did you say you were going out?" Wayne asked Auntie Em who stood watching Ollie, Rion and Nicky walk laughing out of the mews.

"Gemma and I are going out at about nine fifteen."

"Could you let me into Nicky's before you go? I'll finish up at 1A and then do the quotes before going to meet the others."

Auntie Em put her head to one side and looked at the builder grinning in front of her. 'Ah, smile SMILE and still be a villain,' she thought to herself.

"Of course Mr Watson," Auntie Em turned on her heels and was soon in her house.

Wayne walked up the mews. There was only a small bit of bathroom ceiling that still needed plastering. He didn't have to finish it he realised. He could just wait until nine fifteen, get the painting and be out of there.

But something was stopping him.

He combed through various emotions, hoping against all hope that he wasn't experiencing decency or some other softness. Feeling any sort of feelings was severely amateurish. With relief he worked out that what was stopping him was professionalism. He had been paid to do a job and so couldn't leave before it was completed. The fact that he was going to rip them off afterwards was different – that was another matter and should be treated as such.

His conscience appeased he entered lA.

At the other end of the mews Auntie Gem had a surprise for Emma. "You'll find this interesting," she said as she put a large manilla envelope on the sitting room table.

Auntie Em opened it to find it contained a folder marked: *In Strictest Confidence.*

"This isn't the original is it?" she asked.

"Of course not."

Emma settled on the sofa and began to read the report prepared by Mr Paul, the assistant manager at Peters & Peters. It was the inside account on the poisoning of the canal.

"Do you feel strange Ol?"

They were on the towpath heading for Little Venice when Nicky asked the question. Rion skipped ahead of them, excited to be out for the evening.

"Isn't that what we smoke this for?" Ollie took a last hit of the joint before throwing it in the canal.

"No, it's not that, I mean," Nicky struggled to find the words but failed. Was she just feeling guilty about having set up Wayne she wondered? Well, forget that, he was the one deceiving them wasn't he? "Nothing, it's nothing," she murmured, but the nagging feeling wouldn't leave her.

Ollie put his arm around his friend, "You're still upset about the Kakapo aren't you?"

"Maybe," Nicky hugged him.

Ollie had gone to see Nicky a couple of nights before to find her in floods of tears in front of a nature programme. Between sobs she explained about the Kakapo, a rare flightless bird found only in New Zealand that at one time was down to its last known member. For fourteen years local ornithologists heard its lone mating call as the bird made its arduous daily trek up to the top of the mountain. For fourteen years its call went unanswered.

And then nothing.

The Kakapo had never found its mate. It had died the last of the species, unhappy and alone.

"But the story wasn't all bad was it? They discovered another community of Kakapo on an outlying island didn't they?"

Nicky smiled weakly, "I guess."

"Maybe it's just Halloween sweetheart. The change of the seasons?"

"The full moon?" added Rion.

"The night when spirits walk the earth? Or – " Ollie lit his lighter and placed it under his chin, the flame giving his face a ghoulish glow, "the fact that the weed is called 'Mausoleum Madness'?"

"All of the above I think," Nicky decided to shrug off the creepy feeling. "Is there another spliff?"

"We have Jake to thank for this," Ollie pulled out another matchstick-sized joint from his tin. "So make sure you do when you see him."

"They're still here!" Rion gestured to the brightly coloured barges anchored to the towpath. "I walked past these on my first day and for some reason they soothed me - well, all except one of them."

Ollie read the name of the first boat, "Morrisco?"

"No! That sounds like a ballroom dance don't you think?"

"The Tango, the Merengue, the Morrisco," Ollie rolled the word around his mouth, "could be." He pointed to two colourful prancing figures painted on the side of the barge, "Must be something like that."

Nicky could see the name of the middle barge, "Longfelloe?"

"Named after a literary buff who couldn't spell?" Ollie wondered.

Rion didn't get it, "Refers to the size of the boat doesn't it?"

"Or the size of his – "

Nicky cut him off, "Enough Ol!"

"So it must be," Ollie walked up to the final boat, "Home Sweet Home?" He returned to the Longfelloe where Nicky was struggling to light the joint.

Rion nodded.

"I couldn't imagine such a place then, but now," she linked arms with Ollie and Nicky, "thanks to you, I have one of my own."

Ollie couldn't handle the mawkish silence.

He looked at his watch, "You know if we have to be at St Mary's by seven we'd better hurry."

Nicky choked on the hot, dry smoke burning her throat.

"Wait a sec," she wheezed, passing the small spliff to Ollie.

"When are we meeting Wayne?" Rion asked.

"Ten thirty at the look-out on the brow of Primrose Hill."

"We can also meet there if one of us gets lost." Nicky was fairly sure Wayne wasn't going to turn up but hadn't the heart to tell Ollie. That had to be what was making her feel uneasy – all the deception, the trickery. "Do you have your phone?" she asked Rion.

"It hadn't charged yet, but that's ok, I'm with you two. C'mon!" Rion pulled at their arms.

Nicky threw the roach to the ground and stubbed it out with her heel, "Let's go!" She hoped her enthusiasm didn't sound too feigned.

In the darkness of one of the barges someone had listened to their entire conversation. The eavesdropper made a mental note: "Ten thirty, look-out, brow of Primrose Hill."

19

FIREWORKS

The wine from dinner, and countless mini-spliffs, had helped no end but by nine o'clock Nicky still hadn't managed to shrug off the feeling of unease, in fact it threatened to derail her whole enjoyment of the evening.

From Primrose Hill they looked over the glittering cityscape that was central London.

"Do you see there?" Nicky pointed to a mass below them, beyond the fairground in the darkness.

Rion looked hard but couldn't see much of interest.

"It's London Zoo."

"Where the pandas are?" the young girl asked.

Ollie nodded, "You know, that would be one of the main reasons to live in Primrose Hill."

"For the pandas?"

"Not especially, but for the zoo. Imagine," he took a deep breath through his nose as if smelling the open plains of the Serengeti, "you would wake up in the half-sleep of morning, listening to the lions roar, the monkeys screech and believe you were on safari somewhere in Africa."

"Just waiting for some deranged gamekeeper to mug you, rape you then steal all your camera equipment?" Nicky shook her head, "No thanks."

"You know you can walk from Meanwhile Gardens all the way to the zoo along the canal?"

"Really?"

"Yup, you just turn left at Little Venice instead of going straight on as we did to get to St Mary's. There are a couple of parts where you have to cross over a road but it's pretty straightforward."

"Can we do it sometime?" Rion asked excitedly, seeing another London adventure unfold before her eyes.

"Of course."

"Speaking of St Mary's, are you going to see Jake on Sunday?" Nicky asked Rion.

They had only managed to see Jake for the last ten minutes of visiting time but that had been long enough. He had been very weak but grateful for their company.

"I can't make it tomorrow but – " Nicky continued.

"I didn't realise he was a particular friend of *yours,*" Ollie said pointedly to Nicky while nudging Rion in the ribs.

"He's not!" Nicky protested, "but the poor guy's in hospital and besides, there's something about a helpless man in bed – "

Ollie sighed, "Isn't there just?"

" – that brings out an incredibly maternal instinct. Didn't you get that Rion?"

Rion grinned, "I think I'm a bit young for the maternal instinct Nicks."

"It's like some hidden Florence Nightingale gene hidden in every woman."

"And some men too sweetheart," Ollie chipped in.

Nicky sighed, confused at this sudden appearance of feminine instinct within her. "Weird," she muttered. "Just weird." She turned to see Rion entranced by the lights of London. The young girl's face in the half-shadow of night made her think suddenly of Merlijnche de Poortje.

It was then Nicky had the most ghastly feeling. She couldn't have been so stupid, she thought, could she? Could she?

"Oh my God!" Nicky glanced at her watch. It was nearly nine fifteen. Hopefully Wayne would still be there.

"Nicks?" Ollie looked over, concerned.

The photographer gazed around her in a panic, "I have to go." Nicky felt physically ill. "I'll be back for the fireworks at ten thirty or I'll get you on the mobile," she hurriedly kissed Ollie and Rion on the cheek before racing down the hill towards Regents Park Road and the passing taxis. "I'll explain later!" she yelled.

"Is she ok?"

Ollie shrugged his shoulders, "I've been asking that question for longer than I care to remember."

Auntie Em looked on in satisfaction as Wayne's pickup rattled down the mews for what, she hoped, was the last time. She had known he would try to get into Nicky's at the earliest opportunity.

She hadn't been wrong.

The builder had called her at half past eight to inspect the bathroom ceiling at lA. His workmanship was good, there was no doubting that side of things. From there she had let him into Nicky's house.

"He won't be back will he?" Auntie Gem asked.

Smiling she sat beside Gem at the table, "No," Emma said honestly. "I don't believe he will."

She tapped the folder Auntie Gem had handed her earlier that evening. What with all the Halloween trick'n treaters – another regrettable American habit that had been steadily gaining in popularity – disturbing their peace along with other goings on in the mews, it had taken Auntie Em quite a while to get through the report.

"What are we going to do about it?"

Auntie Gem put on her coat before helping Emma into hers. She gave a sly chuckle, "I'll tell you over supper."

In the taxi speeding towards Meanwhile Gardens Mews Nicky was frantically trying to contact Auntie Em and Auntie Gem, but the phone just rang and rang.

She continually pressed the re-dial button on the small handset before putting her hands together and beginning to pray, "Dear God, please let Wayne still be there. Please let Wayne still be there," she repeated over and over in a desperate mantra.

The taxi-driver looked into his rearview mirror before stepping on the accelerator. He hated Halloween, all the weirdos were out and proud but it was always the ones who weren't in costume that you had to watch for.

They made the journey in record time. Arriving outside the small entrance to the mews the driver stopped.

"No, inside!"

The driver turned back to face her, "Miss, I won't be able to turn round."

"Just do it!" Nicky ordered.

Before the cab had pulled up outside her house Nicky had jumped out. She threw a twenty pound note at the driver.

"Keep the change!"

Fumbling for the keys she managed to open her door, run up the stairs and was confronted by the sight she had been dreading.

The mantelpiece was empty. There was no sign of the valuable miniature. Wayne, and so Candida, had kidnapped Merlijnche de Poortje.

There would be no ransom demand.

❧

Ollie and Rion had just finished their second go on the dodgems when the call came through. Shouting to make himself heard above the sound of the fairground Ollie answered the phone. "Hello!" he laughed into the mouthpiece.

He could hardly hear the voice at the other end.

"Ollie it's Wayne."

"One second mate," Ollie quickly moved away from the madness of the bumper cars to a quieter spot near the shooting gallery. "Have you finished at Nicky's?"

"Yes."

Ollie thought Wayne's voice sounded somehow different, even that single word sounded cold. "Are you ok?"

The builder thought it best to get straight to the point, "I won't be coming tonight. In fact my plans have changed completely."

"There's not much happening here anyway. I'll stay for the fireworks and then come back."

"I'm not going to be here mate."

"Well, I'll see you tomorrow then."

Wayne stopped for a second. How could he make himself clearer?

"I'm not going to be here tomorrow *either,*" he said firmly.

"Well – " Ollie began, slightly thrown at the way the conversation was going.

"It's best we don't see each other again. Something's come up."

"Like what?" Ollie asked starting to get rattled. "What are you saying?"

"I'm saying we're over. It's me not you. I can't explain."

"Can't or won't?" he asked angrily but Wayne had

already clicked off the phone. Ollie looked up to find a large cuddly toy grinning down at him from the shooting range. It was some grotesquely sweet bear of an indescribable green. "What are you looking at?" he kicked the side of the range making the stall shudder.

A potentially violent voice from the other side made him think twice about hitting any more fairground property.

"Ollie?" Rion ran up.

He put his arm around the young girl, "I hate it when they say – 'It's me not you.' It's so damn condescending isn't it?"

"Who was that Ollie?"

"I mean – does he think I can't take it if he says, 'I don't fancy you anymore?' or, 'You never put the cds away, it drives me crazy,' or even, 'Your dog makes me sneeze'?" Ollie punched the air. "You can use that excuse with people who have pets can't you? 'Oh my allergies have flared up, I can't live with you any longer' – why couldn't he have used that one?"

"Ollie?" Rion asked concerned.

"He dumped me Rion. I've been dumped."

"Wayne?"

Ollie nodded, "I'm the dumpee, I'm Stig of the Dump, I'm Dumper Dumps of Dumpsville. I'm – " running out of things to say Ollie simply shrugged his shoulders, " – going to get drunk." He shoved his hands in his pockets, "I'll be rotten company, I always am when I'm pissed, so you wait for Nicky," Ollie glanced at his watch, "she won't be long."

Rion looked at the crowd gathering on Primrose Hill above them, "You're not going to stay for the fireworks?"

Ollie shook his head, "We'll come back on Bonfire Night – it's bigger and better and only next week."

"You'll be ok?"

"I'll tell you tomorrow. You have money?"

Rion nodded, patting her wallet in her front pocket, "Auntie Em gave me a twenty."

Ollie hugged the young girl to him, "Wait at the look-out for Nicks. She'll be here soon."

Wayne parked the pick-up outside Candida's flat in Holland Park. He was glad the job was over. All that remained was getting his bonus and getting out of there.

He could see Candida at the second floor window but didn't get out of the van. Instead he pulled his battered workbag to him and pulled out the gilt-framed miniature – Merlijnche de Poortje gazed back at him from the shadows.

It had crossed his mind on more than one occasion that he could simply try and flog it for a better deal. But that went against his principles. He also hadn't a clue who to approach about a painting. Whoever he went to would rip him off, that was clear. He might as well stick with Candida.

Had it all been worth it?

He had done two jobs, been paid for one and would soon be paid for the second alongwith a handsome bonus for successful recovery of the item. He'd also had a lot of great sex – that couldn't be discounted – but had it been worth it? Wayne wasn't sure. He smiled. He could think about it next week when he was in Florida couldn't he?

With the painting in his hand he walked quickly up the glasscovered walkway to the front door. Candida's voice came through the intercom before he could press the buzzer.

"You're late."

The door clicked open. Deciding not to take the small, woodpanelled lift he ran up the stairs to the second floor. The door to the flat was open.

"Where is it? Where is it?"

His employer was standing in front of three elaborate

mirrors in the hall of the elegant apartment. She wore a floorlength peach silk nightgown with tiny straps over the shoulders, a string of pearls and heels. Normally this would have got a rise out of Wayne but on this occasion he just wanted to exit fast.

Wayne gave her a flash of the painting, "Where's the money?"

Candida sighed. She went over to the antique French commode with its spindly legs, picked up a bulging envelope and waved it at Wayne.

"This is a bit ridiculous isn't it?" Candida kicked the envelope along the parquet floor where it span into Wayne's feet.

"You're the one into cop shows."

Wayne picked up the envelope and flipped through the wad of deliciously crisp fifty-pound notes.

"Is it all there?"

That was something I won't miss, he thought, the haughty sarcasm.

"Good enough," he grunted.

He put the painting face down on the dresser and left.

Wayne had hardly got to the first floor when he heard a scream. As he hurried out the front door to the van he heard sash windows crash open on the second floor above him.

"You bastard!"

Wayne looked up to find Candida smashing the small miniature on the windowsill. She threw down the gilded frame, shrieking in rage as it splintered on the concrete beside the pick-up, missing Wayne by inches.

"What the hell are you doing?" he shouted up, but all he could see was Candida ripping the painting from the board. She looked at the canvas for a moment then shrieked even louder.

The backboard came next. It bounced harmlessly off the windscreen before landing on the ground. Finally Candida scrunched the canvas into a ball and threw it down. She slammed the window and vanished from sight.

Deciding it best to make a quick getaway Wayne picked up the oddly crinkly ball of canvas and hopped into the van. It was only when he was safely through Notting Hill Gate that he pulled over.

Wayne smoothed out the ball, immediately feeling that it wasn't canvas but some sort of thick paper, "What the hell – " Now that he held it in his hands, without the disguise of the glass and frame, it was obvious that it was a photographic image cleverly touched up.

He turned the paper over to find a message written on the back.

"With love from all at Meanwhile Gardens Mews"

They'd known all along! Wayne laughed. He'd been done and it had never felt better.

He was still laughing as he drove east through the city, heading for Dagenham and home.

The fireworks started fifteen minutes late but were worth the wait. As Halloween had long ago been hijacked by the Americans it was only fitting that the sizeable expat community sponsored the display.

Rion looked on entranced as blue, red and dazzling white flashpoint streamers flared into the sky. These were followed by all manner of giant Catherine Wheels spinning for all their brief lives were worth, magic lanterns that loomed out of the darkness, enormous rockets that seemed to touch the moon before exploding in a riot of deafening bangs and glittering stars, fireballs of myriad colours flashing over Regents Park, Jack-o'-Lanterns, Fireflies and Will-o'-the-Wisps blazed, gleamed and glittered in the moonlit night. It was magic made all the more so by the domed silhouette of St Paul's Cathedral in the distance.

The blackout, when it finally came, was preceded by a dazzling display of pyrotechnics. Six flares sped towards the stars. At their zenith a distant muffle was heard heralding their separation into white blooms that slowly unfurled as they fell through the blackness.

Another puff and the small white blooms blossomed into larger blue petals and fell further. A louder pop right above their heads and the large blue petals burst into scarlet and became even bigger. In their final incarnation they loomed over the open-mouthed crowd like the tendrils of some gleaming, astral plant that had somehow lowered the ceiling of the sky, appearing so close you felt you could touch it.

A smattering of applause greeted this final display.

Rion looked at her watch. It was after eleven. She looked around anxiously for Nicky but there was no sign of the photographer. On the other side of the lookout she noticed a man looking at her.

"The animals must be driven crazy by it all," he said gesturing to the dark mass of London Zoo below them.

Rion looked round to see who he was addressing but it was apparent he was talking to her.

"I have two cats and they hate any sort of fireworks, imagine how a lion or tiger might react."

Rion hadn't noticed the man during the display but that wasn't surprising, she figured, as she had been staring skywards the entire time. The man wore a Trilby hat which, on anyone else, might have looked trendy but atop his fleshy face it looked rather comforting, rather old-fashioned. What slightly disturbed Rion was how he looked at her.

"Sorry for staring," he said, "but do you live near Golborne Road? It's just I think I've seen you near there." The man didn't want to alarm her by mentioning exactly where he'd seen her.

"Yes," Rion felt relieved. He had seen her around that's all, she thought, he had recognised her. Why, she was almost a Londoner now wasn't she? "Yes, I do actually."

The man's eyes twinkled, "I thought so!"

"Is this the only lookout on Primrose Hill?" Rion asked.

"If not someone is waiting for me somewhere else – anyway they've probably gone by now." The man's face looked sad all of a sudden. "Have you been stood up too?"

"I guess so. Sort of anyway. Funny coincidence how we're both from the same area and we've both been stood up at the same place," Rion couldn't help herself smiling but the girl was too young to realise there was no such thing as coincidence.

The man's face broke into a grin, "Isn't it?"

"Well," Rion said. "I'd better be going."

The man saw his chance slipping away. "Would you like to share a taxi back?" he asked hurriedly.

Rion hesitated.

"It would be cheaper."

Would Auntie Em allow it Rion wondered?

"I mean if you wouldn't mind?"

Rion was in a dilemma. She needed to get home. It was obvious Nicky wasn't going to turn up.

"You could see Salt and Pepper," the man gave a bashful smile that made Rion warm to him, "they're the cats," he explained. "And then go on."

Why not Rion thought? He was polite. He seemed ok, besides he liked animals didn't he? He probably wouldn't hurt a fly. "Ok. That would be nice," she said overcoming her initial hesitation.

They walked down the slope to Prince Albert Road that separated Primrose Hill from Regent's Park. With the firework display well and truly over the street was busy with countless people trying to get cabs. At the first glimpse of a yellow light scores ran for the vacant taxi.

As yet more people scrambled for the few available taxis Rion noticed several badly dressed men waving others over to their parked cars. The cars seemed to be old, mainly in a milky, off-brown colour and to have more than their fair share of dents.

"We could get a mini-cab," she suggested.

The man followed Rion's gaze, "You don't want to get in one of them," he said. "Can't be trusted. You never know where you might end up. They're just as likely to drug you as drive you anywhere."

Well, at least he had her safety at heart Rion thought. She walked over to the side of the road. Below her she could see the moon reflected in the dark waters of the Grand Union Canal. Several couples strolled along the towpath beside it. Remembering Ollie's earlier words she turned to her companion, "We could take the canal couldn't we?"

The man couldn't believe his luck. The young girl was now suggesting a walk that would take them right past his front door.

"I wouldn't do it myself of course, especially not at night, but I'll be alright if I'm with you won't I?"

"Of course you will," he reassured her. "It should only take about forty minutes."

"Probably faster than if we had to wait for a taxi isn't it?"

The man looked at the crowds still waiting for taxis, "Probably. We'll also go right past my front door. I live on a barge on the canal you see."

"I've always wanted to live on a boat," said Rion dreamily.

"Really?" This was getting better and better the man thought. "I'm moored opposite Jason's Restaurant in – "

"Little Venice!" Rion said excitedly. "What's your boat called?"

"Longfelloe."

Rion clapped her hands. She knew she was ok now. "I know exactly where it is! We walked past there this evening!"

The man didn't want to tell her he knew.

They went down the stairs to the towpath. Before they had gone a few steps Rion stopped. She offered the man her hand, "My name's Rion by the way."

"I'm Nigel," he shook her hand formally.

They walked on beside the silent waters of the canal. As they vanished into the darkness of the first tunnel the man said, "But my friends call me Gorby."

20

HUNGRY HEARTS

Nicky charged out of her house as soon as she saw Gem 'n Em come down the mews. "You didn't take your phone did you?" she said accusingly. "I've called everywhere trying to find you – Maramia Café, La Galicia, Thai Rice, even E&O – "

"That's abit above our price range angel," Auntie Em smiled.

"Where've you been?"

"At the Ripe Tomato, child," Gem replied.

"In All Saints Road?" Nicky smacked her palm to her forehead. She should have known the small family run restaurant would have been where they were. "The most terrible thing has happened," she wailed as she followed Gem 'n Em up the stairs into their sitting room. "He's got it, he's got it," Nicky couldn't stop babbling. "After everything he's got it!"

Whilst Auntie Em opened a bottle of wine Auntie Gem sat Nicky down in one of the overstuffed armchairs on each side of the fireplace. "I mean she's got it, she's got it!" Feeling overwhelmed by pronouns Nicky simply wailed, "Oh, *they've* got it!"

Auntie Em poured a glass of wine and gave it to Nicky. The photographer gulped it down in one before handing it back for a refill. Auntie Em obliged then went into her bedroom returning seconds later to the main room.

"I'm so stupid! How could I – ? Oh he'll kill me!"

"What are you talking about dear?"

Nicky looked up at Gem 'n Em through tearfilled eyes. "The painting!" she sobbed. "Wayne's got it!"

"Well he would have done if I hadn't gone into my room to check," Auntie Em pulled the miniature from behind her back and handed it to the distraught photographer. "Not that I didn't trust you angel," she said hurriedly.

Nicky looked at the original painting of Merlijnche de Poortje in her white stole. "Is this – " she blinked back the tears. She didn't have to finish the sentence for she could see it was the original. "Oh Auntie Em, imagine!" Nicky curled up in horror. "It would have been awful. I've been burning in Hell ever since I realised my mistake!"

"In these situations it's best to check and doublecheck. Isn't that right Auntie Gem?"

"That's what I taught you child," Gemma looked up for a second before turning her attention back to the report that so interested her.

Without being asked Auntie Em refilled Nicky's glass. The photographer gulped it down as she had the previous two, still finding it hard to believe the crisis was over.
"Aren't you heading back to Primrose Hill?"

The photographer shook her head, "I'm going to get pissed Auntie Em. I think I've earned that – and – " she clinked glasses with Emma, " – so have you!"

Auntie Em put the bottle of wine beside Nicky, "I find I can't drink like I used to. It makes me so – so uncertain."

Nicky filled the glass to the brim but sipped this one more slowly. The feeling of unease that had plagued her all evening was slipping away. A couple more glasses and she could wave it goodbye.

"But if you have any of the other?" Auntie Em made a rolling motion with her fingers.

Nicky reached into her pocket for the two small joints Ollie had given her and put them on the table.

Auntie Em took one, "And Rion's ok?"

The photographer nodded, "She's with Ollie."

Ollie woke early on Sunday morning after an eighteen-hour sleep and went for a jog. The canal was empty at that time, the anglers hadn't set up and, as Sainsburys wouldn't be open for a while, there were no Sunday shoppers clogging the towpath. Since it was Hum's first jog since being assaulted Ollie decided to do the shorter run. Instead of turning left out of Meanwhile Gardens and heading for the cemetery he turned right and made his way down to Little Venice.

He lumbered under Carlton Bridge and past the bus depot, increasing his pace as the busy Westway curved above him. The run was painfully satisfying, every step a reminder of the abuse he had put his body through on the Friday night that had so easily stretched into Saturday afternoon. His creaky joints told of hours on various dancefloors, the sweat imbued his t-shirt with the residue of poisons his body was eager to get rid of. Memories of the evening were characteristically vague and that was how Ollie preferred it. All that remained of the long night was the feeling that he had indeed enjoyed himself – and that was the main thing wasn't it? Wrapped up in his thoughts about Wayne Ollie soon found himself jogging past the council blocks and the string of canal boats on the approach to Little Venice.

Unbeknownst to him Rion lay trussed and gagged in one of the prettily coloured barges. A crack in the let in a bit of light and the outside world. The young girl couldn't believe her eyes when she saw Hum's face at the porthole.

The hound wagged his tail and began to bark upon seeing his friend.

Rion tried to say something but all that came out was a muffled throaty sound. With Herculean effort she managed to get her hands free. Rion ripped the tape from her mouth, hopped over to the porthole and banged heavily on the glass. If Hum was there Ollie or Auntie Em wouldn't be far away.

"Help!" she yelled. "HUM!"

The door opened quickly, hands pulled her away from the porthole, snapped shut the small curtains and threw her back on the bed. Before she could scream Rion felt the now familiar, sickly sweet smell of chloroform and lost consciousness.

Hum's excited barking broke into Ollie's thoughts. He turned round to see the dog frantically pawing the side of a barge.

"Hum!" he called but as usual the hound was intent on doing his own thing. Ollie jogged back to find a rather frumpy couple coming up on deck. "Sorry," he said dragging Hum away.

"Is the door closed Ted?" the woman asked.

"Yes Mary," her companion replied.

The woman smiled sweetly at Ollie, "We have cats you see."

Ollie clipped Hum to the lead. He carried on the short way to the Canal Café before turning round and heading back the way he came. He was glad Hum was on the lead for the dog went berserk as they passed the Longfelloe. This time [illegible] couple had been joined by someone else. Upon seeing [illegible] vaguely familiar looking man, wearing an old-fashioned Trilby, returned below decks.

"He doesn't normally mind cats," Ollie gasped as he passed them.

The couple smiled and waved. When Ollie was out of hearing range their manner changed. "That must *never* be allowed to happen again," Mary said angrily.

"We'll move her tonight," Gorby removed his hat and lightly drummed his fingers against his birthmark. "I've rostered everyone off. We won't be disturbed."

"Make sure we're not," Ted said curtly.

"But in any case I'll dose her up. She won't be giving us any trouble."

Ollie jogged slowly into the mews with Hum trotting at his heels.

"Good boy!"

The dog smiled up at him, his mischievous eyes shining behind his fringe.

"He's so much better isn't he?" Auntie Em called from the middle of the mews where she was loading the spacious old Citroen with a blanket and some baskets. She went to examine Hum. His cuts had almost healed, the bruising almost gone. The only sign of the vicious onslaught were several bald patches where assorted beaks had ripped the fur from his body. "We're going blackberrying on Wormwood. Care to join us?"

"Hum would I'm sure Auntie Em. I'd love to but Johnson's coming round for the TQ lunch – do you think Rion might like to go?"

"Are females allowed?"

"Of course they are – as guests. I'd like to get her together with Johnson. He's been muttering something about needing an assistant for this Glamourista column he's doing."

"Well, she could do that, couldn't she?"

"As long as Johnson doesn't bully her too much, but he seemed to like Rion from Nicky's shoot last week."

"It'll be much better her working for Johnson rather than for Glamourista directly. All she'd do there is make coffee and get trampled on all day."

"Can she handle Johnson though?"

"I think you'll find Rion can handle most things. Johnson and a TQ lunch will be a breeze."

"Is she up yet?" asked Ollie.

Auntie Gem, Sunday papers in hand, joined Emma by the car. "Let her sleep in. She probably needs it!" Gem winked at Ollie who knew how Nicky, like himself, needed little encouraging to party on a Friday night. Ollie wondered where Nicky had taken the young girl.

"I've put a map through her door saying where we'll be."

"At the magic bush at the top of the Scrubs?"

There was one particular blackberry bush on Wormwood Scrubs that, like some plant of myth and legend, could be stripped of fruit one day only for the next its brambles to be full of the sweet juicy berries. It also stayed in fruit much later than the others due, some said, to it being situated above an ancient spring that warmed its roots.

"Where else?" Auntie Em bent down to stroke the dog. "Hum seems to be on the mend sweetness." She straightened up to look him level in the eye, "What about you?"

"I'm ok," Ollie answered honestly.

Auntie Em looked at Gemma, "Shall we tell him?"

"You can't say something like that in front of someone," Ollie protested, "unless you *are* going to tell them."

Auntie Gem took a deep breath. "Tell him," she said.

When they had finished the story about Candida, about Wayne, about the real and the fake Merlijnche de Poortje, about everything except how Nicky had nearly ruined it all – that could wait for a later date – Ollie just smiled. "You know, I thought I'd be more cut up about Wayne but I'm not and that," Ollie paused for a second to think through his words, "makes me feel surprised and pleased."

Auntie Gem put her arm around him. "It makes us feel surprised and pleased too child."

"Maybe I'm growing up eh?"

"Maybe," Auntie Em planted a gentle kiss on his cheek, "but aren't you going to ask if it's true?"

"Oh, I know it's true. You know how?"

Gem 'n Em shook their heads.

"Well, there were several things I was being wilfully blind to but I saw a number on his mobile. At the time I wasn't sure whose it was but now, well there's no doubt it was Candida's," Ollie smiled. "Basically he was a hired gun wasn't he?"

Auntie Em nodded, "More like a sex pistol I'd say sweetness."

"Just how much do you remember of Friday night?" Johnson asked Ollie.

They were in the middle of a group of twelve gay men seated around a table in the basement of the Hungry Hearts Diner. The restaurant on Kensington Park Road was the venue for the Tragedy Queen of the Week club to decide who, amongst them, had had the most pitiful week and so was worthy of the title. Johnson had been begging Ollie to take him for ages.

"Not much. The normal really, rampaging through Soho, a couple of e's...."

"How Essex," Simon sniffed from opposite.

"...clubbing at Popstarz," Ollie continued. "Then afterhours at some dive south of the river before staggering back here and going to bed yesterday afternoon."

"The only tragic thing about that," Johnson sighed, "is that I can't do it anymore."

"And StJohn didn't pop up at any time?" Lyle asked from the far end of the table.

The mere mention of the name was still enough to make Ollie furious and sad at the same time. He did have a fleeting memory of StJohn's loathsome face looming out of the blur of the evening. Ollie wasn't sure if this could be classified under reality or false-memory-induced-by-hallucinogenic-drugs syndrome. Ollie managed to rein in his feelings before answering Lyle. "I can't really remember too much, I was trying to put things in place on my run – "

"You run?" Peter squealed from his place beside Simon. "God, how butch!"

"Don't knock it – jogging tightens up everything," Murray said. "I tried it once but," he dismissed the subject with a flutter of his hands, "it was too much effort."

"Does wonders for your calves though."

"Yes," Johnson agreed, "but it's easier to get implants." He was enjoying himself immensely. "I know the most – "

They were stopped by a rap on the table.

"Boys, be quiet," Tim commanded. The banker was chairman for the week and had been running a tight ship. "It's Ollie's turn."

"I bet StJohn remembers," Lyle continued. "Afterall a fist in the face is pretty hard to forget."

Peter nudged Alan. "I told you he's butch," he whispered.

"So what if I did hit him?"

"There's no what ifs about it Ollie. He has the shiner to prove it."

"He's lucky it wasn't worse then isn't he?"

Murray looked questioningly at Johnson who whispered behind his hand, "StJohn was driving the car in which James died."

Lyle leant forward on his elbows. "He says if you ever go near him again – "

"Don't tell me what he says. If StJohn wants to say anything he can tell me to my face."

Although normally thriving on any sort of drama the table had hushed to a rather threatening silence. Again Tim took control. "Well," the chairman cleared his throat, "I don't think having a night out in Soho – even if you did descend into Essex type drugs – "

"It must have been Wayne's influence – he was from Dagenham you know," Johnson threw in.

" – counts as anything tragic," Tim continued. "And whilst having a handsome hunk ditch you – "

"And rip you off," Ollie pointed out.

" – merits a couple of points it's nothing that hasn't happened to several of us – "

Even though it was Johnson's first TQ lunch he threw himself into the proceedings with all the ease of a founder member. "You should be so lucky!"

"Lucky, lucky, lucky," Alan sang in imitation of Kylie.

"Wayne was," Johnson continued, "I hate to use the term but nothing else will suffice – drop dead gorgeous and sure, it might be seen by some that to have someone paid to seduce you – "

Ollie had a feeling that wouldn't go unnoticed.

"Wait!" Peter called from the end of the table. "Did you say 'having someone *paid* to seduce you'?"

Johnson nodded.

"Well, that's pretty tragic and should get a couple of extra points – Tim?" Peter looked to the chairman.

"You should be so tragic!" Johnson interrupted.

"Tragic, tragic, tragic," several voices chimed before subsiding into giggles.

"If any of you," Johnson gestured around the table, "had seen this guy you would have been throwing money at him to get him to even smile at you. It wasn't like Ollie was paying him."

"Still a couple of extra points are due for the novel twist," Tim confirmed.

"Did he say he loved you?"

"No."

"So what's the harm?"

"It just sounds like uncomplicated, no-strings-attached adult sex."

"Does anyone remember such a thing?"

"Is there such a thing?"

"Johnson was right," Murray finished off his glass and poured another all in one fluid motion. "The tragedy is it didn't happen to any of us."

Alan couldn't see what all the fuss was about. "It just sounds like an early Christmas present to me, a stocking filler perhaps," he said raising his glass to Ollie.

An early Christmas present? Ollie smiled. That's how he would choose to see Wayne.

The final vote was decided over coffee and brandies.

"I'm so glad cigars are not an option these days," Ollie sniffed his Cognac. "I loathe the things."

"Me too," Johnson said. "If I'm going to put an eight inch Cuban in my mouth it's not for smoking – you know what I'm saying?"

"I hear you!" Murray, smiling flirtatiously, moved closer to Johnson.

"He said an eight inch Cuban not a one inch Scot, Murray," Jason hissed from Ollie's left.

The chairman rapped on the table. "I've tallied up."

Talking immediately ceased. All eyes were on Tim.

"Whilst Alan scores for being mistaken for Prince Edward and Murray scores for being thrown out of the Met Bar after being sick over Tracey and Kate…."

"It was only over their shoes!" Murray exclaimed, giving Johnson's leg a quick squeeze under the table.

"Lyle doesn't score for having his best friend punched by another member here."

All eyes looked at Ollie.

"That's really vicarious tragedy and doesn't count. I get some marks for booking a massage and only getting a massage – "

"Shall we get out of here?" Johnson whispered to Murray who nodded enthusiastically. The lifestyle enhancer took out his black American Express card and flashed it at the waiter. The gesture didn't go unnoticed by Tim.

"But the rest of you: whilst it might have been upsetting to have ugly builders re-doing your wetroom – "

"They were a fright, all the neighbours could see," Peter piped up opposite Ollie.

" – and being clamped is no doubt a pain it doesn't come under the heading of 'tragedy', Ollie scores for having his dog being beaten up by some geese and other aspects of his situation have certain merits but, on balance, the tragedy queen for this week for having cruised his own father is – "

Before the chairman could finish Johnson again flashed his black American Express card in the air.

"Sorry, *was* going to be Jason," Tim corrected himself. "We have a new winner, a late entrant," Tim grabbed Johnson's credit card and waved it at the others. The sight of the black card elicited a few 'Ooohs' and knowing smiles. "The winner on account of having a black American Express card, and therefore having to pay for everyone's lunch, is our newcomer – Johnson Ogle!"

Tim sat down to much applause.

"But I – " Johnson glared accusingly at Ollie. "You should have told me!"

"Then I wouldn't have had a free lunch."

Johnson then looked at Murray who threw up his hands. "Nor me."

Johnson pretended to be hurt but secretly was rather pleased. In his world any attention was better than being ignored, any prize better than nothing.

Ollie came back to the mews to find Auntie Em outside his house. In one hand she held a tray on which were three small bowls covered with clingfilm. With the other she knocked on his door.

Ollie ran up and took the precariously wobbling tray from her, "Here let me."

"I was just going to put these in your fridge," Auntie Em said taking one of the bowls from the tray.

"Good day?" he asked.

"Wonderful angel although," Auntie Em gestured to the bowls that were filled with blackberries, "these will be the last I fear."

She left a bowl on Ollie's doorstep before crossing to the house opposite. Nicky's door opened after a single knock.

"For you sweetness," Auntie Em handed her offering to the photographer.

"Mmmmm!"

"There's something rather satisfying about picking your own food isn't there?"

"The old hunter/gatherer instinct?" Ollie wasn't so sure. "I think it would pall if you had to do it everyday."

"I'm quite happy with the exchange system – you know, 'I give you money you give me what I want'," Nicky said.

"I'm not talking about the basics, – pulling up potatoes, cropping cabbages – "

"You don't like cabbage Auntie Em."

" – harvesting beans – "

"Or beans," Ollie reminded her.

"Work with me here angel," she paused. "But the yummy stuff, picking berries, finding scallops on the beach, fishing for salmon. That I would find rewarding you know?"

"Perhaps," Ollie said half-heartedly.

"Still the ideal is having Mr Christians deliver isn't it?"

"You're not wrong there." Nicky looked at the single remaining bowl on the tray, "Is that for Rion?"

"It would be greedy to have *two* sweetness."

"No, I mean is she in?"

Auntie Em looked at Ollie who shrugged his shoulders. "There was no answer when I knocked at about one o' clock," he said.

"I knocked yesterday afternoon but she must have been out," Nicky said.

"She would have been sleeping it off after her night out with our boy here."

Puzzled by the remark Ollie looked at Auntie Em. "She wasn't out with me. I haven't seen her since Friday night," he went on. "I left her waiting for Nicky at Primrose Hill."

"But you didn't go back did you sweetness?"

"You know I didn't Auntie Em," Nicky replied.

Emma looked worried. "So you both haven't seen her since Friday night?"

"No," they said in unison.

Ollie ran over to the door of 1A at the entrance to the mews. "Rion!" he shouted before giving the front door three sharp knocks.

When there was no reply Auntie Em took the spare key from the large metal key chain and let herself in.

"Rion?" she called up, "it's only us." Followed by Ollie and Nicky she went up the stairs into the empty sitting room. Everything looked untouched since Friday. The door to the bedroom was closed. "Rion?" she called again cheerily. Auntie Em put the bowl of blackberries in the fridge before approaching the closed bedroom door. "Rion?"

Ollie and Nicky hung back as Emma knocked on the door then entered. The bedroom was as empty as the rest of the house.

"It doesn't look like the bed's been slept in," Nicky said.

"Where else could she be?" Auntie Em wondered.

Ollie looked around the small room, "I know she had plans to visit Jake yesterday."

"Let's see if she turned up. If not – " Auntie Em didn't allow herself to think of what might have happened. "Let's cross that bridge when we come to it shall we?" she said hastily.

Ollie immediately went outside to phone St Mary's. When he came back up his face said it all. "We're going to have to cross that bridge Auntie Em," he said. "She never showed up yesterday."

Rion felt dreadful. She had a splitting headache and was chilled to the bone. She thought twice about opening her eyes not knowing what she'd find before them. So many times she'd awoken recently to find the oddest things going on.

People approaching her, stroking her hair and saying, "She's perfect, just perfect."

She could remember walking with Gorby down the canal after the fireworks and then waking up restrained on a boat, she had some dim memory of seeing Hum's face at the porthole, of some peculiar long swords, of being taken on the boat somewhere at night, hurried through darkness, the whistle of a train – and now where was she?

It had all seemed like a dream yet she had felt very much awake throughout – very much awake but unable to talk, unable to move.

She remembered repeatedly trying to pinch herself yet found she couldn't. However now she tried and could definitely feel her fingers on the top of her wrist. What's more her hands weren't restrained and, she moved her legs, nor were her feet.

Maybe it had all been a dream. Maybe this time when she opened her eyes she would find herself with her new family in Meanwhile Gardens Mews. She would be lying on her bed with the window wide open – that must be why she was so cold.

Realising she couldn't wait any longer, Rion slowly opened her eyes.

She found herself in a small enclosed space that at first glance appeared to be a bricked in railway arch. In front of her metal bars ran from floor to vaulted ceiling, separating Rion from the front of the chamber. Directly opposite, on the other side of the bars, a dusty, highbacked chair faced her. The whole space had a sacrosanct, almost ghostly feel to it. This effect was increased by the lone candle flickering in an alcove by the enormous iron door, which, for some reason, had a peephole in it looking out.

This last bit of information confused her. If she was in

prison surely the peephole would be outside looking in?

As her eyes adjusted to the gloom Rion could see the elaborate chair was covered in what once must have been expensive, dark green velvet. Dulled silver studs formed a pattern on the seatback. To one side and behind her was a wall, the bricks had long ago lost their red warmth and were now a cold, grimy grey. A fine mesh grille separated Rion from the other part of the rear chamber so that, in all, she was caged in a quarter of the damp space. On the other side of this finer mesh large boxes had been piled up on evenly spaced shelves that rose to the ceiling.

So she was in a railway storage arch, perhaps beneath a station – that was clear – but what was she doing here? And how was she going to escape? She listened for the rumble of trains but couldn't hear any.

Everything was deeply silent.

21

ANGIE ON THE CASE

"And you say she was homeless?" Inspector Devine asked, his pen poised over his notebook.

Auntie Em nodded, "Before she came here she was anyway. She slept rough in the cemetery."

"Rion had family in Bridlington I think," Ollie added.

"So she was a runaway?"

Ollie exchanged a glance with Auntie Em and Nicky realising how that made it sound. "Well – "

"Did you also say she was sixteen?"

"And a half," Ollie added helpfully.

The inspector closed the notepad with a deft flick of the wrist. "Emma," he began before correcting himself, "Ms Nelson. In our experience we've found that most of these teenage runaways return home."

"Unless they're captured by darker forces first," Nicky said indignantly.

"She wasn't hanging around Kings Cross was she?"

"Not that I know of," Nicky admitted.

"Or the amusement arcades in Soho?"

Nicky shook her head.

Inspector Devine sighed. "We haven't much to go on at this stage. I'll put the word out, we'll try and locate her parents and if she hasn't turned up by the end of the week we'll go from there. Have you a likeness of her?"

"I do." Nicky dashed into her studio, returning to the mews with a photo she had taken of Rion after Johnson's shoot.

Ollie felt a wrench to his stomach when he looked at the picture. It was a hauntingly beautiful black and white image of Rion with her hair falling around her shoulders. "This makes her look older than she is," he said.

The inspector put the picture with his notepad, "We'll be in touch." As he made his way out of the mews he stopped and turned round, "I suppose Sir, that you have an alibi for Friday night?"

Ollie looked at him in disbelief.

"He has to ask angel," Auntie Em whispered.

"I'm sure StJohn StJohn will vouch for me."

The policeman began to write on notepad, " S- I – ?"

"Spelt Saint John Saint John," Auntie Em helped. "Pronounced Sinjin Sinjin."

They watched until Inspector Devine had disappeared around the corner.

"I thought you said he was tame," Ollie protested.

"He is, but there's nothing much he can do until – " Auntie Em's voice trailed off.

"Until a body turns up?"

"Oh angel don't say it."

"Don't even think it," Nicky said glumly.

"It's all my fault. I should never have said she could move into the unlucky house. It was bound to happen."

"I should never have left her."

"And I should have gone back for her!" Nicky wailed.

Ollie put his arms around both women. "C'mon we can't all reach for the blame – if that was the case none of us are guilty and all of us are guilty."

"You know Halloween is really the old Celtic festival Samhain," Auntie Em blew her nose. "Our ancestors considered it the most dangerous night of the year, when the barriers between the real world and the 'Otherworld' broke down and people were – " she gave a little sob, " – lured to their death!"

Ollie had never seen Auntie Em this distraught. "We don't know if anything's happened to her. Maybe she met some friends – "

"She only knew us!"

"Maybe she went back to Bridlington to get some things and forgot our numbers."

"She wouldn't have forgotten Jake in hospital would she?" Auntie Em asked.

"It's unlikely," Ollie had to admit.

"And she wouldn't have missed her chance at Glamourista either," Nicky was sure of that.

"She's only been missing three days – " Ollie said.

"Today's the fourth!"

"How would you feel if someone said to you, 'You've only been hungry for three days'?"

"Or, 'You've only been in pain for three days'?"

"Three days is a long time angel."

"Five minutes can be an age, I mean ten seconds can seem like forever if you're frightened."

"Ok. OK," Ollie put up his hands to stop the attack. "But what are we going to do?"

Angie Peters was still no closer to her 'big idea' for Glamourista – or her '*grand projet*' as her husband liked to call it. Edwin could say things like that. He made them sound perfectly natural, he'd been educated in Switzerland after all, whereas if she tried it just sounded pretentious.

It was definitely time for her ginseng.

The editor scooped the tarlike liquid from the jar with the tiny teaspoon provided. She melted it in the hot water, screwed up her nose and took a sip. Angie hated the taste of the ginseng but was told it would give her energy whilst keeping her calm.

Boy did she need that.

Her work alone, she thought, practically required ginseng be fed intravenously without even touching on her husband's problems. Poor Edwin would need something aged and malted to get through this crisis. He would probably also require chemical compounds, pink pills with cartoon faces – homeopathy just didn't get a look in under such circumstances.

Pinching her nose she took another sip of the foul liquid and perused the photographs in front of her. They were good, of course, but there was one that particularly intrigued her. The editor of Glamourista picked up the phone and dialled. "Nicky? Sweetheart it's Angie here. The shots are great."

"Which one are you going to use?"

"Hmmmm. The one half in shadow will be perfect for the byline but for the main picture?" the editor glanced at the pictures again. "The one with Johnson's foot on that rather attractive bench."

Nicky was pleased as it would give Ollie a credit. "That's the one I would use."

"Is the furniture maker a friend of yours by any chance?" The editor knew how these things worked.

Unwilling to appear too incestuous Nicky deflected the question, "Ollie? He's a friend of Johnson's."

"Then perhaps Johnson can feature him in his column." Angie held her nose and took another sip of the disgusting potion before continuing, "One picture in particular caught my attention."

"Oh?"

"I don't know why you included it but it's a young girl, very interesting looking, slightly haunted?"

"That must be Rion," Nicky hoped she sounded more surprised than she felt. She had never been much good at lying. "She's Johnson's new assistant. We were playing around with the film after the session ended."

"Could you get her in?"

"I – er – wish I knew how to contact her," Nicky said truthfully.

"I'll be in touch."

Angie had clicked off the phone and already pressed Johnson's speed-dial before the photographer had a chance to say goodbye.

"Johnson darling, it's Angie."

"Angie."

The editor thought Johnson's voice sounded uncharacteristically muffled but bubbled on regardless.

"We have the pictures back. You're going to love them. Nicky might have taken ten much needed pounds off Jim James but she's taken twenty years off you." The editor waited for Johnson's gleeful remarks that were very slow in coming. "And you didn't even need it sweetheart," she joked still waiting for some expression of joy at the news. "You look twenty four in most of them!" Again she waited. "Johnson?"

"Sorry Ange, I'm not myself today."

"How's your column?"

Johnson sighed, "Rather limp but nothing a good dose of viagra couldn't cure."

"The magazine column Johnson."

"In the same state I'm afraid. My assistant – "

"I was just going to ask about her! Nicky put in a photo with your lot and she's just – "

" – vanished Angie."

"Sorry?"

"She's vanished. Disappeared off the face of the earth. It's too sad. Ollie – "

"The furniture maker?"

"Designer," Johnson corrected. " – thinks something terrible has happened to her. The police aren't interested at the moment. It's all just awful."

"She's probably just met someone."

Johnson sounded doubtful, "She didn't seem to be the type."

"They never do, do they? She'll turn up, you'll see."

"The column might have to wait."

So that's what this is about Angie thought.

"We can help with that sweetheart, just give us a couple of ideas."

Johnson made some noncommittal sound down the phone.

"We could do something on your friend Ollie – that would be easy wouldn't it?"

Johnson brightened up, "And someone could ghost it for me?"

"That's what we're here for sweetie," Angie swirled the ginseng dregs around the glass, grimacing as she swallowed for the final time. "You know you can call me anytime but especially call if your assistant shows up – she'll be perfect for something here. What did you say her name was?"

"Rion. Rion Ward."

It hadn't been a good few days for Sir Edwin Peters. The week had started badly and got worse. The unfavourable report had come out on Monday, depressing the shareholders and the value of the shares. Events had so compounded that he now found himself being interviewed by some arrogant little prick on *Business This Week*.

The only consolation he could wrest from this ghastly situation is that no one watched the lunchtime programme. Who in their right minds would?

"On Monday the report appeared in SCIENCE about independent investigations into Peters & Peters the UK's largest organic, environment-friendly, pesticide manufacturer– "

The answer came through to him as he listened to the interviewer witter on: his shareholders and prospective shareholders would be watching, he thought gloomily – that's who.

"You described your pesticides as 'like a neutron bomb' – that doesn't sound like a very environmentally friendly claim does it Sir Edwin?"

"On the contrary," Sir Edwin replied, "it sounds like the most environmentally friendly claim of all. The insects and baddies are all killed whilst the flowers, fruit and cell structure of the plant remain intact."

"But how did Peters & Peters change, almost overnight, from chemical usage to organic? Normally it takes years – "

Sir Edwin interrupted him, "But it did take years. It merely seemed overnight," he grated his teeth behind the smile he flashed at the interviewer. God, he needed a Scotch. "I would remind you that the plant had been passed by the D.T.I. on no less than four separate occasions."

"So the leakage – "

"Well, of course a part of the company remained producing – er – " Sir Edwin racked his brain for the right word, " –

unorganic – ” Was that the correct term? “ – er – material but that section was away from the main production centre. To my knowledge the leak has been found and checked.”

“Is there anything not to your knowledge?”

Sir Edwin silently counted to ten.

“Does the Queen know everything about what goes on at Buckingham Palace?” Sir Edwin hoped his voice didn’t betray his annoyance. He had been advised to stay calm and contrite. “Does the Prime Minister know everything about his party? Does – ”

Just as Sir Edwin was warming to this theme the interviewer interrupted, “Judging by the recent reshuffle I would say the Prime Minister makes it his business to know *everything* about his party.”

“Obviously things happen without my knowledge but as chairman of Peters & Peters the buck must stop with me.” Sir Edwin turned to look directly at the camera, “I take full responsibility for whatever has happened.”

Watching their boss’ performance on tv the staff of Peters & Peters judged it to be quite an honest one. As they drifted back to work Auntie Gem sought out Mr Paul.

“Is he guilty?” she asked the young assistant manager.

“Of what?”

“Poisoning the canal?”

Mr Paul thought for a moment. “Perhaps we went too quickly,” he said tactfully. “It’s like Olympic athletes – ”

Auntie Gem looked blank.

“The unknown ones?” Mr Paul prompted. “They come out of nowhere to win three gold medals. I mean progress like that doesn’t go unaided does it?”

Auntie Gem was sure it didn’t. “So what aided him?”

Mr Paul rubbed his thumb over his forefingers, “Friends at the D.T.I.”

"And he knew all along?"

Mr Paul smiled, "What do you think?"

Auntie Gem wasn't sure what to think but, remembering how dangerously ill Jake had been as well as the devastation of the fish, eels, frogs and her beloved heron, she knew what to do.

Angie was waiting for her husband upon his return from the *Business This Week* studio. She had placed a bottle of Laphroaig on a silver salver in plain view on the hall table. Beside it two empty tumblers waited expectantly. Also on the salver was a porcelain pillbox containing two of his favourite pink pills, neatly broken into halves.

Edwin's weary face lit up when he saw her. "Things can't get any worse can they? I mean, they can't take away my knighthood or anything can they?"

Angie thought it might well be grounds for divorce if they could. Again she reminded herself to check where the title would go should the subject be more than just mentioned.

"I'm sure they can't darling," she said in her most soothing of voices. Picking up the silver salver she moved through to the elegant sitting room. This was perhaps Angie's favourite room in the house. With its view over the garden, its large Conran sofas and its 'real' antique furniture it always reminded her of how far she had come.

Angie filled the thick tumbler with Scotch, sat her husband on the sofa and gave him the pillbox. "I have something to tell you."

Edwin looked at the floor, "Go on. Tell me you have a lover, tell me you want a divorce. Kick a man when he's down why don't you?"

"Don't be silly Edwin," Angie crossed over to the marble fireplace, switched on the gas and lit the bowl of fake coals that glowed so convincingly real. "By tomorrow everything will be ok. Trust me."

All it had taken were a few calls to confirm that Rion Ward was indeed on the missing persons register. After that another call brought her the result she wanted.

Angie gently kissed her husband on the forehead. "And it's all thanks to you Edwin."

The early November sun threw feeble rays across the room as she told her husband what she had done.

22

THRICE BURIED

Rion judged it had been three days since she had been taken from the barge but couldn't be sure.

Most of the time she was kept in the near-darkness of what she had now decided was not, in fact, a railway arch but some kind of cellar, an old coalhole perhaps or some other sort of bunker. Rion still couldn't figure out who the elaborate chair belonged to, or what the boxes on the shelves on the other side of the cellar contained, but she was in no hurry to find out.

She also wondered about the two peculiar swords beside the door.

Her watch told the time but the young girl had no idea if it was noon or the witching hour. There was no sense of night or day in the secret place where they had hidden her.

Rion still didn't have a clear idea of who 'they' were, nor what 'they' wanted, but she had a feeling that when things were clear 'they' might not be too pleasant.

A distant scraping, a muffled clang followed by footsteps on flagstones heralded the arrival of one of her keepers but which one would it be? Gorby? Ted? Mary? Or the new one?

The door opened with a groan. Age and damp had swelled the heavy oak so that it needed a push to make a gap wide enough for a person to slip through.

"Oh it's you," she was relieved to see it was the new one. A silent young man of twenty nine entered. His pointed eyes were set too close together, a tightly cropped beard moulded the shape of his chin, in his hand he carried a brown paper bag.

"Don't close the door," Rion said trying to peer through the gap into the dimly lit corridor. In the few seconds before the timer kicked in she saw shadowy, barred alcoves much like her own. "It's so stuffy in here, the fire gives me a headache – can't you turn it off for a while?"

After the initial chill of the first day a gas fire had been brought in and left on permanently. She had also been given a man's thick Arran sweater, which smelt of damp, an old duvet and several blankets that softened up the worn mattress.

Despite her repeated questioning no one would tell her why she was being held prisoner. The fact that she was being looked after, or at least not overly mistreated, reassured her in some way. Perhaps they had got the wrong person, perhaps they thought she was the daughter of some incredibly rich, doting father who would pay a king's ransom to see his daughter again.

Perhaps.

What worried her about this scenario was how they would react when they found out that her family had no money and couldn't care less what happened to her.

"Are you going to talk to me today?" she asked.

In reply the young man handed a styrofoam cup of soup and a clingfilm wrapped sandwich through the bars to her. Hearing the ticking timer click on Rion again tried to peer through the gap in the door, but the young man blocked her view.

What she saw next threw her more than slightly.

Another young man, the spitting image of the one already in the room, stuck his head around the door.

Rion suddenly had a dreadful thought – was the heater spewing poisonous fumes that were affecting her vision?

"Please switch off the fire," she said shakily. Rion held onto the bars to stop her legs buckling, "I think it's leaking."

She took a breath to steady herself then realised that, if the fire was leaking gas, this might be the wrong thing to do. Unsure whether to hold her breath or not Rion sat down on the mattress and hoped that when she opened her eyes there would only be one of the young men, like there had been yesterday.

It was not to be.

The mirror image entered the room and whispered to his twin who repeatedly pointed to the other side of the fine mesh grille. Ignoring Rion who had slumped on the mattress they put their noses right up to the bars on the other side and peered through at Rion knew not what.

Satisfied at what they saw they stepped back and turned their attention to Rion. Again the first twin hurriedly whispered to his brother.

"Can't you let me out just to over there?" Rion gestured to where the twins stood on the other side of the bars beside the elaborate chair. "You can close the door – it's not like I'm going to run anywhere is it?"

This question brought another bout of whispering during which the recently arrived twin, who it was clear was the senior, kept his eyes on her.

"We'll turn off the fire, and maybe let you come out here, if you do something for us," Senior said.

Rion immediately noticed he had a slight country burr to his voice. She got up from the mattress but stayed near the back wall. "Like what?" she asked suspiciously.

"A favour for a favour," he replied.

Rion was surprised to find Senior didn't have a creepy smirk like Gorby did, a mute, almost scared smile like Junior, or even a threatening grin like Ted & Mary, he had, rather, a natural, almost friendly sort of smile.

"Such as?"

Senior nodded to Junior who took a large key from a nail on the wall. After some fumbling he managed to open the latch allowing the bars to swing open.

Rion felt momentarily confused without the barrier in front of her. Cautiously she stepped through into the other side of the cellar. She ran her fingers along the handrest of the once grand chair.

"Whose is this?" she asked.

"The Countess of Rosleagh's," Senior replied.

Rion sat gingerly on the faded green cushion causing a small cloud of dust to flare up. She looked at the twins, "But what is it doing here?"

Senior gestured in front of her to the part the twins had been so interested in, the part screened from her side by a fine mesh grill. "She wanted to be with her family," he said.

For the first time Rion looked through the bars to this hitherto concealed side. On the middle shelf directly at eye level, Rion saw what could only be a large coffin. It was covered in the same faded green velvet as the chair, the sides and corners lined with dulled silver studs.

"The seventh Earl of Rosleagh," Senior explained.

Instead of revulsion or fear Rion felt a strong sense of fascination. On the shelf immediately above the Earl was a smaller coffin covered in the same faded velvet. Beside it was a bouquet of ceramic flowers, gleaming porcelain roses with intricate lead leaves, kept as if fresh under a dome of glass.

"The Countess?" Rion asked the twins who nodded.

"She died many years after the Earl and used to come here, almost every day Gorby said, to be with her husband and children."

"Children?" Rion asked.

She followed the twins' gaze to the top shelf. In a row were six small coffins ranging in size from, perhaps, a five-year-old's to the tiny coffin of an infant.

"Don't worry they can't get out," Junior joked. "They're thrice buried – wood within lead within wood."

Rion, her eyes welling up, simply stared at the sad row of six on the upper shelf.

Senior switched off the fire. He opened the door a fraction, satisfied himself that the light in the corridor was switched off, then opened the door wider. Rion felt the deliciously cool draft clear away the stale, fumey air.

"Now for your side of the agreement," Senior said moving closer to Rion who instinctively shrank back. He smiled, "I'm not – " he corrected himself, " – we're not going to touch you."

Rion kept her back to the bars.

"For your increased freedom while we're around all we ask is that you keep quiet."

This puzzled Rion. Had she been screaming in her sleep she wondered?

"Do you see there?" Senior pointed to a small box at the feet end of the Earl's coffin.

Rion nodded.

"We want that and intend to get it but you mustn't let anyone else know," he pulled closer.

Rion shrank back. "What's inside?" she asked.

"The family jewels!" Junior crowed. He grabbed a metal staff from the door, poked it through the bars and wormed the thin end under the box. He levered it up and let the studded box fall, the gems inside rattling satisfactorily.

"Beck!" his brother silenced him with a glare.

"Doesn't the same key fit? I mean can't you just open the bars like you did on my side?" Rion asked.

"They were sealed up after the Countess was laid to rest," he pointed to the locks that had been soldered shut. "She wanted the family together for all time, never to be disturbed."

"And you intend to – ?"

Senior slowly moved his head up and down. He took a metal file from his pocket and made sawing motions, "Very carefully. But if you tell – " he scraped the file across his throat. The meaning was clear.

The twins jumped at hearing a distant sound followed by the timer clicking on. "Quick!" Senior whispered urgently as he bundled Rion into her side. He closed the bars, looked around desperately for the key before realising his brother had it. Junior quickly threw it to him but before Senior had the time to lock Rion in the door groaned open.

Gorby entered. In his hand he carried a newspaper. After some curt whispering to the twins they all left, locking the door behind them.

Rion heard them vanish down the flagstone corridor. After a second she realised she hadn't been locked in her side. She slowly opened the bars before hearing feet dash down the corridor. A key turned in the heavy vault door and Senior rushed in.

"I have to do this," Senior took the key from his pocket, locked Rion back behind her bars and replaced the key on its nail by the heavy oak door.

"Wait!"

Rion's call stopped Senior at the door. He looked back.

"Where is Rosleagh?" she asked.

"Ireland."

"Is that where we are?"

Senior simply hurried out, making sure to lock the vault behind him.

Rion was left with the Earl and Countess of Rosleagh and their six children, wondering how on earth she had got into their family vault in Ireland and what had caused the twins and Gorby to make such a speedy departure.

Although it was scant consolation, Rion thought, she at least had all the time in the world to think about it.

23

SURPRISING NEWS

Ollie had picked up Jake from hospital that morning. They had decided to set off to Bridlington in order to track down Rion's parents and hopefully Rion.

Jake had insisted on collecting something from his home before they set off. As he clambered back into the van Ollie saw what Jake had picked up – the battered tobacco tin no doubt filled with the cemetery's finest.

"What's this one called?" Ollie asked with a smile.

"Kensal Green," Jake replied. "I've been dying for a draw for what seems like ages."

"You were only in St Mary's for a week!"

"Ah, but a week without weed is a long week indeed."

Ollie laughed. "I would have brought some in for you, baked a cake with it or something, if I hadn't been so damn preoccupied."

Jake waved away his concern, "No matter." He opened up the tin, took out the large silver Rizla and began rolling a joint on the Road Map of Great Britain. "My tolerance will be lower now anyway," he grinned. "It'll be a better buzz."

They were soon zooming up West End Lane onto the Finchley Road and Hendon Way. With Hum already asleep in the back they manoeuvred their way through the junctions of Brent Cross, merged with the correct lane and found themselves, with surprising ease, at the start of the Ml. The vast concrete motorway stretched northwards before them.

"That wasn't too bad was it?" Jake asked. He lit the joint he'd been waiting so long for and, out of respect to the driver, passed it to Ollie first.

Before taking the proffered spliff Ollie had to find out something. "Where's this on the scale between Mausoleum Madness and Headstone Homegrown?" he asked. "If it's the former it's best I don't have any."

Jake smiled. "Kensal Green is probably the lightest, most scintillating of all the crops. It's the mimosa of marijuanas."

Ollie took two quick puffs and handed it back to Jake, waving the joint away when it was offered back to him. "I could handle some tunes though. The adaptor thingy's – " Ollie reached over and opened the glove compartment, causing a stream of cassettes to spill over Jake's feet. " – here somewhere."

Jake looked at the van's ancient radio/cassette player, "Does it work in these old machines?"

"Not old mate, vintage," Ollie grinned. "Works the same as any other."

Ollie popped the ipod adaptor into the car stereo, quickly glancing down at the battered cassettes between Jake's worn Timberlands, "If you see anything embarrassing there it's probably Nicky's."

"Liar!" Jake plugged in the adapted cassette and scrolled through the selection. He grunted occasionally before finding one that met with his approval. "Is she seeing anyone?" he asked.

"Who? Nicky?"

Jake nodded.

"She's been off men for a bit." As soon as Ollie said that he realised it might give the wrong impression. "I don't mean she's into women or anything – at least not that I know of – " he added hastily. "Why?"

Jake ignored the question, sat back in his seat and gave a satisfied sigh, "I love this."

Ollie listened as crashing guitars kicked into the start of Learn To Fly by the Foofighters. "Mmmmm. I love it too." He was buzzing lightly now. Jake had been right. The Kensal Green batch had all the sparkle of a champagne cocktail. They were soon singing along to the song's chorus before the heavily vibrating van got Ollie's attention. He looked at the speedometer to find he was doing 85mph. "That song always gets me going. It's great to run to," Ollie smiled.

"It's great to wake up to."

Ollie eased off the volume, and the accelerator, until they were doing a quieter, more legal 70mph. It wouldn't do to get stopped, not with a tin full of grass and the van smelling like a gathering of Rastafarians had taken up residence.

"You know I saw them in concert years ago."

"Nicky and I saw them at the Astoria."

"Upstairs or downstairs?"

"Downstairs."

"Left or right side?"

"If you were facing the stage it would be on the left. We were next to the speaker stack, although I think the fact that Matt Dillon was in the vicinity – "

"With Brad Pitt?"

"Yeah," Ollie laughed, " – was the deciding factor in Nicky's choice of location."

"I was in the same place! It was so great wasn't it?"

"It was so great I bought the T-shirt *and* the poster. I felt like I was twelve years old."

Jake chuckled at the image before asking, "Can I be dj?"

"You're in charge," said Ollie. He looked at the fields

speeding by. "You know if I won the lottery I'd have that song on permanent loop in my Jag. As soon as I opened the door – bam! there it would be."

"Yeah," Jake said dreamily. "If I won the lottery I'd have the gasometers opposite me painted acid yellow and Trellick Tower painted turquoise."

"The day the world turned day-glo?"

"You bet."

"There's a gasometer on the way to Brighton that's painted bright blue," Ollie said, remembering with a pang of sadness the many journeys he had made to the south coast with James.

"I'd vote for a council with such an enlightened policy wouldn't you?"

"Are you eligible to vote?"

"Not at the cemetery where would they send the forms?"

Ollie smiled, enjoying the grass, enjoying the drive, the music and Jake's company.

And so the miles went by, tunes were played and replayed, the friendship strengthened, joints rolled, crisps, chocolate and fruit pastilles eaten. It was only when they stopped at a petrol station outside Doncaster that the reason for their journey was rammed home to them.

When Ollie finished walking Hum he returned to the van to find Jake, his arms filled with crisps and other goodies.

"Despite the current mode of transport I didn't really see you as 'white van man'," Ollie joked seeing a copy of the Sun under Jake's arm.

"I thought you should see this," Jake unfurled the tabloid newspaper. On the front was Nicky's black and white picture of Rion under the headline.

"Top Supermodel Missing!"

❧

Rion woke to the sound of metal upon metal. With the heater switched off it was cold in the vault, but the chill was preferable to the stuffy, gas-fired fumes of before.

She yawned, stretched and looked at her watch. Although she had only been asleep for little more than an hour it felt like days. Sleep had turned into something of a pastime here. With nothing to read, and precious few people to talk to, there was little else to do.

Through the heavy door, open ajar, she could see shadows dancing in the gloom accompanied by the occasional grunt of exertion.

"Gorby said it'll make her more valuable."

From his voice Rion could tell it was the twin she had named Senior. So she *was* being held for ransom!

"But won't it make it more dangerous?" Beck, the junior of the twins, asked.

The shadows came closer together. Another clash of metal brought a grunt before they danced apart. It seemed to Rion the twins were involved in a fencing match. She remembered the curious long swords she had seen in the barge. Rion looked over to the door where they were normally kept but the weapons weren't in place. The twins must be fencing enthusiasts or something peculiar.

In this Rion was not far wrong.

"Why should it?" Senior asked.

Rion could see the outlines of the Rosleagh boxes through the fine mesh. She felt comforted by their presence, and oddly grateful, it was like they were watching over her in a benign and loving way.

Rion looked around the vaulted cell to see if anything had changed since she'd been asleep. The guttering candle had been replaced by a tall, cleaner burning one, the Countess' chair still faced her family, a Sainsburys bag lay crumpled on the floor beside it. Rion didn't know they had Sainsburys in Ireland but didn't think too much about it. Her attention went back to the newspaper on the chair. She could see it was the Sun, if only she could see the date.

Rion's scream brought the twins rushing in. They found her one hand over her mouth, the other pointing at the newspaper on the other side of the bars.

"Is the fire on?" she desperately wondered if the leaky heater was again affecting her vision, but Rion could see the gas bars were unlit.

Her voice caught in her throat as she looked at the tabloid's front page. There was no mistake – well there *had* to be some mistake she thought, what else would explain her face on the front of Britain's biggest selling tabloid?

"Didn't know you were a supermodel," Beck's voice contained a hint of admiration and more than a hint of jealousy.

Rion didn't know either. "I – er – ," she began. She had to play this cool she realised. This meant that speaking, at least at this stage, was inadvisable. Abandoning any attempt at putting her thoughts into words Rion simply gestured through the bars for the newssheet to be passed to her.

The photographer used her sweetest of phone voices, "Justin it's Nicky." She thought about adding 'again', but decided that might sound facetious. She wanted to stay on his good side. At least at this stage.

"She's gone home," Lady Peter's personal assistant replied.

"Did you give her my messages?"

"Of course," Justin didn't bother to hide his irritation.

"Give me her number Justin. It's important."

The PA's sigh was clearly audible down the phone.

Nicky paused for a second. Although she felt ridiculous saying the next part Nicky thought she should give it a try, "Angie would *want* you to give it to me." Isn't that how you do it – plant a hypnotic suggestion in their mind, give it added emphasis and let them obey you?

"Do you want the obvious answer to that?"

Nicky realised her suggestion hadn't been hypnotic enough. Before she could repeat it Justin continued in his brusque fashion that bordered on unpleasantness.

"Lady Peters has had a very busy day. I know she and Sir Edwin have things to discuss. I'll tell her you phoned. Again."

"She would *want* – " Nicky began.

"I can't give you her home number. She left strict instructions not to be called."

"But – "

"But nothing."

"Well fu – " Nicky caught sight of Auntie Gem covering her ears. Thinking of an inoffensive expletive all she could come up with was, "Go boil your head!" which she shouted into the mouthpiece.

Auntie Em pulled the phone from her and placed it on the handset. "You don't want to say anything you might regret," she advised.

"Don't worry. He'd already put the phone down."

"Try Johnson again," Auntie Em suggested.

The lifestyle enhancer, incommunicado all day, answered after the first ring.

"Sweetie it's Nicky."

The silence was broken by what sounded like a muffled sob.

"Johnson?"

"It's too terrible isn't it?"

"About Rion?"

"I blame myself of course."

Typical, Nicky thought, make it about you. Much as she loved Johnson he never missed a chance of moving centre stage. She didn't encourage him by asking him exactly why he was to blame.

"Do you think she's been white-slaved?"

The question threw Nicky slightly.

"I – "

"Or starring in a blue movie?" Johnson continued, his voice beginning to rise in hysteria. "I've been reading all these dreadful, dreadful stories about ketamine – "

"Johnson I need Angie's number."

" – being slipped in drinks and the girls unknowingly finding themselves in a porn film – "

"I need Angie's number Johnson."

" – or waking up to find themselves being gangraped – "

"Johnson – "

" – or worse!"

Nicky couldn't – and certainly didn't want to – imagine anything worse. She sighed heavily. "We're all upset about Rion but there's a good chance nothing untoward has happened to her."

"After nearly a week?"

"Ollie and Jake have gone to Bridlington to see if she's gone home and – "

"That's the last place she'd go!"

"And the first place to look."

"Maybe at this very moment she's lying in a ditch or – " Johnson's voice trembled with emotion as his mind raced through all the macabre possibilities that Nicky was simply unwilling to hear.

"Johnson I need Angie's number urgently. It's about Rion."

Realising Nicky was reluctant to listen to his paranoia Johnson reeled off the Holland Park number. "Don't tell her I gave it to you."

Nicky put down the phone to find Aunties Gem and Em looking at her from the sofa.

"What did he say?" asked Gem.

Unwilling to give them a glimpse into Johnson's fevered and, hopefully, unfounded imaginings, Nicky simply said, "I have the number."

The editor of Glamourista switched on the fire in the panelled library. Her husband sat in his favourite armchair engrossed in the Sun. He had read and re-read the lead article on the missing young girl – a stroke of genius bumping Peters & Peters from the front page. Edwin folded his hands behind his head, leaned back and smiled, impressed once more by his wife's PR skills.

Angie refilled the Baccarat tumbler with Laphroaig and handed it to her husband. "Well?" she inquired.

"The only thing I'm not too keen on is the 'beleaguered husband' bit."

Angie rolled her eyes. "Really Edwin," she said, unable to hide her exasperation. "With Peters & Peters under fire from consumers and ministers alike, the value of the company in freefall and a PR blunder of such enormity it'll need a mountain of sandbags to shore up, I think beleaguered is the kindest description they could use."

"Just joking! It's a great – "

"After all they could have used 'useless'."

Edwin looked hurt, "Steady..."

"'In the shit' would fit," Angie continued.

"It's nice to see your poetry skills haven't left you," her husband sniped.

"Or even 'totally fucked'!!"

"They would never say that! It's a family newspaper."

"As the half-naked girl on page three proves," Angie retorted.

Edwin couldn't figure out how they had started bitching when all he had wanted was to thank his wife for taking the focus off him.

The ringing phone stopped their bickering turning into something nastier.

"Is Conchita in?" Edwin looked anxiously at his wife.

"I told her to take the night off."

"Answerphone on?"

Angie shook her head. "It's probably for me anyway," she said as she picked up the phone.

"Angie?"

The editor immediately knew who it was.

"Nicky. Sorry I haven't been able to call – things have been so hectic."

"Some days are like that."

"If only they were just days sweetie." There was a pause before Angie purred, "Where did you get my number?"

"You gave it to me at Wanda's – remember?" Nicky lied, remembering the editor's merry state after several glasses of Krug too many.

"Of course," Angie knew she hadn't given Nicky her phone number. She made a mental note to tick off Johnson. "It's just that I have to be careful otherwise all sorts of people – stylists, writers, photographers – " Angie let the point sink in, " – not you of course – " she added quickly, but not quickly enough, "will be phoning me at all hours."

Nicky let the intended slight slip.

"It's about Rion isn't it?" Angie continued. "You might think it strange but I just had to help. Especially after her photo came in with Johnson's – it's like fate isn't it?"

Auntie Em listening on the extension with Gem rolled her eyes.

"Also she was going to be Johnson's assistant therefore directly linked to us, directly linked to the family at Glamourista."

Poor Rion, Nicky thought, from one dysfunctional family to another.

"As a result I felt personally involved. When I saw the photo I called up Johnson straight away and said, 'that girl would be wasted assisting you'. I said it in a more diplomatic way of course – "

"Of course."

"She should be in front of the camera," the editor continued, "such bone structure and those eyes – "

"So you did it out of the goodness of your heart?"

"What else could I do? I *had* to help."

"Making up some story and getting her on the front page of the Sun – "

"Was the best thing, no? Firstly, people will be looking out for her, and secondly it'll do wonders for her career whenever she does show up. At the very least she'll have the cover and main story in that month's Glamourista."

Edwin chose that moment to make up for his earlier seeming ingratitude.

He opened the small fridge that some trompe-l'oeil specialist had disguised as part of the library shelves, and removed the everpresent bottle of pink Roederer 1999. Brandishing two fluted glasses at his wife he smiled and began to open the champagne they were so fond of.

"It's very upsetting I know – "

The pop of the cork was clearly audible at the other end of the phone.

" – and I can't tell you how devastated I am, but something good will come of it. You'll see."

As the phone clicked off Auntie Gem asked, "Was that a bottle of champagne being opened?"

"No doubt to mark her devastation," Nicky said dryly.

"But how does she know Rion?" Auntie Em asked.

"She doesn't. There was a mix-up in pictures.....she's just up to something."

"By the sound of popping corks it seems to be working."

"So she doesn't care about the girl?" Auntie Gem enquired.

"All she cares about are her title, the magazine's circulation and her husband – in that order."

Knowing Sir Edwin's crime, and unwilling to see him get away with it, Auntie Gem was sure more than ever that she had to do something. Obviously it was too late to do anything this Friday, but the next would be perfect.

24

STINGS LIKE A BEE

It had been easy to find the Ward household. All it had taken was a question to the landlord of the Hod & Carrier in the centre of town. Among the pub regulars, who were surprised as any to have found the family of a supermodel in their midst – even a supermodel no-one had heard of nor seen in the media – the consensus was that the Wards lived on the estate on the outskirts of town near Hildethorpe.

Ollie and Jake doublebacked on themselves before heading along the deserted, windswept seafront. "Is this where Dracula came ashore?" Jake peered through the windscreen at what should be Bridlington Bay but the night, and the rain, kept the immense sands from view.

"Wasn't that Whitby?"

"Or even Grimsby?"

Ollie sighed out noisily. "Imagine living somewhere like Grimsby – maybe it's a lovely place but the name alone," he shuddered, "would soon have you on Prozac."

"Life would have to be grim in Grimsby," Jake agreed.

"Whereas somewhere like Redcar couldn't fail to be a fun, soft-top down, wind-in-the-hair kind of place could it?"

"You've never been there have you?"

"No."

They stopped for directions at a chippie to find they were

closer than they thought. Standing behind a trio of raucous teen girls who guffawed at everything they said, then mimicked their southern accents, Jake and Ollie succumbed to hunger.

On the counter were copies of that day's tabloids, the Sun amongst them.

"You're gay aren't you?" one of the trio asked Ollie.

Before he could answer the second girl pointed to a particularly large sausage in batter, "You'll be having the savaloy then won't you?"

"Rather than the fish!" the first one added.

The girls fell about laughing. Not for the first time Ollie wondered at the perception, and foul language, of teenage girls.

"Is he your boyfriend?" the third asked curiously.

"No. He's straight."

"So there's a chance for us is there?" the middle one flicked her hair in an exaggerated fashion that bought another bout of uncontrollable giggles from her friends.

Jake winked at her, "Depends doesn't it?"

"On what?" the first one asked.

Jake pointed to the copies of that day's Sun lying on the counter. "On you telling us what you know about Rion," he said.

"D'ye mean Marion Ward?" the middle one sneered.

Ollie nodded, remembering that she would be known as Marion up here.

"She used to work in Tanya's Salon."

"Plain as wallpaper."

"Dull as piss."

"Quiet as a mouse."

The girls stared them down.

"Anybody would be quiet as a mouse next to you three," Ollie ventured with a smile.

This bought a round of "Oooohs," as if someone on a game show had admitted to something risqué or intellectual.

"Where is Tanya's Salon?" Ollie asked.

"Buy us our tea and we'll tell yer," the first one said.

Ollie went to the payphone on the wall. "Is Directory Enquiries 118 118 up here as well?" he asked Jake.

"We're not another planet you know," said the second girl.

Ollie dialled the six numbers. He got no further than 'Bridlington' before one of the girls pushed the receiver down.

"We'll tell yer."

At that moment the assistant grabbed a newspaper from the counter and wrapped their order. Beneath the plaice and chips liberally doused in vinegar Rion's face stared out at them.

It had been a long day.

Remembering Rion's account of her family life Ollie and Jake were unsure as to whether they could deal with a man such as her father at this time of night. They decided to head for Tanya's Salon instead.

The 'Ladies Hairdressers (Men accepted)' was found easily enough. It was in the middle of a small shopping arcade at the back of the main street. Several lights glowed through curtains in the flats above the precinct.

Peering into the darkened salon they were surprised by a voice from the flats, "Don't be doing anything silly now lads."

They looked up to find a woman leaning out the window above them.

"Do you know where we can find Tanya?" Ollie asked.

"She's gone away."

"Just our luck," Jake said to Ollie. "When's she going to be back?" he shouted up.

"If you're journalists she won't talk to you."

"We just want to ask about Rion."

"So you *are* journalists."

"No – we're – " Ollie began. He looked up to find the woman shaking her head in disgust. As she was about to close the window he added, "Tell Tanya we're friends of Rion from London."

"And how's she to know that?"

"Tell her it's Ollie of Meanwhile Gardens Mews."

The window slammed shut.

"It was worth a try," Ollie shrugged his shoulders. "Where to now?"

"Somewhere to stay?"

Ollie looked around the deserted mini-mall. It had begun to rain again. "Well, I'm not camping on the beach that's for sure, and neither is Hum – even if he is dressed for it."

The hound smiled up at him uncertainly, pleased to be out of the van but uncomfortable in the chunky red coat Auntie Gem had knitted for him.

"I don't know. I could easily rustle up a shelter, there's probably masses of driftwood and – "

"No! A November night dodging raindrops on Bridlington beach...such a thought should never, ever be imagined. Besides what would Dr Gidwani say?"

Jake threw up his hands.

"Better a lumpy mattress in some b & b than – "

" – a sandy one on Bridlington Beach?" Jake was unconvinced. "Starched sheets and paper thin walls over fresh air?"

Ollie wasn't listening. His attention had been taken by a light that had come on at the end of the salon behind him.

"Jake shhh!" he pointed to the silhouette coming towards them. "Maybe she'll know where we can stay."

They watched as the figure appeared to glide through the corridor of upright hairdryers in the darkened salon. As the figure came closer they could see it was the woman from the window.

She unlocked the glass door and beckoned them in, "I'm Tanya."

The woman led them between the portable basins to a smaller room entered by saloon doors. This side room didn't have such an overpowering smell of hairspray. It was also filled with sunbeds.

Near the entrance was a table piled high with women's magazines – magazines Rion would have escaped in Ollie thought sadly. Posters of empty tropical beaches lined the walls.

Tanya gestured to the tanning machines, "I don't use them myself but my clients can't get enough of them. It seems the more unsafe they're declared the more they want them." She went over to a sink beside which was a sideboard filled with mugs, "Tea?"

As she filled the kettle with water Ollie took a good look at the woman he knew to be Rion's best friend. She would be about five foot were it not for the thick platform slip-ons she wore. She was probably in her forties Ollie thought, but looked several years younger – a testament to the creams and therapies open to her as owner of a beauty salon. Her blonde hair was not obviously coloured. It was lightly teased and swept back in the fashion of a restrained Dolly Parton.

If there was such a thing.

"Sorry I was abit unfriendly before. There've been a couple of break-ins recently and journalists have been sniffing round. Who's your friend?"

Jake went over with hand outstretched, "I'm Jake."

Tanya smiled, "Pleased I'm sure." She returned to her tea-making.

"And this is Hum," Ollie gestured to the hound who was on his best behaviour.

"Milk and sugar?"

"Please," Jake and Ollie said in unison.

"Rion used to talk alot about you. You sent her savings to my house. She told me she kept her ipod and other things here," Ollie said.

"I used to pay her a pittance of her wages in cash, the rest I kept safe for her. Her father just drank everything she took home. If her sisters had seen the ipod it would've been fought over and broken within minutes." Tanya bought a plate of chocolate digestives towards them. She sat on the only chair, a rickety white plastic number and gestured to the tanning machines, "Have a seat, please." Ollie and Jake gingerly sat on the closed sunbeds. "Several journalists have been asking odd questions. Really," she snorted in disgust, "you'd think from the article that the Ward house is a place of happy childhoods. I tried telling them it's really West country but–"

Ollie and Jake looked questioningly at each other.

"Are we in the wrong place then?" Ollie asked.

"Should we be in Bristol?"

"Devon?"

"Somerset?"

"'West' country?" Tanya repeated, then seeing their confusion explained, "As in 'Rosemary and Fred'"

"Ah," Ollie and Jake got it.

" – but it wasn't the angle they were looking for. Mar – "

Tanya corrected herself, "Rion was lucky to get out when she did."

"We were going straight there but decided, from what Rion said, that perhaps Mr Ward should wait for the light of day."

"I'm not sure whether he's worse drunk or hungover – those are the only two states you'll find him in. Either way he's a nasty piece of work."

As the kettle whistled to a boil Tanya got up and emptied it into a teapot in the shape of a thatched cottage. "What's happened to Rion? Has she vanished?"

They told her all they knew.

When they'd finished Tanya said, "The only reason she'd come to Bridlington would be to see me and I haven't heard from her since she phoned all excited on Halloween."

"The night she disappeared," Ollie again felt guilty.

"She was all bubbly after the photo shoot with your friend."

"Johnson?"

"No, the photographer."

"Nicky?"

Tanya nodded, "Since then – nothing. But she's ok. I can feel it."

"We have to believe that."

"No. She is ok," Tanya said with certainty. "Rion and I – " she looked at the floor for a second before returning her gaze to Ollie and Jake. "You might think this stupid but – " Tanya shrugged her shoulders to show it didn't matter, "Rion and I have some sort of bond, it's what makes us so close."

"Like telepathy?"

Tanya wasn't sure, "Not as clearly defined as that. It's not words or anything, just feelings. I would always know exactly how she was at every second of the day. That's why it was so great when she went to London – yes there were bleak moments but in general happy feelings, sometimes verging on the joyous, came through."

"How is she now?"

Tanya paused for a moment to find the right words.

"For the past week I've been sensing she's more confused than fearful. Something's happened alright, but what and where I couldn't tell you." She got up to fill the kettle. "What I *can* tell you is she certainly wouldn't come back to see her family."

The following morning, having spent the night cocooned in the sunbeds, the brittle tanning elements softened by blankets, Ollie and Jake bade Tanya their farewells.

"Sorry again about the accommodation but it would have been more comfortable than upstairs. You wouldn't have got a wink all night with my lot."

Ollie quickly scribbled his number on a scrap of paper, "Call me if anything changes."

The Ward household stuck out from the other dismal semis on the estate by its hideous stonecladding. Jake checked the number again. "This is it: 328 Stovolds Avenue."

As the van drew up outside they could see the net curtains twitch.

Ollie looked at Jake, "Ready?"

"As I'll ever be."

With Hum growling by their side they went through the latch gate into the front garden that had been completely concreted over.

"'West Country'," Ollie pointed to the expanse of stone where not even a weed could be seen.

Jake shuddered, "Let's hope there's just soil under that."

The door opened before Ollie could knock. A young woman stood before them. Ollie figured she must be about twenty, although with her hair in pigtails she looked alot younger. Behind her he could see two other young women, Rion's sisters Ollie guessed, peering out from the first doorway. They also had their hair in braids and looked equally childish.

"Yes?" she enquired in a peculiar mix of insolence and nervousness.

"Unless they're offering money I'm not talking," a man's voice slurred from a nearby room. A crashing sound followed. Ollie and Jake watched as the other two sisters were elbowed out of the way and an illkempt man lurched into view. It could be no one else but Mr Ward.

"Did you hear me?" he staggered to the door and stared at them through bleary eyes. The man slapped his nearest daughter on the head, "Get me a Guinness if you know what's good for you."

The unfortunate girl scurried out of view.

"I'm selling my story to the highest bidder but," he bared his stained, English teeth, "I'm open to better offers."

Ollie again felt comforted by Hum's low growling.

The first daughter ran back with a can of beer that she opened, lightly spraying her father with foam.

"Now look what you've done!" he roared.

The girl dodged out of his way and ran back inside the house.

Mr Ward turned his attention to the two young men on his doorstep. "Did you hear me?" he asked again.

As he took a large sip from the can Ollie made a point of looking at his watch. It was ten thirty.

The gesture did not go unnoticed by Mr Ward. "The stress of Marion vanishing has done this," he leered at the can of beer in his hand. "This is all her fault," he put his face up to Ollie's, the rancid alcohol fumes caused the young man's eyes to water.

"I've agreed to go with the Sun, still negotiating but – " Mr Ward's face changed to something that on anyone else would probably be a smile but on him was more like a scowling smirk, "give me fifty pounds and – "

Unable to stomach any more of this Jake interrupted, "Mr Ward."

"Alright, alright, make it twenty five."

"Mr Ward," Jake began again.

"A tenner and that's my last offer."

"We're not – "

"Give us a fiver and I'll see you right."

"We're not giving you *anything*," Ollie said firmly.

Mr Ward squinted at them, confused all of a sudden, "You what?"

"You heard," Jake said. "We're friends of your daughter's from London. We came to see if you might know where she might be but it's obvious she wouldn't come here."

"Now lads if – "

"You burnt her wrists with cigarettes you fucking monster," Ollie couldn't contain himself.

Surprised by where the conversation was going Mr Ward regained his natural state. "So what if I did?" he glowered, wiping his nose on his sleeve. "She's my daughter isn't she?"

"So what if you did?" Ollie repeated enraged. "This is what!" he clenched his fist and sent it straight towards Mr Ward's eye. Rion's father fell back. His head hit the floor with a satisfying crack.

Jake was stunned for a second, "Ollie?"

Ollie rubbed his hand. As a nervous reaction he gave a winded laugh. The three daughters whispered amongst each other from the end of the hall but did nothing.

"Is he...?" Jake didn't dare say the word.

Ollie looked at the supine figure. "Oh my God," he said nervously, realising for the first time what he might have done.

Jake pulled him by the shoulder, "C'mon."

Hum rushed into the house and gave a quick nip to the man's exposed ankle before running out again.

As they left through the latchgate they heard Mr Ward groan.

"C'mon!" Jake said more urgently.

Before they had gone a few yards a bellow was heard signalling Mr Ward was conscious once more. Ollie and Jake hopped in the van, did a quick u-turn and sped from the estate.

Jake laughed, "Rocky Marciano, Muhammed Ali, Ollie Michaelson!"

"Do you think he's alright?"

"I hope not! I bet he won't even remember it though. Guys like that exist in permanent blackout." Jake chuckled and gave Ollie a playful punch, "Floats like a butterfly, stings like a bee!"

25

DANCE IS RELIGION, RELIGION IS DANCE

What was going on? What *was* going on?

Rion still hadn't got over the picture of herself on the front of yesterday's Sun. *Tipped for the top by the editor of top-selling Glamourista* ran the headline. What was going on? she asked herself for the umpteenth time.

As soon as Rion saw the accompanying picture of Lady Peters she knew exactly who she was – Jake's lady friend with the dazzling turquoise pumps. But why hadn't Jake told her about the editor of Glamourista when he knew Rion's ambition was to work there?

Perhaps he didn't know. That could be the only explanation. The connection must have been through Nicky and Johnson. Rion was certain they knew Lady Peters, they'd said as much hadn't they?

But why was Lady Peters tipping her, tipping Rion for the top? And the top of what exactly? It seemed so unfair! Here she was being acclaimed for something, when she was hidden God only knew where unable to take advantage of God only knew what.

What was going on?

A raucous filing broke into her thoughts. After a brief stint with a powertool Senior and Beck had returned to manually severing the cast iron bars.

"I bet you wish you had that electric saw!" Rion said with her knack for stating the obvious. The miniature Black & Decker they had brought in yesterday, whilst making their work easier, had nearly been their downfall. Rion's surprise appearance on the front of the Sun had meant frequent unannounced visits from Ted, Mary and Gorby who came to wonder at their newly valuable prize. The sound of a powerdrill would have been hard to explain.

Rion had hoped to engage the twins in conversation but Senior simply grunted whilst Beck ignored her completely.

"How long do you think it'll take you?" she asked.

Senior shrugged his shoulders, "As long as it takes."

Rion watched as he carried on sawing with Beck. It seemed every few minutes another fresh blade was needed, the teeth of the previous one soon dulled and bent useless.

"They didn't want to make it easy for you did they?"

Rion got tired just watching them and then got tired *of* watching them but there was nothing else to occupy her mind in the Rosleagh vault. She felt her several attempts at conversation had been discouraged: what subject could she pick that would bring forth more than a grunt and a monosyllabic reply?

In the corner by the door she saw what could provide a good topic. She waited until the next break, which wasn't long in coming.

"What do you do with those swords?"

Beck brushed his hair away from his face, "You'll find out soon enough."

Rion had already decided she didn't like the more junior of the twins. The combination of weakness and power reminded the girl of her father.

"Shhhh," Senior glared his brother into silence.

"Do you fence with them?" she continued.

"Something like that."

"If this was *Give us a Clue* I'd be out by now wouldn't I?"

The twins didn't even grunt a reply.

Rion tried again, "Well, what makes them so special?"

Senior looked at the floor in a gesture of humbleness that made Rion suddenly warm to him. "You'll only laugh," he said. "People always do."

"People that don't understand always do," his brother corrected.

"Try me."

Senior held Rion's eye for several seconds, closely examining her face for any reaction to what he was going to say. Just when Rion was tempted to look away Senior broke the silence, "We're Morris Dancers."

Conscious of the watching twins Rion knew her first reaction – a smirk – would be the wrong one. She managed to control herself by opening her eyes wide as if madly interested.

"You don't think that's funny?" Beck asked.

"Most people do," Senior added.

"Someone even wrote a book called, 'I'll try anything once except Incest and Morris Dancing'," his brother said in disgust.

"Maybe if they knew more they wouldn't laugh, I mean loads of things seem funny at first don't they?" Rion gushed.

The answer seemed to please the twins.

Encouraged Rion carried on, "What people see are men with bells on their toes waving hankies in the air – " Rion saw the twins exchange a quick look and realised she mustn't be seen to be taking the piss. " – when I'm sure there's much more to it than that isn't there?"

Senior was unsure for a moment whether to confide his

passion or not. Again he examined Rion's face but could discern no hint of amusement. "Much more!" he said, unable to contain his enthusiasm.

"People only mock what they don't understand," Rion echoed Beck's earlier thought. She knew she was on the right track when Senior jumped up, his eyes gleaming in the candlelight.

"Exactly!" Senior strode to the end of the vault, executed a neat spin on one heel then strode back. "They don't realise that the dance is a sacred act – dance is religion and religion is dance." He pulled his brother to his feet, "C'mon. I'll be the Foreman."

Beck wasn't as willing as his twin but upon his urging followed his steps. Their legs swayed and flashed as they moved in complex co-ordinated rhythms. Occasional high leaps punctuated the steps as they came to an end of the stanza. The moves were then repeated backwards.

Although at first finding it difficult to conceal her amusement Rion was soon gripped by the hard and fast pace of the dance. Mesmerised by the swirls and patterns she was relieved when the twins, with a final leap, came to face each other and stopped. Breathing heavily the twins broke the trance and moved away from each other.

"Well?" Senior asked, his chest rising and falling.

Rion didn't know what to say and so, impressed, just opened her mouth and shrugged her shoulders.

"Those steps are the same as the ones danced in the courts of Celtic warlords."

Rion managed to regain her powers of speech, "It's so complicated."

Senior smiled, "The more intricate the steps, the more the need to concentrate, the more the conscious mind is occupied, the more the spirit is able to soar."

As Rion took it all in Beck spoke up, "Every birth, marriage and celebration, each planting, harvest and change of the moon, each sacrifice," Beck paused, "each death.... "

Rion didn't notice as Senior glared at his twin to stop.

" – for all of these the dance is needed."

"It's the way to communicate with the Gods," Senior said.

"But the success of everything depends on the accuracy of the steps, of the ritual."

Deciding his brother had spoken enough Senior pulled him to his feet. "Let's show her something different." He went over to the door, picked up one of the long swords and tossed it over to Beck who caught it with ease.

Rion, all trace of amusement gone, watched entranced as the twins again went into the demanding, repetitive steps this time accompanied by intricate swordplay.

26

HUM ON THE CASE

The journey up from Bridlington had been easier than the journey down. They had made much better time – at least forty minutes Ollie calculated – on the previous day. As Ollie swung the van through the cemetery gates Jake gestured for him to pull over.

"Let's walk down. It deflects attention and – " Jake yawned, " – I need to stretch my legs."

"So does Hum."

In his red coat the hound bounded past the monuments and mausolea of Centre Avenue. Ollie didn't bother calling to Hum who wouldn't come to him anyway. The dog knew Ollie waited with collar and lead – there were too many scents in the cemetery for him to waste time at his master's side.

Ollie never ceased to be amazed at the tombs on this, the cemetery's main thoroughfare. Pyramids, sphinxes, winged cherubs, griffins, canopies, columns and sarcophagi all vied for attention in the maze of burial plots.

As they came to the Anglican Chapel Jake stopped, the top of his tree visible above the hillock in front of them. "It's good to be home isn't it?"

Ollie smiled, "It will be when I get there."

Before Jake could head for the canal they were stopped by a woman's distant voice, "Ollie! Ollie!"

They turned to see a figure hurrying along the muddy track beneath the huge chestnut trees. Ollie waved, instantly recognising who it was. "What's Nicky doing here?" he wondered.

Within a few moments the photographer arrived breathless beside them. "You drove right past me!" she complained. Unused to the sudden bout of exercise Nicky steadied herself against Ollie, "I was having lunch at William 1V – "

Ollie looked at his watch. "Until four 'o clock?"

"It was with a stylist," Nicky gasped, "and you know how they can talk."

Ollie nodded in sympathy.

"Good trip?" she asked.

Jake put his head to one side and thought for a second. "It was interesting," he conceded. "I'm sure Ollie'll tell you about it."

Whilst Nicky caught her breath Ollie whistled for Hum.

"Where's the hound?"

"Last seen scampering – " Ollie gestured through to the colonnade on the near side of the chapel, " – thataway."

Ollie whistled again – but no Hum. For the third attempt he whistled with more authority, more threat, more of a, 'if you don't come back now I'll be very angry', kind of edge.

Nothing.

"You'd better go ahead," he said to Jake. "Who knows where Hum might be?"

"Make sure you stop in before you go. There's a tin of Kensal Green with your name on it," Jake bowed his head in farewell and set off down Terrace Avenue towards the canal.

"A batch of sparkling marijuana never did anyone any harm eh?" Nicky took his arm as they wandered beneath the porticoes onto the flagstone terrace.

"Hum," Ollie called as if he had a present for him, a frisbee perhaps, or rawhide bone. He expected the dog to come tearing out of some hiding place at any moment, to jump up – eyes sparkling with amusement – before sitting at his feet, tail wagging, awaiting the patting and petting that would tell him all was ok.

"Do you ever think of dog training?" Nicky asked, her breathing almost back to normal.

"There are times I think of little else," Ollie replied. "Hum," he called again, trying to keep the annoyance from his voice.

Nicky put up her hand as a muffled barking was heard. "What was that?"

Ollie listened but the unclear sound had stopped. "Hum?" Again they heard a muted barking. They followed the sound, which appeared to be coming from the side of the chapel. Ollie whistled once and was rewarded with another round of barking. "It sounds like he's scared but where is he?"

They ran to the back of the chapel, soon discovering a metal grille about eighteen inches wide that lined the side of the building.

"What's down there?" Nicky asked.

"The cellars or foundations I imagine."

"Hum!" Nicky's call brought forth a pattering of feet. "Here he is!"

The dog, looking snug in his little red jacket, appeared out of the darkness below them.

"How did you get down there?" Ollie asked in exasperation.

Hum gave a friendly bark in reply before heading back into the shadows.

"Hum!" Ollie put the authoritarian tone in his voice. It did the trick. The hound returned under the grille. He looked at the worried faces above him, wagged his tail and grinned before vanishing into the darkness once more.

"Dog school, dog school, dog school," Ollie muttered. "Try and keep him here if he comes back."

"How??"

"I'll go and see if anyone's around." Ollie dashed to the front of the building but the chapel, as always, was closed. A clumsily typed notice on the door told him that tours of the cemetery and catacombs took place every Sunday at 2:00pm. Ollie suddenly had a dreadful thought. He ran back to where Nicky waited above the grille.

"Can't we just leave him there for a couple of days?" Nicky said. "It might teach him a lesson."

"It's tempting," Ollie had to admit, "but I think we should get him out as soon as possible because – "

"You're too soft on him Ol."

" – because I think he's in the catacombs."

Nicky came to the realisation Ollie had come to moments before. "You don't mean – ?"

"I do. Imagine the fun he would have with shrouded corpses."

"Or human bones," Nicky shuddered, macabre images of a marrow-hungry Hum filling her mind.

They quickly found what they were looking for. Beside the colonnade a section of metal grille had rusted and collapsed inwards. About ten feet below stone glistened damp and hard. Looking down they could see a narrow ledge running halfway along the wall.

"If nothing else we'll at least be able to get back out."

"We?" Nicky asked.

"Of course," Ollie began lowering himself through the narrow space. "I'm not going in there alone."

Cursing Hum, Nicky followed. Her feet easily found the

ledge and from there she jumped to the floor, landing beside Ollie with a thump that echoed across the flagstones.

"Are you ok?" Ollie whispered.

"Sort of."

"Curiosity killed the cat, Hum," Ollie muttered. "What might it do to a stupid hound?"

Or an even stupider human? Nicky thought unhappily.

Ollie lifted the collar of his coat and pulled it tighter around him. His eyes slowly adjusted to the gloom. He could see a passage stretching into the darkness at the end of which was another dim shaft of light. That must be the other side of the chapel Ollie realised. He could also make out the outline of another passage cutting through the middle of the building.

"Hum!" he whispered.

"Why are you whispering?" Nicky said out loud. "Who's going to hear you?"

"Who's going to hear me?" Hearing his own voice gave Ollie a measure of confidence. With a hint of a swagger he set off into the unknown and rather scary.

"Wait for me!" Nicky hurried behind him.

Floor-to-ceiling archways lined the passage. Some were caged with iron bars, some had been bricked up and others were closed by solid iron doors with elaborate gothic locks.

"As if dying wasn't bad enough imagine being put somewhere like this!" Ollie exclaimed.

"D'you hear anything?"

Ollie stopped and listened but there was nothing to alert him to Hum's presence. All that could be heard was an occasional dripping as water seeped from the ground above into the underground chambers. There was no hint of the traffic or trains, nor of the planes stacking overhead getting ready to land at Heathrow.

"It's so quiet," Ollie said amazed. "Some might say a deathly hush filled the space."

Nicky gave a reluctant chuckle, more of nervousness than of mirth, "Or a deadly silence."

A sudden shiver flared down Ollie's spine. He jumped swiftly to the centre of the passage, the vision of skeletal hands reaching through the bars had suddenly become unbearable.

Nicky whistled softly. "Hum!" she implored, but there was nothing, not a distant bark, not a muffled patter of paws, nothing.

Coming to the main passage Ollie looked up and down to find countless other corridors opening off it in some strange subterranean grid.

Nicky whistled again and was rewarded by a flash of colour running across the centre passageway several corridors up. In his little red coat, she thought, this was too Julie Christie, too *Don't Look Now* for words.

Ollie strode purposefully onwards until something happened to stop him in his tracks. He felt it first around his face as it exploded up from the ground. Yelling with both hands raised he pushed it away and jumped back, still pummelling the air with his hands. This incident caused Nicky's already frayed nerves to shred further. Unable to restrain herself she let out an alarming scream.

It took a while for them to realise what had happened, even longer for their hearts to slow down. The startled pigeon fluttered a few yards down the nearest side corridor before stopping and twitching nervously.

"Go towards the light!" Ollie shooed the bird towards the dim glimmer at the end of the passage. The bird hopped a few steps but was unsure. "Towards the light!" he hissed, feeling uncomfortably like a new age guru preaching to his disciples.

"Set it free Ol!"

"But – " Ollie was unsure on two counts; unsure whether he could catch the poor bird even if he wanted to and unsure whether he could find his way back to the broken grille anyway. He took a deep breath in the hope it would make the decision making easier. "Maybe this is his home," he reasoned. "Maybe freeing it would leave a nest of hungry chicks – " before Nicky could comment Hum's familiar bark was heard. Saved from the ornithological dilemma Ollie moved quickly on, his eye taken by faint phosphorescence on the wall ahead of him.

Nicky had also seen the odd gleaming. "Is that a light switch?"

"I bet it doesn't work," Ollie jabbed the button with his fist. To his relief three bare bulbs, evenly spaced along the dank walls, fizzled into action. Lines of side passages stretched before him in the wan glow. The entrances to some were closed with thick doors whilst others remained open.

"There he is!" Ahead of them Hum slipped into a side corridor through a heavy door open ajar. "Come here!" Ollie ordered now totally fed up with the hound. "I have three words for you Hum – " he said the words slowly and clearly: "Battersea. Dogs. Home."

As if to express the dog's indifference the lights chose that moment to go out.

"I'll get it," Ollie fumbled his way back towards the switch. As he pressed the oddly luminescent circle he jumped back screaming, feeling warm flesh and fingers beneath his own.

When the lights flickered into their dull wattage what Ollie saw caused the cry to die in his throat and to rise in Nicky's. Illuminated in the glow was a bald man with an impressive purple birthmark across the centre and side of his head. Ollie knew who it was in a second – the unfriendly cemetery guard who had been sniffing around Rion's place on the canal.

Gorby also recognised Ollie.

"I – " Ollie began but his chest was still constricted with fear.

"How did you get down here?" Gorby asked in a mystified, although slightly menacing, tone.

"My dog – " Ollie took in a huge gulp of air, " – must have fallen through somewhere."

In the silence the guard slowly looked Ollie up and down. "Haven't we spoken about this sort of thing before?" he asked.

Ollie knew full well they had but refused to answer.

"If he'd been on a lead this wouldn't have happened."

"And if the area around the chapel hadn't been so unsafe this wouldn't have happened," Nicky retorted. "Imagine if a child had fallen down here, you need signs at the front warning of the danger."

Feeling the guard's eyes on him caused an involuntary shiver to ripple through Ollie's body.

"Where's the dog now?" Gorby asked.

As if on cue a snarling was heard from where Hum had vanished moments before.

Ollie made for the corridor with the huge door open ajar, but was stopped by the guard. "Stay here," Gorby ordered.

As another snarling was heard, this time louder, Ollie pushed past the guard, "You want me to get my dog I'll get him!"

Quickly followed by Gorby and Nicky, Ollie shoved open the heavy door. He found himself in a side corridor like all the others. Several of the vaults in this smaller passage had been bricked up although some remained caged and open to view. Light spilled from under one closed with a door.

It was from this one that again the snarling began.

"Hum!" Ollie called.

The door to the vault opened a crack and a man with tightly set eyes peered out. He held the struggling, snapping dog at arm's length in front of him. Just as it seemed Hum was going to deliver a nasty nip to his captor the man dropped him, nodded to the guard and quickly closed the door. The dog continued pawing at the iron door upon which a coat of arms could be seen. Ollie picked Hum up, held him close and took a quick glance through the spyhole. Even though it was made for inside looking out Ollie could see a blurred image of what looked like three people.

"It's a private vault," Gorby pulled Ollie away from the peephole. With one arm firmly around the young man and the other around Nicky, the guard shepherded them out of the passage.

Inside the Rosleagh vault Beck had his hand over Rion's mouth while Senior stood with his back against the door. In a fury Rion bit into Beck's fingers. "Help!" she yelped before Senior and his twin restrained her.

The dog struggled in his arms upon hearing the stifled cry. "What was that?" Ollie asked.

Gorby gave no indication of having heard anything. "What was what?" he asked impatiently.

"Didn't you hear it?" Nicky, unsure whether she had heard anything or not, spoke up in support of Ollie.

"Hear what?" the guard firmly closed the door before they could go back to the small corridor. "I must ask you to leave. Our clients come here to be with their loved ones. They do not appreciate intrusion in any form." Gorby gestured for them to follow him down the central passageway, "Please."

Ollie looked back, he sensed something was going on but didn't know what to do.

Gorby again began to shepherd them down the centre passageway. "Please," he said more firmly.

They shrugged off the guard's grip and followed.

"What are your names?" Gorby took a small pocketbook from his jacket.

Without thinking Ollie answered, "Oliver Michaelson." He could have kicked himself as the words spilled out. How many times had he told Nicky never to give your real name to officials in dodgy situations?

Nicky remembered Ollie's oft-repeated advice even if he hadn't. "Carina Fitzboodle," she replied coolly.

Gorby jotted the names down, snapped the notebook shut with a flourish and returned it to its place. After twenty yards he turned off the centre passageway onto some narrow stone stairs that wound their way up to the ground level. Nicky and Ollie followed a few paces behind, Ollie inwardly cursing his own stupidity.

They walked in silence through the neglected chapel, its once grand ceiling depicting the heavens now sadly showing signs of decay, before leaving through the main entrance.

"Keep your dog on a lead," Gorby said.

Before Ollie could think of a suitable reply the enormous chapel door clanged shut behind him.

"I can't believe you gave him your real name!" Nicky said astounded. "How many times – ?"

"I know. I know," Ollie stood under the Doric columns. After a few seconds lost in thought he turned to his friend, "There were three people in that vault."

"Are you sure?"

"No – well, yes, – I think so," he kicked the ground in exasperation. "God Nicky – who knows?"

Nicky put her arms around him, "Maybe they were just mourners like he said."

"Maybe," but Ollie wasn't convinced.

Defiantly keeping Hum off the lead they set off towards the van. In his preoccupied state Ollie forgot to collect his tin of Kensal Green that Jake had so kindly kept for him.

"Get her ready," Gorby pulled Beck to one side. "Do you need any more?" he whispered out of reach of Rion's hearing.

"K?" Beck asked, referring to the horse tranquillizer they had been using to subdue the young girl.

Gorby nodded.

"There's loads left."

"Make sure nothing goes wrong." Before Gorby left he took a quick look at Rion who sobbed on the mattress, her face to the wall.

"When do you expect to move?" asked Senior.

"Soon enough."

Enough time, Senior hoped, to retrieve the jewels and return the bars to their original state.

Senior peered after Gorby as he left down the corridor. Satisfied that he had gone the leader of the twins returned to the Rosleagh vault. "Come on," he went to unlock Rion's section, "stop the waterworks."

Still sobbing the young girl looked up at him. Her eyes were red from crying. In a rage she got up from the mattress and clung to the bars. "What do you want from me?" she screamed at the twins.

Senior rethought his plans to let her out and put the key back in his pocket.

Rion was scared.

But for the first time since her ordeal began she dared to

hope. The sight of Hum had at once confused her and raised her spirit. It meant she must still be near Meanwhile Gardens – at least she wasn't in Ireland – it also meant people were looking for her. Where Hum was, Ollie and the rest couldn't be far behind.

It didn't take her long to figure out that she must be in the catacombs beneath Kensal Green Cemetery.

The twins observed her, Beck blankly, Senior more troubled. Rion felt her eyes well up again. She returned to the mattress, held the blankets tightly to her and stared at the damp, pockmarked bricks. After a few seconds she reached into her back pocket. Rion removed the cutting of Blondin and smoothed it out. She stared at the familiar image of the tightrope walker with the frying pan in hand, the waters of Niagara crashing beneath him.

What would he have done?

Behind her the twins carried on sawing, each minute bringing them closer to the Rosleagh jewels they were so determined to possess.

All was quiet when Ollie finished recounting the recent events in Bridlington and in the catacombs. Gem 'n Em looked at each other in slight bewilderment before Auntie Em stood up and went to the phone, "Neil should know about this." They listened in silence as she tried dialling up her tame inspector, but without success. "Neil's off duty until tomorrow. They wouldn't give me his mobile number."

"We'll phone him first thing," Nicky reassured her.

"What do you think was going on in the catacombs?"

"Only Hum knows don't you boy?" Ollie stroked the dog that had squeezed on the sofa beside him. "There aren't many times I wish he could talk but this is one of them."

Hum pricked up his ears as if aware he was being talked about before scrambling from the sofa and dashing down the stairs. A knock at the door followed.

"I'll get it," Nicky said, following the dog.

Gem 'n Em and Ollie strained to find out who it was but all they could hear were muffled voices. Moments later Jake appeared.

"Thought you should know the guards at the cemetery have blocked off Heron Point – there's still a way in of course, at least to old lags like me," he smiled. "Also," Jake handed a battered tobacco tin to Ollie, "you forgot this."

"Thanks mate. You didn't have to bring it round though. I could have collected it tomorrow."

"Yeah, well, I – " Jake shuffled his feet before looking up.

Ollie wasn't the only one to notice the slightly bashful smile that passed between Jake and Nicky.

"Would you like to stay for supper Jake?" Auntie Em asked quick as a flash. "We have plenty."

27

UNCOMMON JEWELS

Rion woke to excited cries. She turned to see Beck reaching through the bars for the studded green velvet box that lay at the foot of the Earl of Rosleagh's similarly clad coffin.

"This is it!" Senior crowed triumphantly.

Beck's hands inched towards the jewel box, "Nearly there!" With a yelp he touched it, got his fingers around the back and manoeuvred it into his other hand. Slowly, slowly he pulled the studded box out until he held it, arms trembling, before his brother.

"Feel the weight of it!" Beck said impressed.

Rion looked on as Senior took the box from his twin. He balanced it in his hands and shook it slightly, smiling with satisfaction upon hearing the jewels inside rattle about.

Beck sat down on the Countess of Rosleagh's elaborate chair. "Open it!" he implored.

Senior examined the box from all angles. He tipped it upside down, grinning each time the stones rolled from one end to the other. After a while he found what he was looking for.

"You don't get craftsmanship like that any more," he pointed to the rose on the Rosleagh coat of arms. "D'ye see?"

Beck looked closely at the studded velvet box. "See what?"

Rion tried to make out that she wasn't interested but looked on from the corner of her eye.

With the thinnest blade on his penknife Senior lifted a petal of the intricately carved rose. "There," he identified a tiny, narrow slit, "that'll be it." Senior poked his blade through the slot and wriggled it about. He smiled when the top of the box sprang open.

"Yes!" Beck clapped his hands in excitement.

Rion had given up the pretence of being disinterested and looked on with curiosity.

"Well?" Beck asked with bated breath as Senior peered in. "What do you see?"

Unable to bear the silence Beck grabbed the box from his brother. He reached in with one hand, rummaged around and brought up a shiny object the size and shape of an old worn cricket ball. The uneven rock was of so dark a red it was almost black.

"What the..." Beck's voice trailed off as he looked at the object, trying to make out what on earth it was.

He placed the box on his knee and reached in. His fingers closed around smooth oval objects. Opening his palm Beck found two reddish/black stones there, both the size and shape of duck eggs. "Rubies?" he asked hopefully.

Senior pulled out another object from the jewel box. This was also of the same reddish/black as the others but was flatter and somewhat elliptical. He placed it with the cricket ball and duck eggs.

Beck looked at his brother as a child might upon discovering there was no such thing as Father Christmas. "They're not jewels are they?"

"They might be," Senior said hopefully. He scratched his head, trying for the life of him to think what they might be.

"Maybe this is what they look like uncut," Beck began,

his imagination fired up once more. "Maybe this is how raw emeralds are."

Senior caught some of his twin's enthusiasm, "The darkest sapphires perhaps!"

Beck's eyes flashed, "Or black diamonds!"

Rion scoffed. Having been at school more recently than the twins she had already guessed what they were. A chuckle grew into a chortle that grew and grew until she had to hold on to the bars to support herself, her body doubled up, convulsed with loud, rollicking laughter. She finally slowed to a more modest giggle that subsided into a half-smile and smirks.

"You don't know what they are do you?" she asked.

Beck looked at her in annoyance whilst Senior turned away. Seeing their faces caused another outbreak of hoots and cackles. After her time in confinement Rion took release in the laughter that wracked her body. Each time the bouts subsided all it took was a glance at the objects or a look at the twins' expressions for her to burst into uncontrollable hysterics.

Finally she was able to rein in her merriment. "Don't you ever watch those programmes about the pharaohs and ancient Egypt?" she asked between giggles.

The twins looked at her suspiciously.

"If you did you'd know the secrets of embalming."

"So?" Beck asked, his irritation at an all time high.

"So?" Rion managed to force down a giggle that was brewing in her belly. "You'd know they remove the internal organs first."

Beck shrivelled his nose. "You mean they're – ?"

Rion nodded, "His heart, kidneys and liver!" Rion felt the giggle grow and grow. "If you look in the 'jewel box,'" she couldn't help sniggering, "you'll probably find his stomach and intestines as well."

For some reason this struck her as funnier than the others. She doubled up again before collapsing on the bed, her eyes streaming tears of laughter. Rion wrapped her arms around her stomach that was aching from the strain.

Her laughter was unfortunately shortlived.

What happened next stunned them all into a horrified silence. A strange knocking was heard coming from inside the bars. They looked around before Senior gasped, "It's the Earl!"

As one they looked at the shelf at eyelevel. The studded coffin in faded green velvet was beginning to rattle and jump about as if caught in an earthquake.

Or as if something inside was trying to get out.

The twins exchanged a horrified look. There was a second of silence before they all screamed.

Beck had turned a ghastly white. "Phone Gorby!" he gasped.

"But – " Senior gestured to the space in the bars, to the mess, to the studded velvet box, " – what are we going to tell him about this?"

"Just phone him!"

"And let me out of here!" Rion hugged the wall as far away as possible from the angry Earl. Although she was separated from the Rosleagh coffins by a heavy wire mesh it seemed much, much too close. "I'll tell Gorby about the box," she threatened.

Senior glared at the young girl before unlocking her side. "Is the drill still here?"

Beck swooped on a bag in the corner. He pulled out the Black & Decker, "Yes."

"We'll say we used it to try and do something to the coffin."

Beck looked wildly at his brother, "Do what?"

"I don't know – something!"

Senior threw the Earl's internal organs into their box and hurriedly shoved it through the bars where it landed some way from the rattling, juddering coffin.

Gorby sat in front of the computer in the gloomy office, playing and replaying the film of Rion running laughing around the grave of Princess Sophia. The carefree young girl was perfect...she really was. The jangling office phone broke into his reverie. It was the twins – what would they do without him?

Senior clicked off the phone, "Thank God he was upstairs." He grabbed Rion by the hand and ran into the corridor. Beck swiftly followed. "Leave all the talking to me," Senior slammed the vault door. "And you," he looked at Rion, "don't say a word."

They waited in the dimly lit corridor, flinching at every rattle they could hear through the vault door. After what seemed like an age they heard footsteps racing down the outside corridor. The heavy door was flung open and Gorby stood there, his head gleaming under the lightbulb.

"What on earth is going on?" he asked, slightly out of breath and more than surprised to see the twins and Rion outside the Rosleagh vault.

"The Earl!" Senior hissed.

"What?"

Beck gestured to the closed door that bore the oppressive coat of arms, "He's alive!"

Gorby had now heard the peculiar rattling. He put his head to one side and listened. Fearlessly he opened the heavy door and walked in. The twins and Rion peered nervously after him.

"How long has this been going on?" Gorby asked in a remarkably cool manner, Rion thought, for someone standing before a rattling coffin.

"A couple of minutes," Senior said hurriedly. "We drilled through the bars to see if – "

Gorby stopped him. "You drilled through the bars?" he boomed, his voice echoing around the small space.

The twins looked at each other nervously.

"Yes," Senior said almost timidly.

"With what?"

Beck rushed over to the bag in the corner and pulled out the Black & Decker. "With this," he thrust the miniature powertool at Gorby before running back into the corridor.

"Have you a drill head?" asked Gorby. "Quick!"

Beck glanced at the rattling coffin and weighed up his chances. Crossing himself quickly he dashed back into the vault, grabbed the bag and ran out with it. In the safety of the corridor he pulled out the small pack of attachments. "Found it!" he waved the drill head at Gorby.

"What are you waiting for?" the guard urged.

"Holy Mary Mother of God," Beck began as he charged over to Gorby. With shaking hands he changed the head on the powertool, all the while reciting the names of saints and the various promises he would keep if they would only let him out of there unharmed. With a final twist Beck secured the drill head and returned it to Gorby.

"Anyone got a match?" Gorby asked.

"He wants a cigarette!" Senior whispered amazed to Beck and Rion. He reached in his pocket and pulled out a box of Swan Vestas which he threw at the guard.

Gorby reached into the inside pocket of his jacket and withdrew a ballpoint pen. He pulled out the ink cartridge with his teeth to leave only the plastic pipe.

Rion looked on agog. "What's he doing?"

The guard started up the powertool and began drilling a hole in the coffin. He got through the first layer of wood with ease, the subsequent layer of lead took longer. Finally they saw his hand jerk forward. Gorby quickly removed the drill. He filled the hole it had made in the Earl's coffin with the barrel of the ballpoint pen.

"Ooooh," Rion said in disgust. She pinched her fingers over her nose as an overwhelming stench filled the space.

Gorby pulled out the box of matches and struck one on the bars of the vault. As the sulphur ignited he held the flame to the barrel of the pen protruding from the coffin. A whooshing sound was heard as a flare of green and blue flames shot halfway across the room.

Watching from the corridor the twins and Rion jumped back in horror.

The flare grew smaller. The flames changed from their initial colours to a more normal orangey red until with a final gasp they petered out altogether.

It was noticeable that the rattling had stopped.

"It's ok," Gorby said, seeing the awestruck expressions staring at him. "This sometimes happens with the older coffins. The gases just build and build until they reach feverpitch. Lead coffins have been known to explode. Imagine," he looked at Rion and smiled, "what a mess that would cause."

Gorby gave the drill to Senior, "We need to move." He looked around the vault, "I feel we'll have visitors tomorrow."

Before the guard left he reminded the twins. "Make sure she has something to eat and *drink,*" he said pointedly. "We don't want her getting dehydrated," Gorby winked at the twins who nodded their understanding.

Even after the long drive from Bridlington, the wine and

spliffs at dinner, Ollie found he couldn't sleep. By all rights he should be dog-tired. Hum certainly was. Ollie could hear the hound's gentle wheezing from deep under the covers. His mind raced back to the vault in the catacombs – who had been in there? Were they still there?

Ollie inched his way out of bed, careful not to disturb Hum from his nest under the blankets and duvet. He dressed quickly, found his torch and tiptoed down the stairs. It crossed his mind to take the dog but in this situation, where stealth might be needed, it was best to let sleeping dogs lie.

Feeling peculiarly defenceless without Hum Ollie avoided the canal. He ambled along Kensal Road, empty at this time of night, to the top of Ladbroke Grove. From the middle of the bridge Ollie looked over the shadowy mass of the cemetery. Remembering Jake's words he tried the side door adjoining the Dissenters Chapel. He was both relieved and troubled when it opened to his touch.

Now there was no turning back.

Steeling himself Ollie slipped into the cemetery. It wasn't as scary as he thought it would be. There was no need for the torch. The nearly full moon guided him along a small path by the canal that would, he reckoned, join Terrace Avenue.

Before he got halfway he stopped, his attention taken by the gentle puttering of an engine through the darkness. Moving closer Ollie could see a barge was moored on the cemetery side of the canal just below Rion's old home. His curiosity piqued he crept forward.

Rion knew when they brought the tea that it would contain something extra. She also knew how she was expected to act had she drunk it. After fifteen minutes the young girl allowed her eyes to blank over and let her limbs fully relax.

The twins soon noticed.

"Give her another while," Senior said, "then let's take her down."

Propped in the Countess' elaborate chair Rion watched as the twins finished clearing up. They quickly soldered the bars together. After a lick of paint no one would ever know of their misguided attempt at robbery.

Senior stepped back to admire his handiwork. "As good as new eh?"

"Or as old," replied his twin. "No one'll come in here for years anyway."

"Unless the Countess or one of the children should become overly gaseous," Senior chuckled nervously. "Gorby said he expected a visit though."

"Well, they won't find anything will they?"

Senior took a last glance around the vault. "You'd never know we were here."

"You'd never know she was here."

Satisfied that no trace of their stay remained Beck pulled Rion to her feet. Acting entranced she was led along the passageways and up through the darkened space of the main chapel.

When they left the building it tested all of Rion's powers not to jump for joy. By the light of the half-moon everything looked so bright – and so beautiful she thought, feeling a hymn stir in her chest. After the staleness of the catacombs the crisp night air tasted so good! She thought of running there and then until she felt the twins' arms firmly grip her own.

Behind her blank eyes Rion looked to see where they were taking her. She tried not to show her excitement when they went down towards her old home on the canal, down past Jake's!

As they trudged on the side of the muddy track, Rion flopping zombielike between the twins, she looked for the most opportune moment. She seized her chance where the track veered towards the hidden house in the trees.

In a burst of strength Rion struggled to free herself. "Jake!" she screamed, "Jake!"

Although caught unawares Senior and Beck quickly overpowered the young girl.

Rion wasn't able to call out a third time. Beck's hand over her mouth, suffocatingly close to her nose made sure of that. Still struggling she was hurried along the track, past the neglected graves and through the hole in the railings.

Ollie froze. It was Rion! He was about to move from his hiding place when he heard muffled curses nearby. He watched as two men carried Rion to the waiting narrowboat. The young girl kicked and scratched but was no match for the strength of the twins.

Ollie waited until all was quiet. The last thing he heard was a sound behind him. And then nothing.

The twins weren't happy.

"What d'ye bring him for?" Senior asked.

"He knows the girl."

"Finish him off. Leave him here," Beck said.

Senior agreed, "Who's going to look for a body in a cemetery?"

But Gorby had other plans. He carried the unwelcome visitor aboard. As they cast off Ollie lay crumpled on the floor of the wheelhouse, neither in this world nor the next.

They had stopped within the hour. Above them a junction of the M4 curved in the darkness.

"This'll do. Tie up," Gorby ordered.

The twins did as they were told.

Ollie was still dead to the world. He didn't so much as groan as Gorby pulled him from the floor, slung him over his shoulders and carried him from the barge. "I won't be long."

Gorby trudged up the winding concrete steps. He carried Ollie over his shoulders as a fireman might carry someone from a burning building.

But Gorby wasn't going to be saving anyone's life tonight.

The guard slowly made his way above the tunnels and deserted underpass. He was breathing heavily by the time he came to the upper level. The motorway was quiet at this hour. All that could be heard was a distant rumble as juggernauts raced each other through the night. Gorby placed Ollie in the middle of the nearside lane. Powerful headlights bore down on them from the distance.

Perfect. Crushed beneath an 18-wheeler the young man would be unrecognisable.

And impossible to identify.

28

WARNING SIGNS

"This had better be good," Inspector Devine said to Nicky as they pulled up in front of the Anglican Chapel in the middle of Kensal Green Cemetery.

"Something is definitely going on down there. We felt it yesterday."

"I can't act on feelings."

"But you can tell from their faces, it was something really suspicious!"

"So suspicious that Mr Michaelson couldn't be bothered to show up?"

Nicky also wondered where Ollie was. It was most unlike him not to be here. Even more unlike him to leave Hum alone.

"I've got better things to do as well you know. I'm only doing this as a favour to Em – " he quickly corrected himself, "to Ms Nelson. Don't make me regret it."

The door on the side of the chapel was open for once. The Inspector gave a polite knock.

Oh God, Nicky thought, he's not going to say 'ello 'ello 'ello is he?

Before her fears could be confirmed or otherwise, a woman's voice cheerily trilled, "Come in!"

The Inspector pushed the door open and led the way into

a cold, rather dismal office, a colourful print of Picasso's L'Arlequin doing little to brighten the space.

A woman looked up from behind the desk. She had a kindly, plump face and glasses that were too big for her. Her tweed jacket, faded and worn, was the sort favoured by great aunts in the country – a breed to which she no doubt belonged. In front of her was a postcard rack crammed with black and white images of some of the cemetery's more famous monuments.

There was something curiously familiar about the woman although Nicky didn't think she had seen her before.

"Can I help you Superintendent?"

Auntie Em's tame policeman coughed slightly to clear his throat. "It's Inspector actually Madam," he flashed his badge at her. "Inspector Devine, Notting Hill Police Station."

The woman toyed with the double strand of fake pearls around her neck. She put her head to one side in what Nicky hoped was not a coquettish manner. "Inspector," she deferred.

It was! She was flirting with Inspector Devine.

The woman came out from behind the desk. Her skirt, of the same tweed as her jacket, stopped just below the knee to reveal calves of a surprising thickness.

"I'm sorry to trouble you Madam it's just – " the policeman stretched his neck from side to side as if this would ease his discomfort, " – we've had reports of odd goings on in the catacombs."

The woman opened her eyes wide. "Really?" she said, clutching her pearls in alarm. "What sort of goings on?"

"That's just it Madam," the policeman again cleared his throat to try and cover his embarrassment. "We're not exactly sure but if we could have a quick look?"

"I hope it's not serious," the woman said flustered.

The Inspector used his most soothing of voices, the voice that eased the trauma from even the most disturbed of victims. "I'm sure it's nothing but we have to investigate every lead – "

"Of course," the woman said, indignant at the thought it could be any other way.

" – no matter how false they may turn out to be," the Inspector's eyes slid round to Nicky who was looking elsewhere, her attention taken by the numerous toy figures gathered in clusters on the cabinets and shelves of the office. The small figures, all of dancing masked men in white knickerbockers, had the kitsch appeal of holiday souvenirs, perhaps memories of a trip to Spain Nicky thought.

"Let me get my husband. He knows more about the catacombs than I do." The woman opened a side door through which Nicky could see a stone staircase spiralling into the darkness. "Ted!" she called in her shrill voice, "we have visitors. Ted!" She turned back into the room, "He'll be here in a second. I'm Mary by the way, Mary McGrath."

"We've also had reports of kids sleeping rough in the cemetery," Inspector Devine said. "You haven't seen any young girls bedding down – "

Mary cut him off. "Absolutely not," she said firmly. "We did have an old boy in a chamber by the canal but he died last year. The place has been blocked off now."

Whilst waiting for Mr McGrath to appear Nicky took a closer look at the print on the wall.

"Picasso was a mystic of course," Mary said upon seeing her interest in the masked dancer. "His model for this was a Morris Man. He wasn't the only one inspired by their ancient dances."

Nicky wasn't sure what to make of this. "Really?"

"They go back to Celtic times you know," Mary said as if sharing a secret.

"The Morris Men or the dances?"

"Both."

Before Nicky could fully digest this information Mr McGrath entered the room. He was the perfect counterpart to his wife in that he gave off the same air of restrained jollity and wellworn tweed. He also looked slightly similar to her which, Nicky thought, was rather sweet. Maybe that's what happens to old couples, they turn into each other after forty or so years together. With a pang Nicky thought back to her own life. She began to wonder if she would ever spend her life with someone, someone she might begin to look like after forty years.

As Nicky pondered her lack of coupledom, introductions were made and reasons for the visit given. She was jolted out of her thoughts by a gentle nudge in the ribs. Nicky glanced up to find herself being looked at with some concern by Inspector Devine and the McGraths.

"I said, 'Were you with Mr Michaelson who visited us yesterday?'" Ted repeated.

Nicky decided that attack was the best form of defence. "I hope you're insured."

The couple seemed slightly taken aback. "Excuse me?" Mary queried.

"Insured?" Ted repeated, equally mystified.

"Yes. Corporate liability," Nicky said. She ignored Inspector Devine who tried to silence her with a glare.

Ted shook his head. "Corporate liability?" he asked somewhat incredulously. He looked at his wife and shrugged his shoulders. Mary shrugged her shoulders in return.

"Yes. If anyone injures themselves in the catacombs – "

Inspector Devine cut her short. "Shall we?" he gestured to the door.

Ted exchanged another perplexed look with his wife before leaving the room.

"Don't push it," the policeman warned Nicky before following.

They walked through the chapel and down the stairs Nicky had come up the previous day with Ollie and Gorby. Within seconds they were in the damp gloom of the catacombs.

"We have had a problem with vandals in the past. They seem to get in through the surrounding grille." Ted had recovered his composure. He turned to look at Nicky, "Is that how you got in?"

"That's how Mr Michaelson's dog *fell* in."

"And which corridor was it?"

Nicky took her bearings, "Give me a minute." She walked up the central passageway to the heavy door she remembered from the previous day. "I think it's this one."

"Ah," Mary sniffed, "you think?" She exchanged a look with Inspector Devine.

Nicky pushed the door open. "Yes!" she said excitedly. "This is it." She looked at the arched vaults stretching down the corridor.

"You're sure?" Ted asked.

Nicky quickly found the age-darkened bronze door emblazoned with the Rosleagh coat of arms. She nodded excitedly to the policeman, "I'm sure."

"Ah, the Rosleagh vault," Ted looked through the many jangling keys until he found a suitably solid one. He checked the attached label, turned the key in the heavy lock and pushed the door that opened with an uncomfortable groan. "Some of these old vaults have lights but the Countess, so I've been told, preferred candles." The tall man took a flashlight from his pocket and stepped into the vault. Nicky, Mary and the Inspector followed. "We did have some trouble here yesterday," Ted shone the torch at the shelves of coffins in front of him, focusing on a large one that rested by itself at eyelevel. "The Earl's coffin was about to – this is not for the squeamish I'm afraid – " he looked at Nicky and the Inspector, " – but the coffin was about to explode."

Inspector Devine wasn't sure what Ted had said. "Excuse me? Explode as in – " he gestured with his hands, " – boom?"

Ted nodded. "The gases just build and build until – well you can imagine I'm sure."

Mary shuddered before whispering, "Mess."

The policeman looked at the coffin with newfound respect.

"It was only the quick thinking of Mr Dwight that saved the day."

"Mr Dwight?" the Inspector remarked.

"My second-in-command."

"Is he the one with a birthmark," Nicky patted the side of her head, "here?"

"Yes. "

"Can I speak to him?" the Inspector asked.

"Under normal circumstances yes, however Mr Dwight's just begun his annual leave. Where's he gone this time darling?"

"He's abit of a rambler our Nigel: is it Hadrian's Wall?"

"Or Offa's Dyke?"

"Well, he took the train yesterday to Carlisle."

"Or was it Carmarthen?"

The couple were unsure.

"But can I speak to him?" Inspector Devine continued.

"Mr Dwight is not a fan of the modern world – he hasn't got a mobile phone – "

"And is not on email, " Mary laughed. "He won't even use the one here!"

"How convenient," Nicky said under her breath but loud enough so the policeman could hear.

"Gorby – er, Mr Dwight," Mary quickly corrected herself, "might call in sometime from one of the b&b's along the way. If he does we'll ask him to contact you."

"Mr Dwight did mention the couple in his report of the incident." Ted turned to Inspector Devine, "You can see that if you'd like." He shone the flashlight around the small space. "As you can see no-one has been here for years."

"Does anyone else have access to this section?"

"Of the public?"

The Inspector nodded.

"The Worth-Bassingtons are the only ones now – Lady Chessy's a regular, she was here yesterday in fact – they have the vault next door you see," Ted explained. "All the others have died out."

Nicky looked at the Earl's coffin. She could see the blackened half-melted barrel of the pen sticking out of it like some crazed, stunted stalactite. "Bit of a coincidence Mr Dwight being around just at the right time."

"There are warning signs," Ted said in a tone that suggested everyone would know that. "In fact it was Lady Chessy who alerted us. You can call her if you like," he said to Inspector Devine.

Nicky looked for any evidence of Rion, or any evidence of recent occupation, but saw none in the damp vault. Gently sniffing the air she thought she caught a faint whiff of paint but couldn't be sure.

"Lady C's a bit eccentric but reasonably coherent if you catch her on a good day," Mary smiled. "If you'll come upstairs I'll give you her number."

Inspector Devine left the vault. "That won't be necessary."

With Mr Dwight's report under his arm the Inspector walked back towards the panda car where Nicky waited. "I hope you're satisfied Ms Dixon," the policeman gave a last wave to the McGraths who watched from the top of the chapel steps before Mary ushered Ted inside.

Nicky was not entirely successful at keeping the sarcasm from her voice, "What do you think?"

"I think you have an overactive imagination. I also think you should stay away from these people." Inspector Devine got in the car and wound the window down, "I'll let you know if there are any developments. You can find your own way back?"

Without waiting for a reply he drove off.

Nicky watched as the car headed for the main gates. She looked around but the McGraths had gone back inside. As she was mulling things over a four-note whistle caused her to look up. There behind Princess Sophia's sarcophagus she could see Jake.

"I didn't want to come in with the copper about, it could get complicated."

Nicky nodded. How would you explain to a member of the Constabulary that you lived in a treehouse in a cemetery? It would lead to just too many questions.

"Does this look familiar?" Jake took something from his inside pocket and gave it to Nicky.

It was a small, muddied newspaper cutting folded in two. Nicky opened it and recognised it immediately. "Of course!" she exclaimed, looking at Rion's most treasured possession – the image of Blondin crossing the Niagara Falls. "Where on earth did you get it?"

Jake lent against the huge podium that supported the princess' marble tomb. "That's the funny thing," he didn't understand it himself. "I saw it this morning on the track going down to the canal."

"The one that goes right past your – "

"The very same, right past the – er – door." Jake took out the everpresent tobacco tin, removed a half-smoked joint, lit it and inhaled deeply. He held back a cough as the fragrant smoke tickled his lungs. Jake handed the roach to Nicky who declined the offer.

"I really shouldn't," she said.

Jake insisted, "No, you really should. You might need it when you hear what I have to say."

Intrigued Nicky took a hit. She returned the joint to Jake who finished it in one sizzling puff.

"I got back last night at about twelve thirty and soon crashed. Anyway I had the strangest dream," Jake shook his head as if still not believing it. "It can't have been long after I went to bed but I could have sworn I heard Rion calling my name."

Nicky looked up but didn't say anything.

"As in the manner of dreams I didn't really pay too much attention to it at the time. I just thought I'd been thinking about her alot and that must have permeated my subconscious somehow. Also the tree makes odd sounds sometimes the branches moan and groan – this isn't the first time I've thought someone's calling me when it's only been the wind."

"That must be sort of spooky being in a cemetery and all."

Jake shrugged. "Anyway this morning, as I said, I didn't think too much about it until I was going to work and found this on the track. There are also other things."

"Like?"

Jake began walking down the muddy path beneath the chestnut trees. "You'll see. I thought you could maybe tell your friend in blue."

"That wouldn't do any good," Nicky dodged a puddle. "He's just a plod and is doing this for Auntie Em. I think he feels he's done his part – he won't be doing us any favours that's for sure."

"How many people did Ollie say were in the vault?"

"Three."

Jake nodded as if it was all fitting into place. "Where is he by the way?"

Nicky sighed. "It's weird. He should have been at the meeting this morning but never showed."

"He seemed keen last night though didn't he?"

"Yeah, he did. I mean, he is." Nicky couldn't figure it out. "Anyway I got woken earlier by Hum barking to be let out – but no sign of Ollie."

By now they were almost opposite the hidden treehouse. "This is where I found the cutting. Look," Jake pointed to the muddy track, "there and – " he squatted on his haunches, " – there."

Nicky couldn't see anything unusual in the soil, the leaves and gravel that made up Terrace Avenue. She looked again but still there was nothing that would strike her as even remotely suspicious.

"Do you see those footprints?" Jake gestured along the side of the tracks back the way they came.

Nicky could see them now. Heavy sets of indentations on either side of smaller ones.

"How many do you see?"

Nicky looked again. "Three?"

Jake pointed them out. "Judging from the size of their feet I'd say two men walking beside – " he pointed to the smaller set, "a child or woman."

"Rion!"

"Perhaps," Jake stood up. "They came down from the chapel – "

Looking back Nicky could see the three sets of prints more clearly now.

" – to here," Jake pointed to where the prints became a jumbled mess, "where they had a struggle and – "

"Rion called out and dropped the cutting which she knew you would find."

" – then subdued her and took her along here."

They followed the set of prints down the hill towards the canal. Turning off at the neglected graves they saw the tall grass lining the narrow track had been trampled to one side. The trail continued through the hole in the fence and down to the water where the prints abruptly stopped.

"To a boat?"

Jake nodded. "It would appear so wouldn't it?"

Rion had drifted in and out of sleep all day. The gentle throbbing of the barge lulling her to rest, every change in the rhythm waking her. The young girl felt for the everpresent portrait of Blondin then remembered how she'd dropped it in the cemetery days before.

Had Jake found the cutting?

Rion doubted it. She feared the wellworn scrap of paper would have been melted by the rain, trampled into the mud, lost forever. Her friends would never find it and, she thought sadly, would never find her. Was she to be lost forever, was that to be her fate? Rion shivered, suppressing the cough that rose in her chest. She clutched the cheap pillow to her, thought of her favourite blue-eyed singer and told herself she wasn't lost, just undiscovered….

Hearing voices on deck Rion noticed the engine slow down. Through the porthole she could see Beck and Senior's legs in their combats. The thud of ropes on deck, the grind as the boat eased against its resting-place and then silence.

Footsteps clattered downwards. The door creaked open and Gorby stood there. "Here we are," his grin made her shiver. "Your final destination."

Rion knew what would happen next. She didn't even bother to struggle. She just lay there as the handkerchief came closer to her face and the sickly smell of chloroform overwhelmed her.

29

FISH FRIDAY

The rumour had swept through the plant late in the day. It was whispered that Sir Edwin had been seen smiling – nay beaming – a fact Mr Paul confirmed to Gem.

"I don't know how he does it. I just don't know," the young assistant manager put his arm around her, "but if it's true then I think I just don't care."

"If what's true?"

"An announcement is imminent," Mr Paul said knowingly.

Auntie Gem was none the wiser. Upon seeing the tealady's blank face Mr Paul elaborated, "Sir Edwin's got a big press conference planned for tomorrow. He's going to reveal the role – or more precisely the lack of it – that Peters & Peters played in polluting the canal. This is good, good news."

Auntie Gem wasn't so sure. "You mean maybe the dead fish weren't Edwin's fault?"

"That's what the report says."

"Nor the heron?"

"Could've been natural causes Gem."

Gemma didn't like the sound of that one bit. "Whose report this time?" she asked suspiciously.

"The Environment Research Agency's. You can't get

much more independent that that eh?" Mr Paul helped himself to a chocolate digestive and carried on his way.

Later that evening Auntie Gem knelt on the cushion before her shrine. She needed advice and she needed it fast. The following day would be the last one on which she could act. Gem normally went to Emma for advice but this situation was different, this situation required help from above – besides she didn't want Emma to be implicated if things went wrong.

Diana smiled down at her from a huge variety of photographs. Gem could feel the warmth radiating from the Princess of Wales. Just kneeling there made her feel so much calmer.

The old lady offered up her problem to the Queen of Hearts along with a prayer for guidance. Feeling comforted she moved to her bed, switched the electric blanket off and snuggled under the covers.

Her dilemma was now out of her hands. All that was left to do was wait.

The answer came the following morning. It was clear and precise, leaving no room for doubt.

Before Gemma left for work she consulted her oracle. She knelt once more on the cushion in front of the shrine, in her hands the collector's edition magazine that celebrated Diana's life. Gem closed her eyes, letting the pages of the glossy magazine flutter back and forth through her fingers. After a while – it could have been a few seconds, it could have been a minute or longer – she heard the internal voice. At that instant she stopped the pages, her thumb coming to rest on the preordained image.

What photo would it be? What message would it give?

Gem slowly opened her eyes and looked down. When she saw what had been chosen she knew immediately her plan had been approved. The image the oracle had sent was one from early in Diana's life. It showed the young Lady Di, not a princess yet, with Prince Charles at Balmoral. The teenage girl grinned shyly whilst her husband to be stood waist-deep in a river.....fishing.

FISHING!

As clear a message as any. If her thumb had alighted on the one where the Princess, dressed in black, was leaving Klosters for her father's funeral that would have been a clear sign that Gem mustn't take her plan further; or if it had been one on that unhappy trip to Korea, with the Princess looking upset and tearful, that would also have stopped Gem in her tracks, but this one with Diana shyly grinning at the camera whilst Charles *fished* meant that she could now proceed with a clear heart.

Going into the kitchen Gem retrieved the plastic bag from the freezer. She left for Peters & Peters, her conscience now clear about what she was going to do.

Nicky and Auntie Em sat in the house at the end. Both were worried. Ollie hadn't been seen now for more than thirty-six hours.

"He would have told us if he was going away." Nicky looked at the hound lying dejected by the fire, "He certainly wouldn't have left Hum alone."

"Yes," Auntie Em sighed. "It's time to take action." She leaned over and held Nicky's hand, "You do realise whatever we do it's going to be unpleasant."

Nicky nodded.

"We'll have to phone the police – the hospitals – "

" – the morgue," Nicky felt tears prick her eyes. She wiped them away and froze. "Oh Auntie Em!" Nicky nervously pointed out the window.

Emma followed her gaze to see a uniformed policeman walking slowly down the mews.

They hurried out of the house, Hum at their heels.

"Do you know an Oliver Michaelson?" asked the young copper.

"Yes," Auntie Em replied. Her unease was compounded by the gravity of the policeman's demeanour.

"Are you his next of kin?"

"As good as."

Nicky tried to control her mounting hysteria. "What's happened?"

"I have some bad news I'm afraid."

"What's happened?" Nicky shrieked.

"There's never an easy way to do this," the policeman continued.

"Oh God, oh God, oh God," Nicky moaned whilst Auntie Em visibly blanched.

The policeman walked back up the way he came and signalled outside. Seconds later an ambulance rumbled into the mews and stopped behind him.

The driver hopped down, "We cleaned him up a bit." He went to the back of the ambulance and opened the doors, "He was a real mess when he came in."

Nicky nervously peered round to see a dishevelled figure on a bench, a blanket around his shoulders. "Ollie?" she went to help him down. "What's going on? Are you ok?"

Hum gave a joyous bark upon seeing his master.

"You can confirm his identity?" the policeman asked.

"Oliver Guy Michaelson," Auntie Em stroked Ollie's hair. "How did he – where did you pick him up?"

"He was found wandering along the M4 in a somewhat disorientated state," the policeman looked at his notebook, "yesterday midmorning."

"Suffering from concussion. We wanted to keep him in but he insisted on discharging himself." The ambulance driver slammed the doors shut. "We can't be held responsible."

"Says the last thing he remembers is being in a nightclub called," the policeman again checked his notes, before clearing his throat " – 'L'Enfers'?"

"L'Enfers?" Nicky repeated. The afterhours club, a favourite amongst insomniacs and those of a chemical persuasion, was famed for its ferocity.

"I couldn't sleep," Ollie mumbled.

"And when you can't sleep go dancing right?" Nicky hugged her friend, "Oh Ollie."

The policeman approached. "I take it I can release him to your care?"

"Of course officer," Auntie Em signed the proffered form. "And thank you."

They watched as the ambulance reversed out of the mews.

"Bath and sleep is all I need," Ollie said in response to the concerned looks. He patted his pockets but there was no familiar jangling.

"You have a key sweetness?" Auntie Em asked Nicky. "It seems our boy has mislaid his."

Ollie shrugged his shoulders. "Although where I couldn't possibly tell you."

As soon as Nicky let them in Auntie Em marched up the stairs. The first thing she did was put on the kettle. "You'll have tea?"

"Try and stop me," Ollie slumped on the sofa. Hum jumped up beside him and covered him protectively with his paws.

"You weren't at L'Enfers were you?" Nicky called through

from the bathroom. She added an extra dash of bubble bath to the clawed tub before turning the taps on full.

"No."

"Why didn't you tell us you were in hospital? We've been worried sick."

"I couldn't even have told you my name until this morning."

Auntie Em looked at Ollie for a long while. "I've seen you in worse states I must say." She placed the tea tray on the table. "Perhaps you'll tell me about it later," Auntie Em kissed him on the forehead. Before she left she beckoned Nicky over, "Put him to bed after this," she ordered. "Don't let him out of your sight."

Ollie shuffled through to the bathroom. He slowly pulled off his dirty clothes and eased himself into the foaming bubbles. "You've no idea how good this feels."

Nicky waited a few moments but couldn't stay silent much longer. She brought his tea through and sat on the edge of the tub. "What on earth were you doing on the M4?"

Ollie stretched through his body. He aimed to fit his big toe in the tap before thinking better of it.

"It'll get stuck," Nicky warned.

"Probably." Ollie luxuriated in the hot water. He put a generous dollop of shampoo on his hands and began washing his hair.

"The M4?" Nicky prompted.

"I have no idea. Absolutely no idea. The last thing I remember was going into the cemetery. I couldn't sleep, I kept on thinking about the people in that vault – maybe one of them *was* Rion. My mind was just spinning out Nicks. I had to go." Ollie slipped beneath the water to rinse his hair. He stayed under for what seemed an inordinately long time before slowly surfacing.

"But the M4 Ol – what's that about?"

"This is all I know," he guided Nicky's hand to a point on his skull above his left ear. Beneath his hair matted wet Nicky could feel a lump the size of a duck egg. "Lucky I'm thick-skulled I guess."

"And you can't remember anything after the cemetery?"

"Nope."

"PC Plod was a mite peeved you didn't show yesterday."

"It wasn't on purpose believe me."

"There was nothing in the vault of course, and no sign of the creepy guard, but it was interesting. The couple in charge – " Nicky cleared her throat, " – the polite word for them would be eccentric I guess. They were almost made of tweed and their office – ! figures of Morris Dancers *everywhere*."

The recent drama had caused Nicky to overlook the most important part. She quickly filled him in on Jake, Rion's cutting and the theory about a barge.

Ollie wracked his brain: a tweedy couple, figures of dancers and a boat.

"Come on," Ollie got out of the bath and began drying himself. "I've an idea."

Nicky wasn't happy. "But I promised Auntie Em – "

"We'll be back before she will."

"Are you sure you're ok?"

"Like I said, nothing a bath and a sleep won't fix," Ollie gave what he hoped was a reassuring smile. "I've had the bath, I'll sleep later."

Nicky still wasn't convinced.

"C'mon Nicks, I'll take the blame."

Within minutes they were in Little Venice. Ollie hurried down the towpath until he was opposite Jason's Restaurant. "It was here I'm sure," he said but his heart sunk as soon as he saw the barges moored along the canal.

They all looked the same.

Although individually painted their bright colours created a uniformity that made them difficult to tell apart. What made it worse was that all the couples looked similar to each other. There was also a preponderance of tweed and a surfeit of dancing figures woven into the names of the barges.

"I'm sorry Nicks. I made a mistake."

"The mind playing tricks?"

Ollie kicked the fence in anger. "All the fucking time."

It was as if the first floor hadn't heard the apparently good news. The open plan office was silent apart from a jaunty whistling that came from behind Sir Edwin's door. The staff noticeably relaxed when the whistling stopped only to tense up when the jolly tune started once more.

"It's worse when he's happy isn't it?" Miss Collins cringed as the whistling increased in volume.

"Anyone with him?" Gemma asked as her trolley squeaked towards her boss' office.

"Just Mr Paul. He's been in there much longer than usual." The PA pressed a buzzer on the desk in front of her, "Gemma's here with your lunch Sir Edwin."

Hardly had she finished speaking when the office door was thrown open. Sir Edwin stood there smiling, his arms open wide. "Gemma!" he boomed, his bearlike embrace causing the tealady to gasp.

"Stop it," Gem swatted her boss on the shoulder. She adjusted her tunic as he ushered her into his office.

The assistant manager sat on the sofa smoking an enormous cigar and looking slightly ill. "Gem," he acknowledged as they exchanged nods.

As soon as the door was closed Sir Edwin took the trolley and wheeled it towards his desk, "What are you going to do with your Christmas bonus Gem?"

The tealady managed to deflect her boss' fingers that were about to tickle her ribs.

"Paul here is developing a taste for Cuban cigars," Sir Edwin slapped his assistant manager on the back. "Aren't you Paul?"

Mr Paul coughed out a mouthful of smoke. He tried to say something but choked before a sentence could be formed.

The chairman of Peters & Peters continued, "He might be spending his bonus on a trip to Havana eh?"

The assistant manager dodged another slap on the back.

"Show Gem what you've done," Sir Edwin smiled at Gemma. "He's a genius Gem."

The young man gave another cough before stubbing out his cigar in the ashtray. He picked up a poster from the coffee table in front of him and held it up for Gem to see. Mr Paul gestured to the poster and tried to speak but the effort brought on another coughing fit.

Sir Edwin smiled indulgently. "I'll explain shall I?"

Mr Paul gratefully nodded.

"We're putting these up along the canal."

Gemma squinted at the posters. Knowing how much her boss liked the sound of his own voice she pretended she couldn't see the lettering that, in reality, was perfectly clear to her. "You'll have to read it for me Sir Ed-win."

Her boss needed no prompting. "'Danger!'" he read out loud. "'Blue green algae alert. Organic toxin. Do not drink. Contact can be dangerous to humans and animals.'" He beamed at Gemma, "This is the best part." Sir Edwin pointed to a section that was in red. It was also in much larger lettering than the first. "'This announcement paid for by Peters &

Peters as part of its – '" Sir Edwin took a theatrical intake of breath, "'Conservation Research Advisory Programme.'" He looked at Gemma, "What do you think?"

"Do we have an conservation research advisory programme?"

"We do now!" Sir Edwin looked out of the window at the canal below him. "Naturally poisoned – isn't it wonderful?"

Mr Paul looked at his watch, "Sir Edwin." For the first time since Gem entered Mr Paul was able to get through a whole sentence without coughing. "The conference is in one hour."

Sir Edwin lifted the lid from a salver. An unexpectedly pungent aroma filled the room. "Join me for lunch Paul."

The assistant manager wrinkled his nose. "I'm not a great fish eater Sir Edwin."

Faced with such a smell the boss of Peters & Peters wasn't sure whether he was either. "Well," he said replacing the lid, "we don't have to have fish – what else has cook got Gem?"

Gemma did her best to look horrified. "It's Friday Sir Edwin!"

Mr Paul got up from the sofa, "I need some time before the conference anyway." He smiled shakily at Gemma who had begun to lay the lunch on the smoky glass coffee table.

Before the assistant manager could leave Sir Edwin reached into his polished oak executive humidor and chose two cigars. "Practice makes perfect!" he winked at Mr Paul, putting the two Cohibas in his top pocket.

The chairman of Peters & Peters closed the door on his assistant manager. "Am I having fun today Gem or what?!"

Seeing her boss in such an amicable mood made the tealady think twice about what she was going to do. She didn't have to think for long though – her plan had been sanctioned from on high hadn't it?

Sir Edwin disappeared into the small side room where he

kept several changes of clothes. It was also where he kept his wine.

"What sort of fish is it Gem?"

The tealady held her nose as she looked at the lightly poached fillets in their white sauce. "A flat one?" she said hopefully.

Her boss appeared brandishing a bottle of wine. "Red wine with fish, I know it's not the done thing – there's probably a very good reason for it too – but I fancy something a little more fruity, a tad more robust than the normal Chablis," he winked at Gemma. "Don't tell Lady Peters!"

Sir Edwin uncorked the bottle of Merlot and poured himself a glass. "Magnificent," he said, holding up the glass to the light. He took a small sip, savoured the taste on his tongue before swirling the wine around his mouth and swallowing in one. "Have a glass with me Gem."

The tealady shook her head disapprovingly. She ladled consommé into a bowl, placing it before her boss who, worryingly, appeared in no hurry to eat.

Sir Edwin poured himself another glass and sprawled back on the Chesterfield. Stretching his legs he nearly kicked over the bowl of clear soup on the table in front of him.

"Edwin!" Gemma gestured for him to take his feet off the coffee table.

"Let's have some fun first."

Auntie Gem looked at him doubtfully.

"Come on," Sir Edwin patted the sofa beside him. Gem again looked at him before sitting down tentatively on the Chesterfield. Her boss pressed a speed dial on the speakerphone. "Aaron?" he said as a gruff, somewhat threatening voice filled the room, "It's me. Stay on the line."

Sir Edwin pressed the conference call button and dialled another number, "I'm beginning with the Standard."

The London Evening Standard had been one of Peters & Peter's fiercest critics over the recent ecological disaster.

"Tim?" her boss began as the editor came on the line. "It's Sir Edwin Peters here."

A chuckle was heard. "Ah Ed – still polluting the canals of our fair city?"

Sir Edwin let the jibe slide by. "The Environment Research Agency has just published a report you might find interesting."

"I doubt it but go on."

"It shows the canal pollution was caused by blue green algae, a naturally occurring organic toxin – you see I'm not the 'Enemy of Nature' you portrayed."

"So you're not going shooting this weekend?"

Sir Edwin again ignored the taunt. He had the upper hand in this one.

"Your false, malicious reporting wiped millions off the stock value, not to mention the damage to our name and goodwill leaving me no alternative but to sue you on behalf of our shareholders."

Sir Edwin smiled at the long silence that followed.

"Let's have lunch," the editor began. "Harry's Bar. Monday twelve – "

Sir Edwin didn't let him finish, "My lawyer is here. Aaron?"

"Mr Sheridan?" the celebrated libel lawyer's voice, filled with menace and charm, caused Auntie Gem to shiver.

Sir Edwin clicked off the phone. He downed another glass in one and poured himself a third.

"Your soup is getting cold."

"It's not really a consommé day is it? I need something – "

he opened his arms wide before putting them behind his head, " – grander, like foie gras and oysters, like filet mignon, like – " Edwin's desires on power food were interrupted by a light flashing red on the phone. He pressed the button to be met by a loud belching noise.

"I reckon he'll settle before the end of the week," the lawyer's voice filled the room. "Give me another."

Sir Edwin laughed out loud. "Did he squeal?"

"He will do."

Gem's boss rubbed his hands in glee. "Let's do the Guardian."

There followed a series of similar calls. Gem and Sir Edwin listened in whilst his lawyer terrorised newspaper editors before extorting damages from them. Auntie Gem watched anxiously as her plan appeared to slip away.

After Aaron reported back with yet another successful call, Auntie Gem decided to take matters into her own hands. "No more calls until you have something to eat," she said in her best no-nonsense voice.

"But a day like today demands something red and meaty," Sir Edwin said with disappointment, looking at the salver under which he knew was something white and fishy.

Gem took the lid off the silver dish. She put several fillets of fish on a plate, a serving of vegetables beside them and placed the meal before Sir Edwin. "It's Friday," she reminded him, "you always have fish on Friday. Besides," she gestured to the wine, "you need to line your stomach. The conference is in half an hour."

Auntie Gem made sure her boss finished everything on his plate.

"What would I do without you Gem?" he winked at her.

The tealady stayed silent. She poured him a cup of black

coffee before gathering up the plates. As she was about to leave she turned to her boss who was already on the phone. "Have a good conference Sir Edwin," Gemma smiled and closed the door.

30

SHE CAN'T JUST HAVE VANISHED

It was the first of a series of very cold mornings. Overnight frost glistened on the cobbles and pavements making progress along Portobello Road a delicate affair.

The market echoed to the cries of street traders vying to outdo each other in their quest for custom. "Come alive Portabella, come alive!" cried one, his fleshy face red with cold. "Tree buyers where are ya?" shouted another as his neighbour cackled loudly, "Caulis are cheeeeap!"

Auntie Em slipped her arm through Ollie's. "There's something positively Dickensian about this street isn't there?" she said as they passed bundles of Christmas trees piled high against the side of the road. "I half expect to see a sooty-faced urchin in a doorway, cap in hand, going 'penny for the guy guv'?"

"That would have been a couple of weeks ago Auntie Em."

"You know what I mean angel."

Ollie looked at the mounds of fruit and vegetables, at the muffled and gloved traders – their breath coming out in thick clouds – at the stalls stacked with oversized cards and cheap wrapping paper. He knew exactly what she meant. "Who buys their trees this early anyway?"

"Mind yer backs!" a man carrying a tray of steaming

beetroot dodged past them. He almost tripped over Hum who trotted close to Ollie's side.

"Did you tell Gem about my overnight in hospital?"

"No sweetness. I thought it best not to."

"She's been very quiet recently."

Gemma's mood had not gone unnoticed by Auntie Em. "She's been deeply upset about Rion, of course, but also this business at work..." Emma sighed. She was sure there was more to it than that but couldn't figure out what.

"You mean Edwin projectile vomiting over journalists?"

Auntie Em allowed herself a small laugh. "I would have loved to have been there – although obviously not in the front row," she added hurriedly. Whilst it felt cruel to take pleasure in someone else' misfortunes Auntie Em indulged herself anyway, "I gather he only got to 'Ladies and Gentlemen' before he was brought to his knees."

The image had been one of the few things to raise people's spirits recently.

"But how are *you* sweetness?" Auntie Em rubbed the side of Ollie's head. She could feel the nasty bump through her mittens.

"It's gone down don't you think?"

"No after effects?"

"Not that I can tell."

They fell silent as they turned into Golborne Road. It was as if the closeness to the mews brought home the continuing lack of progress in finding Rion.

"Oh Auntie Em," Ollie said frustrated. "She can't just have vanished, she can't have!"

"And Neil wasn't much help?"

"Unfortunately to him she's just another teenage runaway. The police haven't got the resources nor the necessary evidence to proceed further although," he laughed bitterly, "by the time they get the necessary evidence it could be too late."

"We mustn't think that. We're her only family, we're all she's got. She needs us to find her," Auntie Em squeezed his arm tight. "What you're doing is very important."

"It's like she's just disappeared," Ollie said despondently. "Nothing leads anywhere."

Approaching Café Feliz they could see that, even on such a cold day, most of the pavement tables were occupied. "Come for a coffee. I'm meeting Kanwar – we can sit outside with the other hardy annuals and eat pastries 'til we burst."

"Not even custard tarts could charm me today," Ollie kissed her on the cheek. "I've got to dash Auntie Em. Johnson's coming round. He's probably there already."

Ollie jogged into the mews, Hum at his heels, to find the silver Merc parked outside his house. The lifestyle enhancer was talking to Nicky who stood in her doorway opposite.

"And you're sure you don't have his number?" Ollie overheard Johnson ask Nicky.

"No," she grumbled. "How many times do I have to tell you?"

"Whose number are you trying to find Johnson?"

The handsome man turned, embarrassed, "Oh, it's nothing."

Nicky rolled her eyes at Ollie. "Is Jake still coming for supper?"

"Yes."

"See you later then," Nicky smiled and returned to her studio.

"Whose number Johnson?"

"It's not important."

"Johnson!"

"Ok," he smiled sheepishly. "I was looking for a builder – "

"Go to the Heath."

The lifestyle enhancer looked offended. "For some building work."

Ollie didn't believe it for a second.

" – and was thinking of asking your friend – ?" Johnson fluttered his hands as if having forgotten the name.

"Yes?" Ollie knew precisely who Johnson would be looking for.

"You know," Johnson did the fluttering thing with his hands again. "Him," he said pointedly.

"You mean Wayne?"

Johnson clicked his fingers, "Yes!"

Ollie led the way into his workroom, "I'm not giving you Wayne's number."

"But you said he did such good work and – "

"Johnson."

" – besides I wouldn't mind if he nabbed the odd objet d'art – "

"Johnson – "

" – it would be cheaper than some of the rent I've paid for in my life and – "

"Johnson! I haven't got his number and have no idea where to get it," Ollie lied.

The lifestyle enhancer couldn't hide his disappointment. "Oh," he said gloomily.

"Besides I thought you were seeing Murray."

"I am but this would be for building work – honest."

Ollie looked at his friend but wasn't in the mood to take it further. He moved to the central workstation. "What do you think?" Ollie pointed to the half-finished upside down tables Johnson had commissioned. "Hopefully they'll be ready before Christmas."

"No rush."

It was obvious Johnson was still peeved.

"Look mate I can't help with Wayne," Ollie put his arm around Johnson's shoulder. "Want some tea?"

Johnson wasn't sure whether to sulk or not. "Any cakes?"

"And spliff."

As they walked upstairs to the sitting room Ollie asked, "What else is new?"

"I've been to see Angie. Edwin's stabilised but is being kept in for at least another few days." Johnson's sulk vanished at the first chance to gossip. "You know what they're calling him at Glamourista?"

Ollie shook his head.

"Even Angie thought it was funny. They've been through several names. First it was 'Vance', then 'Paris', then 'Ada'." Johnson raised his eyebrows but Ollie couldn't see the link between Sir Edwin Peters and a selection of media tarts. "You don't read the tabloids do you? Chundering celebrities?"

As with so many other things the craze had started in the States. Vance and Paris had kicked things off, a couple of British popsters then took it up before WAG extraordinaire Ada Collaren promptly, and messily, jumped on the bandwagon. After that it was a free-for-all. It had reached the point where some of the more downmarket titles had weekly sections devoted to vomiting celebs.

All this meant nothing to Ollie. "Chundering celebrities? Is that linked to the Size Zero debate?"

"No! Well, it could be I guess – Hugh always says the lead-in to the red carpet at Oscar time is just a barf-o-rama, apparently there's a velvet marquee'd vomitorium or something – anyway, they've settled on calling him 'Bush'," he giggled. "Bush! – get it?"

Ollie didn't. "As in the band?"

"No dumbo, as in Dubya's Dad?"

Ollie still didn't get it.

"Don't you look at those clips I send you?"

Ollie shook his head. "No. I...."

"It's a classic! Remember when George Bush Senior was President he went on a state visit to Japan – or was it China? whatever, somewhere in the East where they value manners – anyway he spewed all over his hosts at speechmaking time. Remember?"

Ollie smiled. "Gem'll like that."

"This'll make you chuckle too," Johnson unrolled the magazine which Ollie could see was called FOLK! On the cover was a picture of dancers in traditional garb. "It's one of Luca's titles. Angie keeps it on her desk as aversion therapy – you know if the subscriptions and advertising aren't great that's where she'll slide to." Johnson flipped through the magazine until he found the page he was looking for. "Look, isn't this precious?"

The page was headlined 'Schism amongst the Morris'. Ollie did a doubletake when he saw the picture underneath. The art editor had arranged the photograph so that it appeared to be ripped in two. On one side were a group of men dressed all in white with red sashes around their waists. Facing them were Gorby, Ted and Mary in full tweed, alongwith a couple of others Ollie didn't recognise.

"I mean what are they going to do – prance each other to death?"

The hour had passed pleasantly enough but Ollie was itching for his guest to leave.

"It's Rion isn't it?" Johnson asked.

Ollie nodded.

"Still no news?"

"Not really."

There was no way Ollie was going to get into the whole catacombs thing – let alone the M4 mystery – the drama of it all would keep Johnson there for days.

"I must say Angie seems to have cooled on that – still she has enough on her plate at the moment," Johnson pulled on his floorlength Ralph Lauren overcoat. "Phone me if you hear from Wayne," he hugged Ollie. "Ciao for now."

As soon as he heard the Merc purr out of the mews Ollie called FOLK! He was immediately put through to the journalist in question. Ollie was relieved when a man answered in a voice both friendly and helpful. He couldn't handle an aggressive hard-nosed journalist at this time – but then, what would hard-nosed journalists be doing working on a magazine like FOLK! anyway?

Ollie got straight to the point. "It's about the article in this month's issue."

"Which one?"

"Schism amongst Dancers?"

"Ah yes," the journalist paused for a second. "I had to ask because I wrote more than several articles in the November issue. In fact I practically wrote the whole damn thing singlehandedly," the journalist gave a nervous laugh. "And I don't mean I wrote it with one hand either!"

I wonder how many times you've said that Ollie thought. He looked at the picture again. The caption confirmed the couple's identity. "It's about Mary McGrath?"

"Ah Mary. One of the experts on the Morris. Her father was king of the Morris Men of course."

"Is he still alive?"

"I wouldn't have thought so," the journalist said slowly. "I know he had some illness. He hasn't been seen for years anyway. They're traditionalists you know, sort of Morris Dancer fundamentalists," the journalist gave his nervous little laugh again. "That was the problem."

"How so?"

"Well, traditionalists want to keep the link to Mummers Plays – "

"Mummers Plays?"

"Yes as they – "

"Wait a second," Ollie interrupted. "What exactly *are* Mummers Plays?"

"Oh, ceremonial dramas typically involving death and resurrection. The Morris used to be closely linked to them in ancient times but that was when the dances were more – er – " the journalist paused whilst searching for the right word, " – involved."

"Involved?"

"Yes, when they used sacrifices and things – goats, sheep, white bulls, young girls...."

Ollie felt a pain as if a needle, sharp and cold, had been jabbed through his heart. "Young girls?" he gasped, his chest suddenly constricted.

The journalist gave what was now his annoying laugh, "Oh yes. Lock up your daughters when the Morris come to town!"

Ollie put the phone down, the most awful thought numbing his mind.

Nicky rushed over as soon as she got Ollie's call. "It's the McGraths!" she shrieked when she saw the picture.

"I told you."

From his bed by the fire Hum cast his eye over Nicky, Ollie

and Auntie Em who pored over the photograph from FOLK! In the background the radio played a mournful tune by one of Rion's heartthrobs.

Ollie got up and angrily switched off the stereo, "I can't bear that song."

"Me neither, " Nicky added.

"And you hear it everywhere!" Auntie Em began. "I was on my balcony this morning, trying not to have a cigarette – "

"How's that going?"

"Not great Nicks, I've got to read Allen Carr again – but I could hear fragments of it on car stereos, from builders' radios....everywhere."

"And if it's not that it's something else," Nicky complained. "They played Protection – "

" – by Massive Attack?" Ollie asked. The song was in his and Nicky's All Time Top Ten.

Nicky nodded, " – on the radio yesterday and I burst into tears! Just couldn't stop it."

"Yeah," Ollie grimaced, knowing how a tune can dagger the heart. He put his arm around Nicky, "But what are we going to do?"

The three friends frowned in silence, their brows ruffled in concentration, one person forever on their minds. A pounding on the door broke into their thoughts.

Jake had arrived early. "I just saw them," he gasped as Nicky let him in. He quickly moved past her and up the stairs.

"Saw who?" Nicky asked to his back.

Jake gave a quick wave to Ollie and Emma before flopping into one of the straight-backed chairs. He collapsed forward onto the table to catch his breath.

Nicky tried again, "Saw who?"

It took several seconds before Jake had recovered enough

to reply, "Them. On a boat."

"Who??" Nicky asked, exasperated at the vagueness of it all.

"The tweedy couple that run the cemetery."

"Ted and Mary?"

Jake nodded. "I'd just got back from Crouch End and was having a post-work spliff on the canal when they chugged past."

Ollie smacked his fist into his palm. "And you're sure it was them?"

"Positive. Isn't their boat called the Morrisco?"

Ollie whistled between his teeth. "But where are they going? And how do we find out?"

"Wherever it is you can bet Rion's there." Jake and Ollie frowned in silence, their brows ruffled in concentration.

"For Heaven's sake," Nicky said, "why don't you just phone the cemetery? You know, pretend to be someone?"

Ollie, Jake and Auntie Em looked at Nicky, looked at each other then looked back at Nicky.

"Oh no," she said.

"C'mon Nicks. I'm crap at lying, I get all tongue-twisted and it just never works."

"Me too," Jake added. "I'm anything but convincing."

"But you know when I lie I have to be someone else and I'm terrible at accents."

It was too late. Ollie was already thumbing through the phone book. "Say it's about the boat or something, their mooring rights, anything just use your imagination."

Nicky looked at her watch. It was six fifteen. "There'll be no-one there."

Ollie pressed the speaker button and dialled, "Just try."

After the third ring Nicky breathed out a sigh of relief, "I told you. I'll do it tomorrow – I swear."

"Shhhh," Ollie gestured for her to be quiet.

After six rings she got up from the table. "They must have gone home. C'mon, who's going to – "

"Hello?" a man's voice with a pleasing burr stopped Nicky in her tracks. She whipped round.

"Hello? Is anybody there?" the voice from the phone asked again.

Nicky quickly sat down. "Er, hello, this is Rhona from Little Venice – "

Auntie Em tried not to cringe as Nicky spoke with an Australian inflection, ending each phrase as if everything was a question.

" – could I please speak with Ted and Mary?"

"I'm sorry they're away. Can I help?"

Summoning all her knowledge gleaned from Australian soap operas Nicky ploughed on, "Aw, jeez, you wouldn't know where I could reach them do you?"

Ollie began scribbling something on the notepad.

"It's real important," Nicky continued. "Are they on the Morrisco?"

Ollie held up the notepad on which he had written, 'Name of Mr Dwight's boat?' Jake shrugged.

"Well, yes," the man said, unsure how much information he should give out. "They are in fact."

"Do you know where they'll be mooring? Will it be with Mr Dwight?"

"Ah, you know Gorby?"

"Of course. He's a – " Nicky was stuck for words, " – a cobber."

This obviously wasn't the answer the man at the other end was expecting to hear.

"Excuse me?"

Nicky thought it best not to repeat her last sentence. She

looked at Ollie who pointed once more to the notepad.

"Please hold," Nicky pressed the mute button.

"What's Mr Dwight's boat called?" Jake asked.

"There's some literary connection," Nicky ground her teeth furiously, "a famous book or something – "

"It's the Ivanhoe isn't it?" Ollie suggested.

"That's the one!" She flipped back to the speakerphone, "Is Mr Dwight on the Ivanhoe?"

"Sorry?"

Nicky thought frantically back to the Halloween walk down the canal. "I mean the Hiawatha? – his boat?"

There was silence for a second.

"Do you mean the Longfelloe?"

"That'd be right," Nicky corrected.

"They'll be moored outside his mother's as always," Senior replied. "Who did you say you were again?"

Ollie pulled a finger over his throat. Nicky nodded.

"You've been beaut," Nicky put the phone down and heaved a sigh of relief.

"Australian?" Jake asked.

"I can't help it. My Scottish is even worse," she shrugged her shoulders. "It just takes over – sort of a defence mechanism against lying I guess."

"Longfellow. Longfellow," Ollie paced back and forth. "Now why – " He took a deep breath, "Back in a sec." Ollie took the stairs in two leaps and ran to his van in the mews.

Moments later he was back, in his hands the Road Map of Great Britain. "I was doing some research on where the canal went," Ollie muttered, searching frantically through the index. "Aha!" he grinned. "17 SP9 416." He quickly found page seventeen, all the while chanting, "SP9 416 SP9 416."

Ollie moved his fingers along the grid until they met.

"Longfelloe!" he said triumphantly.

Nicky and Jake looked over his shoulder to see him pointing to a speck on the map.

"And look," Ollie traced a thin blue line that ran past the tiny settlement. "Any guesses?"

"The Grand Union Canal!" Nicky and Jake said in unison.

Ollie nodded. "Let's go."

"Now? Shouldn't we wait 'til morning?" Nicky asked.

"We need to go tonight," Jake said firmly.

"Wouldn't it be better to go when it's daylight?"

Her reasoning was cut short by the phone. Ollie answered it before it could ring again, "Hello?" After a series of monosyllabic replies he put the phone down. "That was Tanya. Rion's friend from Bridlington."

"The psychic one?"

Ollie nodded, his face ashen.

"What is it?" Nicky asked concerned.

"Tanya just sounded really worried. Rion's 'pulse', as she puts it, is getting fainter and fainter. She says she can't even feel it sometimes."

That did it for Nicky. "We're outta here."

Ollie and Jake needed no convincing.

Nor did Hum.

The dog gave a brisk bark, alert to all the signs of adventure, but this is one he would have to sit out. "You'll look after the hound won't you?" Ollie asked Auntie Em. "His food's under the sink as always." Ollie ran his hand down his dog's back, "You've got to stay here boy. Stay." Upon hearing his least favourite word, Hum settled back into his snug and pointedly avoided Ollie's eyes.

"Don't do anything st – " Auntie Em began but the three had already raced down the stairs and were out the door. She watched them pile into Ollie's van and rumble from the small mews. Auntie Em leant down to stroke Hum behind the ears, "Let's hope they know what they're doing."

Or else, she thought unhappily, there would be only her, Gem and Humdinger left. It would be like something out of Agatha Christie.

And then there were three.

Rion's cough was now a burning wheeze that slid down her chest in a frightening echo of her previous illness.

She could feel herself growing weaker. The weeks in captivity were taking their toll. She was losing her will to live.

This place was much worse than the other. At least in the vault she was never alone. Whilst the occupants had long since ceased living there was still a presence, benign and comforting, in their proximity.

Here there was nothing. No fire to keep her warm, no mattress and worst of all no constantly burning candle. Rion could handle the damp she thought, and even the cold so long as there was a source of light no matter how weak. Her night was only relieved when she had a visitor, but she had fewer and fewer of those.

She knew she was being held deep in the earth. Gorby had said as much when he had brought her here Rion didn't know when. Time in this dark subterranean place had no meaning.

Her 'room' had been carved out of the rock. It was ancient in its roughness. She could feel no brickwork or sign of habitation, it simply appeared as a side tunnel going nowhere. The flimsy wicker door was enforced with the threat of being lost in caves where, Gorby had said with his creepy smile, even those with a map had vanished. Rion was in no doubt that it was best to stay where she was.

All she could do was sleep. But even then she was never sure if this was sleeping or not – all the young girl knew was that she was in the dark with her thoughts, with her dreams and nightmares. It was only when she coughed that Rion realised she was awake.

No one would find her here she thought unhappily.

Hearing the faintest of footsteps Rion felt her way to the front. As her visitors came closer it was apparent they were the twins – at least Gorby wasn't with them. Rion quickly went to the back and lay down. Moments later flashlight bounced off the cell walls.

"She's sleeping," a voice she recognised as Beck's whispered.

Senior's voice was low but urgent, "We should get her some medicine."

"Why?" the younger twin asked. "She'll soon be in the Otherworld."

"It's not right. You know as well as I do it's not right."

"It doesn't matter. It's too late now anyway."

"But – "

"But nothing. We've come this far they're counting on us."

"So is she. She didn't tell Gorby about what happened in the vault did she?"

"So?"

"We owe her one."

"We owe her nothing," Beck said firmly. "We're doing her a favour."

"What is this other world?" Rion's voice in the darkness caused the twins to jump.

Senior was the first to recover. "So you're awake?" he said in his normal voice.

"Now I am, yes." Rion covered her eyes to escape the blinding flashlight. "What is this other world?" she asked again.

"A place where you feel no pain," Beck said.

So they're going to give her more pills Rion thought, but she was past caring. "You mean like when you give me those drugs?"

"Sort of," Senior said without conviction.

"It's the place our ancestors the Celts believed was as real as the physical world and as ever present."

"'Our ancestors the Celts!'" Rion mimicked. "You don't believe in all that. When the Earl's coffin was rattling about it was all 'Mary, Mother of God, Sweet Jesus,' wasn't it? I didn't hear a single Odin or Thor amongst them."

"Maybe – " Beck thought for a second, "maybe because those are Norse Gods not Celtic." He stopped talking upon hearing footsteps echo down the tunnel.

"Who is it?" Rion asked.

"Be quiet!" Senior hissed.

They watched as two figures approached. Carrying a lantern the taller one hugged his companion close to him.

"It's Gorby."

Rion went to the back of the chamber upon hearing the name of her original kidnapper. She hugged herself in an effort to calm her trembling body.

As Gorby came closer it was clear something was not quite right. "Who's he with?" Beck asked puzzled.

The guard strode up, greeting them cheerfully, "Hello lads!" He shielded his companion from view. "You haven't met Ann have you?"

Rion watched the eerily lit figures from the darkness at the back of the cave.

"Er, no, I don't think so," Senior held his hand out. "Hi

Ann, pleased to make your acq – "

Gorby exploded in laugher, his guffaws ricocheting off the hard stone. He roughly pulled the unfortunate Ann from behind him to reveal a lifesize doll in bluechecked pinafore, pigtails and childishly made-up face.

"It's Raggedy Ann – geddit?" again he bellowed with laughter. "Come on, it's practice time." Still chuckling he set off back the way he came. The twins followed, Senior casting a concerned glance back before he left.

Rion shook with fever and fear. She watched as the enormous shadows faded from view. "Nutters," she mumbled to herself. "Complete nutters."

31

WOMEN IN WHITE

Although Jake and Nicky seemed unaffected by the night spent in the van, Ollie had a nasty crick in his neck. He also had a sharp pain darting along the left side of his body that appeared to be even worse than when he had awoken earlier.

"Not much here is there?" Nicky looked at the few houses lining the main road. "No sign of a shop and it looks like there's only one pub."

Within seconds they were in the countryside once more.

"Was that it? Was that Longfelloe?" Ollie asked bemused.

"I guess so." Jake examined the road map on his knees, "You know if you turn back and take the – " he moved his finger down the page, " – third right the road should run along the canal. Let's start there."

Even motoring slowly they were through Longfelloe without catching their breath. Following the sign for Cheddington they soon found the Grand Union Canal beside them. Jake stared intently along its length.

"Spy any barges?" Nicky asked.

"Certainly not downstream, you can see quite a way, but perhaps – " he looked to his right where the canal turned from the road and made its way through some fields and out of sight, "upstream. Pull up somewhere and we'll walk."

Ollie parked on the verge further on from the hump-backed bridge. "Don't forget the binoculars – we can always pretend we're birdwatchers."

They followed the towpath under the low railway bridge and through the reeds. Opposite a small wood they could see the canal vanished right before reappearing on the other side of a headland.

"Maybe we got it wrong," Ollie sighed. "It wouldn't be the first time."

"Maybe the man I spoke to was feeding us misinformation, maybe they know we're here and they're miles away, maybe – " Nicky's musings were interrupted by Jake grabbing her arm.

"Bingo!" Jake put the binoculars up to his eyes. "Yes!" he said excitedly. "It must be them."

They followed Jake's gaze to see a small cottage some way above the canal. "But where are the boats?" Ollie asked.

"Take a look," Jake handed the binocs to Ollie who squinted down the barrels.

"At what?"

"Further on from the cottage see anything? Look under the weeping willow."

Ollie twisted the barrels, focusing and refocusing on the prows of the two longboats sticking out from the overhanging branches. "I can see – yes, it's the Longfelloe!"

Nicky grabbed the binoculars from him, "My turn."

"What do we do now?"

"Let's watch and wait."

They took turns scanning the cottage and surrounding countryside. "There's been no movement at all has there?" Nicky said after fifteen minutes.

"They must've gone out."

"Should we go and nose around?"

Jake looked up and down the water, "Why don't I go? I mean, they know you both don't they?"

Nicky didn't want to miss out on anything. "Yeah, but – "

"You could keep watch over here. If you see anyone just – " Jake thought for a second. "Can you do this?" he cupped his hands, put his lips against his thumbs and blew – a very convincing owl sound followed.

"I used to be able to years ago." Nicky fitted her hands together and blew to be met with a reasonable hooting.

"There you go! How about you Ol?"

"Of course!" Ollie said, keen not to be outdone. He tried as he remembered how but all that emerged was a formless huffing.

Nicky couldn't keep from smirking.

Ollie again breathed hard into his clasped hands but to no avail.

"Well as long as one of you can do it."

Nicky handed Jake the binoculars, "Take these, if you're caught just say you're from the Audubon Society come to examine their egrets."

"Egrets eh?" Jake smiled quizzically and set off.

They watched until he went round the corner and vanished from sight. Within minutes Jake had appeared in the fields on the other side. He looked through the binoculars, in the manner of a bird enthusiast, before carrying on.

"He's a natural," Nicky smiled, "which is more than can be said for you."

Ollie glared at her. He kept practising the owl sound whilst Nicky kept an eye on the cottage. Ollie tried and tried. He finally managed to coax a faint sound from his hands.

"There!" Ollie said proudly. He redoubled his efforts,

soon giving an imitation that would make any Red Indian proud. Hearing the distant call Jake looked up.

"Now look what you've done," Nicky said crossly. "It's ok," she mouthed. "OK."

"As if he'll see that."

Ollie waved his hands flatly in the manner of an umpire signalling four runs. He gave an exaggerated thumbs-up and was relieved when Jake did the same. They watched as Jake approached the pretty cottage with its wooden veranda. He peered through the lattice windows before vanishing round the back.

It was then Ollie noticed someone creep out from the weeping willow. "Who's that?" he wondered.

Nicky knew the person's identity in an instant. Even from this distance the height and stoop gave him away. "It's Ted McGrath. Quick!" Nicky put her hands together and blew as hard as she could. To her horror not a peep emerged. She watched anxiously but Ted was still some way from the cottage. Again she tried but her throat had suddenly dried in panic.

Ollie was trying equally hard but without success. "We can do this!"

"Of course we can."

Both increased their efforts.

"I can do this. I can do this," Ollie chanted, cupping his hands and blowing for all he was worth. He soon felt light-headed but refused to give up.

Nicky looked on jealously as a brief toot sprang into life then faded just as quickly. She glanced up upon hearing a faint rumbling and was confused to see there were no clouds, stormy or otherwise, in the midday skies.

By this time Ted was making his way along the path that led up to the house. After much puffing a stronger sound came from Nicky's hands only to be drowned out by the London to Liverpool express thundering by. Having mastered the technique Nicky and Ollie hooted and hooted to no avail.

Ted was now on the veranda. The last carriages of the train flashed by as Ollie, now very dizzy, continued trying to alert Jake.

With his hand on the door the tall man turned around, looking for what sounded like a pair of jousting owls. Not seeing any he opened the door and went in.

Redfaced, Nicky staggered in a circle before passing out. Ollie carried on for several loud hoots before he too fell to the ground, his body in full hyperventilation. By the time Nicky pulled him to his feet she could see Ted, and a second figure she was sure must be Mary, emerge from the cottage and drive off.

Seconds later Jake ran across the fields. "C'mon!" he shouted.

They needed no further urging. Ollie and Nicky tore down the towpath arriving at the van at the same time as Jake.

"We can probably still catch them!"

They hopped in the van, screeched round and headed towards Longfelloe.

"Which way?" Ollie asked as they sped through the tiny settlement.

"Straight on."

Nicky caught a glimpse of a car disappearing round a bend, "No, there they are! Go right – right!"

Ollie just made the turn.

"Not too fast, we don't want to alarm them," Jake warned.

They stayed at a reasonable distance. "This is ridiculous," Nicky said. "We're the only vehicles on the road, they must know we're following them."

Feeling more Inspector Clouseau than Poirot Ollie edged the van closer. "What are we going to do anyway?"

"Overtake," Jake said, "and cover your face!"

Ollie pulled past the Volvo, his hand to the side of his head as if shielding himself from the sun. Nicky lent down to hide herself.

"It's not them!" Jake groaned upon seeing a young couple stare curiously back at him. "Damn, damn, double damn," he smacked the dashboard. "Turn around!"

Ollie pulled in to let the maroon saloon pass. "We've lost them," he turned to look at Jake who was gnashing his teeth. "Let's get a bite to eat and a drink – maybe find someone to help us."

The only pub in the small settlement was empty apart from an old man dribbling into his Guinness. They got three pints and the promise of a sandwich from the barman, a fresh faced young man, redheaded and eager to please who, despite the gravity of the situation, had Ollie's mind wandering onto other, more pleasurable things.

"They nearly saw me you know," Jake led the way to a table beside the fire. "I don't think they did but it was close."

"We tried warning you," Nicky took a gulp from her beer, "but the sound just didn't come and by the time it did AND the train had passed, Ted was almost in the house."

"He appeared slightly confused as to the desperate birdcalls though," Ollie said. "What did you see anyway?"

"Well, at first I thought the place was empty. All the rooms had dust sheets over the furniture and just looked very unlived in."

"Maybe it's just a holiday home," Ollie suggested.

"Maybe. But in a small room at the front of the house I saw an old woman in a nursing cot being attended to by Mary."

Nicky looked up. "An old woman?"

Jake nodded. "Mrs Dwight perhaps?"

"Gorby's mum?" Ollie combed his fingers through his hair. "Well, it's her house isn't it?"

"Then Ted came in, Mary arranged the pillows around Mrs Dwight and they left."

"Did they say anything?" Nicky asked.

"I thought I heard Mary say something like 'Perfect, it must be perfect.'"

"Hmmm," Ollie sat in thought. "But where did they go?"

Jake opened the much-used road map he had brought from the van. "Let's see," he quickly turned to page seventeen. "We're here right?"

"Yes," Nicky scrutinised the map once more. "Wait a second," she said excitedly, flipping to the symbols page at the front.

"Looking for something?" the barman placed three ham sandwiches, neatly quartered, on the table in front of them.

Ollie looked at the handsome young man who grinned down at him. Feeling Nicky's kick under the table Ollie pulled himself together, "We're here to see some friends but we can't find them."

"Maybe I can help," the barman folded his arms to reveal biceps of a pleasing proportion.

Wary of Nicky's kick Ollie refused to let his mind stray. "Do you know the Dwights?" he asked.

"Gorby?" Jake added helpfully.

Nicky smiled sweetly. "We're friends of Ted and Mary."

The barman looked surprised. "Are you here for the Honouring then?" he said in a low voice.

"That's enough Jason," a voice warned.

They looked over to see a man in his late forties glowering

behind the bar. He had a shock of red hair and strikingly similar features to the young man.

Jason bobbed his head in deference to his father. Without a word he headed back to the kitchen. Before he got halfway across the bar Ollie called him back, "Wait."

Jason turned.

"We're really here to see Mrs Dwight. We understand she's not well."

A peculiar expression flashed across Jason's face. He looked at his father who, with a quick nod, made it clear he was to leave the room.

"Not well?" the older man asked. "Of course she's not well she's been dead these three years."

"Oh – I – " Ollie flustered before giving up. They finished the sandwiches in silence and left.

"All the man said was they were moored outside Gorby's mother's place," Ollie muttered as they walked across the car park, "not that she was no longer with us."

"So who was the woman if it wasn't Gorby's mum?" Jake wondered.

"Haven't a clue," Ollie looked around him. "God, I hate the country," he said with feeling. "There's veiled threats and hints of *Deliverance* everywhere."

Once they were in the van Nicky couldn't hide her excitement any longer, "I've got it!" She quickly opened the road map again. "Do you know what this is?" Nicky pointed to a curious symbol, an elliptical shape with short lines around the outside, that appeared on the map to be a mile or so from Longfelloe.

Ollie shrugged his shoulders as he started the engine.

"It's the sign for a Celtic monument!"

Jake still looked blank.

"It was something Mary McGrath said to me. Her office is full of these weird figurines of Morris Men."

"Yes?" Jake said slowly still not seeing the connection.

"Well, I'm sure she said something about their dances going back to Celtic times!"

"And you think – ?"

"It's the only lead we have."

As they drove out of the car park Jake pointed through the windscreen, "Maybe you're onto something."

Nicky looked to see the pub's shield atop a flagpole: the coloured board showed a figure of a dancing masked man. Feeling they were on the right way Ollie sped up the hill and away from Longfelloe.

They were going down the other side when Nicky shouted, "Look!"

In the picnic area below them stood a lone parked car. Coming closer it was apparent the vehicle was a maroon Volvo saloon.

They parked the van out of sight of the picnic area and walked back.

Jake examined the Volvo saloon. "It's their car alright."

"You're sure?" Nicky asked.

Jake nodded. "I recognise it from the cottage."

"Besides, look," Ollie pointed to something at the front of the car. "Who else could it be?" Whatever doubts they might have had were erased by the little masked men dangling from the rear-view mirror.

"Longfelloe Iron Age fort," Nicky read out loud from the sign at the edge of the picnic area. "Let's go."

There was no one around as they followed the path across a grassy field and up through a small wood. It was only when they got to the brow of the hill that they came upon ditches and spiralling ramparts, evidence of the ancient fortress.

They clambered over the last of the simple fortifications to find themselves overlooking a flattened area on top of the hill. The large space was overrun with gorse bushes, their yellow flowers the only sign of colour in the wintry landscape.

Nicky looked at the dense thickets in front of her, "Where now?"

"Where else?" Ollie pointed to a series of paths winding their way through the prickly bushes.

Jake wasn't so sure. "Have you any string?"

"It can't be that much of a maze," Ollie jumped down from the earthworks, landing with ease on the soft, springy grass. "Come on," he led the way into the undergrowth.

Jake and Nicky watched him go then quickly followed. After several minutes of squeezing over and under gnarly roots, the path opened into a clearing in the middle of which was a small fenced off area.

Jake leapt over the flimsy railings and peered into the centre. "It's a well."

"Be careful," Nicky warned, "maybe the ground is unsafe."

"Have you any change?"

Nicky reached in her pocket and offered up its contents. "This is all I have."

Jake took three pound coins. He gave one each to Nicky and Ollie whilst keeping the other for himself.

"Couldn't you have taken the ten pence pieces?" Nicky grumbled.

"The Gods don't respond to thrift."

Ollie squinted down the well-shaft. "I can't see any water."

"It's probably really, really deep." Jake rolled the pound

coin along the backs of his fingers as any magician might. "Let's do this together, it'll increase the power."

They linked hands.

"Make a wish," Jake said as he closed his eyes.

Ollie did as he was told. "Mine involves Rion."

"Shhh!" Jake scolded, "you're not supposed to say." After a second he confided, "But so does mine."

"Mine too," Nicky whispered

"On the count of three," Jake said slowly. "One – two – three."

The two young men flipped their coins into the darkness while Nicky simply tossed hers in. Instead of a long silence and then a splash they were met by three dull thuds in quick succession.

"It's been boarded up!" Jake said in disgust.

Nicky felt stupid. "We couldn't fish them out could we?" she asked, realising superstition had got the best of her once more.

Mary looked up upon hearing the muted bumps in the wellshaft above them. Several tiny bits of earth and loose stone splashed into the bubbling pool of water in the middle of the large cavern. Mary looked questioningly at the seven dancers, amongst them Senior and Beck, and then at Gorby who stood to one side, an earthenware tom-tom under his arm.

"It's probably a squirrel," her husband said from the shadows.

"Or someone throwing money," Gorby scoffed. "There's one born every minute."

Mary resumed the practice. She hopped from leg to leg with surprising lightness, drilling the dancers – all young men carrying swords – in the intricate steps they had been rehearsing for months. The Raggedy-Ann doll in the centre silently played her part.

After the dancers had executed a number of these sequences to perfection Mary clapped her hands.

"Well done," her voice echoed around the vast underground chamber beneath the hilltop. "Be here at the appointed hour. Check and double-check everything. You know what to do." She cast her gaze on each of the dancers in turn, "Success depends on your actions tonight. Do not let us down."

The dancers clashed their swords then broke the circle, moving away they talked in soft voices amongst themselves.

Seeing his wife's anxious face Ted put his arm around her and pulled her close. "Everything's perfect," he kissed the top of her head. "It's going to work."

"It must do. It's our last chance, " she looked at the seven young dancers. "It all depends on them, it all depends on the accuracy of the ritual."

Nicky, Jake and Ollie made their way out of the gorse bushes. They walked round the low ramparts of the ancient fort, Longfelloe, and the thin line of the Grand Union Canal, visible in the valley below them.

"Where are they?" Ollie scanned the woods for any sign of life.

Jake shrugged his shoulders. "They can't have just disappeared."

"Why not? Others have," Nicky reminded him.

The friends continued along the brow of the hill, soon coming to the point looking away from Longfelloe but towards the picnic area.

Three figures emerged from the woods below: one tall, one shorter, the other stout.

"It's the McGraths!" Nicky said excitedly.

"And Gorby!"

They watched as the odd trio walked across the field to their car.

"They weren't alone either," Jake pointed to a group of five young men coming out from the trees at the same place. Their voices and laughter drifted up the hill as they headed on the path away from the picnic area down towards Longfelloe.

Jake, Ollie and Nicky waited for several minutes before heading along the trail. They turned right where the field met the trees and followed the line of the woods round.

"What do you think?" Nicky asked as they came to a second, smaller path.

Jake took his alignment from the hillfort above them. He nodded his head, "This is it."

They followed this smaller path through the woods until it joined the main trail.

Eyes watched them unseen from the forest.

"What can we have missed?" Ollie asked as they retraced their steps for the third time.

"Shh!" Jake cupped his ear. "Do you hear that?"

Nicky and Ollie listened but all that could be heard was a soft, distant hum. "Traffic?" Nicky ventured.

Ollie wasn't so sure. "We're pretty far from the road though."

"It's water isn't it?" Jake said listening again, this time trying to see where it might be coming from. He looked to the left where he could see a mosscovered cliff face surrounded by dense wood about thirty yards from the path. "It must be coming from there."

Ollie's heart sank as he looked at the branches and fallen trees blocking their way. They quickly began moving the debris to one side. After a second Jake called out, "Look!"

Beneath the logs and brush was the unmistakable sign of a path. They moved another few light branches away to find a clear trail skirting the fallen trees. Before long all three were in front of the rockface from which a steady curtain of water streamed into a pool.

Behind the wall of water a cave was visible.

"Come on," Ollie led the way. Ducking under the water he entered the small cave. Jake and Nicky were close behind.

"Anyone got a lighter?"

Jake took out his wallet, "Even better." He removed what looked like a credit card from his pocket, pressed it and a strong beam of light lit up the wall in front. "If you live like I do you always come prepared."

Nicky couldn't stop herself marvelling as the torch lit up simple ochre drawings of dancing men, "Wow."

"How old do you think these are?" Ollie asked.

Jake shone the flashlight around, lighting up other crudely drawn dancing figures. He moved in for a closer look, "And what do you think they used – blood?"

Ollie and Nicky looked at each other and shuddered.

Bouncing the beam off the walls Jake saw what they had had been looking for. "There we go," he shone the torch to the end of the cave where the beam lit up an opening stoppered by a heavy studded door.

Nicky was the first one there. "There's no lock, no handle."

Ollie examined the door. "Not even a keyhole."

Jake ran his hands over the surface. He pushed against it with all his might but there was no movement. "Come on," he gestured to the others. As one they put their shoulders to the door but nothing, not a fraction did it budge.

Ollie banged it with the flat of his hand to be met with a

deadened thud. "It must be a foot thick."

"At least," Nicky reckoned.

Jake took a closer look. "We're never going to get in there," he shook his head. "There's no way."

"What are we going to do then?"

Jake flashed his torch around. "We should get out of here that's for sure. There's no place to hide if someone comes."

"Back to the vantage point?" Nicky asked.

Jake nodded. "As good a place as any."

Leaving the cave they were again unaware their every move was being followed. They replaced the brush and branches where the hidden track joined the main trail before heading up to the hilltop fort with its views over any and all arrivals.

"We should have got some more sandwiches," Nicky said, feeling her stomach grumble.

"I think we were lucky to get out when we did."

Ollie agreed with Jake, "The landlord was hardly the most welcoming was he?" There's no telling what he might have done." He watched the full moon rise over the end of the valley. "It's so beautiful isn't it?"

"And so cold," Nicky hugged her fleece tightly to her. "I can't wait until the days start getting lighter."

Their attention was soon taken by headlights coming up from Longfelloe. Instead of driving past as others had done these pulled into the picnic area.

Jake sat up with interest. "We're on."

"What's that?" Nicky pointed to flickering lights approaching from the valley. The sound of voices singing in unison drifted up to the hillfort.

Ollie grabbed her arm. "What's *that?*" he said more urgently pointing to two silhouettes not twenty yards away.

"Do you think they've seen us?" Nicky whispered.

"If not they soon will. Let's jump," Jake said. "I'll follow you."

They landed more heavily than before. Jake tumbled but was on his feet in a flash.

"Stop there!" a man's voice ordered above them.

"Not frigging likely," Ollie hissed as he dashed into the gorse bushes, Nicky and Jake at his heels. They crashed along a narrow track, tripping and stumbling against the roots and undergrowth, their progress shadowed by the yells of their pursuers.

Coming to the clearing in the middle Jake made up his mind in a second. "Get in the well!"

Hearing the crashing come ever closer Nicky followed Jake and Ollie over the rails. They slid down the brick-lined shaft, using their outstretched feet and hands to slow their descent until Jake felt board beneath his feet. He tried not to cry out as first Ollie then Nicky landed on top of him.

With hearts in mouths they heard their assailants stumble into the clearing. "Where could they have got to?" said one breathing heavily.

"There they are!" cried the other.

Nicky closed her eyes waiting for the moment of discovery. The heavy footsteps came closer and closer. Nicky's heart pounded ferociously against her ribs. She could feel her face flush warm as blood raced to her head.

The footsteps came nearer and nearer still then rushed past into thickets on the other side. The voices faded as the men went further away from them.

"That sort of thing could make you religious couldn't it?" Jake whispered. He pulled the creditcard-sized torch from his pocket. The beam clicked on showing them to be some way from the surface. A system of rungs spiralled to the top.

"Let's stay here abit," Ollie linked his arm around one of the metal rungs.

"You bet," Jake said. "I'm not going anywhere." He flexed his legs, feeling the board wobble beneath his feet.

"I wouldn't – " Nicky began but it was too late.

The thin board wasn't meant to carry the weight of one let alone three people. With a nasty crack it snapped, splashing into water not far below them. Ollie held tight to his rung. Nicky managed to grab one above him. Jake wasn't so quick but he was quick enough. In his fall he clutched at Ollie's legs. For a second they dangled there swinging from side to side, Jake sliding lower and lower.

"Hold on!" Ollie said between his teeth, the strain almost unbearable.

"I can't!" with a final gasp Jake let go. He landed to the side of a small spring. "Come on!"

Ollie looked down to see Jake gesturing with his hands. He glanced up at Nicky, "You alright?"

Nicky automatically nodded.

Ollie moved down to the last rung. He swung his legs in the manner of a trapeze artist getting up speed.

"Now!" Jake hissed.

Ollie felt Jake's hands around his ankles and let go. He landed with a heavy thump, Jake pulling him away from the water. Ollie looked round to find himself beside a gently bubbling spring in a large cavern. Dark tunnels led off at the four corners, the whole space faintly lit by a single flaring torch against the far wall.

"I think I've twisted my ankle," Ollie grimaced, the agonising pain causing bile to rise in his throat.

Jake went to support his friend when footsteps could be heard. He looked up, "Someone's coming. Hurry!"

Nicky needed no second urging. She quickly worked her way down until her legs were left hanging in the air.

Jake looked back as the footsteps drew near. "Quick!"

Nicky let go. Her fall was broken by two sets of hands pulling her to safety.

With Ollie in the middle Nicky and Jake hobbled into a tunnel to one side, each step causing Ollie to gasp with pain.

From the shelter of the shadows they saw beams of flashlight enter the space followed soon after by two men. One took the flaming torch from the wall and moved to the well in the centre. He looked up into the shaft through which the night sky could now be seen. "I thought they were going to do that later."

His companion pulled the piece of board from the water. "As long as it's done that's the main thing," he said, his voice tinged with the same pleasing Oxfordshire burr as his colleague.

Their faces caught in the lamplight made Ollie forget his pain for a second. The pair were identical twins.

The next sentence brought the pain back. "Let's return to the girl," the first one said. "They'll be here soon."

The twins wandered back the way they came.

When their footsteps could be heard no longer Nicky whispered, "Wasn't that the guy in the vault?"

Ollie nodded excitedly. "They must mean Rion! Should we go after them?"

"Judging by your ankle I don't think we're going anywhere," Jake looked around the dark cavern. "Don't move."

"Is that a joke?" Ollie asked but Jake had already gone.

Nicky and Ollie watched as he ran across the darkness to the tunnel through which the twins had vanished. They saw Jake creep up the sloping sides to a small ledge of rocks, which he ducked behind.

Within seconds he was back at their side.

"Come on." They half-carried Ollie across the floor and

up to the ledge of rocks, "You should be out of sight up here."

Ollie shifted about until he found the position that caused him least pain. With his back against a rock he found he could peer through a gap in the ledge to get a good view of almost the entire cave.

"I'll go look for Rion."

Nicky looked concerned, "Be careful Jake."

Voices echoed into the cave as Jake made his way down the slope. Some were singing, some laughing, but all joined in a sense of excitement. Jake hurried back up to hide behind the ledge. "Too late!"

They watched as the McGraths entered at the head of a crowd of perhaps twenty people. Mary was dressed all in white. On top of her head was a simple crown. Her husband wore a frock coat and a black box hat. The people behind carried a tree trunk on their shoulders which they placed beside the bubbling pool. Under Ted's directions the trunk was raised, its top nearly touching the ceiling. Mary looked at the open wellshaft above and nodded in satisfaction.

Others followed, many – but not all – in white. The worshippers carried flowers and small branches which they scattered around the upright trunk, creating a semblance of a garden in the ancient cavern. More torches were lit and placed in grooves in the rock hands had carved for them centuries before. Soon the vast space trembled with a flickering light.

Hidden behind the ledge Ollie, Jake and Nicky watched as Mary and two women, also dressed in white, entered the tunnel beneath them.

32

CEREMONY

The twins tensed as people approached, their shadows dancing along the wall before them.

Beck kicked the floor. "I don't like it."

"You'll do as you're told," Senior ordered. He moved near the young girl but saw the drug was already taking effect. Communication was impossible.

Mary came up to the flimsy wicker door. "Is she ready?"

"Ready for you," Senior let Mary in, her two companions close behind.

"And she's had the drink?"

"About ten minutes ago." Although he had not wanted to give Rion the blue-tinged tablets Senior knew it was best she be drugged. The girl hadn't struggled this time. It seemed she had resigned herself to whatever fate lay in store for her.

Mary beamed, "Good!"

As the women removed her clothes Rion had a last musing before the ketamine overwhelmed her: maybe this is what death is like, she thought, everything a blur, vaguely awake but unable to move, unable to do anything. She always thought she'd be cleverer than this – maybe her parents had been right afterall.

"She is perfect," one of the women said as Rion stood naked before them.

"Just exquisite," her companion caressed the girl's long hair. Rion gave no reaction. She just stared at the middle distance, oblivious to everything around her. "And intact?"

"Of course," Mary replied primly.

Rion was dressed by the three women in a simple white dress that touched the ground. Her long hair was combed to fall loose around her shoulders. A crown of woven flowers was placed on her head.

Mary couldn't hide her pleasure. "She *is* perfect isn't she?"

At that point Rion gave a loud throaty cough before flopping back into her semi-conscious pose.

Mary whipped round, the smile ripped from her face. "She's supposed to be in excellent health!"

"She is, it's just the cold in here," Senior said hurriedly

"It won't work unless she's 100%," Mary put her face to Rion's and looked her level in the eye. Satisfied the cough was a one-off her smile returned. "It's time."

Her two companions went either side of Rion. They linked their arms through hers and stood behind Mary who moved out of the cell, Rion and the companions two steps behind.

"It's not right," Beck complained again.

"You're right," Senior agreed. "It's *not* right."

"I don't mean *that*," Beck frowned at his twin who had an annoying habit of changing his words around and giving them a different meaning. "*That's* what we're meant to do." Beck shook his head unhappily, "We'll never get away with it."

"*We* will."

Mary and the other dancers waited for them where the tunnel joined the main area. Mary glared at the twins as they got into line behind her. She took one last look to check everything was in order before she nodded at Ted and smiled.

The procession began.

Holding hands Mary and Ted stepped into the large cavern. Gorby followed, a fool's hat jangling on his head, the tom-toms under his arm.

The crowd hushed upon seeing their King, Queen and Fool move at a stately pace to the well, the starry night sky visible through the shaft above them. On one side of the spring stood the tree surrounded and bedecked with flowers. Colourful ribbons radiated out at six points from the trunk. On the other side was the cot bearing the shrunken figure of Gorby's mother. With her head wrapped in a bonnet the poor woman gazed with blank eyes at those assembled, spittle dribbling from the side of her mouth.

Mary rapped the ground three times with her wand. There was immediate silence. "We thank you all for attending this Honouring to my father," she said regally, her voice reaching every part of the hall. Mary bent down to kiss the frail person in the cot.

Ollie sat up with a start. "Do you mean," he whispered, "that's her dad?"

"Must be," Nicky said confused.

Mary continued in the same powerful voice, "This midwinter night of the moon we will strengthen our bond with the Gods through tribute and dance as has always been done." She gestured to the trunk next to her, "As the tree appears dead in Winter before Spring weaves her spell so we call on the Gods to bring life to their trusted servant in this midwinter of his life and let Spring fill his body this year!"

Shouts of acknowledgement and support rang out from the crowd until Mary held up her hands for quiet. She cast her gaze over the assembled before bursting into a triumphant smile, "See what the Gods have provided on this most special of nights." Mary nodded to the tunnel.

The crowd gasped as the two women companions stepped slowly from the shadows. Their arms were linked around Rion who shuffled unsteadily between them, her mind and body lost in a dense fog.

Nicky bit her clenched fist to keep from screaming.

Mary knelt by the pool in which the very edge of the moon was reflected. "Let Sister Moon add her power!" Mary scooped up a handful of water which she flicked gently over her father and then over Rion. Again she rapped the floor three times with her wand. At this signal Gorby began a solemn beat on the tom-tom he held beneath one arm.

Hearing the drum the six dancers entered. They were dressed identically in white shirt and breeches with gold buttons, red stockings and a red sash around their left arm. They had bells on their legs, tightfitting black velvet caps and white eye masks to further conceal their identity. Swords rested in silver scabbards on their sides. As each entered they extinguished the flaming torches until only two remained.

The dancers formed a circle around Rion who was held against the tree by the two woman companions. Each picked up the end of the ribbon in front of him, giving it a short tug to check it was tightly secured to the trunk. At some hidden signal one dancer moved around the tree, his ribbon securing Rion to the trunk. He was followed by another going the opposite way and then another so that soon all six of the dancers were weaving in and out of each other as they went their different ways, dancing around the tree as they might a Maypole.

As one they ended. The dancers returned to their original points of the circle where they stood facing the centre, the points of their swords resting on the ground in front of them.

The two women companions moved away from the tree leaving Rion there, her neck, body and arms bound to the trunk with the thick ribbon.

Mary looked on in satisfaction. She nodded to Gorby who slowly increased the beat on the drum.

The dancers moved slowly round the ring. They pointed their swords towards the centre, clashing the blades in time with the drum. Patterns of jagged angles were created with swords that the other dancers would jump into and out of. As the beat increased so did the speed of the dancers. They executed turns and half-turns, switching positions across the circle, sometimes dancing singly, sometimes in pairs, but all the time clashing swords that drew sparks in the cavernous space.

The patterns quickly changed. From the circle they moved to file formation performing a series of steps, their feet moving so quickly it was hard to follow without becoming dizzy. When they had finished one sequence it would be repeated in reverse order, the steps demanding perfect muscle control. Circles and spirals, weaving both inwards and outwards, were traced on the floor upon which feet battered as if trying to awaken Spring in the enfeebled old man.

As the tempo increased so the bells on their legs jangled ever louder, the dancers jumping higher and higher over swords in a kind of contest. A section of the audience started clapping in time with the drum. This spread and spread until everyone present apart from Ted and Mary, who retained their regal disposition throughout, were lost in the frenzy of the moment.

For a second or two Ollie forgot where he was, mesmerised by the spectacle before him. He was hypnotised by the speed and agility of the dancers, the clapping and drumming inducing a sense of euphoria in him. It was when he found himself tapping the ground that he suddenly woke up.

"This isn't the last night of the Proms," Nicky hissed in disapproval

"What are we going to do?" Ollie realised unhappily that with one ankle out of action it was fanciful to think he could do anything

Jake obviously had the same thought. "You can't run anywhere – they'd soon have you tied to the tree next to Rion."

"We've got to do something though."

"Just wait until the time is right."

"How will we know?"

"*We'll* know," Nicky said decisively.

The full moon was now directly above the wellshaft. It sat atop the funnel so that, to the celebrants in the cave, it appeared there were two moons so perfect was the reflection in the pool.

This was the sign Mary had been waiting for.

"Stop!" her voice rising above the din brought immediate silence. All that could be heard were the panting dancers, their bodies exhausted, as they leant on the hilts of their swords.

It was time for the second and final phase.

In an exaggerated gesture Gorby plucked a quill from his pocket. He raised it above his head and thrust it through the centre of the drum, the taut skin making a loud crack as it was pierced. He now began to push in and draw out the quill, causing a horrid monotone sound, like a booming bullfrog, to fill the space.

The two women companions came out from the crowd to take their place beside Rion. They were joined by a dancer, his sword by his side. With a quick flick his blade cut the ribbons from the young girl. She was led to the middle of the circle then left alone, swaying like wheat in the breeze.

To the sinister sound the dancers held the hilt of their swords to their shoulders with one hand, whilst grasping the tip of the sword belonging to the man in front with the other. With swords raised above their head they did a small turn and approached Rion, their hands opening and closing making it appear as if the blades were a giant scissor.

Coming closer the circle was made ever smaller until hands were linked with wrists, creating a hexagon of blades that was placed over Rion's head.

Behind their masks two of the dancers exchanged glances.

Ted and Mary, the King and Queen, approached. Mary held a silver chalice in her hand. She looked with concern at her father who lay mewling in the cot beside the silvery moonlit pool.

The sinister monotone stopped.

All that could be heard was the slicing of swords as the blades scissored ever closer.

Ollie looked at the others, "We have to do something!"

"And how!" Nicky replied.

"And now!" Jake helped Ollie to his feet.

"Stop! Stop! Stop!" all three cried from the ledge of rocks.

After a second of stunned silence the most unexpected sound was heard: that of a walkie-talkie crackling into life followed by a man's voice shouting, "Go! Go! Go!"

Ollie, Nicky and Jake watched amazed as uniformed police swarmed into the cavern beneath them. One of the officers rushed to Rion, protecting her with his body from any danger.

"It's Auntie Em's tame plod!" Nicky exclaimed. "The one who came to the cemetery that day."

Angry shouts and screams filled the air as the celebrants

were carried away. Huge flashlights flooded the cave, dazzling the worshippers further.

Blinded by the glare people staggered into the arms of officers waiting by the main entrance. Others dashed into tunnels hoping to escape the police who rushed everywhere, collaring and cuffing with alacrity.

Ollie, Jake and Nicky took one last look at the mayhem before easing their way down. They hobbled over to Rion who was being put on a stretcher. The young girl looked pale, glassy eyes staring blankly in front of her. Behind her Mary's father was being attended to.

"Will she be ok?" Jake asked a paramedic.

"She's suffering from hypothermia and has obviously been drugged but yes," he nodded, "with attention and rest she should be fine."

Ollie held Rion's hands. Her fingers felt so cold against his.

"She can't hear you," the paramedic advised.

Ollie felt a tiny pressure against his thumb.

"It's Ollie. Nicky and Jake are here too. You're going to be ok," he looked at the young girl's face and could swear he could see tears welling behind her eyes. "You're going to be ok."

Choking up Ollie, Jake and Nicky watched Rion being stretchered through the melée and away.

"May I have a word?"

They turned to find Inspector Devine beside them. "You nearly ruined a complex operation."

"But – "

The policeman put up his hand to stop Nicky. "I said you *nearly* did."

"I thought you didn't believe me."

"You were right. Then I checked to see if Lady Chessy could shed any light on the situation in the catacombs – "

"And?"

"It turned out she died more than twenty years ago." Inspector Devine looked at them earnestly. "You see I'm not such a plod after all."

The three friends remained silent.

"And also, well – " the policeman smiled, " – what's the betting we don't find two of the dancers?"

"So you were tipped off?" Ollie asked.

"That would be telling wouldn't it?" He made to leave then turned back. "By the way, where did you hide?" Upon seeing their confusion Inspector Devine continued, "When you jumped off the ramparts and ran into the bushes?"

"So it was you!" Jake exclaimed.

Ollie smiled. "That would be telling wouldn't it?"

33

ALL'S WELL THAT ENDS WELL

Christmas Day dawned cold and got colder. The snow started to fall in big flakes shortly after nine fulfilling Yuletide wishes of children and grown-ups alike. It clung to the balconies of Trellick Tower giving the enormous block a softer, dusted feel.

By early afternoon the snow had been blown in to drifts that settled unevenly in the mews below. Inside the large house at the end Christmas lunch was slowing down. Rion had been released from St Mary's the previous week since when Auntie Em hadn't let the girl out of her sight. She couldn't cope with a third bout of illness, especially not with the news she'd heard about Rion and the possible plans for the New Year. Fully recovered the young girl sat at the festive table between Auntie Em and Ollie. Opposite were Nicky and Jake. Auntie Gem was ensconced on the sofa captivated by the bumper edition of Eastenders.

Above them all, in her niche on the chimneybreast, Merlijnche de Poortje cast her calm gaze over the proceedings.

"When's the TQ of the Year lunch Ol?" Nicky asked.

"On the 30th."

"What are your chances?" Auntie Em asked.

"Hopefully fairly slim," Ollie pushed his chair away from

the table and undid the top button on his trousers. If there was one thing that would top off a miserable few months it would be by being voted Tragedy Queen of the Year. "I think Pete's in the bag with that one."

"What did he do?" asked Rion shyly.

"Oh his ex-boyfriend was getting married."

"Ouch," Nicky shuddered in sympathy.

"It gets worse," Ollie stretched out and put his hands behind his head. "You know the part in the service where the priest asks, 'Is there anyone here who knows of good reason why these two etc etc'?"

Auntie Em guessed what was next. "He didn't?"

Ollie nodded. "Fell into the church – literally – belted out the first couple of verses and a chorus or two of 'It Should Have Been Me', before the bride's brothers threw him out."

"The poor boy."

"He's ok now though isn't he?"

"Oh yeah. He was miserable for a while, in fact he checked into a clinic he was feeling so sorry for himself, then he stopped drinking, lost two and a half stone and is now seeing a Swedish footballer who's crazy about him."

"And you think that's going to win him TQ of the Year?"

"The first bit will. No question."

"Shouldn't it win him some other trophy like 'Most Admired' or 'Most Improved' or – "

"We don't have lunches like that Auntie Em – where would be the fun?"

The elegant woman didn't answer, suddenly distracted by the thought of seeing Kanwar later that day – now *that* would be fun.

Nicky took advantage of Auntie Em's silence. "Did I tell you Andy called? He's back from Japan and was asking after you."

"Really?" Ollie tried to feign disinterest which was never one of his strengths. He took a sip of wine and slowly wiped the side of his lips. "You know I sent him a text thanking him for his help with Hum – never heard back."

"Well, you know how texts can get lost in the ether, and what with being in Japan….."

"Actually I sent him three texts and a voicemail." Ollie suddenly had a desperate urge to look at the tv. "What's going on in Albert Square Auntie Gem?"

"Ollie!" Nicky said indignantly. "Andy wanted to know our, well more specifically *your* plans for New Year's."

"Aren't we going to Lloyd and Clive's?"

"That's what I told him."

"What so he can snog me rotten and give me some false name?"

"I thought you said he was a great kisser."

"He was but I'm not into closet cases."

Welcoming the distraction Ollie reached for the ringing phone but Auntie Em got there first. She handed the receiver to Rion, "It's Tanya. Take it in my room."

As soon as Rion had left the room Auntie Em turned to Nicky, "Have you told her yet?"

Nicky shook her head, "I'll tell her when she gets back."

Auntie Em rubbed her hands together in glee.

"Tell Rion what?" Ollie asked.

"Just something I heard from Angie."

"Where are they spending Christmas by the way?" Ollie asked anxious to move the conversation away from Andy.

"Anguilla. Edwin went a couple of weeks ago, immediately after he got the all clear. Angie left on Thursday."

"I think the staff at Peters & Peters were rather relieved he couldn't attend the Christmas party," Emma smiled.

"And certainly not give any speeches," Ollie grinned, "not after his last explosive performance. I saw it online – in technicolour!"

Auntie Gem didn't join in the accompanying laughter. Pretending she hadn't heard she remained engrossed in the cliffhanging destruction bringing the Christmas edition to a close. They would never know the role she played in bringing Edwin to his knees.

Ollie looked over at the sofa upon hearing the Eastenders theme tune. "Good episode Gem?"

"You know it child," Gemma pressed the mute button on the remote and returned to the table.

"Aren't you going to watch the Queen's speech?" Jake asked, his arm around Nicky who snuggled in closer.

"Don't you – " Auntie Em began then stopped. "Of course you weren't here last year."

"Or the years before," Ollie laughed. "This is one of those difficult times for Gem. Torn between loyalty to the Royal Family and idolatry of Princess Di – and recognising the feelings the Queen had for her daughter-in-law – she has to compromise don't you?" He poured a glass of port and handed it to Gemma who bobbed her head, smiled but remained glued to the set.

"She does this by watching the speech but with the sound down," Nicky explained.

"She should be in politics," said Jake getting out the battered tobacco tin.

"So what – " Nicky stopped and listened but could still hear Rion chatting happily on the phone in Auntie Em's bedroom. " – was the deal in the end? I mean with the McGraths and the creepy guard?" her voice had sunk so low to be barely audible.

Ollie breathed out deeply, letting go the mystery and

tension of the past weeks. "Auntie Em got it all figured out."

Emma took a sip of champagne, letting the bubbles tickle her teeth before swallowing. "Well, from what I can gather it was a mid-winter ceremony chosen to symbolise the point where the sun was the most enfeebled, like the poor woman's father."

"But why didn't they hold it on the winter solstice then?" Jake interrupted.

"It was the winter solstice to *them,*" Auntie Em stressed. "It appears they were traditionalists keeping to the old calendar which, of course, is several days out."

Jake, Ollie and Nicky nodded their heads. Auntie Gem was still glued to the Queen's speech.

"And they wanted a virginal girl because she obviously represents purity, but they also hoped her blood, her vigour, would replenish the old man. They also believed the Gods would smile on such a sacrifice."

"I still can't get over that," Nicky shuddered

"And the chalice would catch her blood which would be mixed with water from the well and drunk, then – "

"We don't need to hear any more of *that*," Auntie Gem said primly without taking her eyes from the Queen of England.

"Quite," Ollie agreed as the Queen's Speech turned into the Christmas edition of Top of the Pops.

The mood in the room lightened as Rion reappeared, returning the phone to its base. "Tanya sends everyone her love," she smiled.

"When's she coming down?"

"Some time in January."

Auntie Em drew in the air over her teeth as if concerned. "Nicky has some news for you sweetness," she took Rion's hand. "Maybe you'll be somewhere else in January."

Rion's eyes welled up. "But you said – "

"Shhhhh," Auntie Em hugged the young girl to her. "It's good news angel."

"Rion," Nicky took a drag on the joint. "Angie had a call from H – " she began to cough, " – from H – " the dry smoke tickling her lungs caused another outbreak.

"Who?" Rion asked nervously.

Nicky waved her hands about as she spluttered and gasped, trying to name the celebrated designer.

"For goodness sake," Auntie Em said, "shall I tell her?"

Nicky, her face puce, nodded.

"From Hitherto Williams. Apparently she saw your picture and has made enquiries about booking you for the couture collections in January," Auntie Em's eyes twinkled as she looked at the young girl, "in Paris!"

As Ollie and Jake whooped and cheered Rion just felt her face flush a very deep, very hot, red.

Nicky had regained her powers of speech. "It's not confirmed but there's definite interest. She'll be in London in a couple of days and wants to meet you."

Rion didn't have time to think. In the next instant Nicky had pulled her to her feet. "Turn it up! Turn it up!" she pointed to the screen where a successful girlgroup were getting ready to sing one of their hits.

The photographer also grabbed Ollie and Auntie Em as Auntie Gem increased the volume.

"I can't dance to this," Auntie Em complained.

"Don't worry," Ollie gestured to the tv where the girls were going lamely through the motions, "neither can they."

Nicky arranged them all in the shape of a diamond. Watching the screen they followed the all-girl group as they rotated round, slowly putting their feet in and out in time with the music.

Gemma offered her hand to Jake, “Shall we?” Grinning they eased their way into the diamond, soon clicking their fingers, shuffling their feet and giggling with the rest of them.

Hum watched from his leopard-print bed by the fire. He rolled over on his back, stretched and let out a deep sigh.

All was well with the world.

THE END.